# Advance Praise for *An Act of Injustice*

"*An Act of Injustice* brings it all home, a study of crime long forgotten but one that should be remembered in this day and age of reversing verdicts of the innocent."

-- Andrew Armitage, *Owen Sound Sun-Times*

"Ray Argyle has created a panoramic and absorbing read in this compelling tale of life in Victorian Canada. He brings to light the prejudice and struggle for equality facing so many – in particular, the fallout from wrongful criminal conviction. As his main character reminds us, 'you have to listen to both sides if you want to get at the truth.'"

-- Jeanette Lynes, author of *The Factory Voice*

"In *An Act of Injustice*, Ray Argyle has written a multi-layered combination of murder mystery, love story, and sociopolitical study, an historical novel rich in detail and complex characters, shedding light on issues that still plague our justice system today."

-- Diane Schoemperlen, author of *This is Not My Life*

**Library and Archives Canada Cataloguing in Publication**

Argyle, Ray, author
        An act of injustice / Ray Argyle.

 Issued in print and electronic formats.
ISBN 978-1-77161-229-6 (paperback).--ISBN 978-1-77161-230-2 (html).--
ISBN 978-1-77161-231-9 (pdf)

I. Title.

PS8601.R48A63 2017        C813'.6        C2016-905911-1
                                         C2016-905912-X

Published by Mosaic Press, Oakville, Ontario, Canada, 2017.
MOSAIC PRESS, Publishers
Copyright © 2017 Ray Argyle
Printed and Bound in Canada
Designed by Courtney Blok

ONTARIO ARTS COUNCIL
CONSEIL DES ARTS DE L'ONTARIO
an Ontario government agency
un organisme du gouvernement de l'Ontario

We acknowledge the Ontario Arts Council
for their support of our publishing program
We acknowledge the Ontario Media Development Corporation
for their support of our publishing program

Funded by the        Financé par le
Government           gouvernement          Canada
of Canada            du Canada

MOSAIC PRESS
1252 Speers Road, Units 1 & 2
Oakville, Ontario L6L 5N9
phone: (905) 825-2130

info@mosaic-press.com

# Ray Argyle

# Contents

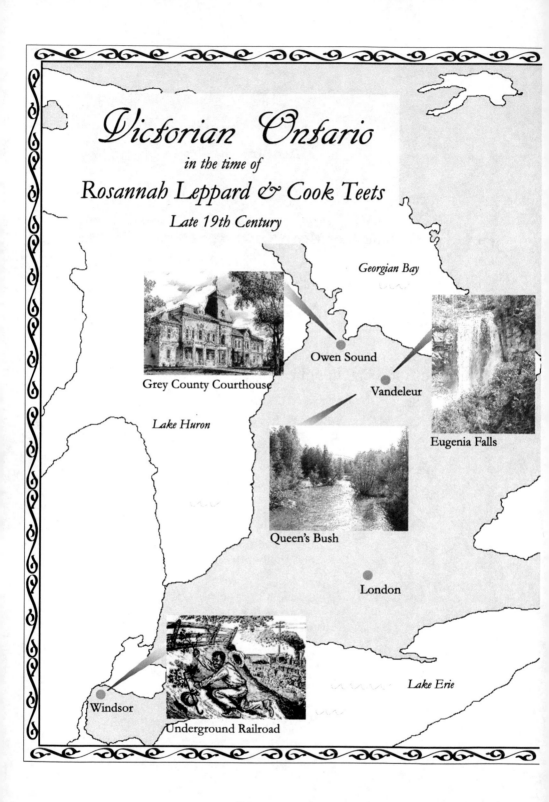

*Victorian Ontario*

in the time of

Rosannah Leppard & Cook Teets

*Late 19th Century*

Georgian Bay

Grey County Courthouse

Owen Sound

Vandeleur

Eugenia Falls

Lake Huron

Queen's Bush

London

Lake Erie

Windsor

Underground Railroad

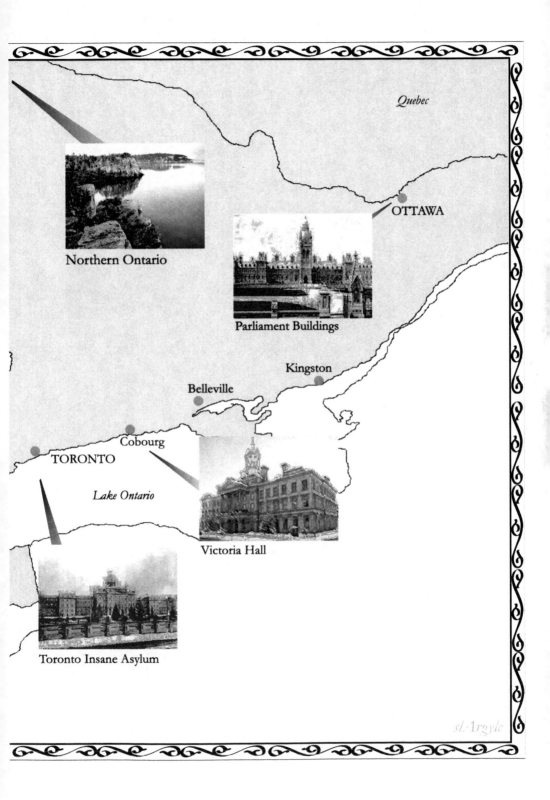

Quebec

Northern Ontario

OTTAWA

Parliament Buildings

Kingston

Belleville

Cobourg

TORONTO

Lake Ontario

Victoria Hall

Toronto Insane Asylum

sd Argyle

# PART I
## THE JUDGMENT OF MEN

There is no crueler tyranny than that which is perpetrated under the shield of law and in the name of justice.

Charles de Montesquieu

It is more important that innocence be protected than it is that guilt be punished, for guilt and crimes are so frequent in this world that they cannot all be punished.

John Adams

# Prologue
## ROSANNAH AND THE NIGHT

### October 31, 1883

Rosannah awoke in the dark, feeling edgy. Her headache had eased, replaced by a restlessness that brought on a foreboding that something was wrong. At twenty-five, she'd known the hurt of vanquished love and the pain of childbirth, but this was different. She stirred uneasily, not wishing to disturb others asleep in the house.

It was a simple place, not much more than a cabin where Rosannah had been raised with a dozen brothers and sisters. The one room log house had been built by her parents, James and Molly Leppard, from trees they'd felled and trimmed, using few tools and a lot of sweat. It clung to a hillside where her father held title to six stony acres overlooking the Beaver River Valley, opposite the village of Vandeleur. The Leppards were one of the poorest families in the slab of territory between Lake Huron and Georgian Bay called the Queen's Bush. It was here that immigrants and sons of farmers and failures from the cities – each seeking a second chance at life – were extending the frontier society of Ontario.

Rosannah knew every footpath within a half-day's walk of the house. An hour's hike took her to The Gravel, the only decent road in this lonely countryside. She sometimes hitched a ride on a passing wagon for the journey to Munshaw's Hotel, where she'd always find a willing man to buy her a glass of beer.

It was cold in the house on this night of the thirty-first of Octobor, 1883, and the fire in the stove had burned out. Now fully awake, Rosannah gathered her blanket around her. She wondered what life would hold for her two little girls sleeping below in the trundle bed they shared. Her angels, she

3

called them. One was four years old and the baby was not quite two. How difficult it had been to care for them without a father. She couldn't have done it without Mother, but it was clear Mother's patience was running out.

Rosannah remembered the men she'd been with. First there'd been Father Quinn, the Catholic priest. She detested him for what he had done to her when she was only twelve. He taught her she had something men wanted and they'd pay for, in money or in other things. By the time she was fifteen, there'd been boys her own age and men she'd met at village socials or the blacksmith shop or general store. Later, there was David Rogers, to whom she'd been briefly married. And Leonard Babington, whom she had never married but had dearly loved.

Six weeks ago, Rosannah had defied her Catholic mother by marrying the Protestant, Cook Teets, in a Presbyterian church in Toronto. He was thirty years older than her, and she was still getting used to being Rosannah Teets. It was all going to be different married to Cook. He was the kind of man she had always wanted: aloof when he encountered coarseness, a spendthrift when he was gripped by passion, compliant when he sought affection. They would have a home together as soon as he could find a place. It was too bad Mother wouldn't let him stay here. Or that Cook's mother wouldn't permit her to set foot in the Teets house. Rosannah had learned long ago that most Catholics and Protestants couldn't abide each other, and there was nothing she could do about it.

The small sounds of the night – the creaking of a timber or the distant yelp of a coyote – were upsetting to Rosannah. She thought she heard singing, and then someone fiddling with the latch on the front door. She lit a candle and went to investigate, but no one was there, just the dog lying at the doorstep. The first light of dawn was now showing itself through the thin blankets that hung as a canopy around her bed. Rosannah had been thinking how worthwhile life was going to be when the tingling began. It started in her stomach. In a little while it brought on cramps, followed by spasms of pain that led to convulsions. She heaved and arched her back, seeking relief. Her chest grew tight. It was hard to breathe. Spittle ran down her chin and her muscles went rigid. She felt a hot wetness beneath her. She was losing control of her body. She flung out her arms and whispered, "Dear God, why are you punishing me?" In a moment, she began to scream.

# Chapter 1
## CAUSE AND EFFECT

### November 1, 1883

Leonard Babington settled deeper into his captain's chair, emitting a slight sigh of satisfaction. Amid all the relics he had acquired on taking over the *Vandeleur Chronicle* – an ancient printing press, a grimy type cabinet, assorted pieces of well-worn furniture – only the chair gave him comfort. He relaxed against its wrinkled and cracked black leather cushions, taking pleasure from the way they molded to his body, a form as spare and unembellished as the chair itself. He broke off his study of yesterday's Toronto newspaper – Grave Crisis in Balkans, read its headline – when he heard the click of the latch being lifted to open the front door. It was barely eight o'clock and he hoped his early visitor might be an advertiser come to pay his bill or a reader with subscription money in hand. Leonard unfolded himself from his chair and went into the hallway to welcome the visitor.

Constable John Field, out of breath and looking mournful, stood at the still open doorway. He was not the visitor Leonard had hoped for. Field's arrival usually signaled a tragedy of some sort – a killing in a beer parlour brawl or possibly a drowning in Georgian Bay.

"There's trouble at the Leppard place," Field said. It was clear he regarded this as important news. "Somebody's tried to poison Rosannah Leppard. I'm going over there now. Want to come with me?"

Leonard's heart heaved and he felt faint with shock. He tried not to let his face show his alarm. Any trace of agitation would confirm the suspicion no doubt lurking in Field's mind that any news of Rosannah Leppard would be of more than passing interest to him.

It was like Field to look for notoriety in everything he did, Leonard thought. The Constable for Artemesia Township, that backwater in the Queen's Bush of Grey County, was paid only for the days he worked on police business – a dollar fifty a day. Every mention he could get of himself in the *Chronicle* was a reminder to the men on the township council that he'd been doing his job, well and faithfully.

Leonard had worked for the *Toronto Globe* before being caught up in a messy situation that cost him his job. He'd worked as a stoker on a Great Lakes steamship and had taken over his hometown *Vandeleur Chronicle* after its publisher had fallen ill, deep in debt. He struggled to master the tasks of selling advertising, writing up the news, and nursing the old Washington Press that churned out two hundred sheets an hour. On top of all that, he'd had to keep on hand a generous supply of booze to discourage itinerant printers from wandering off after their first payday. He was thin and fair-headed, thirty years old, and lived alone in the estate house his parents had occupied until they'd passed on.

For Leonard, the news Field brought was far more devastating than his usual mournful tidings. The Constable's brusque announcement reminded him again of Rosannah's erratic behaviour. There was that foolish marriage she'd made only six weeks ago. Now, he thought, God knows what has happened to her.

Leonard Babington pulled off his ink-stained apron and called out to Tyler Thompson, the printer's devil he relied on to break up the pages after the printing of each issue. "I'll go along with the Constable," he said. "I want you to print up the handbill for the piano teacher and take it to over to the school."

Constable Field decided it would be quicker to cross the Beaver River by footbridge than take a buggy down the East Back Road and along The Gravel, the name people gave to the Durham Road. On the way, buttoning his canvas jacket against the morning chill, Field explained that Billy Leppard, the youngest of the brood, had been sent to fetch him. They descended the path on the hillside known as Bowles's Bluff and came to the footbridge. The water was low this late in the fall and Leonard could see fish scudding up the stream, looking for spawning sites. Small islets, not much more than sandbars, housed stunted pine bushes and outgrowths of sweetgrass. They crossed quickly and in half an hour they were at the Leppard place. Field rapped on the cabin's big wooden door to announce their arrival.

Molly Leppard, Rosannah's mother, opened the door and silently let them into the cabin's single room, a space measuring no more than fifteen by twenty feet. Leonard had been there many times but he had never seen it as it was now. The room was crowded and smelled musty, a combination of sweat and dampness from an overnight rain, and stale odours from cooking. A table was littered with dishes and scraps of food. Clothes were scattered on chairs and an empty whisky bottle sat on a cabinet next to some carpenter tools. Molly Leppard, still in her nightdress, motioned the men forward with a vague wave of her hand. Her hair looked stringy and her face pallid against her eyes, red from crying. Leonard recognized Bridget Leppard, Rosannah's sister, sitting in a rocking chair. Mary Ann Leppard, wife of one of Rosannah's brothers, stood behind her. Two small children played on the floor. There was a bench along the far wall, and on the floor in front of it, a man sat crumpled up. Leonard recognized him as Rosannah's husband, Cook Teets. He was muttering to himself. Leonard could barely make out his words. He was repeating, over and over, "She's gone, she's gone." Everyone's eyes were red from crying.

"Mrs. Leppard, what's happened here?" Constable Field asked. "How is Rosannah?"

Molly Leppard gestured toward the far side of the room, where a blanket hung from the ceiling partly concealed a washstand and a bed. There was someone in the bed.

"Rosannah's gone," Molly said. She held onto the back of a chair as she spoke. "She died this morning, in awful pain. It was like she had taken poison."

Leonard felt a shiver, followed by more pounding of his heart. He was confused and he hoped that somehow it might turn out that Rosannah was still alive.

"I'll have to examine the body," Constable Field announced. Leonard looked over his shoulder as Field lifted the blanket off Rosannah. Her body was arched upward, as if she was trying to lift herself off the bed. The constable bent over her, listened for a heartbeat and finding none, checked her pulse. "Sure enough dead," he declared.

"I'm going straight to Dr. Christoe," the Constable announced. Leonard knew that Dr. William Christoe, the coroner, had an office next to the Township Hall in Flesherton. He would tell Field what he must do in a case of suspicious death.

"I don't want anybody to leave, or touch the body," Field added.

A half hour later, Leonard was back at the *Chronicle* and Constable Field was on his way to see the coroner. Leonard learned later that Field had taken Rosannah's body to Dr. Sproule in Markdale for a post-mortem examination. The coroner had telegraphed Alfred Frost, the Crown attorney in Owen Sound, for instructions. Word came back that an inquest should be held and Dr. Christoe scheduled this for the next morning. He spent the evening rounding up six men. He told them to be at the Township Hall at nine o'clock, prepared to listen to whatever evidence might be presented. It would be up to them to determine what, or who, had caused the death of Rosannah Leppard.

When the inquest jury assembled in the council chamber of the Township Hall, almost every seat was filled in the small public gallery and Leonard Babington had to squeeze into the last vacancy in the front row. The furnace was stoked up against a November chill and before long people began to slip out of their coats. Dr. Christoe called Cook Teets, but he denied any knowledge of the cause of Rosannah's death. A neighbour, Scarth Tackaberry, claimed he'd seen Cook in possession of a bottle of strychnine, but Cook denied it. That was when the jurymen asked for a break. After huddling in a corner, they announced that no verdict was possible without knowing whether poison had been the "positive cause" of death. Dr. Sproule said he would send Rosannah's stomach organs to Toronto for examination.

The break in the hearing lasted two weeks. Leonard Babington thought a lot about the case. He was unable to fathom how Cook Teets would want to kill Rosannah Leppard. Nothing like this had ever happened in Vandeleur. To the casual visitor, the village seemed smug and placid, an unlikely place to contemplate the act of murder. Leonard knew better. Vandeleur was as filled with jealousies, family quarrels, and sexual promiscuity as any other town. Having been born here, Leonard absorbed without question the sentiments of his elders in matters of faith, morality, and Protestant respectability. Any public recognition of sex was regarded as a horror, and modesty in women's dress was insisted on at all times. Neighbours carefully scrutinized each other's observance of the Sabbath. These traits had to be inculcated early in the young, backed up by stern discipline.

Vandeleur had four churches, an Orange Hall and a cemetery in which Rosannah Leppard was laid to rest three days after her death. There was a schoolhouse from whose flagpole flew the Union Jack. An assortment of blacksmiths, livery stables, and dressmaker and drygoods shops served the village. Its buildings were made of lumber hewed at Jacob Teets's sawmill, as were the cedar shingles on their roofs. A scent of newly sawn wood and fresh paint could still be detected in the newer stores. They were spaced irregularly along both sides of a quarter mile stretch of the Beaver Valley Road, and most bore false fronts that affected the pretence of a second floor. Cedar and pine trees surrounded the village and birch and poplars grew in sunlit spaces between the green forest and the road. Twenty-four children were taught, for a time by Leonard Babington, in the one-room schoolhouse of School Section Number Eleven. Leonard was a good teacher despite never having set foot in a classroom, having been entirely home schooled by his parents. Later, he had that stressful and disappointing stretch at the *Toronto Globe*, before finding himself the proprietor of the *Chronicle*.

The prominent families, the Babingtons, the Teets, and others attended one of three Protestant churches – Anglican, Methodist, or Presbyterian – leaving the Catholic church to watch over a flock of mostly poor, mostly Irish believers like the Leppards. Mail arrived twice a week at the post office in James Henderson's general store, everyone's favourite stopping place. A bucket on the counter was kept filled with whisky. Customers were encouraged to help themselves. People came and went, but the Beaver Valley Road, clinging to the west shoulder of the valley as it made its way to Georgian Bay, was the one constant feature of the place.

Leonard lived next to this notoriously unreliable course. In winter the road was covered with glacier-like sheets of ice and in spring it became mired in gumbo. Often, he had to throw down planks to get his horse and wagon over a treacherous section. Among his earliest memories was being told how neither he nor his mother would have survived his birth had not the husband of a skillful midwife carried her the last hundred yards through the mud to the Babington place. Thomas Kells claimed his wife had birthed most of Vandeleur, but insisted it was he who had given birth to the village. He named it after the Irish estate where he'd worked as a gardener for the Vandeleurs, a Dutch family grown wealthy on trade with Ireland. His story was readily accepted, Vandeleur not being important enough for anyone to argue about its name. This village of six hundred souls had never known notoriety, but Leonard sensed this was about to change.

When the report came back from the medical examiner in Toronto, the coroner, Dr. Christoe, hastily reassembled the inquest jury. He told the jury the presence of strychnine in Rosannah's organs had definitely been confirmed. It took only a few minutes for the the jury to conclude that Cook Teets had used strychnine to "feloniously poison" his wife. Leonard noted there'd been talk of a four thousand dollar insurance policy, of which Cook Teets was the benficiary. Constable Field was dispatched to arrest Cook at his home. He offered no resistance, and Field took his prisoner by train to Owen Sound, where he turned Cook over to the governor of the county jail.

Leonard headed his article THE FATE OF A BRIDE. The crime, he noted, had "sent a tremor of excitement" through the community. His story added that Cook's possession of the poison, together with the incriminating insurance policy, "supplied the motive for the suspected crime." But Leonard felt compelled to report that testimony had indicated "strychnine is a poison that generally acts very quickly, producing death in from ten minutes to four hours." To this fact he dutifully added: "The evidence so far goes to show that Cook Teets was not in the company of his wife for a period of twelve hours or more before her death."

# Chapter 2

## THE PLEA

### November 3, 1884

On the morning that Cook Teets came to trial, a year after Rosannah's death, Leonard Babington rose at dawn in his room at Coulson's British Hotel, his usual stopping place in Owen Sound. When an hour's wait failed to produce hot water for a morning bath he decided, reluctantly, to forego the pleasure of the tub. He shaved from a chilled basin, a three-day stubble resisting the blade of his straight razor, and dressed quickly. Stepping carefully around patches of ice, the residue of an unseasonably early storm, it took him twelve minutes to trudge the five blocks to the courthouse.

Leonard hurried through the vaulted front door of the Grey County Court Building and up the narrow staircase to the courtroom on the second floor. He paused at the top of the stairs to look out the big windows at the harbour and saw dark water lapping against its docks. It looked as bleak as he felt, ghost-like and all but empty with winter on the way. In other seasons, it offered a sanctuary where vessels on runs to the Upper Lakes, Chicago, and Minnesota found respite from treacherous gales that could turn Georgian Bay into a seething ocean of froth and foam.

He was glad to be able to claim the last seat at the table set up for newspapermen who had come to cover the trial. Cook Teets was just now being brought into the courtroom, shackled in handcuffs and leg irons. Finally, Cook was to face a jury to answer to the murder of the girl Leonard had loved. He was convinced of Cook's guilt, but apprehensive at what the trial might reveal. It would, Leonard knew, force Rosannah's mother to confront unwanted ghosts from her past. Just as it would stir up bitter memories of his own that he had no wish to recall. He looked forward to the end of the trial when he could put Rosannah's life and death behind him. It was time to start thinking about his future and what he would have to do to make a success of his newspaper. Find a good wife, build up the *Chronicle*, make it a real paper, more than just the "local rag."

Leonard scanned the faces of the four men settled at the newspaper table. He exchanged glances with the two he knew, Henry Heatherwood from the *Owen Sound Advertiser* and Andy Fawcett, the editor of the neighbouring *Flesherton Advance*. The other men introduced themselves as reporters from Toronto. They represented the *Globe* and the *Evening Telegram*. Leonard felt edgy in their presence, knowing they might find out about his past relationship with Rosannah.

"What are the folks in Vandeleur saying about this case?" the *Telegram* man asked.

"That it's a God-awful shame and a horror, that girl being poisoned," Leonard Babington replied. "We're just a small place so everyone feels they've a stake in the trial."

"Why is it," the *Telegram* man wondered, "that the most ghastly crimes seem to occur in these out-of-the-way places? There was the Donnelly family – Black Donnellys, they called them, and Irish, too – all but wiped out by a vigilante gang, down near London. Nobody ever convicted."

"We've had no such gangs around here," Leonard said. "People here are mostly law-abiding. They're used to hard times. They have none of the niceties of life you enjoy in Toronto. They might as well be living in Transylvania." Leonard was determined to say nothing of his own, earlier experience as a reporter in Toronto. Nor of the fact he had known Rosannah or that he had written a stinging story about Cook Teets when he shot at a gang of boys who had pelted him with snowballs. Fortunately, the bullets had gone astray.

Leonard realized that for the Toronto newspapermen, this must be just another dreary murder trial, albeit in a bucolic setting. He hadn't been sure how to answer the *Telegram* man's questions. He only knew that for settlers in the Queen's Bush, life was a struggle to survive on what they could extract from its stony soil, be it meagre crops or wild game bagged by shotgun or fishhook.

Leonard looked around to see how many people from Vandeleur were in the courtroom. His attention focused momentarily on Scarth Tackaberry, a tall, ruddy-faced man who had wrapped his legs under the bench in the second to last row. He knew Scarth only slightly, one of another of the large families that lived in the Beaver Valley. Scarth's father had come from England but the family had Irish blood. They were a tribe Leonard had never cottoned to. Sly and mischievous, Scarth had been expelled from the Vandeleur school at the age of eleven after setting fire to the hair of the girl who sat in front of him. He had never gone back. Later, there were rumours he'd been having his way with Rosannah Leppard.

Huddled in the front row were Cook's mother, Margaret Teets – an old lady, nearly ninety – and his sister, Sarah. Leonard thought they looked shrunken, as if trying to make themselves invisible. Beside them sat Cook's oldest brother, Nelson Teets. He had run the family's sawmill and furniture workshop since the death of old Jacob Teets. Nelson sat upright, bowing to no one despite the embarrassment of his brother's arrest.

To Leonard and most others in the courtroom, Cook Teets was a familiar sight. Leonard knew him as a man of broad shoulders and thick chest, with cloudy blue eyes. Today, the bushy black hair that covered Cook's head and face gave way to a beard turned prematurely grey. He sat upright, his hands clenched at his knees. He stared toward the courtroom windows, seemingly unmoved by the gravity of the charge against him.

The crowd, aroused by the sight of the accused, muttered its scorn but quieted when Angus McMorrin, the clerk of the court, bellowed "Oyez, oyez, oyez, all rise, this court is in session, the Honourable Mr. Justice John Douglas Armour presiding. All persons having business before the High Court of Justice, attend now and ye shall be heard."

McMorrin thumbed through a bundle of court papers. When he found the sheet he sought, he read out the charge and turned to ask: "Cook Teets, how do you plead, guilty or not guilty?"

Leonard shifted his view to Cook. He was convinced his plea would make not a whit of difference to the outcome of the trial. He could barely disguise his loathing of the man. How could someone possessed of his senses kill his beautiful young wife, a woman half his age and the mother of two little girls? In Leonard's mind, there was no forgiving Cook.

Judge Armour, who had travelled to Owen Sound from Cobourg to preside over this sitting of the Fall Assizes of the Ontario High Court of Justice, let the seconds tick into a half minute while he waited for a response from Cook.

"How does the prisoner plead?" he finally demanded. Leonard Babington thought his voice communicated a loss of patience. At last, Cook Teets rose to his feet.

"Not guilty," he answered. His voice was firm and clear.

Judge Armour nodded imperceptibly. Leonard dipped his pen into the ink well on the table in front of him and inscribed the date on a pad of white paper: Monday, November 3, 1884. Looking up, he noted a mural of the Coat of Arms of Great Britain and the Empire that dominated one wall. A Union Jack was affixed to one side of it. A full-length portrait of a stern Queen Victoria hung on the other side. There were no Canadians more loyal to the Crown than the people of Grey County, he told himself.

Jury selection took less than half an hour. Three farmers – described as yeomen in the jury's warrant – were chosen, along with a warehouseman, two shopkeepers, a bookkeeper, a retired ship captain, a deckhand, a stone mason and two blacksmiths. Most were dressed in their Sunday best and they shifted about in their elevated seats, a little nervous but secure behind their wooden railing.

Leonard was surprised to see a Negro, the stone mason Henry Johnson, on the jury. His small home and acreage would have barely met the four hundred dollar property qualification, a rule that ensured juries were filled with men of quality. When the Grey County board of selectors suggested to Sheriff Moore that Johnson's name be added to the roster, they must have never expected he would be called.

James Masson, the lawyer defending Cook Teets, had used his right of challenge to veto three prospective jurors but had raised no objection to Johnson.

Nor had Alfred Frost, charged with prosecuting this case. He was known to be proud of the role his father John Frost had played in providing sanctuary for hundreds of Negro runaways who had reached Grey County via the Underground Railroad They lived first as squatters, clearing off trees and planting crops on what had been forestland. Then came the government survey and when the value of the land was set at a dollar fifty an acre, few could pay the price. Most gave up their homes and drifted to towns like Owen Sound. Now, those who had taken to town life were getting the vote and Alfred Frost would not have it said he treated coloured people less fairly than whites. Anyway, Leonard thought, Johnson was as entitled as any man to the dollar fifty a day juror's pay. And his inclusion was not likely to have an undue influence on the outcome.

The afternoon before the trial, on the train that carried Leonard from Vandeleur to Owen Sound, he had encountered Rosannah's parents, James and Molly Leppard. He took a five-dollar bill from his pocket and offered it to Molly. "Get something for the children," he said. Molly waved his hand away. "I'm can't think about that. I'm to testify tomorrow," she said, turning to stare out the window. "It'll be hard, very hard." Her coolness surprised Leonard. "You know I'd want them to have this," he said. Again, Molly refused the money. "We might be poor but that doesn't mean we take charity from you."

Leonard sighed as he looked at Molly sitting with her husband and her daughter Bridget in the second row of the courtroom. She gave no sign of recognition. She didn't need to act so prim and proper, he thought. It still hurt him that she'd rejected the money he'd offered her. After all, he'd known the Leppards for years and had visited them many times before moving to Toronto. Molly had been welcoming enough then, although he had known she would never have permitted a Methodist boy like him to marry her daughter.

Cook Teets, Leonard thought, seemed almost too large a man to fit into the space allotted him in the prisoner's dock. Leonard watched him tilt his head to one side. He looked older than his fifty-four years. A bandage fashioned from a white handkerchief covered an inflamed eye. His skin, pale from his incarceration, made a sharp contrast against the dark blue of his shirt.

The jurors gazed intently at Cook Teets, their looks fixed on the thick eyebrows that weighed like small anvils on his forehead, the circles under his eyes, and his straggly beard. Leonard knew that Cook was seeing none of the particularities of their faces. The singular fact about the prisoner, a reality that by now had manifested itself to everyone in the courtroom, was that Cook Teets was blind.

# Chapter 3

## A BOY AND THE DARK

### November 29, 1842

Cook Teets felt feverish and confused as he listened to the formalities that began his trial for murder. By concentrating on the sounds and smells of the courtroom, he was able to unravel much of what was happening around him. He blinked unconsciously when the time came to answer to the charge he was facing. His lawyer had told him to plead not guilty. He had stood to speak. When he sat down his mind shifted to the day when he had awakened to find himself blind. If that hadn't happened he wouldn't be here, he thought.

As a boy in Marcellus, New York, before his father moved the family to Vandeleur, Cook had been a gentle child, often bullied by his schoolmates. It was another snowy November day – Monday, the 29th – when Cook was twelve years old that Otis Freeman, who fancied himself the toughest boy in the village, had gathered his gang on the steps of the schoolhouse.

"About time we taught this little runt a lesson," Otis told his minions, pointing to Cook. "Teacher's pet ... always trying to get on the good side of old Mrs. Holmes." Cook thought this a good time to run off. The price of sticking around would be at least a roughing up and quite possibly a bloody nose.

Cook and Otis were in the same class, even though Otis was three years older, the result of him having failed three different grades. Otis had been picking on Cook for months, mainly because he made an easy target. Cook was small for his age, reticent and unskilled in such boyish pastimes as choking kittens, setting snarling dogs on each other, or using slingshots to kill songbirds.

When the boys began to pelt him with snowballs, Cook ran faster. He looked back to see if they were gaining on him. A wet snowball hit him in the face. It stung like blazes and he knew even before he crumpled to the ground that a good-sized rock must have been imbedded in it. He felt blood gush onto his nose and into his eyes. He heard Otis shout, "Don't nobody say I threw that or you'll be sorry." Cook blacked out while he lay in the snow and when he came to he was aware only of the silence of the street and the grey fog that covered his eyes. He stumbled home to be cleaned up and put to bed by his mother. When he awoke the next morning he was unable to see, and thought his eyes had been bandaged. When he put his hands on his face and found nothing there, he cried out in terror. He couldn't understand that he was destined to live in a world of darkness.

Cook's parents sent for a doctor but the only advice he could offer was to keep the boy's room darkened. Cook stayed in bed for three weeks and tried to understand what being blind would mean. "Why did this happen to me, Mum? I never did anything to Otis Freeman. How come he put a stone in that snowball? What's going to become of me?"

"I don't know but your father has spoken to Mr. Freeman and he's given Otis a good thrashing. The doctor says if we keep your room dark, you might get to see again." Cook never did get his full sight back and it was not until many years later he learned that the stone that had hit him had detached the retina of one eye. An inflammation followed that led to blindness in his other eye. He was told prompt surgery might have saved his sight but no surgeon had been available to perform such a miracle.

Cook never went back to school. He learned to rely on other senses – hearing, touch and smell – and guided by his three brothers and encouraged by his sister Sarah, led a life not too different from that of other boys. As he grew older he began to detect shapes and shadows in the void of his sight, but he remained pensive and shy, seldom volunteering his thoughts.

Cook's father Jacob Teets had served a long apprenticeship before be-coming a master cabinet-maker. His family had come from Germany. Jacob moved his wife Margaret and Cook and his three brothers and sister Sarah to the Queen's Bush the year that Cook turned twenty-four. "That country's got free land," Jacob told his wife. "And fine stands of hardwood. Good for making furniture."

Torn from his familiar surroundings, Cook became dejected and morose. Only when his brother Nelson started teaching him to make furniture did he begin to assert himself. "You're doing a good job," Nelson told him every day. "If ever you need anything, you'll always have me here beside you."

Jacob, being one of the first into the district, had taken up a grant of fifty acres of Crown land just north of the new village of Vandeleur. The land had rolling fields, sandy soil, and a clear pond fed by springs. The pond released a stream that flowed into the Beaver River. Jacob built flues to divert the stream toward a waterwheel that he used to power a large circular saw he had brought from Toronto. He knew that the property's ample stands of maple, elm, birch and pine trees were its most valuable asset. He harvested the trees carefully and chose the best wood to make tables, cabinets, commodes and bed frames.

"The pieces are sturdily made and nicely finished," one of his first customers told him. Word spread and before long most families in nearby townships owned at least one piece of Teets furniture. The work enabled Jacob to keep his family comfortable and prosperous.

In comparison to the Teets and the Babingtons, the Lepppards lived in dire want, yet in their own way were serenely content in the log house James and Molly had put up on the land they occupied near Eugenia Falls, where the Beaver River tumbled over a seventy-foot precipice to the valley below. Molly kept the house going between giving birth to nine more babies, chasing deer from her vegetable garden, and stocking a root cellar with turnips, potatoes, carrots and beets.

Molly gave birth to their new home's first baby unattended except by a neighbouring woman. When a priest called on her a few days later, Molly had no idea what to name the little girl. "Why not Rosannah?" the priest suggested. "A Godly name, it means Rose of Grace." Molly agreed, and the child spent her first three months in a basket before being put in a tiny bed with her sisters Elizabeth and Bridget. They played on the drafty floor that winter, moving outdoors as soon as the snow melted. Later, they ran barefoot in the mud and by the summer of her second year, Rosannah had put her toes into the river and had learned to balance on Elizabeth's lap atop their horse, Sadie. As she grew older, Rosannah liked to tag alongside her father as he tended his crops, milked his cow, and herded a half dozen sheep. He often said she was of more help to him than either of her brothers, who were bigger and stronger. He didn't mind if she forgot to say her prayers at night and when Molly complained he told her, "The girl's fine, just let her be."

James relied on the few dollars he earned from the oats and corn he grew, supplemented by occasional carpentry jobs. He accepted that he would always be poor, and blamed his lack of wealth on the independent spirit he'd inherited from his father and grandfather. They had refused to kowtow to the selfish and mercenary "best families" who had come early to Upper Canada.

James aimed to be his own man, even if he couldn't be rich. "It's said I'm stiff-necked," he told his wife. "My family's always been that way. Better that than bow down to people we have no use for."

Those he had no use for included Jews – although James had never met one – all coloured people, the local Indians, and any farmer who owned more land than his family could cultivate on their own. He didn't particularly like Catholics but being of a practical turn of mind, he readily accepted Molly's insistence that their children be raised in the Church of Rome. He was not unkind. Unlike many men he knew, James Leppard did not beat his wife. He disciplined his children only enough to make them obedient, for a time.

Unschooled – except in profanity – and illiterate, James Leppard was ignorant about many things but he did not lack intelligence. He could be shrewd in his business deals. Sometimes too shrewd, as when he let a crop of perfectly good barley rot in its field rather than accept an unfair price from the miller in Vandeleur. He understood the care that animals needed if they were to supply the family with milk, eggs and meat. He knew when and where the fish were most likely to bite and could tell, by scents in the night air, when a herd of deer presented an opportunity for a kill. He could splint a child's broken arm quicker than the limb could show a bruise. These were valuable assets in the struggle to survive in a place where a visit to a doctor involved a half day of travel. Some of this knowledge he'd gained by instinct and some he'd figured out himself. But most of it was handed down from his father and his forefathers. He was rich in the lore of country life, absorbed from the wisdom of generations on the land.

# Chapter 4

## INTO THE QUEEN'S BUSH

### September 30, 1854

**O**utside the Grey County Court Building, the wind was picking up speed and threatening to bring more snow to the leeward side of Georgian Bay. In the courtroom, James Leppard shifted in his seat beside Molly. When she reached to hold his hand, her gesture reminded him of the day they'd met. It was at the fall fair in the tiny Ontario community of Colgan, the last day of September of 1854, and Molly had been sitting behind a table filled with gourds of all sizes, shapes and colours. She had green eyes and red hair and spoke with an Irish lilt that fascinated him.

"Are you enjoying the fair now, dear sir?" she had asked, her mouth curling into a smile. They were in a field where hundreds of visitors had gathered for a plowing match and horse races, the sale of home baking and sewing and knitting, and the showing of prize cattle. It had been a year since James, now eighteen years old, had left home and found work as a hired man. James lingered at the girl's table as long as he dared. Molly O'Malley, he learned, was new to the district, sent from Toronto to serve the family of Edward Edinborough, the biggest landowner in the district.

"They wanted us out of Toronto," Molly told James. "We were dying of the typhoid in Montreal and Kingston. They figured all us Irish carried the disease in our veins. We wouldn't be here but we were starving in Ireland. No more potatoes, nothing to eat. We had to get out.

"I'm seventeen now," Molly said. "Mrs. Edinborough says I'm old enough to be thinking of making my own family. She says if I find a husband who's willing to work for them, we can stay with them forever." She smiled and

21

blinked her eyes in the sunshine. "But maybe I'd sooner go off somewhere, just to see what life might bring me."

James took it as a hint she'd like a man who could free her of the servitude of the Edinborough household. He told her he had felt the same way in his home village of Hope,* three day's walk to the east. "It was a religious colony, the Children of Peace," James said. "I felt trapped there, watched over every moment of the day. I couldn't wait to leave."

Three months after meeting Molly, James attended a Christmas social at St. James Roman Catholic Church. He had spoken with her several times and now, he decided, the time had come to get serious. "I think we should get married," he said. "What do you think?" Molly showed no surprise at James's question. She's probably been expecting me to ask, he thought.

"You'd have to become a Catholic," Molly answered.

"I don't mind," James replied. He'd do anything to capture this lovely young girl.

The traditional Catholic wedding ceremony was attended by several of Molly's aunts and uncles and a few friends. After their wedding, the babies came along quickly. The first, Thomas, was a big boy who came into the world with a head of curly red hair. The next three babies died in a cholera epidemic.

James also learned it was not easy for a Catholic – even a nominal Catholic, like himself – to find fair treatment in a place where the religion of Rome was considered an alien intrusion, something to be detested and feared.

"We have to get out of here," James told Molly. "They don't want to hire me and when they do, they won't pay nothin' at all."

Molly had relatives in the new territory of the Queen's Bush that reached all the way to Georgian Bay. She encouraged James in the idea of moving there. "My brothers in Grey County will put us up until we get our own place," she said. "They say there's free land there."

James sold their few sticks of furniture and with Molly, the boys Thomas and Joe and their sisters Bridget and Elizabeth, the Leppards set out. They took turns riding the single horse James owned, picking up the Sydenham

---

* Now called Sharon

Road as it curved toward Georgian Bay. After five days they reached the new settlement of Flesherton. They found it as untidy as the other villages they'd known. At the general store, James bought a bag of flour and asked directions to Thomas O'Malley's clearing. He was told to branch off the road to the right, follow a path through the bush for four miles, and he would soon come on to the place.

They heard the hogs before they could see the shanty that Thomas and his brother Joseph had erected. The animals were rooting in a ditch where garbage had been thrown. A man rushed out of the shanty, shouting at the hogs. He stopped suddenly when he saw James, Molly and the children. "Those hogs'll eat anything," he cried, "and there's poison weed in that ditch. But I'm mighty glad to see you all, never thought we'd live long enough to welcome you."

It was Thomas O'Malley, Molly's eldest brother. "Sister, it's a blessed thing to see you," he said. He was barefoot and wore only an old pair of overalls and a torn shirt. In a few minutres, Thomas's wife Mary, their two children and his brother Joseph were adding their welcomes. After driving the hogs back to the pigsty Thomas set about preparing a barbecue in an outdoor fire pit.

The meal of pork ribs was enlivened by talk of what the brothers had accomplished in their two years on the land. That summer they had harvested eighty bushels of wheat and twenty-five bushels of oats, along with Indian corn, potatoes, turnips and in the spring, fifty pounds of maple syrup.

"It is mighty lonely up here, like living in the forest. But you get used to it," Thomas told James. "No cussed neighbours to bother you. About the only problem we have is bears, they come around trying to eat up the oat crop or snag a hog. Soon fall will be here and the bears will need to fatten themselves for winter. They're cantankerous and dangerous. You can help us keep watch tonight."

Along about ten o'clock, as the mosquitoes and gnats made good meals of the men, a horrible noise came from a paddock behind the shanty. "Bear's got a hog," Joseph shouted. A huge black bear had a sizeable hog in its jaws and was shaking it like a terrier would shake a rat. "Let's go after it," Thomas hollered.

The chase carried the three men and their dogs into the woods, just shy of a cedar swamp. James carried a flintlock rifle, a relic of the War of 1812. He caught up to the bear as the dogs were nipping at its flanks. James fired. A cloud obscured the moon and the forest fell dark. He waited for the smoke from his rifle to clear. James saw the bear, now dead, huge and black, lodged against the trunk of a pine tree. He had shot it in the heart. The two dogs chewed at its hind leg. He watched the porker as it struggled in the weeds, covered in blood.

A week later, having decided to leave their children with Thomas and Mary, James and Molly set off to find land for themselves. They followed the Boyne River to where it merged with the Beaver River below the raging torrent of Eugenia Falls. Looking up, they saw a green and purple escarpment and once having climbed it, a vast stretch of high tableland. "There has to be good land here free and clear," James declared. "Why, we'll live like kings once we get a cabin up."

The free land that James Leppard thought he would find in the Queen's Bush was no longer free. He had arrived too late, and had to satisfy himself with six gravelly acres still unclaimed, a rough and stony patch of land reached by a trail that lead from the Eugenia Falls. It was all that remained of a fifty-acre lot where the rest of the land, looking decidedly more promising, had been deeded to an earlier arrival. Even so, he had to pay two dollars an acre. Custom dictated that he cultivate crops and put up a habitation as a claim to permanent ownership.

As poor as the land might appear to other eyes, to James Leppard these few acres were a treasure. They changed him from a footless wanderer to a man of property, proud to own the land on which his children scurried about in their play. It was a start. That was what counted, and he was sure it would someday lead him to richer property and a better future.

"We've got a good crop of stones but this land isn't worth a damn," James told Molly one night after he'd spent twelve hours dislodging rocks and carrying them to the side of a field he hoped to plow.

"I suppose you're going to blame me for us coming up here," Molly answered. "When I think how easy I had it before I married you, I'm sorry for the day we ever met."

"Don't say that Molly," James said. "I know I'm the one that wanted us to move off on our own. We've just got to stick together, that's all we can do. Things will get better." He drew Molly to him and stroked her hair. She sobbed, then looked up and James saw a small smile come over her face.

"I'll never leave you, James. But I'm so tired."

"If I could get together enough money to buy some proper stuff for farming," James said, "we'd be a lot better off. A good plow and a reaper would set us up just fine."

The day that James took a bag of potatoes to Henderson's store, intent on trading for tea and sugar, he heard of a way to earn the money he so desperately needed.

"Why don't you go up to Owen Sound," Mr. Henderson told him. "They say there's jobs on the lake boats for shipwrights. A good carpenter like you should be able to do that kind of work."

When James got home he talked to Molly about this new opportunity. "If it means you can come back with a few dollars, go ahead," Molly told him. "We'll manage without you somehow."

All that summer James worked the boats sailing into Georgian Bay and the big lakes, Huron, Michigan and Superior. He tore up and replaced deck planks, repaired cabins, and once dove underwater to patch a rudder damaged on an uncharted rock, saving a trip to dry dock. That happened near the rapids at Sault Ste. Marie, and the captain decided to tie up for a day to give his crew a rest.

James wandered into town. On a bluff overlooking the river, he found a Roman Catholic church. Near it sat a building whose front doorstep sagged to one side. It would not be hard to fix, James thought. While he watched, a nun emerged and walked to the church. James presumed he was looking at a convent. There must be a Mother Superior about.

When James knocked on the door nothing happened for a long time. Finally, it opened a crack. He saw in the dim light a woman wearing a nun's habit. He gave his name and offered to repair the sunken doorstep.

"Wait here," he was told. After a few minutes the door opened again and another nun came out. They talked. She said she was Sister Bernadette and that yes, the doorstep needed fixing. The building had been an old warehouse before it was taken over by the Sisters of St. Joseph.

Sister Bernadette agreed to give James a meal and pay him a dollar to fix the doorstep. He'd work first, and eat later. When James lifted off a foundation block, he realized he was into a bigger job than he'd expected. Summoning Sister Bernadette, he asked permission to go into the cellar.

"Is that really necessary?" she asked. "It's not very nice down there. We try to stay out of it. Just do what you can to shore up the doorstep."

A hopeless task, James told himself. He would have to get into the cellar. There was a trapdoor just around the corner. Lifting it revealed the source of the problem. The floor of the cellar had sunk on one side, causing the beams to lean crazily. It was a wonder the whole building hadn't collapsed.

James noticed several mounds of fresh earth. He began to poke at one pile, and felt something hard. Scraping away the dirt, he found a wooden box. He heard footsteps, and saw Sister Bernadette make her way into the cellar.

"Whatever are you doing?" She sounded alarmed. "There's no need to poke around like that."

This was when the awful thought came to James. He'd heard stories about this sort of thing. Babies buried in convent cellars. Children of the nuns, their fathers priests. The babies baptized, and then drowned in the baptismal water. A Catholic ritual.

James had never been comfortable in the Catholic Church. It wasn't just that he'd felt discriminated against back in Adjala Township. Growing up Protestant, he'd heard tales of Popish evil and had been warned against mixing with Catholics. Now he understood why.

"You've got babies buried here," he blurted. "When did you bury the last one? Look, there's fresh earth. No wonder you didn't want me down here."

"Oh dear God," Sister Bernadette answered. "Is that what you think? I knew I shouldn't have let you start this job."

"But you did, and now your secret's out."

"There's no secret. No babies. It's all lies. Slanderous, despicable lies, spread by spiteful Protestants. They hate us. They write evil books about us. Like that book by that dreadful woman in Montreal, claiming to reveal the confessions of a nun. We're forbidden to read it."

James had heard tales of misbehavour between Catholic priests and nuns. There must be some truth in all the stories, he thought. "Explain what's been going on, then," he demanded.

The explanation Sister Bernadette gave James was that in the early days of Sault Ste. Marie, settlers had hidden guns in the cellar of the storehouse. They were to be brought out only when needed for protection against Indian raids. They'd been forgotten for years. When the nuns heard about the buried weapons, they decided to dig them up, one or two at a time, so as not to cause suspicion. They sold the guns and used the money to help the poor.

"There could be no greater sin than taking the life of an innocent babe," Sister Bernadette said. "Unless it be the sin of breaking our vows of chastity, poverty and obedience. Holy vows. We are all brides of Jesus Christ. We would never betray Him."

James dug about some more as Sister Bernadette watched. "Go ahead, open it," she told him when he had dug a box clear. The box was long and narrow. He broke it open. Two old flintlock rifles. He held one up.

"This don't mean there's no babies down here," he said. He felt shamed by the accusation he'd made. But neither was he prepared to admit he had been wrong.

"You can see for yourself there's only guns," the nun told him. James grunted, a muted response intended to commit him neither way. He told Sister Bernadette it would take at least two men to repair the sunken beams. He had no time to finish the job. There were other piles of dirt in the cellar, but he never bothered to disturb them.

When James got home, he told Molly what had happened. He was convinced he had found a secret burial ground where infants had been sacrificed to save the nuns from shame and the Church from scandal.

Molly was aghast at his story.

"Never, no not ever will I believe you. Don't you dare say anything to anyone about this. True or not, you're not to repeat it. You'll burn in hell if you do."

"Maybe so, but I can no longer be a Catholic," James said. "And I'll do better when people know I'm not one. Stay in the Church if you want. Let the children believe whatever you tell them."

"You'll pay for this, James. And the rest of us, too. We'll all suffer God's wrath."

James tried but could not get out of his head the image of babies being buried in the convent cellar. He remembered his own little ones, especially Rosannah. She was a beautiful child, always cheerful. Despite her rebellious ways and the problems she caused, she was his favourite of all his children.

After Rosannah turned thirteen, James noticed she no longer kept him constant company as he went about his chores. One day, James discovered her behind the barn, crying while she cradled a kitten.

It took James a long time to coax Rosannah into telling him the cause of her tears. A bit at a time, the truth came out. It concerned Father Quinn, the priest at St. Agnes Catholic Church. Now he understood why Rosannah had been distancing herself from not just her father, but from her brothers as well. Father Quinn had kept her in the sacristy one afternoon, where she'd been folding vestments and alter cloths.

"Father Quinn asked me if I was still pure. I told him yes. He said he must do something so I would stay pure. Then he put his finger in me, down there. And something else, too. He told me only God would know, and I must tell no one.

"Daddy, it hurt, why did he do that?"

James held his daughter close to him, and cried. The tears of the two mingled, springing from a shared bitterness. "It's all right, Rosannah," he told her. "You don't have to go back to that church anymore. But don't tell your Mother why. It would kill her." He knew it would be useless to complain about the priest. His anger grew within him and one day, when he could no longer contain his hatred, he went to the Church. He intended to beat Father Quinn, and perhaps even kill him. When he got there he found a new priest had arrived in Vandeleur just that morning. Father Quinn had been sent to Toronto.

When the census taker arrived in 1871, James put himself down as having no religion. He made his desertion irrevocable when he applied for membership in the Loyal Orange Order, the Protestant organization brought to Canada from County Armagh in Ireland.

On the morning of Rosannah's death, James was on a ladder fitting a final spar into place for the roof of Pat Burns's new barn. He'd barely begun the task when his boy Billy ran into the farmyard. It was a little after seven o'clock.

"What's the matter, lad?" James asked when he saw Billy standing below him, breathless and tearful.

"Something awful's happened to Rosannah. I think she's died. Ma says she's been poisoned. She says to come home right away."

# Chapter 5

## THE FIRST WITNESS

### Morning, November 3, 1884

Molly Leppard, mother of the murdered Rosannah, was the first witness to testify at the trial of Cook Teets. Leonard Babington saw this as a clever strategy on the part of the Crown. Molly's testimony on the events surrounding her daughter's death would be sure to harden the attitude of the jury toward the accused. The Crown's careful preparation of the case against Cook Teets would make his conviction a certainty, Leonard thought. He was satisfied there was no chance of himself being called, as he'd seen Rosannah only that one time since his return from Toronto.

When the clerk Angus McMorrin called Molly's name, she rose from her seat and made her way to the witness box. Leonard leaned forward at the press table, eyeing her intently. Although more than a year had passed since Rosannah's death, Molly was dressed for mourning. Her black wool dress sagged loosely on her body, revealing little of a figure that was still shapely despite forty-eight years of hard living and many pregnancies. On her head she wore a small black hat bearing a limp artificial flower. A tattered veil descended over her eyes. After Angus McMorrin had sworn her in, Bible in hand, Molly settled into the witness box. It was large and ornately carved. Once seated, she made the ritual Sign of the Cross, lifted her veil, and adjusted her spectacles.

Alfred Frost, a towering figure at six foot five, took up his position in front of Molly, rocking slightly on his heels. He was said to have acquired the habit when he'd worked as a youth on the boats sailing out of Owen

Sound. Leonard, who was good at ferreting out information, had learned this was the first murder trial of Frost's career. There were reports he and Judge Armour were old friends and that they'd articled together at a law firm in Cobourg, down on Lake Ontario. The prosecutor paused in his rocking, as if to set his feet more solidly, and addressed Molly in a voice designed to convey kindness toward her.

"Now, Mrs. Leppard, the court would like to hear in your own words all you know of what transpired the night your daughter Rosannah died. You were with her at that time, the night of the thirty-first of October of last year?"

"That's right, she was at home with me on the farm."

"And how old was Rosannah at the time of her death?"

"Twenty-five years of age on the twelfth of July, the same year she died."

Twenty-five years of love and sorrow gone in a few hours of horror, Leonard thought. Molly had worked alongside her husband, James, during desperately hard times. She'd helped trim the logs that went into their house, dug and planted a garden year after year, pulled weeds, and chased off un-welcome animals. She'd put up vegetables and crab apples for the winter, and made flour sacks into dresses for her girls. All that time, growing more tired and weary, she'd tried to raise her children in the faith she'd absorbed back in Ireland.

Alfred Frost was keenly interested in hearing everything that Molly could remember about how Rosannah had become entangled with Cook Teets.

"What do you know of your daughter's marriage to the prisoner?" he asked.

Molly took off her glasses, sighed, and hesitated before answering. Leonard thought the prosecutor's question would allow Molly to share the distress that she, as a good mother, felt over her lively daughter's decision to take up with a much older man of a different religion, and blind.

"I know a little something," she finally said. "I tried to keep an eye on Cook whenever he came around. One morning, I saw them together at the fence. He'd been pressing her to give him an answer about getting married."

The fence Molly was referring to was the zigzag split rail fence that James had thrown across the back of their property. It kept the cow in the meadow and deer out of the garden.

"Where did they go to live after their marriage?"

"They ran off so quick Cook hadn't gotten around to finding a place to live. He remained at his mother's house and she remained with me."

Her answer seemed to perplex Judge Armour. He leaned over his dais, a quizzical look on his face, to ask Molly, "How far is it from your place to where the prisoner lived?"

"There are two ways. By the road it would be five or six miles but by the path that crosses the river and goes through the bush, it would be about three and a half."

Judge Armour nodded, causing a flutter in the tangle of long white hair that tumbled onto his shoulders. Leonard judged him to be well into his fifties, a little on the heavy side, like most prosperous men. Molly bowed her head when Judge Armour spoke, as if she were afraid to look at this commanding figure in his black judicial robe.

By now, Molly was beginning to jerk her head as she spoke. It was a mannerism she fell into when she was nervous. She'd say a few words, pause, then jerk her head, as if she'd been surprised by something.

Alfred Frost asked Molly how long Rosannah and Cook had continued their separate living arrangements.

"From the day of their marriage until her death, except for the time they went visiting his folks in Michigan."

Leonard was impressed with Molly's answer, mainly because he knew she found it difficult to pin down an exact time for just about anything. He wondered if she'd been rehearsed. He remembered how she would get confused when different things were talked about at the same time. They got jumbled up together. She relied on her husband to tell her when it was time to slaughter the hogs, or kill a turkey for Thanksgiving.

Leonard knew the Leppards went without many things, but that didn't seem to matter to Molly. She had told him, in the days when he used to visit Rosannah, that their place had a coziness that even her home in County Mayo had lacked. The single room of their cabin had two windows, both facing the front. For the longest time, neither held glass; a luxury James could not afford. Molly had covered them with animal hides she had boiled and beaten with her shillelagh and a stone until they were porous enough to allow light through. Hand-hewn boards eventually replaced the dirt floor. Their furniture consisted of a table, a stove, an ancient armoire, a long bench that sat next to one wall, and beds that were separated by blankets hung from the ceiling.

To Leonard, the cabin gave off a miasma of unpleasant smells – dried sweat, dirty garments and cooking fumes. At one end of the room a loft held discarded tools and a few sacks of potatoes. Except for a Bible, there was not a book in the place. Molly had told Leonard the Leppards were a story in themselves. It was clear to him she was aware many folks looked down on them, as they did on anyone who cooked, ate and slept all in one room. Still, such intimacy didn't seem to bother her. Family was everything, Molly used to say. She found pride in her family's ability to overcome hardship and survive a crop lost to frost or flattened by hail.

As these thoughts were running through Leonard's mind, Alfred Frost shifted his questioning from Rosannah's marriage to how long the Leppards had known Cook Teets.

"Oh, a long time," Molly said. She added that various Teets had visited the farm while her children were growing up. Lately, she said, Cook had come alone with his dog Cromwell. It was a Labrador Retriever that went everywhere with him. Cook's blindness didn't stop him from wandering the roads around Vandeleur as long as he had that dog, Molly added.

Alfred Frost listened patiently. "Now, Mrs. Leppard," he interjected, "can you tell the court when it was that you became aware of Cook's interest in Rosannah?"

"It was after he came to ask Rosannah if she would be willing to go up to the Teets's place and work for his mother," she said between jerks of her head. "I'm sorry I ever allowed it. If my oldest, Tom, had been around, he'd have kept Cook in his place. It's hard for a decent woman to raise a family. People around here don't have no morals at all."

"I'm sure many would agree," the prosecutor responded. "But just tell us what happened the day Cook came to hire Rosannah."

"I saw Cook coming up the trail from the little footbridge over the river. It was muddy and I saw his boots and overalls were dirty. I didn't want him in the house. I said to my husband, 'The way that man gets around, you'd think he could see.'" Her head jerked to one side. Leonard thought she was having a nervous reaction to the pressure of being on the witness stand.

Molly said Cook had stopped when he got to the fence and called to ask if he could come in. He said he wanted to speak to Rosannah. By then, Rosannah was at the door watching Cook. Rosannah called out to ask him what he wanted.

"He said his mother needed help. Cook said the house was too much for her since Mr. Teets died, so he wanted to know if Rosannah could come up and help her. He allowed, of course, that she'd have to move to their place."

"It didn't surprise you that Mrs. Teets needed someone to help out," Alfred Frost said.

Molly said she wasn't a bit surprised. "She's going on for ninety and she was alone in the house except for Cook." Molly added that everyone knew her other children had gone off and set up their own families. Her eldest son Nelson ran the sawmill and employed three or four men at the Teets's furniture shed.

"And what was Rosannah's reaction to all this?"

"Oh, she was excited. Especially when she heard he'd pay her five dollars a month. She said if she could leave the babies with me, she could do a real good job for Mrs. Teets. She said she would use the money for things the children needed."

"Rosannah didn't mind leaving the children with you?"

Molly snorted at the prosecutor's question, and jerked her head.

"Mind? She was glad to get away from them. I don't mean she didn't love them. Sure she did. But she never got any help from their fathers, and I think she thought it would be like a holiday, going up to the Teets's."

Molly added that Rosannah claimed to have been married to David Rogers, the father of her youngest, but they were divorced. Molly didn't believe this. If there'd been a divorce, she said, it was one of those Queen's Bush divorces.

Hearing this, Alfred Frost smiled. "Whatever do you mean, Mrs. Leppard, a Queen's Bush divorce?"

"You know," she said, "when people just walk away from each other. If the law don't work for you, folks around here just ignore it."

Leonard had heard the expression. He knew it took an Act of Parliament to register a divorce and no one in Vandeleur would spend money on a piece of paper to say they're no longer married. If you were a Catholic, you wouldn't get a divorce even if you did have the money.

Alfred Frost parried Molly's explanation. He changed the subject, asking her, "You raised no objection to her taking the job with Mrs. Teets?"

"Wasn't any point. I said to my husband, may as well let her go. I have to take care of those kids anyway. Rosannah was all happy, said she'd go anytime Mrs. Teets needed her."

Cook came for Rosannah the next morning, Molly said. He arrived in a four-wheeled buggy driven by Homer Jessup. Rosannah and Cook climbed together into the back seat.

Molly told Alfred Frost that Rosannah returned home every few days to visit her children and help with a few household chores. It seemed she was happy working for Mrs. Teets. Molly was surprised, therefore, when Rosannah came home after a month to announce she had left the Teets household.

"That old woman didn't really need me," Molly said Rosannah told her. "Rosannah said Cook's mother didn't like the way she did things. She kept telling her she would cook and clean herself. Rosannah said Mrs. Teets couldn't get used to having someone take charge of her house."

"Did you believe her?" Alfred Frost asked. Molly said she wondered if there was any other reason. She thought Mrs. Teets should have been glad to have somebody relieve her of sweeping, cleaning and cooking.

Alfred Frost summed up what they'd heard so far. "So Rosannah has spent a few weeks with the Teets's, and now she's back home. Can you tell the court if she continued to see Cook?"

"They couldn't leave each other alone," Molly said. "Cook came around almost every day. I couldn't see why Rosannah would want to encourage him, an old man like that, blind and all. And he wasn't a Catholic. Rosannah knew I wanted her to marry a Catholic."

"You didn't want Cook calling on Rosannah?"

"No, I didn't. I used to watch them, sitting close together on the bench beside the stove. Whispering all the time." Another jerk of her head.

"Did you have words with Rosannah about this?"

Molly lifted a wisp of hair that had fallen onto her face. She paused before answering. Leonard thought she must be debating what to say.

"We had words," Molly admitted. "I was fixing the fire one day and I figured the time had come to lay down the law. I told her, you go off and get yourself pregnant again and I'll have another brat to look after. I reminded her I was her mother, and I was putting my foot down. I told her that if she saw him one more time I'd disown her."

Leonard imagined the scene. He knew Molly had a sharp temper and he remembered Rosannah telling him how, when she was little, her mother had used a wooden spoon to spank her and her sisters. There would have been a good deal of screaming back and forth.

Alfred Frost asked Molly if she could explain the cause of her daughter's disobedience. Leonard thought he'd like to have an answer to that, as well.

"I can't explain it," Molly said. "Except that Cook must have made her all kinds of promises. Must have said he'd buy her anything she wanted. His brother always gave him money."

Molly fell silent. Watching her, Leonard wondered if she was thinking back on Rosannah's life, perhaps trying to understand what it was that had brought her and Cook together. Molly stared around the courtroom before jerking her head toward Judge Armour. She took up her testimony, hesitating every few words.

"Cook came back the next morning," Molly said. "Rosannah went outside to talk to him. They were out there for quite a while before she brought him into the house." Molly hesitated, tried to speak, but seemed to be choking up. "That was when Rosannah told us what they'd decided," she said. She was sobbing now. "Rosannah said she and Cook were going to get married."

Everyone in the courtroom could see that Molly's emotions had gotten the best of her. Judge Armour told Alfred Frost that his witness might wish a chance to regain her composure. "Recess for fifteen minutes," the judge announced, rising from his seat.

# Chapter 6

## THE ELOPEMENT

### Recess, November 3, 1884

**M**olly was grateful for the few moments she had been allowed to pull herself together. Thinking about the testimony she had given, it seemed her whole life had been a series of misfortunes and blows of various sort. First the famine in Ireland when many of her relatives had died. The awful voyage across the Atlantic and the fever that had broken out followng their arrival in Canada. After she married James, there was one baby after another. She'd grown tired of the sex that marriage required and after four or five babies, she was exhausted by all that fucking. There, I've said it, Molly thought. Dear God, how I hate that word. And what kind of life would Rosannah have had to endure if she'd lived?

Molly could not forget how Rosannah's announcement of her intention to marry Cook Teets had hung in the air. The day had begun beautifully, a glorious spring morning, the first of June, 1883. Cook had arrived at about noon, and before Molly had the chance to serve him dinner, Rosannah blurted out their intentions. Everyone needed time to take it in. She had turned to her husband, showing surprise and shock on her face.

James Leppard was the first to speak.

"Cook, aren't you married already?" he asked.

"I was, but Ann Jane left me. We're divorced now."

Molly knew of Cook's marriage to Ann Jane Sargent, a farm girl from the next township. Divorce? Another one of those Queen's Bush divorces, of course. He'd only have to go to a different church in another town to get married again.

James kept at Cook, wanting to make sure how things stood between he and Ann Jane. At least James wants to know they're all finished, Molly thought.

"Are you sure it's all over between you?"

"She's gone up to Owen Sound. Haven't seen her for over a year."

James turned to Rosannah to ask if she really wanted to marry Cook.

"Now Rosie, are you sure you know what you're getting yourself in for? Do you really want to marry him?"

"I do, Daddy. I love Cook."

"If you're sure that's what you want, Rosie, and Cook, if you can support her, then it's all right with Mother and me."

Molly felt betrayed by her husband's declaration. How many times would she be taken by surprise today? Molly was determined that if Cook was to be her son-in-law, Rosannah would at least have a Catholic wedding.

"What priest will you have? Where will you get married?"

Rosannah promised her mother all that would be worked out, not to worry about it. Molly, feeling somewhat better, started dinner preparations. James produced a bottle of Gooderham & Worts Bonded Stock whisky from the armoire and filled cups for himself and Cook. Rosannah and Cook sat arm in arm on the bench against the wall. She reached up and caressed his smoothly-shaven face. Watching her, Molly thought you had to admit it – blind or not, Cook was a well-turned-out man. Had a fair bit of money, must get it from the family furniture business. Lots of people bought their tables, their chairs, their chests of drawers from the Teets's.

Cook seemed quite ready to spend money on new clothes for Rosannah. "We'll go and see Mrs. Carson and get her to make up a nice outfit for you," Cook told her. "Would you like something new for the wedding, Mrs. Leppard?" Molly didn't think so.

James asked Cook if he'd made arrangements for the children in case anything happened to him or Rosannah.

"It would be a smart thing for both of you to get some insurance so the children would be looked after," he said.

Perhaps Rosannah was on the right track after all with Cook Teets, Molly thought. But still she worried about them having a Catholic wedding. She'd have to talk to Rosannah tomorrow about the arrangements. More than anything, she wanted to make sure her daughter would share in God's reward.

That night, Bridget swept the house before everyone settled down. While Molly turned back the covers of her bed, she listened to Rosannah sing a lullaby to her children. A pretty voice, you have to allow her that. If only she behaved as well as she sang.

When Molly awoke the next morning and crossed the room to check on Rosannah, there was no sign of her. The children played on the floor beside an empty bed.

"That girl's gone off and done something foolish," she told Bridget, who had begun to dress the girls. Molly's greatest fear was that Rosannah and Cook had run away together. The more she thought about Rosannah's reckless behaviour, the angrier she became.

Rosannah did not come home that day or the next. Molly spent the time speculating endlessly on what her daughter was up to. She hoped Rosannah and Cook hadn't been married by some Protestant priest. That would be the end of her. On the second night after Rosannah's leaving, just as Molly was about to bolt the front door, Rosannah showed up.

"It's me, Mother," she said as she came into the house. She smiled and dropped her small carrying bag on the floor.

There was only one thing Molly wanted to know.

"Are you married now, Rosie?" she asked.

"That's all you care about, isn't it, Mother. I may as well tell you, Cook and I got married in Toronto."

"Do you have your wedding certificate?"

"Yes, here it is."

Molly hardly glanced at the official looking paper. Too bad she couldn't read. She cared only if they had had a Catholic wedding.

"Were you married by a priest?"

"No, Mother, a Presbyterian minister married us."

Molly looked at her daughter, unwilling to believe what she'd heard. For all the years she had struggled at Vandeleur, what she had wanted more than anything was to pass on her Catholic faith to her children. Even as a child Rosannah had defied her, refusing to be the compliant and religious daughter Molly had always hoped for. A rage built within Molly as her sense of betrayal mounted. Her face flushed and when she spoke, her voice was high-pitched as her words tumbled from her mouth.

"In that case, you can take Cook Teets and go to Hell. Because that's where you're going, anyway." With a scowl, she ripped the wedding certificate into pieces. "Where's Cook now?" she demanded to know.

"He's gone back to his mother," Rosannah answered. "She didn't want me there, and I know you don't want Cook here. He's going to find us a place of our own."

Rosannah went to her bed, drew the blanket that hung around it, and nothing more was said that night. The next day the household settled back into its quiet routine. Molly didn't see Cook for several more days. When he did show up, it was to collect Rosannah to take her to Michigan for a visit with his brother's family. When Rosannah came home several days later Molly thought she looked unwell. She was convinced her daughter was pregnant, but Rosannah denied it.

Two days after Rosannah's return, Cook showed up at the Leppard place about four o'clock, in time for tea. Molly was standing by the stove when Rosannah went to the door to meet him. Molly wondered what her husband would think of this. He'd been away since Rosannah's return home, finishing the new barn for Mr. Burns on the Tenth Concession. It would be good to have him back.

"How are you, Rosie?" Cook asked. "I've been to Flesherton to buy some tools."

"I've been sick to my stomach all day," Rosannah told Cook. She led him to the long bench backing against the wall. They sat down and she put her head in his lap. He stroked her hair while Molly set out a pot of black tea, a jar of her own strawberry jam, and a loaf of freshly baked bread. She hacked off several thick slices. A tin pail filled with milk drawn that morning from the Leppard's cow sat in the middle of the table. Cook pulled the bench over to the table and returned to his seat next to Rosannah. Molly sat at the end in a Windsor chair, the one item of furniture in the Leppard house that had been crafted by a Teets workman. Rosannah nibbled a bit of bread and said she wasn't hungry.

"Cook, I've never felt the same since you gave me that glass of wine at Munshaw's hotel."

"But that was a week ago," Cook protested. "That can't be what's bothering you." He sipped on his tea. No one said anything. It was getting dark – the onset of fall had brought an early twilight – when Cook got up and announced he had to get home to his mother. Molly glanced at her clock, saw its hands stilled at half past two, and remembered it had a broken spring.

"Come over to Eugenia Falls with me, Rosie," Cook said. "I want you to see a place we can rent."

"Cook Teets, I cannot," Rosannah answered. "My head aches and I'm still sick at my stomach."

"Well, come a little piece with me then," Cook pleaded.

Rosannah slipped a shawl on her shoulders and went outside with Cook. They sat on a flat rock near the fence. Molly watched as the two hugged and kissed. A little later, Cook stood, untethered his dog, and turned to go home. Rosannah came back into the house.

"We'll be moving in a few days," Rosannah said. Her voice faltered as she spoke. She stumbled toward Molly's bed and threw herself onto the straw mattress. Holding her head in both hands she cried, "Mother, I have an awful headache."

"Take a spoonful of your medicine," Molly told her. Dr. Griffin's medicine would calm her nerves. Ease the "female hysteria."

"Let me have the bottle," Rosannah demanded. "Don't need a spoon." She lifted the bottle to her lips and took several gulps.

As Molly settled Rosannah into the trundle bed she shared with her children, she heard a knock on the door. "If that's Scarth Tackaberry, keep him away from me," Rosannah called out. "I can't stand that man." Molly fastened the blanket that shielded Rosannah's bed and went to the door. She found Scarth standing there. He came in and sat down, saying he wanted to talk about ways to control the rabbits and raccoons that infested his garden. Molly was anxious to be rid of him.

"I'm tending to Rosannah, she's sick," she said. "Better for you to come back another time."

Scarth Tackaberry wasn't so easily put off. He badgered Molly about the best way of getting rid of pests. How did strychnine compare with other poisons? Molly didn't like his questions, or the way he kept fingering his beard, all frizzy and reddish brown, while he cast searching looks around the cabin. It took Molly an hour to get rid of him.

Rosannah woke up shortly after Scarth left. She got out of bed and stood by the stove. Molly was darning a pair of her husband's overalls. She worked by candlelight and squinted to follow the path of her thread. Rosannah said she felt hungry.

"Put on the kettle," Molly suggested. "Make yourself a cup of tea. It will settle your stomach."

"I don't feel like tea. I'll have milk."

It was impossible to satisfy that child, Molly thought. Whatever she suggested, Rosannah had a different idea.

Rosannah poured milk from the pail and cut two thick slices of her mother's bread. She spooned crabapple jam from the jar Molly had placed on the table.

"That's more than I've seen you eat all week," Molly told her.

Rosannah ate the bread and drank the milk. When she was finished, she and Molly lit their pipes and smoked before going to their beds. They avoided any discussion of Rosannah's marriage. Instead, they talked of the weather and discussed the vegetables that had to be put in the root cellar for the winter.

When Molly went to say goodnight to Rosannah, she noticed a small purse hanging on the wall, over her bed. It was open and she could see it contained a carefully folded piece of paper. She said nothing about this to Rosannah. Later, Molly drifted off to sleep. She thought she heard some kind of singing coming from far away.

At about midnight Molly heard Rosannah call to her. "There's somebody at the latch," Rosannah said. "I'm scared."

"It's just the dog," Molly called from her bed. "You know he rolls against the door in his sleep. Go check the door if you don't believe me"

Molly listened as Rosannah got out of bed, lit a lamp, and made her way to the front door. Rosannah found it fastened the way Molly had left it. To make the door more secure, she stuck a knife between the latch and the frame.

"I suppose you are contented now," Molly said.

"Now I can sleep," Rosannah answered.

Some time about dawn — it was still dark — Molly was awakened by a scream from behind the blanket that sheltered Rosannah. Everyone in the house heard the cry. Molly stumbled as she struggled out of bed and hit her head on its iron frame. She found Rosannah tossing in agony, her arms and legs flailing as she arched her back against her mattress. One arm struck Molly and a coiled fist caught her in the face. Rosannah was foaming at the mouth and her eyes stared out blankly.

It was Rosannah's scream, mournful, drawn out and rising in pitch, that Molly remembered as Angus McMorrin's voice jarred her out of her reverie.

# Chapter 7

## 'POOR ROSIE WON'T SPEAK AGAIN'

### Morning, November 3, 1884

The recess ordered by Judge Armour ended when Angus McMorrin stood up, called out "Oyez, Oyez," and told everyone in the courtroom to rise. The jury filed in and the judge mounted his dais, bowing slightly as he did so. Leonard Babington wiped tears from his eyes at his remembrance of Molly Leppard's testimony. He had memories of a different Rosannah, a happy young girl who enjoyed her farm chores, loved her chicks and rabbits, and had a flashing smile for any young man. He thought of the times they had been together, and of how he had hoped someday to marry her. Now, waiting to hear more of Molly's account of Rosannah's death, he lowered his head and gripped his pen so tightly he was uncertain whether he would be able to go on with his notes.

Alfred Frost crossed his arms and and propped them on his chest as Molly returned to the witness stand. He brushed one hand across his forehead and looked down at his shoes.

"I hope you're feeling better now, Mrs. Leppard," he said. He added he would ask her only a few more questions.

"Can you tell us what you did when you heard your daughter's cries?"

Molly said she rushed to Rosannah's bedside and found her frothing at the mouth. "I sprinkled her face with water and bathed her forehead with a cloth. Her mouth was closed tight. I tried to pry her mouth open with a kitchen knife but I couldn't. Her teeth were locked together."

"So you just bathed her forehead?"

"Yes, I put cold water on her. I could tell she was in pain all over. When I saw her stomach was swelling, I asked her did anyone give you poison? She motioned up and down with her hands five or six times and made a sign I took as 'Yes.'"

Molly appeared much calmer now than before the break. Leonard admired the way she had gotten hold of herself. He thought any woman who had endured the life she had led must be tough and resilient, and Molly was showing both these characteristics.

Alfred Frost circled between the witness box and the jury after hearing Moilly's latest answer. Turning back to Molly, he asked if Rosannah spoke while in these spasms.

"A few words after I brought her around with the water," Molly said. "I applied hot cloths and flannels thinking she might be cold in the stomach. Then she went into another fit. She vomited, and messed herself. When I saw it was no use, and she was dying, I told Bridget to take word to Cook Teets. She stopped at Scarth Tackaberry's house and Mrs. Tackaberry went on to the Teets's place with Bridget. They got Cook. He came."

Leonard noted that nothing in Molly's evidence had so far linked Cook directly to Rosannah's murder. To convince the jury of his guilt, the Crown was going to have to rely on circumstance. That would include any damaging facts about Cook's behaviour on hearing of the loss of his wife.

"Now tell the jury, Mrs. Leppard, at what time did the prisoner arrive at your house on the morning of your daughter's death?"

"I'm not sure, I guess about eight o'clock."

"What time? What time did she say?"

The interjection came from Cook Teets. He'd been squirming in his seat, changing the bandage over his eyes, leaning his head on his hands, and giving vent to deep sighs. Molly's testimony was clearly disturbing to him.

"I can't hear her. I've got to hear those lies," Cook said, standing up, his agitation apparent to everyone in the courtroom. He went as if to get out of the prisoner's dock.

Molly looked to Judge Armour on his dais, as if for protection from Cook.

"Get the prisoner a chair," Judge Armour said. "Let him sit beside his lawyer."

Angus McMorrin, the clerk, hurried to put a chair in place. Cook, with the help of James Masson, fumbled his way to the seat. Everyone was surprised at Cook's outburst. Cook ran his hands over his face, scratched himself on the neck, and rubbed one arm. After a minute, Alfred Frost returned to his questioning.

"What did the prisoner do or say when he came into the house?"

"He came in and went across to the bed. He felt around her body and said, 'Poor Rosie, she won't speak to me again.' He moved away from the bed and went to sit down. I got up to give him a chair but he said he would rather sit on the floor. He had his back to the window and he gripped his head. I don't know if he was really troubled or was just pretending. He was saying as if speaking to himself, 'Poor Rosie, it is me that caused this.'"

"In what tone did he say this?"

"Just a kind of a whisper to himself."

"Anything more?"

"I was on the other side of the room, crying. Bridget was trying to quiet the children. They were bawling for their mother. Mary Ann kept running out the door, as if she wanted to get away."

Alfred Frost asked Molly how long Cook had stayed with Rosannah's body. She said he'd stayed all day, even after Rosannah's body was removed.

"Did he say anything more about the deceased?"

"I remember him saying to my husband, when he came home, 'Mr. Leppard, my calculations is all done with. It's all over.'"

"Did the prisoner ask you how Rosannah took sick or anything of that kind?"

"He never asked any question about her death to my knowledge."

It looked to Leonard as if Molly, who had seemed strong at the outset of this latest round of questions, was begnning to wilt. He wondered how much more of this she could take.

"Before your daughter's death, did you say anything to the prisoner about taking his wife to their own home?"

Molly admitted she was anxious for Cook to take Rosannah and the children to a place of their own.

"He kept putting it off. He allowed he would have a place in a day or so. He said that a few days before she died. He calc'lated he would rent the old Pedlar place."

Alfred Frost took a moment to consider his next question. He stared at the ceiling, put his hands behind his back, and glanced at the jury before looking again at Molly.

"Mrs. Leppard, I am sure the jury would be interested in hearing about the paper in your daughter's purse, the one you mentioned at the inquest last year. Can you describe it for them?"

Leonard remembered how that had come up at the inquest, but no one had paid any attention to it at the time.

"It was a little paper folded at both ends like a doctor would give you with a dose of medicine. I found it in her purse on a nail over her bed."

"Did you see your daughter take anything in the way of medicine that evening?"

"I never saw her take anything except what Dr. Griffin give her in that bottle. She was always into it. But come to think of it, she might have taken somethin' else without my seeing her."

That poor girl would have taken just about anything, Leonard thought. He had wondered if whatever it was that Dr. Griffin was dishing out had addled Rosannah's mind.

At this point, Alfred Frost brought up the matter of strychnine. It was the first time in the trial that anyone made mention of the poison.

"And what about the strychnine that you spoke of at the inquest?" he asked Molly.

The question caused Leonard to reflect on a possible connection between Dr. Griffin's medicines and whatever it was that had killed Rosannah.

Molly put her hands on the witness box and leaned forward with her answer.

"The prisoner was at my house before he and Rosannah went off to the States," Molly replied. "We had some onions on the table. He said they were the best he'd ever tasted. Rosannah told him someone was stealing them out of the garden. He said, 'Why don't you catch them?' I told him it was a pretty hard thing to catch a thief between night and daylight."

Far from being worn out, Molly was wound up now and the words poured forth without a break.

"He said, 'I'll give you what will catch them. You take two or three rows across your garden, get a needle and put some strychnine in the onions in those rows and you'll catch the thief.' I said I wouldn't do that. The prisoner wanted me to do it. He offered it to me different times."

"Did Cook Teets say if he had any strychnine, or where he kept it?"

"He said he had plenty of it, in his trunk. He got it in the States. He said he would bring it the next day. I told him if I had it I might poison my own children by mistake. I didn't want any lives on my head."

"How often did he speak to you about the strychnine?"

"At different times. I am sure he did three or four times."

Alfred Frost was finished with his examination. "Thank you, Molly, you've been most forthright. Your witness, Mr. Masson."

When James Masson rose from his chair he tugged on his suspenders and looked, in turn, first at Judge Armour, then at Molly and finally at the jury. Leonard thought he must feel frustrated with the testimony he'd heard. Leonard had asked around about Masson and had been told he'd moved to Owen Sound from Belleville, another Lake Ontario town, and that he prided himself as a shrewd judge of character. He was known to be a man with military experience, having served in the 18th Regiment of the Canadian Volunteer Militia. Leonard wondered why he hadn't been called back to duty, with rumours of all that trouble with half-breeds and Indians in the North West. What facts might the lawyer bring out that the court hadn't already heard?

James Masson's first question of Molly opened up a new line of inquiry.

"When Rosannah came home from her trip to Michigan," Masson asked Molly, "did you suspect she was again in the family way?"

"I thought that," Molly said.

Leonard knew this line of questioning could be uncomfortable for Molly.

"Rosannah was married before, I believe?"

"She went away from home," Molly replied. It was obvious she wasn't going to admit to any marriage.

"That man she married, you knew nothing at all about him?"

"His name was Rogers, that was all I knew about him. She came home about three weeks after she went off with him."

"That wasn't the first time she had run away from home?"

Leonard thought Molly looked as if she was again on the verge of collapse. She was breathing more rapidly now and she gasped as she struggled with her answer.

"She used to leave home from time to time, if that's what you mean."

"I put it to you, Mrs. Leppard, that your daughter was hardly a chaste young lady. She'd had two children out of wedlock. She was having affairs, running around with one man after another. Isn't it possible one of these men, one of the many she'd thrown over, might have had it in for her?"

"I never gave any thought to that."

"But you wanted to get rid of her? Did you order her away?"

"Yes, I wanted her away."

"Were you violent to her after she was married to the prisoner?"

"I talked to her pretty sharp, but I was never violent."

"Didn't you threaten to knock her brains out with a poker?"

"I never threatened that."

"Didn't you hear she had tried to throw herself in front of a train?"

"I never heard about that."

"And how do you account for that black eye you had when you testified at the inquest? Did you and your daughter have a good punch-up over her marriage to a Protestant?"

"Like I said, her arms were flailing around when she was in a fit and her fist hit me in the face."

James Masson was going hard at Molly Leppard, Leonard thought. He wondered if Judge Armour would allow this line of questioning to continue. So far, he'd made no move to interrupt Masson. The lawyer continued with his cross-examination.

"Was everything going on smoothly between your daughter and the prisoner before her death? They appeared to love one another?"

Molly stared out at the gallery as she pondered the question.

"Well, he pretended to," she said.

"He pretended?" Masson asked, his voice rising. "How can you say he only pretended to love your daughter? Do you have any evidence he didn't love her?"

"No."

Cook's lawyer pressed Molly with more questions. He asked why she hadn't sent for a doctor and whether Rosannah might have eaten anything besides bread and jam during the night. He wanted to know why Molly had distorted what Cook had said when he arrived at the Leppard place that fateful morning.

"You have testified you heard Cook say" – and here Masson made a point of examining his notes – 'Poor Rosie, it is me that caused this.' "You went on to say that he told your husband, 'Mr. Leppard, it's all over.'"

"That's right," Molly said. As she answered, she seemed to shrink into the witness box.

"And that is the extent of what he said about his connection with her death?"

"I've told you just as I remember it."

James Masson paused for a moment. He scratched his nose and cupped his chin in one hand. Leonard thought Molly must have hoped he was finished with her. But the questions kept coming.

"You've told us Cook Teets was speaking in a whisper. You admit you were on the opposite side of the room. And that the children were crying. How can you be sure you heard him correctly?"

"I know what I heard."

"Mrs. Leppard, did you at any time hear Cook Teets say he had killed Rosannah?"

"Not in so many words."

"Did you hear him say he had poisoned her, or he had murdered her?"

"No, but that's what he meant."

"What he meant! How do you know what he meant? It seems to me, Mrs. Leppard, that when Cook Teets saw his wife dead, he was stricken with grief, the grief of a loving husband and an honourable man. He was distressed at having brought Rosannah into a marriage that ended in such catastrophe. You admit you heard no admission of guilt."

Molly looked up at Judge Armour. The judge seemed fixated on the lawyer's questions.

"Your Lordship, the defence moves that all Mrs. Leppard's testimony of Cook Teets's remarks on the morning of Rosannah's death be stricken from the record. The jury must be told to disregard all she has said in that connection."

Alfred Frost bolted from his chair.

"Objection, your Lordship. I implore you to stop this outrageous harassment of the witness. She has given an honest account of what she saw and heard. She doesn't deserve this treatment."

Judge Armour shifted in his seat.

"The jury will disregard the opinion of the witness as to the meaning of the prisoner's comments. Her conclusions are inferential and not evidentiary. But as to the balance of her testimony, I see no reason it should not stand. And Mr. Massson, I advise you to treat the witness with more respect."

"Most assuredly, your Lordship," James Masson responded. He had one other issue to deal with.

"Mrs. Leppard, did you know that Rosannah's life was insured?"

"Yes, of course."

"Was that your idea, or your husband's?"

"I don't know whose idea it was."

"But you thought that if the beneficiary was disqualified by having committed a criminal act, you might lay claim to the money? A lot of money, more than four thousand dollars."

"I never thought any such thing."

James Masson shook his head, and ended his questioning with a sarcastic flourish:

"I'm quite sure, Mrs. Leppard, the jury will take that into account."

Molly had been two hours on the stand, and it was obvious to Leonard that she was exhausted. By the time Judge Armour called for adjournment a few minutes before noon, Leonard was feeling sick to his stomach. He had listened with mounting dread, remembering how yielding Rosannah had been in his arms. The pain in his gut told him of the agony she must have endured. He rushed from his seat at the newspaper table, down the stairs and onto the street where he stood, hands on his hips, retching. He heaved again and again, as if that would cleanse him of the knowledge of Rosannah's suffering. But nothing came, other than the taste of bile that filled his mouth.

# Chapter 8

## THE TALE OF WAHBUDICK

### October 15, 1869

Molly Leppard's testimony carried Leonard Babington back to the days before he'd lost Rosannah, when they'd rambled together through the woods around Vandeleur and hiked into the Beaver Valley. Leonard had not spoken with Rosannah in the last months of her life but he'd listened to stories about how she had carried on with different men. He found such talk upsetting, and he wondered if the medicines she had taken, laced as they were with opium and alcohol, had affected her ability to think straight. Considering all the impulsive things that Rosannah had done, nothing shocked him like her sudden marriage to Cook Teets. Leonard felt he had been betrayed, and that led to anger over the fact she'd chosen to marry a man so much older and so handicapped by his blindness.

Molly's testimony also stirred in Leonard memories of the high hopes he'd had when he'd first become a teacher and he'd hardly known Rosannah, before his life had begun to fall apart.

When Leonard was twelve, his father inherited five thousand pounds on the death of Grandfather Babington. Erasmus Babington squandered a good part of it on an ostentatious two-story stone house, complete with a tower, that he shamelessly named Vandeleur Hall. He had a forty-gallon barrel of whisky hauled up from a distillery in Toronto. The liquor became an essential part of the wages of the workers who built the house.

Leonard took a keen interest in its construction. His father had told him he wanted their home to be different from that of other settlers. He took Leonard with him as he drove along the concession roads looking at the homes of better off farmers. Most favoured Ontario Gothic or Wilderness Georgian architecture, simple variations of old forms adapted to the needs of a cold and remote land. Erasmus decided on a different but still functional plan. He had a house built of stone in the shape of an "L" with a tower of not inelegant proportion. Affixed to the tower was a portico supported by timber and stone that lent an impression of a grand entranceway. It opened on a foyer with a hearth that in winter assured a warm welcome to visitors. Erasmus had river rocks of various sizes set around each window and door, providing a pleasant contrast of color and texture. And as if to measure time, he had cast into the concrete lintel above the front door the date of construction - 1868. It was put in place on Leonard's fourteenth birthday, and the boy thought of it as a sign of his growing up.

Erasmus furnished Vandeleur Hall with the most fashionable and expensive pieces shipped from London and Philadelphia and hauled at great cost by horse and oxen from Owen Sound. A handsome rosewood table covered in marble dominated the foyer. The dining room featured a cut glass chandelier, a walnut dining suite and a sideboard of carved walnut. The headboard on Erasmus's and Esther's bed was seven feet high, of solid walnut, so heavy two men were needed to carry it into the house. In the parlour, a sofa covered in crimson velvet sat below a tapestry of cabbage and vines. The room was filled with chairs, small tables and miscellaneous bric-a-brac. Flowered wallpaper adorned every main floor room except the foyer, which was painted in a simple slate grey.

It was here that Leonard grew up as the only child of this mismatched British couple. He was a quiet but happy boy whose light hair, whitened by the summer sun, gave him the appearance of a towhead. Erasmus and Esther insisted that Leonard be schooled at home and that he become a literate British gentleman, no matter how primitive their surroundings. His exposure to books had come in his first year when his father read to Esther and Leonard by lamplight every night.

Leonard was reading by his fourth birthday and by seven he had devoured *Robinson Crusoe* and *Gulliver's Travels*. He was happy in his solitude but due to there being few visitors to the Babington home, he grew up uncomfortable with strangers. Leonard preferred to wander in the forest when he was not at home reading or attending to the few chores his mother had assigned him.

The first time a neighbour brought his two children to visit, Leonard had run out of the house to hide behind a large elm tree.

There was one boy who, like Leonard, preferred the company of animals in the forest over people. Tom Winship lived three miles away on an acreage fronting the Beaver River. He went to the Vandeleur school until he was twelve, but Leonard had met him much earlier when their parents worshipped together at the Methodist Church.

One October afternoon, when the air was warm and the sun bright, Leonard and Tom played in the yard of Vandeleur Hall with Leonard's dog, Toby. Erasmus was intent on fixing a fence and the boys, in their roughhouse play, were getting in his way. "Go and play some place else," he told them. Leonard had heard fish were spawning and he decided to take Tom down to the Beaver River to watch them swim upstream to lay their eggs. The route was downhill through thick bush, and they would have had an uneventful outing except that Toby, a black and white water spaniel who loved to chase birds, caught sight of what he took to be an injured pheasant. It was a hen playing decoy to protect her young, but Toby neither knew nor cared and chased the bird back uphill, well away from where the boys had entered the woods. Leonard and Tom followed.

The hunt for Toby took them into a thick stretch of woods broken by clearings filled with blueberry bushes. In one, Leonard sighted a herd of whitetail deer. "Shh, look at how they're grazing in the grass," he whispered to Tom. Unseen by the boys, a large mountain cat known to locals as a cougar, moved stealthily toward them. Leonard caught sight of a tawny blur leaping into the clearing. The blur landed a few feet from a doe munching grass at the edge of the clearing. A second leap carried it onto the back of the helpless animal. The rest of the herd dashed into the bush. Leonard grabbed Tom's arm and the two ran in the opposite direction. An hour later they were reunited with an exhausted dog. By then, neither boy had any idea where they were. The slanting rays of the sun were on their backs as they settled down at the foot of a giant cedar. Both fell asleep.

When Leonard awoke, it was dark. He told himself he had to stay calm. There was nothing to panic about. He shook Tom awake, and told him they should remain where they were. Later, they heard coyotes wail in the dark. In the cracks between the treetops Leonard saw the moon rise and dapple the forest floor with brightness. He worried they'd be in trouble when they finally got home.

As the night became chillier, the boys clung together for warmth. Leonard wondered, as they sat with their arms around each other, what it would be like to hold a girl. He'd heard older boys tell of stealing kisses from girls at school.

"Have you ever kissed a girl, Tom?"

"Naw, don't like them."

"But if a fellow had a chance to kiss a girl, how would he go about it?"

"Don't know," Tom answered. "Maybe like this."

Tom planted his lips squarely on Leonard's mouth. Leonard felt warmth that spread into his arms and chest. The kissing lasted several minutes. After, they took turns cuddling with Toby. They slept fitfully through the night. In the morning the ground was covered with a dusting of frost. The first rays of the sun warmed their faces.

Leonard knew they would have to turn around to get home. Tom saw bear tracks in the frost and the boys agreed they were lucky not to have been attacked during the night. Two hours later they wandered into Leonard's front yard. A gang of men was milling about and asking questions of his father.

"I see them," one shouted. Leonard saw his father break from the group and rush toward them.

"Where have you been?" his father demanded. "Are you two all right?"

A neighbour took Tom to his house where his tearful mother wrapped her arms about him. After, Tom's father gave him a stern talking to and for good measure, a severe licking. Erasmus was guilt-stricken for having turned the boys away from his work on the fence. He saw no reason to punish him. As if to make sure all was well with Leonard, he insisted on taking him for a check-up by Dr. Griffin.

"Nothing wrong with the boy that a few good meals won't fix," the doctor said after examining Leonard.

"He's a little thin for his age," Dr. Griffrin added. "You need to fatten him up."

Leonard realized later that the experience changed forever the relationship between himself and his father. What should have been nothing more than a childhood misadventure, he knew, had turned into a calamity of immense proportion. From that day on, Erasmus showed an increasingly irrational fear for Leonard's well being. The boy felt hounded day and night, his father rarely letting him out of his sight.

"We don't want you falling in the river or being attacked by a bear," Erasmus told him. "You've got to learn it's dangerous in the woods."

Leonard could never understand his father's distress. He came to recognize it as but one signal of the dark mood into which Erasmus was descending. His father had warned him that what he called "self abuse" would lead straight to mental derangement and other horrifying consequences. These warnings haunted Leonard. Every time he did it, he descended into despair. In time, without any real awareness on his part, feelings of guilt and apprehension began to seep into other aspects of his life.

It was not long before Leonard began to resent the constant watch his father kept on him. With his resentment came a profound curiosity that would shape his personality for the rest of his life.

When Leonard asked his father about the Indians who had once hunted and fished in the Beaver Valley, he got the usual settler reply that they had done nothing with the land and were a thieving, lazy lot, treacherous and none too bright. Leonard doubted his father was entirely correct in his measure of the red man, but he had no way of judging; natives were rare in the Beaver Valley and he had never spoken with one.

Leonard often searched out a large rock or mound of earth where he could stand and recite poems or deliver speeches to his imaginary troops. One day, not a hundred feet from where Eugenia Falls thunders into the chasm carved by the Beaver River, he began to voice aloud the lines of his favourite poem. Where the pools are bright and deep, he bellowed, Where the grey trout lies asleep, and so on until he had recited all six verses of *A Boy's Song*. It was a poem Leonard's mother had taught him. His voice competed with the roar of the Falls but unknown to Leonard, he was not alone. When he fell silent, he heard someone speak behind him.

"Who are you talking to, boy? The eagles that fly with the clouds, or the fish that swim in the river?"

Leonard turned, shocked and embarrassed. He eyes fell on the first Indian he had ever encountered. The Indian wore his hair in a long ponytail and an eagle feather rose from the back of the leather band that ran around his head. His jacket was of deerskin and it was decorated with beads. He wore leggings from his waist to his ankles and moccasins on his feet. A black leather sheath holding a knife hung from his belt.

"I was just practicing my verse," Leonard said. With that, he slipped past the Indian, called to his dog, and ran home.

Two weeks later, at a clearing on the riverbank, Leonard sighted a wisp of smoke rising into the trees. Curious, he went closer and saw a man crouched near a small fire, not far from a wigwam that had been set up in the shadow of a large cedar tree. The shelter was covered with sheets of bark. An animal hide hung over what seemed to be an entrance way.

The Indian saw Leonard and beckoned to him.

"I have just cooked a fine trout in clay," the Indian told him as he rose from his haunches. "If you are hungry, come and share my meal."

After that, Leonard became an almost daily visitor to the Indian's wigwam.

"My father was Wahbudick, a chief of the Chippewa of the Saugeen," he told Leonard. "He wanted me to learn the ways of the white man. He didn't want me to be cheated and stolen from as he was. He sent me to Owen Sound to be schooled by the priests. They gave me the name of Louis Joseph. I told them I didn't want any white man's name. I go by what my people called my father, Wahbudick."

The story that Leonard heard that day was utterly different from anything he would ever be told about the Indians. It taught him a lesson he would long remember – that you have to listen to both sides if you want to get at the truth.

"When our people first walked on earth," Wahbudick said, "they called themselves Anishinaabeg. It means the 'true people' in English. When the white men arrived, they made up their minds to steal our land. My father, the chief, would never agree to sign the white man's treaty, so they conspired with his enemies to push him aside. The new chief went ahead and put the mark of his clan, his doodem, on the treaty. We lost over a million acres of Indian territory. That is why we call it the Great Theft.

"We were treated in this manner after giving corn and tobacco to the white man, teaching him how to tap the maple trees, and how to stop scurvy. What did he give us in return? Smallpox and alcohol."

The day after the first heavy snowfall of that winter, Leonard found Wahbudick and his wigwam no longer at the river. He assumed the Indian had retired to a reserve. He missed his friend and wished he could have learned more about Indian life. Leonard knew now that not all the wonders of the natural world could be explained by what he heard in church on Sundays or what his father told him.

Leonard first set eyes on Rosannah Leppard the summer after he'd encountered Wahbudick. He had been rummaging around the site of Wahbudick's wigwam, hoping to find a forgotten trinket when he saw a thin girl carrying a tin pail. She was barefoot and wore a pair of overalls that were now a washed-out blue. She had brown hair and freckles and Leonard guessed she had been picking blueberries.

"I've never seen you around here," Leonard said. The girl looked at him. "They're not your blueberries, are they?" she asked. "I guess I can pick them if I want."

"Course you can," Leonard said. He asked her if she was alone and when she said she was, he told her he was surprised her mother would let her wander around in the woods. "I go anywhere I want," she answered. Leonard told her his name and said he lived on the Beaver Valley Road. Rosannah gave her name and asked him why she had not seen him at school.

"My mother teaches me at home," Leonard said. "I'd like that," Rosannah answered, "but there's so many children at our house I don't think my mother could ever get around to that. Anyway, she can't read or write."

Leonard wondered what else he should say to this girl. More than anything, he thought she was too thin, but he did like her eyes, which were brownish and sparkled when she looked at him. And she smelled nice, unlike most people who seldom washed the sweat from their skin. As he was having this thought, he saw something in the dirt and knelt to pick it up.

"I used to know an old Indian who camped here," Leonard said. "He must have left this behind, it's an arrowhead. He taught me lots of things. Told me how to make tea from cedar tips. Cures headaches and stops coughing. If you mix the tips with wood ashes and the gall bladder of a bear, it will make your teeth white and cure bad breath." Leonard also told her the Indian had said the concoction made a man strong with a woman, although he didn't understand the exact meaning of this.

Rosannah laughed. "I think you're making that up. There's no Indians around here."

"Not anymore, but there used to be," Leonard said. He told her other things about Wahbudick and offered to help her pick berries. After they'd filled Rosannah's pail they sat on the riverbank and talked some more. They told each other they would meet again. Leonard watched her carefully before she headed off, lest he forget what she looked like. He saw her only once more that summer, when a fresh crop of blueberries had ripened, and then only for a few minutes. But he remembered her tiny toes, the pale eyebrows over her eyes, and the way her hair hung down her back. He thought about Rosannah a lot, especially about how he wanted to kiss her. He was seventeen and he had been thinking about the time he and Tom had kissed. He was sure it would be different with a girl.

Rosannah had told him the coming school year would be her last. She was thirteen now and her mother needed her at home. One evening that fall, Leonard decided he would slip out of the house and walk to the Lerppard place. Rosannah had given him rough directions and when he got there, he realized it was a much poorer place than Vandeleur Hall. He crouched behind the split rail fence, hoping to catch a glimpse of Rosannah. Children ran in and out of the house. As dusk fell and the sky darkened, he saw Rosannah come out by herself. She was carrying a basket. She stopped at a line strung from the house to a shed and began to lift clothes from the basket and pin them to the line. He watched as she tucked her hair behind her head before stretching her arms to reach the line, revealing bare knees and the swelling of a girlish breast line. Once she'd emptied the basket, she returned to the house. Leonard stayed for another half hour but saw no one else. He went home, dodged his father who was reading in the sitting room, and snuck into bed. He thought about Rosannah until he fell asleep.

Leonard knew he should not spy on Rosannah but his desire to see her overcame any sense of guilt. He went back to the Leppard place for the next three evenings but saw Rosannah on none of them. On the third night, his father caught him slipping in through the back door and Leonard had to make up a story about noises in the barn. He decided it would be safer, and that he'd be more likely to see Rosannah, if he went to the Leppard place in daylight. He made his next visit late in the afternoon. After only a few minutes crouching at the fence, he saw Rosannah come out of the house and go to the shed. She came out carrying a rake. He whistled to get her attention. She smiled and waved, and came to the fence and asked him what he wanted.

"I just wanted to see you," Leonard said. "I liked it when we picked berries together. I wish I was in school so that I could see you every day."

"Well, you're not," she laughed. "And I don't think you should hang around here. If my mother sees you, she'll run you off."

They sat crouched on one of the limbs of the split rail fence and talked. Leonard could feel the warmth of her breath as she spoke. He told her he liked to read books that his mother received from England, and said he would read to her some time. Rosannah said they had no books in their house and if they did she wouldn't have time to read them. Helping her mother care for her sisters and brothers took all her time.

Leonard asked Rosannah what she would do when she no longer had to go to school.

"Help with the kids and look for a husband, I guess," Rosannah said. "Then I can have my own place and children of my own."

Leonard thought that was normal, because that's what he expected girls to do. But for himself, he knew he wanted to see other places besides Vandeleur.

"That's fine for you but I'll probably go to Toronto," Leonard said. "Of course, I'll have to come back someday to take over from Father. I expect to do some exciting things before then."

Leonard wanted to kiss Rosannah but he wasn't sure how to go about it. He was surprised when she asked, "Would you like to kiss me?"

He didn't answer. Leonard pecked her cheek, and Rosannah turned her face so that he could kiss her on the lips. When their lips touched he saw that Rosannah had closed her eyes. He closed his, and in a moment felt the wetness of her mouth. He wanted to keep the kiss going but Rosannah pulled away from him.

"I know about men," she said. "Something happened to me a little while ago. Maybe I'll tell you about it sometime. But one kiss, that's all you can have. Now you have to go."

# Chapter 9

## A DIFFERENT KIND OF GIRL

### June 14, 1872

It was on Leonard Babington's eighteenth birthday that he decided to become a teacher. Never having been inside a school, his idea of a classroom was constructed out of idle remarks collected from village children and of comments he'd overheard from adults. Becoming a teacher, he reasoned, would give him his best chance to free himself from his father's control. His choice led to a serious rift between them, which was surprising given Erasmus's insistence that Leonard be raised with an appreciation of learning. In the years since Leonard had become lost in the forest, Erasmus lived with the fear he could lose his son for good. He wanted him to stay at Vandeleur Hall and live the life of an English gentleman on the frontier, rather than launch himself on a path that might take him God knows where, with possibly unknown consequences.

"What harm can come to me in a schoolhouse?" Leonard asked of his father. "It'll be a lot safer than staying here on the farm where any kind of accident can happen."

"At least when you're at home I can keep an eye on you," Erasmus said. "I don't want you running off again like you did that time in the bush."

Leonard considered his father's fears ludicrous. He was determined to take the examination that was given every year to applicants for a teacher's position. His mother encouraged him to sit for the school board test.

Sherman Bailey, the superintendent of School Section Eleven, conducted Leonard's examination. It took place in the little Vandeleur log schoolhouse after the teacher and the children had left for the day.

The superintendent extracted a folder from an inside pocket of his coat. He looked over his glasses at Leonard. "The first thing you have to do," he said, adjusting his glasses as he glanced at the paper, "is to show you can intelligently and correctly read a passage from any common book. You'll find one on that desk. Read me a bit from it."

Leonard went to the desk and picked up the book. He saw it was *The Luck of Roaring Camp*, by the American writer of western stories, Bret Harte. He flipped it open and began to read: "We were eight, including the driver. We had not spoken during the passage of the last six miles ..."

"That's enough Leonard. I see you can read just fine. Now, spell out the words from this sentence: 'The world is an enormous place and it is filled with opportunity for any man who is a British subject.'" A few seconds went by as Leonard circled the table, repeating the sentence and spelling out its words as he walked. Mr. Bailey followed him with his eyes.

"You can sit down, you know." Leonard had spelled each and every word correctly. He didn't want to admit he had been too nervous to sit.

"You must also be able to write a plain hand," the superintendent told Leonard. "Go to the desk and copy something from that book you were just reading." He wrote in a flowing hand, free of smudges or errors, finishing with a swirl that marked his signature and the date. Leonard handed his sheet to Mr. Bailey and awaited his reaction. The superintendent nodded, smiling.

Next had come a series of questions on arithmetic and a discussion of the elements of English grammar. There was a brief lecture by Mr. Bailey on the importance of maintaining discipline, followed by an admonition to be seen in church each Sunday and to lead a pure, moral life.

"A good schoolmaster must serve as a model of rectitude for his students," he added. "And must never hesitate to use the strap."

Mr. Bailey appeared to be pondering what he had told Leonard. He mashed his lips together, frowned, and replaced the folder he had withdrawn from his coat.

"Your answers are exemplary, Leonard," he said. "I'll notify the Board and you can expect to start in September. Twenty dollars for the school year."

Mr. Bailey had one more thing to say to Leonard:

"Most folks around here can't read or write. We've got to do a better job in raising up our children. We'll be counting on you to see to that."

The single room in the Vandeleur school was filled with six rows of desks in various sizes, designed to fit children from tykes to strapping teen-age boys. The room contained a globe, a pull down map of the world showing the British Empire in red, and a blackboard that ran along one wall. A Waterman & Waterbury stove stood at the back of the room. In cold weather, it was the job of one of the older boys to keep it supplied with wood. On wet days, clothes and boots steamed away their dampness beside it. There was much excitement when mice, seeking a warmer home than the woodshed fastened to the side of the school, ran into the classroom and darted among the desks. There were outhouses for boys and girls at the back of the property.

Leonard welcomed two dozen children of varying ages that fall. Enrollment dropped off to fewer than twenty during the winter. Not many had warm clothes and sometimes children stayed home because they had no shoes.

He took care to arrive home each winter night by dark. If marking papers kept him late, his father hounded him as to where he had been and what he had done. "I have my responsibilities," Leonard told him. "I can't come home until I've marked the students' papers and prepared the next day's lesson." Erasmus's attitude infuriated Leonard. He tried not to show disrespect.

It was not long before Leonard learned that a schoolroom could offer distractions to a young man such as he. Every few days, one of the older girls would try to get his attention by letting their bodies touch when they passed by him.

In his first year, it was most often Abigail, a younger sister of Rosannah, who did her best to fascinate Leonard. But it was Rosannah, who returned to the school from time to time to collect her sister, who held his interest.

Leonard knew he had grown up a good-looking young man. He was tall, with long limbs and slim fingers. When he looked in the mirror, he saw a pleasant face with clear blue eyes and a high forehead. His light brown hair was parted on the left. He shaved faithfully every day – not many in Vandeleur did – and he did his best to dress with care. Leonard knew that his most distinguishing physical characteristic was seldom noted, for which he was thankful. He had a sunken chest, an abnormality which caused him to sometimes suffer heart pains. A side effect was that he was often chilly. Fearing ridicule, Leonard took care to camouflage these aspects of his make-up.

His compulsion to do so gave rise to empathy for those who were unable to disguise more evident handicaps.

Leonard indulged in petting and kissing with a number of girls by the time he was sixteen. He lost his virginity during a stroll with the visiting niece of the local storekeeper. They made love cradled by a tree that stood not more than twenty feet from the edge of Eugenia Falls. The sound of rushing water drowned out their tentative cries.

Leonard was caught by surprise when Rosannah invited him to a Leppard family picnic in the spring of his second year of teaching. As he considered what she had said, his eyes scanned a face that showed traces of freckles, but one that liked to laugh. He smiled and said he would like to come.

When Leonard arrived at the river he found Rosannah was alone. "There's lots of food," she said. "Nobody else could come." Leonard noticed Rosannah had brightened her lips with some kind of colouring. He felt a pleasurable anticipation of what the afternoon might bring.

Leonard had carried his fishing pole with him. It gave him the chance to divert their conversation in an innocent direction. He noticed a large tree had fallen into the water. "Come, that looks like a good place to fish," he said. Together, they clambered onto the log and lay, face down, staring into the water. They watched fish swim beneath the overhanging branches, in water so clear they could see the pebbles on the bottom. Leonard pointed out the profusion of flowers blooming on the river bank: hepatica, the white trillium, Lady's Slipper, crimson bloodroot, adder's tongue, and others.

"That old Indian I told you about taught me how to make native medicines," Leonard said. "Did you know that cedar tips mixed with witch hazel can heal an injury quicker than anything?" When Leonard mentioned the Indians had a remedy for what the white man called melancholia, Rosannah showed a sudden interest.

"Maybe I should try it," she said. "Dr. Griffin says I have the women's disease, hysteria. I can't help it if I get excited, or if some days I just don't feel like doing a thing. All the women in my family are like that."

Their conversation halted when Leonard felt a tug on his line. He had hooked a large trout that was not about to surrender without a fight. When it ran to deep water, he played it carefully and worked his way from the fallen tree onto the shore, where he slowly brought it in. He ran a stick through its gills and left it secured in a few inches of water.

Rosannah and Leonard returned to the blanket where they had eaten lunch. Nothing happened that afternoon short of tentative kisses and preliminary caresses. Leonard might have been embarrassed had his nervousness not held his libido in check, for he was too uncertain of himself to become hard. Yet the intimacy of their togetherness created a bond that gave him a sense of belonging. It was a feeling unlike anything he had ever known. He knew she was a girl of a different kind.

All that summer Rosannah and Leonard were inseparable. Leonard told her stories he had heard from his parents, and he read to her from books that his mother's family had sent from England. He felt compelled to draw Rosannah into a discussion of what he had been reading – usually stories or articles from Blackwood's magazine, or novels or art books.

On the day they went to Eugenia Falls to watch a tightrope walker attempt to cross the gorge on a cable, Rosannah listened quietly as Leonard talked of the books he'd read. At the Falls, they found a large crowd had gathered to watch the unfolding drama. A poster announced a ten-cent charge to see Arthur Wilson attempt to cross the five hundred foot chasm on a two-inch strand of cable. The Great Blondin had recently conquered the Niagara River and Wilson was but one of many imitators going about the country with similar stunts. Bets were taken on whether he would fall seventy feet to his death on the rocks below.

The spectacle excited Rosannah and Leonard. Wilson carried a long pole to balance himself and Rosannah clung tightly to Leonard as the crowd alternately gasped and held its breath while the daredevil aerialist teetered, then recovered his footing, and finally dashed safely to shore. Everybody clapped and cheered but all Leonard was aware of was Rosannah's breasts pressed against his arm and back. When Leonard readied their buggy to go home, he chose a seldom-used back trail. After about twenty minutes, the trail widened into a clearing and Rosannah suggested they stop and rest. He pulled up the buggy and turned to Rosannah. He told her he had something to say.

"We've been seeing each other for awhile now. I want to keep on seeing you. I'm in love with you."

Rosannah smiled and held out her arms to him.

"I've been wondering if you were ever going to say that."

In a moment, they were in each other's arms. Leonard breathed in the sweetness of her smell, a mix of fresh air and sweat, and the scent stirred him deeply. He found himself lifting her down from the buggy to sit on the blanket he'd thrown onto the grass. Their kisses led to a frantic shedding of clothes. Leonard finished quickly. After, Rosannah still clung to him, grinding herself against him.

Later, as they neared the Leppard place, Rosannah brought up the matter of his always wanting to read to her.

"You're always telling me about people whose lives have nothing to do with ours," she said. Leonard thought she might feel humiliated for knowing so little of the things that interested him.

"You don't want to be ignorant, do you?" he asked her.

"I'm not ignorant Leonard. I just don't know very much of the things you like to talk about. You're always so serious, and I just want to have fun, like we did today. Why don't you kiss me again?"

Leonard did, and that ended their small argument. But he realized later it was an omen of things to come. The more Leonard tried to interest Rosannah in matters removed from her daily cares and concerns, the more she resisted his efforts – as she put it – "to make a lady of me." Her only goal, it seemed to Leonard, was to live unfettered by convention or responsibility. He dismissed her claim that she wished only to marry a rich husband. "You'll never find one around here," he told her.

When Leonard got to know Rosannah better, he found out that she was addicted to morning and evening doses of a mixture prescribed by Dr. Griffin. The bottle it came in was labeled Dr. Shiloh's Cough and Consumption Cure. He'd read about such potions in *Blackwood's* magazine. Their main ingredient, the article warned, was a generous portion of alcohol laced with a considerable amount of opium. Leonard worried about the effect of such stuff on Rosannah. Too much of that would kill a person, he told himself. When he smelled tobacco on her breath, she confessed she was using a pipe a day. Another recommendation by Dr. Griffin.

"I don't think smoking does you any good," Leonard told Rosannah.

"And your medicine – I imagine you feel better taking it, but it just makes you want more. It could be dangerous."

Rosannah frowned. "Dr. Griffin says I should take it, so I don't see why you should tell me not to. Professor Babington!"

Leonard said no more on the subject.

Smoking and medicine were not the only things that affected Leonard's view of his relationship with Rosannah. There was religion, too. Leonard made no secret of his family's Methodist connection. But he knew Rosannah's mother was a devout Catholic who would insist her children marry within the faith of Rome.

The time Leonard raised the possibility of marriage he was quick to add, "Of course, I could become a Catholic. You're a good Catholic girl, aren't you?"

"If you think I am, then I am," Rosannah answered. She offered no encouragement to Leonard, either toward him becoming a Catholic or of their getting married. He decided he would say nothing more about it for the time being.

On Leonard's next visit, he thought Rosannah looked glum. She seemed indifferent. There had been a light snowfall and Leonard helped her hang the family washing on a clothesline that was strung between two trees. Her mother and father had gone into Eugenia and she had promised to finish up the wash.

As they were hanging the last blanket, Billy ran up carrying a snowball encrusted in dirt. He threw it at Leonard but missed, hitting a sheet instead. It left a smear of mud. Rosannah was furious.

"Billy, you're going to get a whupping for that," she said. Turning to Leonard, she said, "You can do the job. I'll get you father's razor strap." When she saw his hesitation she added, "If you can't do it, I'm sure I can find someone else who can."

Leonard hated the thought of using the strap on Billy. He had twice strapped boys at school. Both times, he felt degraded at what he had done. He vowed he would not strap another child. When Rosannah returned from the house, strap in hand, he took it and led Billy into the shed behind the house.

Once inside, he told Billy what they would do.

"When I hit the bench with this strap, you holler."

"Aw, maybe you should whup me," Billy said. "I shouldn't have thrown that muddy snowball."

"Doesn't matter, just do as I say."

Every time Leopard slapped the bench Billy let out a cry.

Rosannah seemed in a better mood when they returned to the house.

Their relationship continued pleasantly enough until the day later that spring when Leonard went to see Rosannah with a new book of poetry under his arm. A nice way to talk about love, reading poetry, he thought. She invited him in and they sat on the long bench under the window. He was unprepared for what she told him.

"I'm tired of your acting so high and mighty," she said after listening to Leonard read a poem. "I think you should read those things to somebody who loves you better than me." She was holding back tears as she spoke.

Leonard felt crushed but after a moment, anger boiled up in him. All the things he'd tried to do for Rosannah. She liked to make love, but there's more to life than that. What about friendship, respect, or working together?

"I'm sure I can find somebody who would like me to read to them," Leonard told her. He didn't really mean it.

"I think it would be better if you did, Leonard. We started out having fun, but it hasn't been much fun lately. I feel invisible around you. Please don't come to see me anymore,"

Invisible! How could Rosannah ever be invisible with that alluring body, her lovely face, her beautiful long hair.

Leonard pushed her back onto the bench and as they struggled they slipped to the floor. He had never felt this way. His anger fed his desire to possess her. He wanted to show how he loved her, and to enjoy what he'd come to think was rightfully his. He squirmed himself between her legs and pulled her shift up to her waist. She fought to roll him off but Leonard held her with one arm and with his other arm he pressed her to the floor and kissed her. He was hard now and he unbuttoned his pants and guided himself into her. His lunges caused her to respond and he could feel her relax and her legs envelop him. He came quickly, as much in triumph as in lust. When he tried to kiss her after, she slapped his face.

Leonard lifted himself off her. He looked at Rosannah lying crumpled on the floor. He regretted what he had done. He'd as much as raped her. An apology wouldn't change what had happened. He reached for his coat and left.

Leonard tried to put Rosannah out of his mind but no matter what he did – teaching every day, cleaning out the stable at home at night, reading by candle light until after midnight – he could not forget what had happened. He spent Sunday morning tending his mother's flower garden. He cut five stems that held rich, red flowers and wrapped them in a wet cloth. He set out for the Leppard place, going over in his mind what he would say to Rosannah. He was sure a proper apology would set things right.

James Leppard was fixing a link in the split rail fence when Leonard came into the yard. A dog laid lazily on the ground and chickens pecked among the weeds and wild flowers. Leonard held his bouquet of roses behind his back, and continued on to the house. Molly met him at the door and when she saw the roses, she called to Rosannah. There was no answer from Rosannah but Bridget came quickly to the door. "What's that you've got there? Oh, flowers! I'll take them if Rosannah don't want them."

Nothing was working out the way Leonard had hoped. "Just something for Rosannah," he said. "Can I see her?" As he spoke, Rosannah appeared in front of him.

"I cut them especially for you," Leonard said, handing the roses to Rosannah. She took them from his hand and held them close to her face, enjoying their scent.

"That's sweet of you, Leonard, but you didn't have to do this."

Encouraged, Leonard smiled for the first time since arriving at the Leppard house. "Can we go for a walk?"

They were almost out of sight of the house before either spoke.

"Leonard, it was good of you to bring me those flowers," Rosannah began. "But I really wish you hadn't bothered. Not just because of what happened last time. I've seen this coming. You don't really want me. You want a girl who's been through school, and who cares about all those fancy ideas you get from books."

"Rosannah, all I know is that I love you."

"You think you do," Rosannah replied, a tone of exasperation in her voice. "Do you ever think about what it does to me? How it makes me feel? Knowing that I'll never be able to keep up with you? That you'll get tired of me? My stomach gets tied up in knots every time I see you. Then I have to take more of Dr. Griffin's medicine. It isn't worth it to me."

Leonard didn't know what to say. His carefully rehearsed speeches counted for nothing.

"So you're saying you don't want to see me anymore."

"It'll be better for both of us."

For the rest of the school term, Leonard looked for Rosannah every day, hoping she might come to take her sister home. But she never came again to the Vandeleur school. He tried once more to see her but when he rode Sugar Loaf to the Leppard place he found the house empty. The door was open and he went in and sat down on the bench beside the stove. He looked around, thinking how unpleasant it would be to live with so many people in such a small place. When Rosannah arrived, she was alone.

"What are you doing here, Leonard? I told you we shouldn't see each other again. It hurts too much to see you and it hurts not seeing you. But I'd rather suffer from not seeing you, than the other way around. It's less painful. You'd better leave."

Rosannah stopped in mid-breath, apparently considering what else to say. Something final.

"If you ever come near me again, I'll tell everyone what you did. So if something happens to me, they'll know who to blame."

"I'm sorry for what I did," Leonard said. There was nothing to do now but leave.

Riding home, Leonard reflected on all that had happened. Slowly, the feeling came over him that he should not be so disheartened. By the time Leonard reached the East Back Road, he had Sugar Loaf into a full gallop. He thought of how he'd named him after reading of a certain stony mountain peak in South America. He was his own man again, and he had the road to himself. A warm breeze began to blow and Leonard pushed Sugar Loaf harder and harder. The horse's exuberant spirit soon took hold and by the time they reached The Gravel, Sugar Loaf was running all-out and Leonard was whooping with joy as the trees swept by. The horse slowed to a canter only when the first houses of Flesherton came into view. Leonard turned

Sugar Loaf about and rode back to Vandeleur Hall.

A few days later, Leonard sent a letter of resignation to School Section Eleven. He would not be back in the fall, he wrote. He had made up his mind to go to Toronto. He knew he was in for a great fight with his father. For all the bravado of his wild ride, anything would be better than staying home and facing life in Vandeleur without Rosannah.

# Chapter 10

## THE AUTOPSY

### Afternoon, November 3, 1884

After the midday break Alfred Frost called Dr. Thomas Simpson Sproule, the Member of Parliament for the riding of Grey East. The doctor had performed the autopsy on Rosannah the afternoon of her death. He entered the witness box wearing a Prince Albert coat and a white shirt set off by a blue silk bow tie. His pants were hiked well up on his hips and his polished shoes made a strong contrast against the rough footwear of the men in the courtroom.

Dr. Sproule brushed aside stray strands of hair that fell over his ears. A Walrus mustache drooped onto his mouth. Leonard Babington's father had been an enthusiastic supporter of Dr. Sproule and in one election he'd put on a picnic at Vandeleur Hall where neighbours came to hear a campaign speech. Leonard remembered a long, boring talk on a hot afternoon. Now, he guessed the doctor would have recognized about half the men present as his constituents. He was of Irish Protestant stock, one of the "Belfast Irish," and a staunch supporter of the Orange Order. He was proud to sit as a member of Sir John A. Macdonald's Liberal-Conservative government.

Alfred Frost peered intently at his witness. "Can you tell me, Doctor, if your examination of Rosannah Teets revealed any natural cause for her death?"

Dr. Sproule remembered he had been alone in his office in his newly built block on the main street of Markdale. It was about four o'clock. He had just sent his receptionist, Mrs. Royce, home with a cold when John Field, the constable for Artemesia Township, arrived to say there was an emergency.

75

"One of the Leppard girls died this morning and we need an autopsy," Constable Field said. "There's to be an inquest and they want to know the cause of Rosannah's death. They think she might have been poisoned. We've brought her body. Took us four hours."

Dr. Sproule sighed and put aside the letter he was writing to Prime Minister Macdonald. Field's arrival reminded him how an autopsy always upset him – even though he'd conducted many since coming to Grey County. He thought of how he had endured sights that would cause most people to faint dead away – the man with his guts ripped out when a saw jumped from the log he was cutting, the boy with a crushed skull from a falling tree, the woman beaten so badly by her drunken husband that her face was no longer recognizable. Now, he'd have to undertake a series of acts that no ordinary person would wish to witness. Such was the duty of a country doctor.

Constable Field, with the help of his occasional deputy George Thompson, carried Rosannah's body up the narrow stairs to Dr. Sproule's office. She was wrapped in a blanket and the constable was puffing by the time they got her through the door.

Dr. Sproule asked them to put the body on his examination table in his consulting room.

"Where did they find her, John?"

"She died at home – the Leppard place, you know that rundown outfit across the river from Vandeleur."

Dr. Sproule knew the Leppards as just another poor family, and the thought of them reminded him how he tried not to judge people by the way they lived. A good attitude, he thought, for a man with political ambitions.

"Bring those two coal oil lamps from the waiting room," he asked the constable. "I'll need extra light." While Field brought in the lamps Dr. Sproule washed his hands in a basin. "You can go now, but come back in an hour and I'll have something for you."

"As you say, Doctor. I'll go over to Mrs. Sykes's and have something to eat. I'll be back in an hour or so." Dr. Sproule noticed he didn't mention that would allow him time to enjoy more than Mrs. Sykes's cooking.

After Field left he lit the lamps, raised the blanket covering Rosannah, and found she had been wrapped in a white sheet that bore stains of urine and feces. She was still clad in the nightgown in which she had died. Using his scalpel he slit the gown down the front, exposing her slim, white body. It was quite rigid.

Rosannah's nakedness reminded him of his wife Mary Alice and he wished he was with her, in the home he'd lovingly built. He called it Knarsborough Hall. It was just around the corner and he could be there in five minutes, once he'd finished this awful job.

Rosannah looked perfectly natural in death except for two small bruises on her upper cheeks. The result of postmortem lividity, caused by blood gravitating there, he knew. She looked to be in the prime of life, well developed and well nourished. Having suckled two children, her nipples rose prominently from her breasts. He checked her eyes, nose and throat, and examined her ears. Delicately, he checked her vagina. He concluded there had been no criminal assault.

Dr. Sproule lifted Rosannah's head with one hand and with the other used a razor to make a cut behind her ears and across the back of her head. He peeled away her scalp, reached for a hacksaw, and began to cut into the cranium. This was always the hardest part. Her skull was thick and it took fifteen minutes of sawing before he could lift out the brain. He was tired by the time he was finished. The brain was normal in size and in a healthy condition although the membranes – the dura mater – were slightly congested and the veins contained considerable blood.

With Rosannah on her back, he made a series of cuts in the shape of a Y that began at either shoulder, met midway between her breasts above the rib cage, and extended in a single incision to the pubic bone. Due to the fact blood pressure is absent in a corpse, there was little blood flow. He sawed into Rosannah's sternum and with both hands pried open her breastbones and rib cage. He could see all her inernal organs – her lungs, stomach, liver, kidneys, spleen, and intestines.

Dr. Sproule stepped back, wiped blood from his hands with a towel, and drew a large white handkerchief from his coat pocket. He blew his nose. Adjusting his glasses, he noticed that both lungs contained blotches of discolour measuring about two inches across, perhaps an early sign of consumption. The left lung was slightly congested. Her heart appeared normal and her liver looked healthy. Her stomach cavity contained a small quantity of fluid and considerable gas. He found the bowels of the deceased – better to think of her in that term rather than as Rosannah – nearly empty, as was the bladder. Both organs had a healthy appearance.

Dr. Sproule was not surprised when he found Rosannah had a fetus in her womb. Goddamn it to Hell, he muttered under his breath. From the size and state of development of the child, he thought Rosannah was about four months gone. Because Constable Field had mentioned poisoning, Dr. Sproule removed her stomach, intestines and esophagus, along with part of her liver and one kidney. He placed the organs in two jars, one glass and the other stone. He then restored her abdomen and skull to as normal a condition as possible, discarded the sheet in a garbage pail and wrapped the blanket around the body.

The door to the waiting room creaked open. "You can come in," he called to Constable Field. Dr. Sproule handed Field the jars. "The coroner may want you to send these down to Toronto for analysis. I saw no cause for natural death. I calculate she's likely been poisoned. But by what there's no way I can tell. We'll leave that to the analyst." Constable Field held the jars gingerly.

Alfred Frost's question about the cause of Rosannah's death had put Dr. Sproule in a reflective mood. He chewed his lower lip and passed his hand over his brow. Leonard put a fresh sheet of paper before him, his pen poised to record the answer.

"I saw nothing that would account for death by natural causes," Dr. Sproule said.

"You heard the evidence given at the inquest regarding the symptoms Rosannah showed when she died?"

"Yes, I did."

"From your knowledge of medicine what did these symptoms represent?"

"The arching of the body, the spasms, the inability to speak? To my mind, strychnine poisoning."

The prosecutor asked how quickly the poison could kill. He put his question in lawyerly terms:

"What is the length of time for the operation of strychnine poison from administration until death ensues?"

Dr. Sproule hesitated before answering. Strychnine – from that shrub in India, Strychnos nux vomica. Most people thought of it as nothing more than a good, reliable rat poison. Dr. Sproule knew there were so many factors to consider – the amount of the white crystal ingested, the constitution of the victim, whether food had been recently eaten, the presence of alcohol in the blood. Strychnine is terribly bitter and as little as half a grain could kill. Doctors sometime prescribed strychnine to stimulate the nervous system, or as a laxative. Dr. Sproule had given tiny doses to patients who felt lacklustre or apathetic. When he finally addressed the question Alfred Frost had asked, his words were deliberate and detailed:

"The time between administration and death would depend on the condition of the stomach. If strychnine was taken when there was no food in the stomach, it would be more active, it would be absorbed more rapidly. Death might ensue in half an hour. If the stomach contained much food, it would act slower."

Dr. Sproule's testimony reminded Leonard that Cook had last been seen with Rosannah at tea-time, around twelve hours before her death. Could she have survived that long with poison in her stomach?

"Well now," Alfred Frost remarked jauntily, "we have heard the prisoner and the deceased shared tea and bread. After, they spent some time alone together outside the Leppard house." He let the implication of that statement hang in the air. He must have hoped the jurors would accept the suggestion that Cook had taken advantage of that time to poison Rosannah.

Alfred Frost said he had one more question. Had Rosannah Teets been pregnant at the time of her death? Dr. Sproule confirmed that she had.

Leonard stopped writing and sucked in his breath. This made her murder an even more vicious crime.

"Your witness, Mr. Masson."

Leonard had watched James Masson carefully as he cross-examined Molly Leppard. He felt his performance had not been all that convincing. This didn't surprise him, considering the likelihood of Cook's guilt. The lawyer was going to have to cast serious doubt on the Crown's evidence if he hoped to get Cook off. He would have to find a way to demolish the Crown's theory that Cook had poisoned Rosannah either at tea or when they sat together outside.

James Masson was careful to be respectful in his questioning of Dr. Sproule. The doctor was much admired in the community, not just as a medical man and a politician but as a first-class horseman and a successful breeder of Shorthorn cattle. The two men were about the same age, the doctor forty-one and the lawyer, thirty-seven.

"You've practiced medicine in Grey County for how many years, Doctor?"

"Fifteen. I came up from Toronto, when the old Sydenham Road was just a dirt track. It rattled your bones, I can tell you. Received my medical degree at Victoria College in Cobourg."

"And have you dealt with poisoning in the past?"

"All kinds. There are always people poisoning themselves on the moonshine they mix up around here." There was laughter in the courtroom.

A frown spread across Judge Armour's face before he interrupted the outburst with a raised hand. "I'll tolerate no more such levity."

James Masson pressed on with his questions.

"You say you found the stomach of the deceased nearly empty, Dr. Sproule? And it was in a condition for poison to act rapidly upon it?"

"I would expect it to act pretty quickly. Half an hour or so. If the poison was in a fluid condition, it would act even more rapidly."

Leonard Babington, bent over his notes, jerked his head upright when he heard these words. So much for the prosecutor's theory that Rosannah had died hours after being poisoned by Cook. Leonard was beginning to wonder if Cook could be innocent. Perhaps James Masson was going to make a fight of this trial after all.

"I see by the legal journals," James Masson said, "that three hours is given as an extraordinary length of time for strychnine to kill?"

"I think it would be," Dr. Sproule replied.

Leonard found it painful to picture how Rosannah must have suffered. James Masson had still more questions for the witness.

"Dr. Sproule, I understand the real cause of death by strychnine is that it excites the body. And that death follows by exhaustion?"

"I think that would be one way. If the victim's spasms prevent the action of the heart for a length of time, I don't think there's a chance of recovery."

"The spasms increase in volume and length until they kill?"

"I presume they would."

"And how did you find the heart of the deceased?"

"It appeared in a natural condition, except it was pretty empty of blood. The small amount I observed was rather dark."

So Rosannah's heart hadn't suffered a lot of stress, Leonard reflected. Perhaps she didn't even die of strychnine, but from the alcohol and the opium in her medicine. Nothing had been said about that. Nevertheless, the timing was the thing – that could stand in the way of the jury finding Cook guilty.

"Once again if you don't mind, Dr. Sproule. You think half an hour would be a reasonable length of time for death to have occurred in this case?"

"Yes."

"Thank you, Dr. Sproule. Your testimony has been most important, perhaps the most important we are likely to hear. I have no more questions."

Leonard scanned the faces of the jurors. He saw nothing to tell him how they had received Dr. Sproule's testimony.

Judge Armour glanced at the courtroom clock. It was just past four o'clock. "This seems an appropriate time to adjourn," he announced. "I must caution the members of the jury that you are impaneled for the duration of this trial. When you get to the hotel, there is to be no discussion among you or with anyone else of anything you have heard today. Court is adjourned." Angus McMorrin ordered all to stand. Judge Armour got up and strode from the room.

Leonard was upset. He resented the fact Cook had enticed Rosannah into marriage, an impulsive act she had paid for with her life. Cook had the motive and the means to kill her, even if there was no proof of him having done so. He still thought it was all Cook's fault. If Cook knew of Rosannah's pregnancy, would he have wished to kill his child as well? A small spark of doubt began to flicker in Leonard's mind. He could not forget he had himself once been struck by the poisoned arrow of wrongful accusation. Mistakes were made. He wondered if he had gone too far when he'd written so bitterly about Cook having shot at a gang of boys. Had his story told the whole truth? And if Cook hadn't killed Rosannah, who had?

# Chapter 11

## LEAVING VANDELEUR

### Evening, November 3, 1884

Leonard Babington ate a solitary supper of Georgian Bay bass and boiled potatoes at a nondescript café well away from Damnation Corners, an infamous intersection he was careful to avoid. A block from his hotel, it had a saloon on every corner, each of questionable reputation. These boozy joints had quickly become a favourite of the lawyers, pressmen and hangers-on who had assembled in Owen Sound for the trial. It was ironic, Leonard thought, that just a block away was an intersection known as Salvation Corners, populated by four churches. He avoided both and instead sought out The Tea Shoppe, a place that offered the isolation and quiet he longed for after a day of traumatic testimony.

As Leonard ate, carefully transferring bones from his fish to a saucer beside his plate, he thought about the decision he had made to leave Vandeleur after Rosannah had broken off with him. He hadn't known how he would earn a living. Aside from teaching school, the only worthwhile thing he'd done had been to write nature articles for the weekly edition of the *Toronto Globe*. He'd had ample opportunity to observe the habits of wildlife in the Queen's Bush and he drew on those experiences as he wrote.

Large flocks of passenger pigeons would fly over Vandeleur, sometimes in such number that they took half a day to pass his house. Whenever that happened, the men of the village got out their shotguns and brought down dozens and sometimes hundreds of the birds. Leonard had learned that each hen hatched only one egg every year. He concluded that this reproductive habit, when combined with heavy hunting pressure, meant the flocks were bound to get smaller. He speculated that other wild species might also be pushed to the edge of extinction. These thoughts led him to write one of his best pieces: "Whither that delectable morsel of the skies, the Passenger Pigeon?"

It had been Leonard's habit, ever since the Babingtons moved into Vandeleur Hall when he was fourteen, to rise early on Saturdays and visit James Henderson's general store, where he collected the family's mail and his father's prized copy of the *Weekly Globe* and *Canada Farmer*.

Leonard had gone to the barn and saddled Sugar Loaf for the ride into Vandeleur. He let the normally trim-legged animal amble at his own pace. By the time they got to the store his throat felt like chalk and he was wrung with sweat. The other customers, a couple with a child and a few farmers in to pick up their mail, moved slowly, unaccustomed to such weather. He collected the Babington mail in a damp palm and headed home. He dumped the letters on the kitchen table, pumped two cups of water that arrived cool from the backyard well, and went to his bedroom to compose a letter to Melvin James, the editor of the *Weekly Globe*. In it, he asked to be hired as a reporter. It was his only chance.

Leonard took the letter to Henderson's store Monday morning in time to catch the mail wagon. He was first in line every Saturday and Wednesday for the next month to watch for an answer. Every time, Leonard thumbed quickly through the envelopes addressed to the Babingtons, but there was no letter from the *Globe*.

Leonard helped his father with farm chores — fencing the north meadow, dynamiting stumps, and bringing in hay — while he turned over in his mind what to tell him about his wish to go to Toronto. After waiting a month without hearing from the *Globe*, Leonard decided he must go to the city and confront Mr. James. He would show his determination, spell out his willingness to take on any task, even offer to work for nothing. Anything to get started. First, he had to deal with his father.

"I've been thinking about what I'm going to do with myself," Leonard told his parents when they sat down to Sunday supper. His mother had prepared a stew of beef and suet dumplings, Leonard's favourite meal.

"What do you mean, son, you know I need you here at Vandeleur Hall," his father said.

It always irritated Leonard to hear his father refer to their house as Vandeleur Hall. That kind of stuff might have been all right back in England, but this was Canada.

"You can always hire help," Leonard answered. "Quite a few men have been by looking for work this summer."

"But what would you do, Leonard?" his mother inquired.

"I'm going down to the *Globe*. They like my articles. I'd just as soon not teach school any longer. I could do better as a journalist." Leonard didn't consider he was being untruthful. He was sure he would land a position with the *Globe* once he'd explained to Mr. James how anxious he was to work there.

Erasmus dipped a piece of bread in what was left of his stew. Wiping his dish with it, he lifted the bread to his lips and worked it around in his mouth before swallowing.

"Leonard, why would you want to go and do a damn fool thing like that? Who knows what kind of company you'd fall into? You have no idea what might happen to you. They say it's not safe to walk the streets of Toronto. No, I'll have you stay here. This is where you're needed."

"Father, I don't think you have the right to decide my life for me. I'm twenty-five and I think I'm entitled to my own decisions. I'm going to Toronto in the morning."

"Do that and you don't need to come back," Erasmus barked. He stood up, shoved his chair to the table, and left the room.

"Oh, Leonard, look what you've done." His mother began to cry.

The next morning, Leonard packed his clothes and books into a single valise and left the house before the sun was up. An hour's walk found him at Munshaw's Hotel. It was a substantial two-storey brick building, with eight windows on the second floor, indicating as many rooms. Leonard took a cup of tea from the morning serving girl, Elsa, and waited for a carriage to take him to the train station a mile and a half out of town.

The coaches of the Toronto, Bruce and Grey Railway rolled south through forests and farmland, stopping no more than a few minutes in each village. Leonard's pent-up excitement pushed the quarrel with his father to the back of his mind. He ate the lunch his mother had packed and spent his time looking at the passing scenery and watching other passengers. When the train arrived at the Toronto railway station in a belch of steam and smoke, he gathered up his things and made his way out of the coach. He followed the crowd onto Front Street where he saw a jumble of people and horses unlike anything he'd ever imagined. Carriages jostled in the street while dogs ran after their masters and people greeted relatives and friends in a noisy, jovial spirit.

Leonard found the noise of the city unsettling. Everything he saw was new and fresh – stores, banks, factories and churches. The sun had come out after a shower and the streets, paved with cedar blocks, sparkled in their wetness. Customers were going in and out of the stores. He spent two cents to buy the evening edition of the *Globe* from a newsie at the corner of Bay and Wellington Streets. He decided to wander north on York Street and soon found himself at the Shakespeare Hotel. A bell tinkled when he opened the door. For fifty cents he secured a room. It was clean and neat. He ate supper at a restaurant on King Street and later, he marvelled at the number of people out walking after dark.

The next morning Leonard took breakfast at a coffee house near the hotel and set out to find the *Globe* building. This turned out to be an impressive three-storey brick affair on King Street East, topped by a large globe that rested on a parapet anchored with ostentatious cornices. Its first two floors extended to the height of all three floors of neighbouring buildings. Altogether, the suggestion was one of worldliness, if not Victorian splendour. There was no doubt the newspaper it housed was well established and knew what it was doing.

The *Globe*'s main door was of heavy timber and brass and it swung open as Leonard was about to enter. Three young men tumbled out and he managed to catch a hurriedly thrown remark as the reporters rushed past. "The chief will want everything we can get." Soon, he might be doing the same. Inside, he found a young man wearing a celluloid collar and a black coat. He was behind a counter, peering at a book similar to a hotel register. When Leonard asked for Mr. James he jerked his thumb in the direction of the stairway. "Up the stairs, second floor, first door on your right. Sign the visitors' register first."

Leonard stood outside Mr. James's room, taking in the sounds and smells of the newspaper office. He could hear the dull rumble of a printing press in the cellar. He detected tobacco smoke and other substances beyond his ability to identify: a combination of stale food, sweat, and grime. He nervously knocked on a door slightly ajar, being careful not to force it open. "Come," a voice from within sounded.

"Mr. James, it's Leonard Babington. I didn't get an answer to my letter so I thought I should come and see you."

The face that looked up from the desk bore thick mutton-chop whiskers, a deeply veined nose and tired eyes set behind the thickest glasses Leonard had ever seen. Elbow garters held his shirtsleeves in place and an eyeshade covered his brow. Melvin James appeared to squint to better see his visitor, then rose from his chair and held out his hand.

"Ah, Babington, of course, glad to meet you, delighted you could come in. Sorry I never got to answer your letter. Too dashed busy. Didn't have a thing to offer you. But what a marvel you're here today! We've just lost a fellow. Not Catholic are you? Ah, of course not. When can you start?"

Leonard tried to conceal his surprise. His amazement mounted as James ran on about his plans for coming issues, and what good use he could make of Leonard. At the top of his list was the Toronto Industrial Exhibition, a grand new annual fair that would open in a few weeks.

"It'll show us for what we are – a great city of industry and humanity, God-fearing, British, loyal to the Queen. Most of all, a metropolis of high morals, good family values. Babington, you're just the man to handle it for the *Weekly Globe*. Fresh eyes for a fresh new day."

Thrilled to have fallen into such an exciting job, Leonard spent nearly every waking hour tramping the new exhibition grounds east of Fort York. The ravine that once contained Garrison Creek had been filled in to make way for the great event. The fill-in was the answer to Toronto's ravenous appetite for fresh land within handy reach.

Leonard was at the magnificent Crystal Palace when men and women of high society arrived for the official opening of the Toronto Industrial Exhibition. The Governor General, Lord Lorne and his wife Princess Louise, said to be the favourite daughter of Queen Victoria, came from Ottawa. Leonard watched the Princess inspect all manner of crafts from engraved glass to inlaid woodwork, and took careful note for his readers of her purchases. Remembering his mother's tears when he left, he paid the unearthly sum of four dollars and fifty cents to buy her an engraved hand mirror. He thought briefly of getting something for Rosannah, but decided against it.

For Leonard, the exhibition was a carnival filled with new sights and sounds. He made innumerable visits to the food tent to enjoy the free meals for journalists. He knew that most of the *Weekly Globe's* country readers would never see the fair and he did his best to describe it for them.

Leonard also felt compelled to warn visitors against the seamier side of the great city. One night, he visited a number of establishments that were strung out house after house along York Street, above King Street. It was his intention to determine what went on in each house, and to leave without becoming involved. He stopped at three places and found them untidy and uninviting and the women in them unappealing. The fourth door he opened took him into a small parlor with a settee and two chairs. A bell rested on a table and a sign invited visitors to ring for service. It tinkled gently as he shook it.

A tall woman with striking red hair and a low-cut gown emerged from a darkened hallway. "Good evening, dearie, have you come to see someone?"

"Oh, I'm just looking around," Leonard answered, unwilling to commit himself.

"I'm sure you'll like what we have here," she said. With that, the woman turned and called out, "Mabel and Hortense, come and see this beautiful young man!"

Leonard thought the two girls were the prettiest he had ever set eyes on. Mabel was short, with dark hair and a saucy smile. She wore a revealing blouse. Hortense was bigger and heavier. She had painted her lips a bright red and had applied rouge to her breasts. The effect was to make them even more alluring under her transparent chemise. She took Leonard's hand and led him to a bedroom at the back of the house where both girls kissed him and promised he could do anything he wanted. This was not what Leonard had intended, but he found himself unable to spurn their enticement. Three dollars changed hands and when he left, twenty minutes later, he had no desire to visit any of the other houses on York Street.

Leonard counted ten brothels and eight unlicensed groggeries that sold, he wrote, "maddening liquor to the depraved classes." It was one of the most disreputable streets that ever existed in any city and country folk should stay away, he warned. Inevitably, business boomed after his article was published.

Long after the Exhibition, Leonard was so busy he seldom had a day – even a Sunday – to relax in the big house in Parkdale where he'd taken room and board with Mrs. Metcalfe. The publisher of the *Globe*, George Brown, sent him a congratulatory note. Instead of going home for Christmas he decided to stay and write for the special holiday edition. Little did Leonard realize his article, "A Boyhood Christmas in Vandeleur," would become something of a classic for the paper's readers.

Leonard enjoyed stopping for an idle sip of beer at the Queen's Hotel, a noted hostelry not far from the *Globe* offices. It was here that he met George Bennett, a garrulous printing pressman who singled out Leonard for attention. One day, when Melvin James saw Leonard accept a beer from Bennett, his editor drew him aside. "Be careful of this fellow, he's not a stable sort." Leonard avoided Bennett for as long as he could but one day he found himself caught at the door of the men's washroom. Bennett smelled of drink and swayed unsteadily. He supported himself with one hand on the hallway wall.

"Five years and they're letting me go," Bennett complained. "Can't a fellow miss a day now and then?" He doubled over, coughing, and wiped drool from his mouth as he straightened up.

Leonard considered what he might say. He couldn't just ignore the man.

"Go and ask Mr. Brown if he'll reinstate you." Leonard thought it unlikely the man would follow his advice or if he did, that it would do him much good.

A few days after speaking with Bennett, Leonard arrived home earlier than usual. He took tea with Mrs. Metcalfe and went out to buy the six o'clock edition of the *Evening Telegram*. He'd gotten into the habit of checking the four-page sheet for local gossip that the *Globe* usually chose to ignore.

The newsie was still at the corner of Queen Street and Ossington Avenue when Leonard arrived. "Terrible crime," he shouted, "Mr. Brown shot." Leonard was aghast when he read of the dreadful occurrence at the *Globe:*

We stop the press to record one of the most dastardly and daring acts of violence and attempted murder ever perpetrated in this city. This afternoon, about 4:10 o'clock, an ex-employee of the *Globe*, named George Bennett, entered the *Globe* office and met the Hon. George Brown and shot him with a revolver. Mr. Brown is at the present writing lying in the *Globe* office with physicians attending him.

There must be some mistake, Leonard thought. He had to get to the *Globe* and find out what's happened. He ran four blocks along Queen Street before he could hail a hansom.

Leonard found a crowd milling around the *Globe* entrance. He barged into the lobby where two of the paper's editors, Bill Henderson and Allan Thomson, were surrounded by a gaggle of reporters from the other papers.

"I was sitting upstairs above Mr. Brown's room when I heard a pistol shot and a voice call 'Murder' and 'Help,'" Henderson said. He raced downstairs to find Mr. Brown lying on the floor. Thompson took over the story. He'd heard Bennett demand that Mr. Brown take him back, or give him a letter of reference. Mr. Brown said he couldn't do that. Then he heard Bennett say, "Babington sent me," and there was a shot.

"I saw Mr. Brown lunge at Bennett. He grabbed his revolver. He was holding it in both hands and he said, 'Don't harm him, I've got the pistol.' It was then I saw a bullet hole in Mr. Brown's trousers. He'd been shot in the leg. I took hold of the prisoner while Henderson rushed outside and got a policeman."

Leonard was stunned to hear his name mentioned. He felt a hand on his arm. It was Melvin James.

"The police will want to talk to you, but you'd better get out of here for now," James told him. "Go home and wait for someone to call for you."

Leonard lay awake most of the night. The next morning he read in the *Globe* that Mr. Brown had been taken home and was resting from "a severe flesh wound." That afternoon, Inspector Bonnycastle of the Toronto Police presented himself at Mrs. Metcalfe's door. When he asked for Leonard, she scurried upstairs to get him.

"Ah, Mr. Babington, just a few questions for you," the Inspector said. "How well do you know this Bennett?"

"I hardly know him. Just ran into him at the Queen's. When he told me he'd been fired, I suggested he ask Mr. Brown for another chance. I had no idea he had a gun."

Inspector Bonnycastle made a note of Leonard's answer.

"What you say comes off well enough, but they're unhappy with you at the newspaper. Let me give you some fatherly advice. Be more careful in the future. We'll let you know if we need you." With that, he left.

Later that day, a note arrived from Mr. James. Leonard was to stay home until further notice. Two weeks dragged by while he waited to be called back to work. Bennett had been arrested for attempted murder and Leonard followed the case carefully in the papers. On a cheerful spring day he heard the disastrous news. Mr. Brown had died. Infection and fever had squeezed the last ounce of strength from him.

Early the next morning, Leonard's trembling hands opened an envelope handed him by Mrs. Metcalfe. Inside was a single sheet bearing a one-sentence message from Mr. James. "In light of the unhappy circumstances attending your employment at the *Globe*, it is necessary you consider your position terminated."

Leonard read the three lines of careful handwriting several times. Then he crushed the paper in his fist. He wanted to send an angry reply, a note that would shame and embarrass the editor for such an unjust decision. The idea burned in his brain all that day and night. He awoke the next morning with a headache and a nervous tingling all over his body.

Leonard managed to get some tea and toast into his stomach, and then sat down to write a letter to Melvin James. Seething with resentment, he wrote that what the *Globe* had done to him was unfair and that he should be given his job back. "You've trapped me in a nightmare not of my own making. I have given you no cause for the action you've taken." He delivered the letter that afternoon, leaving it with Robert, who handled the reception desk.

When Leonard returned to the *Globe* the next day, Robert did his best to ignore him. When he finally turned to Leonard, it was to tell him the editor was too busy to see him. "But here's something I was told to give you." He handed over an envelope. It was Leonard's last pay packet. In it, he found three crisp new, four-dollar bills. Were these bits of paper to represent his last contact with the *Globe*? No, Leonard decided. He brushed past Robert and vaulted up the steps to the second floor. The door to Melvin James's office was closed. Leonard knocked once and pushed his way into the room.

The sight that greeted Leonard shocked him almost as much as the letter that had brought him here. A girl he recognized as Loretta, a barmaid from the saloon across the street, was on the editor's lap and he had his hands inside her blouse. She quickly disentangled herself and fled through the open door. "What in damn hell are you doing here, Babington? You're a son of a bitch for bursting in on me like this. I told you, you're fired!"

By now, the blood had drained from James's face, leaving him white with anger. Leonard had been ready to grab hold of him and make him see reason. Instead, he started to laugh. "So, Mr. High and Mighty, is this how you keep Toronto fit for decent families – screwing around with any young woman you can lure in here? I'm surprised I didn't find you planking her." The anger had gone out of Leonard's head, replaced by disgust at what he'd seen. "You're just a hypocrite – you were a hypocrite when you fired me just like you're a hypocrite with that girl on your lap."

"I had good reason to dismiss you, Babington, and you know it. We can't keep someone who's connected with that braggart Bennett ..."

"I wasn't connected with Bennett, I was just stupid enough to try to be kind to him ..."

James interrupted Leonard. " ... and someone with a Catholic name, like yours."

"But I'm not Catholic," Leonard protested.

"You're seen to be Catholic, it's the same thing."

"I wouldn't work here if you paid me a hundred dollars a week," Leonard said. He didn't think of himself as idealistic, but he wanted nothing more of this hypocrisy. He bolted from the room.

The next day, sleepless and exhausted after weeks of worry and strain, Leonard realized there was nothing he could have done to change what happened. With the shame of his firing, he'd never get a job at another paper. He had just enough money for his last week's board and a train ticket home. Once there, he knew, he'd have to deal again with his father's weird ideas and the bitter memory of how he'd lost Rosannah. He thought he'd escaped all that. Perhaps his father was right after all. One never knew when ill fortune might strike, or what bizarre fate could descend on a man, undeserved and unannounced.

# Chapter 12

## ON THE BOATS

### August 20, 1881

Leonard Babington encountered his friend Tom Winship on his second day back in Vandeleur. Tom was saddling his chestnut horse Dart – the name was for the blaze on its face – outside the harness outfitter on the Beaver Valley Road. Leonard expected his boyhood chum to ask about his time in Toronto and why he had come home. Instead, he posed a more painful question.

"Have you seen Rosannah?" Tom asked. "Did you know she's had a baby?"

Tom was the only person Leonard had confided in during his love affair with Rosannah. His question brought back memories Leonard had pushed from his mind. At first, he felt a surge of jealously at the thought she'd taken another lover. Then the idea struck him: could the child be his?

"A baby? When did this happen?"

"A few months ago," Tom said. "A girl. She's out there at the Leppard place. I've no idea who the father could be." Tom delicately avoided any suggestion of Leonard's possible paternity.

That night, Leonard thought about the last time he and Rosannah had made love. It was May now, and if the baby was a few months old that meant he could be the father. The more he thought about it, the more convinced he became that he had to see her. If the child was his, he'd make sure Rosannah got the help she needed to give his daughter a decent life.

The sight of the Leppard place reminded Leonard of the poverty in which Rosnanah would have to raise her child. The vegetable garden showed neglect and scraps of old lumber and a broken wagon axle blocked the path to the back door. A dog roused itself from its place in the shade and began to bark. When he knocked, Molly Leppard answered the door.

"Leonard, where have you come from? We heard you were in Toronto."

"I'm back now, and I'd like to see Rosannah. I'm told you've an addition to the family."

When Leonard looked past Molly he saw Rosannah nursing a baby.

"I'm busy right now," she called to Leonard. "Can you wait outside?"

Leonard and Molly chatted at the door. When Rosannah appeared, she handed the baby to her mother. Leonard caught a quick glance of a fair-headed infant with a pug nose and a firm mouth. It was making the sucking sounds of a nursing baby. Molly took it inside.

"How are you, Rosannah? That's a pretty baby you've got."

"I'm all right, Leonard. It's nice to see you, but I've got my hands full right now."

"That's why I've come," Leonard said. "Rosannah, can you tell me if the baby's mine?"

She replied with the twisted, nervous smile that he remembered from their first days together. It usually meant she was trying to avoid an answer. Or perhaps preparing to face up to the truth. Things would be so much better if they were honest with each other.

"I really don't want to say, Leonard. I'm looking after the baby just fine. I don't need any help."

At least she's not denying I'm the father, Leonard thought.

He heard Molly call from inside the house. "Rosannah, please come in. Lenora's acting colicky."

Leonard locked his eyes on hers. He saw a look of alarm spread over her face. That proved it. There could be only one reason for the baby to have that name.

"I think I know who the father is," he told Rosannah. "You'd better tell me the truth."

"Leonard, what's truth got to do with it? You'll be unhappy no matter what answer I give you. Unhappy if I say it's yours, unhappy if I say it's not."

"If it's mine, I'll help look after it."

"You know what my mother would say. She loves the baby, but maybe she wouldn't if she thought its father was a Protestant. It's better without your help, Leonard. You get me all mixed up with your fancy ideas. I don't want to see you back here, ever."

She turned and went inside. The door fell shut behind her. For a second time, Rosannah had locked him out of her life. Their baby's life as well. It's not as if she couldn't use the money. But for now, there was nothing more to be said. He turned for home. He'd figure out something.

News of the execution of George Bennett came a few days later. The trial jury had debated only two hours before finding him guilty, and he was hanged at the Don jail. "Death was painless and easy," the *Globe* reported.

Leonard spent the month helping his father with a new herd of Shorthorn cattle. Erasmus drove twenty head from Flesherton and hired three men to build new fences. The market for Canadian beef in England was growing and he intended to take advantage of it.

"I might take a load over myself," Erasmus said. "A chance to show them how we've kept up the good family name in Canada."

Leonard found it was becoming harder to enjoy being with his father. Erasmus lived by a stern code of ethics – perhaps a reaction to the loose ways of his youth – that he now seemed determined to impose on his son. No dancing, no gambling, no smoking, no drinking, no casual conversation with women of the village. It was a frame of mind, Leonard knew, that was strengthened by the sermons of travelling evangelists every Sunday at the Methodist Church.

Leonard saddled Sugar Loaf and rode aimlessly into the Beaver Valley. This ride was not like the wild one he'd had the last day of school. The horse drank at the river and after awhile, Leonard found himself outside Munshaw's Hotel. He was hot and thirsty. An ale would taste good, and give him a chance to think about what he should do.

There were half a dozen people in the hotel's dimly lit saloon. The innkeeper Aaron Munshaw, a couple of grizzled farmers, a carefully dressed man who must be a travelling salesman, a slatternly girl, and – in a far corner – Tom Winship. Tom waved at him and Leonard moved to his table. He signaled the innkeeper for drinks.

"Did you ever look up Rosannah?" Tom asked.

Tom's constant questions about Rosannah troubled Leonard. Could he never get her out of his mind? He told Tom he was finished with Rosannah, she didn't want his help, and she wouldn't say if her child was his.

"I don't think I can stick around Vandeleur with things the way they are," Leonard said. "What the hell am I going to do?"

Tom laughed, as if he found Leonard's fix something to make fun of.

"If she don't want your help, to hell her with her," Tom said. "You're damn lucky. And if the old man's causing you grief, you better come along with me. There's work on the boats in Georgian Bay. I'm going up to Owen Sound to be a fireman. Hard and dirty work. But what the hell, pay's good and just a boss to deal with, no woman or old man trying to mess up your life."

Leonard and Tom got off the train at the station on Stephens Street in Owen Sound and walked the quarter mile to the head office of the Georgian Bay Shipping Company. They passed the Mechanic's Institute, several foundries, and assorted ship's chandlers. The docks were filled with stevedores carting goods, passengers waiting for their sailings, and peddlers hawking food and clothing.

Leonard and Tom signed on with the Georgian Bay Shipping Company as firemen for the Australasia, the new sidewheel steamer built in Owen Sound. It was mid-August, halfway through the shipping season, and their jobs were available because some of the farm boys who had signed on earlier were needed at home for the harvest. She was setting records for fast trips to Collingwood, Port Arthur, and Chicago. Four hundred and sixty tons, a beautiful ship, gleaming white, one hundred and eighty feet long, cabins and deck space for a hundred passengers and crew A thirty-foot smokestack, tall enough so that smoke and embers belching from its wood-fired engine blew harmlessly away, above the heads of first-class passengers enjoying the promenade deck.

Captain William Craig had the final word on hiring crew and he shook his bearded head in dismay when he saw Tom and Leonard.

"If I wasn't so short of men I'd never take you two," he said. Tom, who'd always been ready for a second slice of his mother's pie, had a plump, apple-cheeked look about him. Leonard, in contrast, was so thin he might have been an icicle in the last stages of a March thaw.

Feeling reduced to the level of awkward adolescents, Leonard and Tom were put to work pushing wheelbarrows of hardwood up the gangplank and into the Australasia's boiler room.

The ship was to sail for Collingwood at one-thirty. Its boilers would need a ton of wood for the return journey, six hours each way. The chief fireman, Harold Dorsey, warned Tom and Leonard of the need to maintain a steady supply of steam to power the ship's twin paddlewheels, one on each side of the vessel.

"Keep your eye on the steam gauge. When she falls below the blue line, pour on more wood, boys, or we'll end up a drifting hulk out there somewhere around Christian Island."

Leonard found the heat in the furnace room almost unbearable. He felt light-headed and staggered with each armload of wood he carried from the hold. Tom had promised it would be a hard and dirty job. The heat and smoke escaping from the firebox drove all other thoughts from his mind. Grab the wood, heave it into the inferno, slam the fire door, stick your head outside for a breath of fresh air. It took every ounce of his energy to stay on his feet.

Leonard had been aboard only a few days when Harold Dorsey sought him out. He had a warning for him.

"There's all kinds of queers on these lake boats. If I was a good-looking young man like you, I'd carry a knife. Let those bloody hermaphrodites know you're not one to be interfered with."

"I've had no trouble," Leonard answered.

"You will, mark my word."

That night, Leonard told Tom about the warning.

"Don't listen to that shit," Tom said. "Else you'll never make no friends on these boats."

Leonard forgot the warning as his muscles firmed and his waistline tightened while he heaved wood and tended the Australasia's boiler. He relished Captain Craig's slow and careful navigation of the channel off Manitoulin Island and through the shoal-infested St. Marys River into Lake Superior. The insatiable maw of the furnace was less hungry and Leonard was able to catch his breath and look out at the shoreline.

Days of smooth midsummer sailing left Leonard unprepared for the rough waters that autumn winds brought to Georgian Bay. Storms blew up quickly, lashing the deck with rain as waves tossed the Australasia in and out of troughs forty feet deep. He learned what sea sickness meant. It was not until well into his second season that Leonard became accustomed to the torment of rough water. All around, ships were getting into trouble, running aground on shoals, or sinking in bitter storms, sometimes with all hands on board.

As treacherous as open waters, Leonard learned, were the frequent fights among dockworkers and boatmen. He saw black eyes and broken noses aplenty in the saloons he frequented with Tom. Leonard avoided barroom battles but Tom, with a shorter fuse and more likely to object to some slighting remark, incurred the wrath of one of the meanest men on the docks. His name was Orville Compton and Leonard thought him a big sonofabitch, as ugly as he was ill tempered.

Leonard blamed himself for their fight in the saloon at the Georgian Inn. It had been his idea to stop there – the grungiest of the four in Damnation Corners. Tom had wanted to go straight on to supper. They were on their first ale when Compton came by and asked Tom who his "girl friend" was. In a minute, Tom and Compton were struggling on the floor. Both were bloodied – Compton from a lost tooth and Tom from a cut nose and a black eye. The fight surprised Leonard. Tom and Compton had gotten on well before that night. Leonard couldn't understand why the two were now such enemies.

Leonard extracted the truth from Tom during a long night of drinking. Tom had refused that night to go with Leonard to Branningham Grove, the famous whorehouse run by old Meg Matthews. "Guess you still don't like girls," Leonard said. "Come to think of it, you and that Orville Compton were pretty friendly there for awhile. What happened?"

"I went too far with him once," Tom admitted. "You know what I mean. After that, he wanted me to be his boy. But I didn't really like him. I told him to bugger off." Leonard remembered their night in the forest long ago. He and Tom had kissed. Leonard worried that it was his fault that Tom liked being with men.

On payday, Leonard put a five-dollar bill in an envelope and addressed it to Rosannah in Eugenia Falls. He enclosed a note giving his address, and asking her to write to him. No answer ever came, and Leonard sent no more money to her.

On an afternoon in their second summer on the Australasia when it was Tom's job to push wheelbarrows of hardwood up the gangplank and into the boiler room, Leonard noticed Orville Compton had come on board. He led a gang of dockworkers who were hoisting kegs of cargo onto the main deck. Leonard was piling Tom's wood into orderly rows when he heard a shout, "Watch out below." Then he heard the dull thud of a heavy keg hitting the gangplank, and the sound of wood being shattered. A short, sharp scream was followed by a loud splash, and then silence.

Leonard rushed to the door of the boiler room. The gangplank lay twisted and smashed and the wheelbarrow was on its side, partly in the water. Leonard saw Tom trapped under the wheelbarrow. His body was crushed and bleeding.

With the help of Chief Dorsey, Leonard managed to drag Tom up the broken gangplank and into the hold. Tom's eyes were open and seemed to be focused on some distant object. Leonard wrapped his arms around him and felt for a heartbeat. "Get ashore for a doctor," he shouted to Chief Dorsey.

"I don't think there's any need of that," Dorsey said. "Can't you see, he's dead?"

"He's not dead, he can't be," Leonard protested. He put his ear to Tom's chest. Hearing nothing, he began to massage his chest. "Tom. Keep breathing, don't die on me."

"That'll do you no good," Leonard heard a voice say. It was Captain Craig. "Here now, let me get you out of this mess." Leonard moaned and muttered, but allowed himself to be dragged out from under Tom. He sat stunned and silent, his face and chest smeared with blood, as two of the crew carried out Tom's body. Others began a cleanup of the mess and started hammering together a new gangplank.

"We were loading ten barrels of steel rods," Captain Craig said. "The cable snapped. Nobody knows why."

Was it an accident? Or the result of a murderous jealousy? Compton said he had no idea how the cable had come loose. Leonard had not forgotten Harold Dorsey's warning and he sought out the chief fireman to ask him what he tbhought had happened.

"I knew something bad was going to come of your friend's foolishness," Dorsey said. "I've seen it before. I had a brother who went that way. Dead now, too. I always wondered if there was something deep inside him that made him turn the way he did."

It was left to Leonard to put Tom's body on the train for home. Dispirited, he felt Tom's death had been his fault and he wondered whether he should stay on the boats. It worried Leonard all that week, and for long after. He was alone and was sorry he'd not made friends of the other lake sailors. He wrote a long letter to Tom's parents. He told them how easily Tom had made friends but remained silent on their son's choice of companions. Leonard had not been able to stop from sobbing as he wrote the letter. When he pasted the one-cent stamp to the envelope, he felt his head begin to clear. He realized that writing the letter had been a kind of catharsis that helped ease his guilt. Leonard decided there would be no more running away. Not from his memories of Rosannah, not from the stupid mistake he had made at the *Globe*, and certainly not from the boats.

# Chapter 13

## THE STORM

### September 7, 1882

Captain Craig eyed black clouds scudding across the horizon when he docked the Australasia in Owen Sound a little before noon. Weather permitting, he was scheduled for a return run to Collingwood later in the day. Below decks, Leonard Babington looked out a porthole and saw trees on shore bend and break as they were buffeted by the wind. All afternoon, he waited for word from the engineer to throw more wood onto the fire, now banked and awaiting its chance to flare into life. Just before supper, an order came down from Captain Craig: "Cancel the sailing, boys. It's too damn rough to go out there tonight."

The storm raged that night and then all day. The Australasia was riding easily at anchor the next morning when Captain Craig received orders to make his run to Collingwood. The return trip was uneventful and they were back in Owen Sound when Leonard heard a commotion on deck. He found the first mate and the engineer crowded into the pilothouse. Captain Craig had news for them. Reports were coming in of ships damaged and lost. A telegraph gave them details of the sinking of the S.S. Asia. She'd left Owen Sound about midnight and was known to have floundered in mountainous seas. The telegraph said a single lifeboat had carried the only two survivors, a teenaged boy and a girl, to shore. An Indian found them and took them to Parry Sound in his canoe. One hundred and twenty-three passengers and crew had drowned.

"Damn shame," Captain Craig declared. "Bloody want of judgment, leaving port in the face of that storm."

The sinking reminded Leonard of the risks of boating on the lakes and he thought of his parents and how they would have worried about him. He went to the telegraph office and sent them a wire to say he was safe. He felt relieved he'd done the right thing.

As the Australasia was getting up steam the next morning, a messenger came aboard with a telegram for Leonard. He opened the neat buff envelope and read with shock and surprise:

THOUGHT YOU HAD DROWNED. FATHER INJURED. COME HOME. MOTHER.

On the train that afternoon, Leonard wondered what had happened to his father. In a silent Vandeleur Hall he found Erasmus in the back bedroom, heavily bandaged and lying on his back, a light blanket covering an emaciated frame. He thought his father had shrunk, he looked so vulnerable and help-less. Leonard sat with him all afternoon and into the evening. When Erasmus opened one eye and saw Leonard beside the bed, a slight smile crept across his lips.

"I prayed you'd come," Erasmus whispered. "We were blasting stumps. They told me you'd drowned. It shocked me pretty bad. I didn't pay attention to what I was doing."

"That's all right, father. You need to rest now. Don't worry about a thing."

"Promise me you'll stay for good," Erasmus pleaded.

"Hell, Father, I can't guarantee that. But Mother and I will look after you."

Leonard left the bedroom and found his mother in the kitchen. "How in the world did he blow himself up?"

"Erasmus always hated that job, dynamiting stumps. It was so dirty and dangerous. They were out there when Jamie Ross showed up from the Henderson store. He said they'd had word the Australasia had sunk. All aboard supposedly lost. "

She turned her face away and wiped her eyes with a towel.

"Erasmus must have been so shocked he forgot what he was doing. Sam Mellon was helping him. He says Erasmus just stood there. He forgot he'd lit a fuse. When the dynamite went off, he was standing right beside the stump. It threw him over on his back. Tore an eye right out of his head.

"It wasn't until Dr. Griffin got here that we found out it was all a mistake. He said it was the Asia, not the Australasia, that had sunk. He laughed and laughed. Told Jamie he would have to examine his ears."

Leonard returned to his father's room. He was feeling even more gloomy, convinced that what had happened was not his father's fault, but his own. His father had always been afraid something would happen to Leonard, but it was Erasmus who has come close to killing himself.

Leonard saw a tear trickle down his father's cheek. Erasmus tried to speak but his words were no more than a whisper. "Tell me you forgive me, Leonard, for trying to keep you home. I've loved you more than life itself."

"I know, Father, I know." Leonard let his head drop into his hands. He had no doubt his father loved him. He realized their struggle was borne out of his father's wish to mold him into something Leonard could never be.

Sitting with his father, Leonard thought about why his parents had chosen to abandon the England of Queen Victoria and settle in this isolated corner of Canadian backcountry. He remembered having long talks with his mother, and one day having come across a stack of letters packed away in a trunk. Between what he'd been told and what he read, he gradually assembled the true reason for their having come to Vandeleur.

Bit by bit, the story emerged that Erasmus, scion of an eminently respectable family in Derbyshire, knew that as a younger son he could never inherit his father's estate. He had the choice of two occupations: the clergy or the army. Neither appealed to him. While he contemplated his future, he enjoyed carousing with friends in the pubs of Derby and gambling at the tables of the Erewash Club. He took a wife, the estimable Esther Brandreth, a pretty girl who knew much of literature and poetry but little of homemaking. They would have lived splendidly on her income had Erasmus's gambling debts not risen to more than five thousand pounds.

"We have decided you must go abroad," Erasmus was told. "You can count on receiving an annual remittance. I have arranged to clear your debts, but you must never return to England."

"Father, you can't do this to me," Erasmus protested. "I will lose Esther. Honest to God, I'll never gamble again."

His father insisted that all the arrangements had been made and that nothing could be changed. Erasmus was given a choice between Canada and Australia. He chose Canada, thinking, as he one day confessed to Leonard, that because it was closer, he would stand a better chance of some day returning home. On a spring day in 1852, Erasmus and Esther, who had agreed to stay with him and take their chances in Canada, sailed for Montreal. They were on their way to the Queen's Bush in Canada West where a grant of fifty acres, once part of lands inhabited by the Ojibway Indians, had been secured for them in the Township of Artemesia, County of Grey.

It seemed to Leonard that Esther had accepted banishment with less complaint than his father. "Splendid, just splendid," she had exclaimed the first time she saw the Beaver Valley. She and Erasmus stood at the brow of a hill facing the Escarpment, the height of land that ran like a spine through the Queen's Bush, all the way to the tip of the Bruce Peninsula in Georgian Bay. To the east rose a line of hills dappled in sunlight and deep shadows, their gentle shapes testament to thousands of years of glacial erosion. A vast tableland that had once been the bed of a tropical sea stretched behind them to the western horizon. At their feet lay the valley of the Beaver River, which fell over the escarpment into a deep rift at a point known as Eugenia Falls. There, joined by the waters of a smaller stream, the Boyne River, it flowed placidly north to Georgian Bay.

Erasmus freely admitted to his son that he had known nothing of the new land of Canada or what it would take to draw sustenance from the fifty stony acres ceded to him. His remittance brought him money for the family's essential needs, with enough left over to hire settlers to build a log cabin. Eventually, Erasmus mastered farming well enough to assemble one hundred acres that he stocked with diary cattle and planted to wheat, oats and barley. He became a devout parishioner of the Wesleyan Methodist church on the Beaver Valley Road, a stone's throw from the Vandeleur School. Their families in England did not forget them. From time to time Leonard's granddmother sent out fancy ball gowns that had been worn the mandatory single occasion. Esther stuffed them into a trunk and never put them on.

At last, Leonard realized, he had begun to understand the difficult relationship of a father and his son. He noticed that his father had awakened, and Leonard began to speak now of his feelings. "Your whole life's gone into building up Vandeleur Hall," he said. "It's all you cared about – the land, the crops, the house. You wanted to prove to yourself that what happened in England was something that occurred when you were young and foolish. So you tried to instill the same desire in me – to make a glorious thing of this piece of wilderness. But I was born here. I took it as I found it. It was the natural world for me – the forest, the streams, the wild animals."

Leonard waited for his father to say something, but there was no response. Leonard tried to explain how his thirst for fresh experience had driven him to explore the world outside Vandeleur.

"Everyone has to find their own place. You found yours here, four thousand miles from home. I don't have to travel that far to get to know this new country we're building. Canada is young, not even as old as me. I'm going to grow old with it."

Whether it was the shock of seeing his son, of hearing Leonard's refusal to promise to stay in Vandeleur, or simply the exhaustion of staying alive until his son had come home, the breath of life was ebbing from Erasmus. He sighed, closed his remaining eye, and let an arm slip over the edge of the bed.

Leonard's mother had come into the room as he was talking. She flung herself onto the bed and embraced her husband. Leonard let her cry for a few minutes, then gently raised her to her feet and took her to the big bed that Erasmus had brought from Philadelphia. He put a blanket over her. Leonard sat up most of the night, reflecting on the past and thinking of his future.

He dreaded the funeral. "I wish we didn't have to do this," he told his mother. He visited the Methodist minister in Vandeleur, Richard Orgell, to ask him to conduct the service. After hearing a half hour of sermonizing on God's will in life and death, Leonard left the manse feeling more dejected than ever. Worse than the grief he felt at the loss of his father, was the guilt that he once again carried in his mind. His thoughts were of all the slights and disagreements that had come between he and his father. He had been an ungrateful son.

When the service began at the Vandeleur Methodist Church, nearly every pew was full. Reverend Orgell was a thin and tired-looking man and Vandeleur was his fifth or sixth charge, evidence that his spiritual skills were either very much or very little in demand. The service marched with disciplined precision, from the recitation of John 11.25, "He who believes in me will live, even though he dies," through the singing of a hymn from the Methodist song book, and into a prayer commending the soul of Erasmus to God's care.

The words of the minister didn't mean very much to Leonard. His grief had brought on disdain, not for his father but for the sermon he had heard, for the man who mouthed it, and perhaps for the church in which it was delivered. It was his father he had come to honour; nothing he'd heard bore any resemblance to the reality of the parent he'd known. He stood at the end of the service, embraced his mother, and walked out with the four pallbearers carrying his father in his coffin.

All stood with heads bowed as the coffin was lowered into a grave behind the church. Jamie Ross, who had carried the false news of Leonard's sinking to Erasmus, apologized for what he had done. Leonard considered that Jamie had been a fool not to have known the difference between Leonard's Australasia and the Asia, but he saw no point in berating him. "You couldn't help it, Jamie, you were just repeating what you'd been told." Later, neighbours brought food to the house and everyone talked late into the night.

Leonard did his best to help his mother overcome her worries about keeping up Vandeleur Hall. She was uncertain for the future of their property and hoped Leonard would take up where his father had left off. "Who will do the work, see the cattle are attended to, and keep us going?" Leonard promised he would not leave Vandeleur Hall without hiring all the help his mother would need. "We'll get one of the neighbours to manage the fields and look after the cattle," he promised. "I'll get a housekeeper for you and I'll try to come home once a month to make sure you're all right. I'm really not cut out to stay and run the farm. Your books and stories have filled my head with all kinds of ideas. I'm glad they did, but I'll never be content to live the life of a farmer."

# Chapter 14

## THE CHRONICLE

### October 20, 1882

Leonard Babington put the finishing touches to the death notice he had prepared about his father, shortening a sentence here and adding a word there. He kept it brief, mentioning only his father's birth in England, his arrival in Canada, his accident, and the large turnout for the funeral. The day was pleasant and he set out to walk the mile to the office of the *Vandeleur Chronicle* to ask Charlie Ibbotson, the proprietor, to put the announcement in the next issue. Leonard had rarely read the local paper. He thought it a poorly printed and haphazardly edited sheet, content to record the most inconsequential of neighbourhood occurrences. The death of a prominent citizen like Erasmus Babington ranked as major news in a place like Vandeleur.

When Leonard arrived at the *Chronicle* he found Charlie Ibbotson packing letters, paper, an ink well, pencils, and a printer's apron into a cardboard box. Leonard told him he had brought in his father's death notice. "I hope you can put it in this week's paper," he said.

"There's not going to be a paper this week," Ibbotson replied. "Nor next week, either." He was a little man, his head perched forward on his shoulders like a bird's, the result of years spent brooding over cabinets of type. "These old eyes are getting too weak to read a stick of type, and I've been feeling poorly for about a year now. Think I'll just close 'er down. People won't miss it, anyway."

Leonard looked around the office and tried to imagine what it had been like for Ibbotson, working here alone most of the time. He pictured himself amid the mess and disorder of this dusty office, thinking it a poor comparison with his working space at the *Globe*. The thought was a fleeting one, and he pushed it to the back of his mind.

"That's too bad, can't you get someone to take on the paper?" Leonard asked.

"I'd give it away if I could," Ibbotson answered.

Leonard decided he would take his father's obituary to the *Flesherton Advance*, the paper that people in Vandeleur would read once the *Chronicle* stopped printing. He wished Ibbotson well and returned home, intending to travel to Flesherton the next day. He arrived home in time to help his mother serve tea to Sam Bowles, a neighbour who had agreed to look after planting and harvesting and give care to the animals in return for a share of the crop. His daughter Sarah would come around every day to help look after the house.

"The *Chronicle* is closing down," Leonard announced. "Sam Ibbotson says he can't keep it up anymore. I thought of taking it over, but what's its future?"

"Oh Leonard, what a wonderful idea. You must do it."

"I know you'd like me to stay home, Mother, but I'd have to be sure I could make a go of the paper." They talked about it all evening. Long after Sam Bowles had left, Leonard agreed to have another discussion with Charlie Ibbotson. He found the publisher at his house on the East Back Line the next day. A deal was struck. Five hundred dollars would buy the *Chronicle*, assets and liabilities all in hand.

On his first visit to the *Chronicle* as its new owner, Leonard reflected on how his new status would be received by people in the district, especially the Leppards. He doubted if Rosannah ever saw the *Chronicle*, nor her parents, either. It took him only a few minutes to make a circuit of the small office. Idly, he opened the top drawer of a wooden cabinet that stood at the back of the printing room and found it filled with a jumble of tiny brass letters. They were all mixed together, and would have to be arranged alphabetically in their own compartments. Once he got them back in order, he'd learn to pluck them out letter by letter to assemble lines of type. Old pages sat in metal frames on the printing stone. The Washington Press tucked into the corner oozed a mess of black ink. A pile of newsprint sheets gathered dust. Dust was everywhere; there'd been no rain for weeks and from the road a cloud of powdered clay arose every time someone went by. He felt as addled as the day he first went on board the Australasia.

Vandeleur, the community served by the *Chronicle*, took itself seriously and its civic leaders addressed themselves to matters of the gravest import: securing railway connections, celebrating in proper manner the Queen's birthday on the 24th of May, and delivering due respect to the clergy and to men of the law and medicine. Merchants flourished, children were educated, and politicians became entrenched. Men voted Conservative even when high tariffs pushed up the price of farm implements. When they looked for wives, they preferred girls of Protestant families with roots in the north of Ireland or the east of Scotland.

The *Chronicle* occupied a decrepit shack on the Beaver Valley Road. A vacant lot separated it and the Methodist church. There was a small front office, a cubicle for the editor, and a printing room at the back. After straightening out the type Leonard began to clean up the mess of old papers and unopened mail. From the floor beside the editor's desk he retrieved an armful of empty whisky bottles. A few people dropped in that afternoon – a man who complained there'd been no paper for two weeks, and Mr. Heard, the wagon maker from Flesherton who came to pay his advertising bill. It was from Mr. Heard that Leonard learned about the printer's devil, the apprentice to Mr. Ibbotson. Young Tyler Thompson was a smart lad, the wagon maker said, and Leonard should get him back on the job.

That evening Leonard saddled Sugar Loaf and rode down the East Back Line to the Thompson place. Tyler was a fair-headed, blue-eyed lad of fourteen, done with school but fed up with the *Chronicle* because he hadn't been paid the past two months. "I wasn't treated right by Mr. Ibbotson," the boy complained. "I think I should get what's owed me."

Leonard decided to be forthright with Tyler. "I need your help. Somebody who knows how Mr. Ibbotson did things." Everything was settled in a few minutes; Tyler would get five dollars in back wages with a guarantee of a dollar fifty a week in the future, paid each and every Saturday. Tyler's father told Leonard he could count on the boy being at work the next day.

It took two weeks for Leonard to get out his first issue. He decided to use the time to read back copies to find out what had been happening in Vandeleur. A larger paper would never publish most of what passed for news in the *Chronicle.* "Somebody broke a pane of glass in the front window of Smith's harness shop. Mr. R. Cook, agent for the celebrated Ontario Iron Harrow, has sold 25 sets of these splendid devices in Vandeleur. Mrs. R. T. Wilson has a fine brood of young Plymouth Rock chickens just hatched, the first of the season."

Leonard also read more serious news. The Warden of Grey County, it was alleged, had taken advantage of his office to have county workers clear brush on his property. There were several items about Cook Teets, an eccentric blind man Leonard vaguely recalled having seen at the post office. He'd been fined five dollars after Constable Field had arrested him for wandering down the Beaver Valley Road, shouting drunkenly. On another occasion it was alleged he had struck a woman he'd been drinking with at Munshaw's Hotel. The charge was dismissed when she failed to turn up to testify.

Many of the paper's ads, Leonard was glad to note, were the same every week. He'd just repeat them in the next issue. That would give him more time to get out and meet folks. Munshaw's and the Commercial Hotel in Priceville were regulars. The Vandeleur Brick and Stove Works had a nice ad that ran every week, as did the butcher, Joseph Greene, and the Union Carriage Works from Markdale. Then there were the "national" ads that came from Toronto: "Lydia E. Pinkham's Vegetable Compound. A positive cure for all those painful complaints and weaknesses so common to our best female population."

Within a few days, the office had been cleaned up and Tyler had explained Mr. Ibbotson's routine in getting out the paper. Ads had to be collected, news gathered, stories set into type, and the old press had to be wiped down before it could be trusted to churn out another issue.

Leonard soon realized Tyler knew much more than he did about getting out a paper. One night he dreamt of dropping the page forms and scattering type all over the floor. He'd struggled that afternoon to put letters in his typestick and it took him hours to fill half a column. It was a far cry from the *Globe,* where he'd simply handed his copy to an editor; he'd had only to write clearly so the typesetters would not make errors. And there was the matter of printing the *Chronicle.* He knew he needed more help than Tyler could offer, and he went looking for it.

If Leonard needed a reason to take his mind off Rosannah and her baby, he found it in his new adventure as a country editor. The logical place to recruit someone to help him get out the paper, Leonard thought, was another newspaper and so he went to Flesherton where he introduced himself to Andy Fawcett, the proprietor of the *Advance*. Fawcett, a curt and unsmiling type, told Leonard he knew of a printer who had come to town looking for work. He had no need of him, but he thought Leonard might find him across the street at the saddler's shop. "Goes by the name of Harte," Mr. Fawcett added.

The man Leonard encountered at the saddler's shop looked about forty years old and was well dressed, with a slight smile on his face, as if to indicate he was a friendly type. But what Leonard mostly noted was his height – over six feet – and the lanky way he stood waiting to be recognized as someone important. More like a banker than a printer.

"Charles T. Harte at your service," the man said when Leonard introduced himself. With that pronouncement he chuckled slightly. Leonard took it as further evidence of the stranger's desire to demonstrate a good nature. He explained he had just taken over the *Vandeleur Chronicle* and he needed help to get out the paper.

"I'm a journeyman printer," Charles Harte told him. "I did two months subbing at the *Owen Sound Advertiser* and now I'm on my way to Cleveland. Vandeleur, you say? I wouldn't mind seeing your village."

Leonard realized he was talking to a tramp printer, one of the thousands of wandering craftsmen who worked their way from paper to paper and print shop to print shop, often riding freight trains to their next destination. He'd heard of such men at the *Globe* although George Brown would never hire any; he preferred men with family obligations and liked them even better if they were in debt.

The most valued possession of the tramp printers, Leonard had heard, was their membership card in the International Typographical Union. Most drank hard liquor and enjoyed life to the full. Harte, Leonard was to learn, was no exception. Leonard agreed to pay him five dollars a week, supply him with at least one bottle of whisky, and give him a bed in the hired man's cottage at Vandeleur Hall.

Harte proved to be a skilled typesetter and a proficient pressman. He worked with lightning speed to collect letters from the type case, assemble them into lines in a composition stick, and gracefully transfer the column into the forms that made up each page. Leonard worked alongside him, at one tenth the speed. Harte showed Leonard how to tighten the quoins that held the type in its page. "It's like your mother's clothes pin," he told him, demonstrating how to use a key to tighten the grips. Then he inked the form with a roller, laid a sheet of paper on it, and tapped it firmly with a wooden mallet to produce a proof for Leonard's inspection.

During that first week, Harte lectured Leonard on the ways of business he'd observed in the dozens of places he'd worked. Leonard asked why, with all his skills, Harte had chosen to roam from town to town.

"The freedom. I ship my stuff ahead by express, put on my oldest clothes, and go down to the rail yard for a free ride to the next town." He said he stayed away from women – they only tied a man down. He found a change of scenery a welcome relief when he ran into bad conditions – places filled with lead fumes from a hellbox of discarded metal, or where the smell of urine, sometimes used to clean the presses, got into the pores of anyone who stayed in one place too long.

"A printer's life can be rough" Harte said. He claimed to have watched Mark Twain almost get himself crushed when Twain worked on his brother's paper in Hannibal, down in Missouri. "Flywheel flew off the press. Just missed Mark, and smashed a hole in the wall straight into the tavern next door. Brother decided to put a door where the hole was. Wouldn't have to go outside for a refreshment."

When they were putting the finishing touches to Leonard's first issue, Harte announced he would like to write an editorial.

"Come from a long line of writers," he declared. He claimed to be a cousin of Bret Harte, the famous novelist. Leonard told him of the time he had read from the *Luck of Roaring Camp* to get his teaching job. He marvelled at the way Harte composed an editorial about the pleasures of the open road. The printer made it up as he plucked letters out of the type case.

"You've put that together in haste," Leonard remarked, having learned how Harte liked to banter his way through the day. "I hope it'll give us no cause to repent in leisure."

"Leisure, Mr. Babington. That's something you must know a lot about!"

The old Washington Press clattered and groaned as Tyler and Harte fed it sheets of newsprint. Leonard beamed with excitement as he picked up two sheets and folded them together to make the first copy of his first issue of the *Chronicle*. It was dated October 20, 1882. A column on the front page was devoted to the obituary of Leonard's father. A small notice announced that Leonard Babington, Esq., was the new publisher. Several ads and two other news items filled the rest of the front page:

### ARE THERE MORMONS IN VANDELEUR?

We have been informed that disciples of Brigham Young are at the present time endeavoring to make converts to their faith in the Township of Artemesia. We can scarcely credit the rumour, but give it for what it is worth. If it be correct, then the sooner this so-called class of Christians are driven out of the place, the better it will be for the morals of the community.

### HARD ON THE BEARS

Mr. Scarth Tackaberry, who lives on the Beaver Valley Road in Vandeleur, set up a dead-fall on his property this fall, and has succeeded in capturing four black bears, which were foolish enough to investigate the mysteries of the rude but "sartin death bar trap." Folks say bears seem to be more numerous this season than for many years past. There is something more sportsmanlike in shooting than in trapping them, however.

"Congratulations Mr. Editor, you've got a paper," Charles Harte told Leonard, wiping ink from his hands with a rag. Harte opened a bottle of whisky and Leonard took two drinks. Tyler looked on, sipping from a bottle of Sarsaparilla. Leonard's good feeling about the first issue was tempered by a nagging concern in the back of his mind. He knew he couldn't have gotten the paper out without Harte's help, but he didn't like the habit Harte had of lording things over him. Leonard should have brought out the whisky, not Harte. Just a tramp printer, Leonard reminded himself. He better not get too big for his britches.

At home that night his mother read every line of all four pages of the *Chronicle*. "Your father would be proud of what you've written about him," she said. "I liked how you called him an indomitable pioneer, imbued with the spirit of the frontier. I wish I felt some of that spirit right now. But I'm tired, and I'm going to bed." Leonard knew she wasn't well. She'd been failing since the death of Erasmus.

Leonard had not seen Rosannah since his return from Owen Sound. He avoided the Leppard place and had not encountered any of the family in the village. It was by chance as he talked with the blacksmith, Tom Bragg, about an ad — "Horse shoeing a specialty" — that he heard Rosannah had gotten married. Worse, her husband had abandoned her, leaving her with two children to support.

"Married up with Dave Rogers but he's taken off. Knocked her up and she's had another kid. She's back at home with her mother and the brats."

Leonard cringed at the news. Almost two years after their parting, the thought of Rosannah in the arms of another man was still like a stab in his heart. Once again she had invaded his world and stirred hurtful memories of their past. He wished he'd not been told of this new misadventure.

Leonard filled the next month with busy days of selling ads and gathering news. He never seemed to get around to collecting money and he neglected the bills that came into the *Chronicle*. A stack of envelopes had been pushed unopened to a far corner of his desk. He was unprepared when the visitor from the Toronto Paper Manufacturing Company arrived in Vandeleur.

He was a short, fat man with a bald head, dressed in clothes a size too small. When Leonard saw him he thought he looked like a comic character he'd seen in a play at the Grand Opera House in Toronto. The card he gave Leonard bore the name Otis Sampson, General Representative. His mood was brisk and he got right down to business.

"Our records show the *Chronicle* owes a very substantial sum for newsprint," Sampson said. "We have not had a payment for eighteen months. The balance due is one thousand, five hundred and sixty-seven dollars. We require the amount in full. Failing that, we will suspend shipments and pursue a court order for our money."

The crisis forced Leonard to confront the unopened mail on his desk. He was shocked to find bill after bill, almost all addressed to Mr. Ibbotson. The bill from the paper company was not only the biggest but the most important. He didn't have the money to pay it and he couldn't ask his mother to take out a mortgage on the farm. If he lost his newsprint supply, he wouldn't have a paper.

Leonard stewed over the problem. He was reluctant to ask his tramp printer for advice, but he had no one else to turn to. The next morning, red eyed from lack of sleep, Leonard told Harte about his problem. The printer was in the middle of making up a poster for an auction at old Ike Williams's farm. He listened, a quizzical look on his face, as Leonard recounted the threat by Mr. Otis to cut off newsprint and sue the *Chronicle*.

"Aw, they do that all the time," Harte scoffed. "I remember when Mark Twain's brother got behind in payments at the *Hannibal Courier*. He pushed them off with a few dollars and arranged to buy his newsprint elsewhere. Why, he had three or four companies supplying him at one time, and he owed money to all of them."

"I wouldn't feel right not paying what I owe," Leonard said. "I could give them a hundred dollars and pay ten or twenty dollars every month."

Harte chuckled. "You'll be in debt forever at that rate. Here's what you do. Tell Sampson you'll pay up ten cents on the dollar – a hundred and fifty dollars, cash. Otherwise you'll go to their competitor, Laurentide. Those newsprint makers in Quebec hate upstarts like the Toronto Paper Company."

When Otis Sampson returned to the *Chronicle* three days later, Leonard was nervous. He didn't really want to do as Harte had told him. But he realized he had no choice. He made the offer suggested by his printer.

"Impossible, Mr. Babington," Sampson told him. "Not a reasonable proposition. And if you think you can buy from Laurentide, we'll tell them you're a bad risk. I'll have to have three hundred now, and an extra ten dollars on every bundle of newsprint we send you for the next two years."

Leonard saw it as a deal he'd have to go along with. He reached into his desk drawer and took out a cheque drawn on the Bank of Commerce. He'd survived his first crisis. Just as well Harte had been there to give him advice.

While Leonard had been struggling with how to pay off this debt, his mother had been growing more feeble. She'd fallen in her bedroom and Dr. Griffin thought she may have broken her hip. Leonard sat with her all day on Sunday and Monday. That night Sarah Bowles, the neighbour's daughter, stayed at her bedside. It was after midnight that she came to Leonard to awaken him and tell him his mother was asking for him.

He found his mother gasping for breath. When she saw him a smile fluttered briefly on her face before she closed her eyes. It was too late for him to say goodbye. Three days later, another funeral. Another sermon of empty chaff by the Rev. Orgell.

Home after the funeral, Leonard ached with loneliness. The death of his father had been easier on him than the loss of his mother. Erasmus had died accidentally and things like that happen in the country, but Leonard felt cheated at the loss of his mother. He'd been closer to her than to his father and he wondered how he would manage without her at his side to look after him. If only he could turn back the clock and bring her back! He wrote a short, careful account of his mother's life and published it in the *Chronicle* under the heading, A Pioneer Wife.

The death of Leonard's mother caused Leonard to think about whether there was any point in staying on in Vandeleur now that he had lost everyone he loved. He spent several days calculating the reasons he should stay, as against the reasons he should not. He remembered telling Rosannah he wanted to find exciting things out in the world. The murder of Mr. Brown and Leonard's firing by the *Globe* had given him excitement enough for a lifetime. By staying in Vandeleur, he might still have a chance to win back Rosannah. Weighing everything up, he decided he must make a success of the *Chronicle*. Sam Bowles would look after the farm, and Leonard's half-share of the crops would make up for any shortfall at the paper.

The day after Leonard put out the issue reporting the death of his mother, Charles Harte announced he was leaving for Cleveland.

"I've taught you all I can," he told Leonard. "It's up to you now."

Leonard reminded himself that no tramp printer stayed long in one place. For all Harte's know-it-all ways, he'd miss his help, his banter, and his pronouncements on high level matters, be it religion, science or politics. He envied the printer his skill at hurling bright ripostes to any comment Leonard might make. His own bantering skills had sharpened considerably as a result, he thought.

"Collect up your empty whisky bottles on the way out," Leonard told

Harte.

"Thought I'd leave them for you," Harte laughed as he stepped out the *Chronicle*'s front door. "Something to remember me by."

Leonard felt saddened as he watched Harte, a rucksack over his shoulder, make his way onto the Beaver Valley Road.

"Goodbye my bantering friend," he called after him.

# Chapter 15

## THE STRYCHNINE BOTTLE

### Morning, November 4, 1884

When Angus McMorrin called the court to order on the second morning of Cook Teets's trial, Judge Armour held up the proceedings. "I have been told," he said, "that the jurors were forced to spend last night at Coulson's Hotel without benefit of heat. I apologize for that, gentlemen, and I am assured the problem with their furnace has now been corrected. I hope you were not entirely too uncomfortable. Perhaps some of you found alternative warmth." Leonard heard snickering from some of the benches. Judge Armour cast a stern glance toward the source of the noise. "Is the Crown ready to proceed?" he asked Alfred Frost.

"I am, my Lord," the prosecutor answered. He called Rosannah's sister Bridget Leppard as the first witness of the day. Leonard Babington watched her make her way from a back seat of the courtroom. She threw a troubled glance at her mother as she approached the witness box. Bridget was a timid girl, Leonard knew. He remembered her as a pupil when he'd taught school in Vandeleur. He'd learned she could be fearful and diffident, a behaviour very different from that of her rebellious younger sister. How he wished Rosannah had been half as reserved.

Alfred Frost rubbed his hands together, as if chilled by Judge Armour's comments on the lack of heat in the jury's hotel. He began his questioning by drawing from Bridget the fact that Rosannah had complained of being sick after arriving home from Michigan. There had been a rumour that Cook had tried to poison Rosannah more than once. "I thought she was in the family way," Bridget said.

119

Bridget described how everyone had been awakened by Rosannah's screams. "She threw off her bedclothes and trembled like she was in a fit. She leaned her weight on the back of her head. Her legs and arms were all in motion."

When her mother realized Rosannah was dead, Bridget said, she asked her to go for Cook Teets.

"I went down the road to Scarth Tackaberry's house and spoke to Mrs. Tackaberry. Mr. Tackaberry wasn't there. I didn't want to go to the Teets place alone so I got Jane to go with me."

"Did Cook express any surprise when first you told him of Rosannah's death?" Alfred Frost asked Bridget.

"No, he just wanted to know when she'd died, and what she'd said. I told him Rosannah was still warm when I left. I said perhaps she was just in a trance, and might be able to talk when we got back. We stopped at the house of his sister, Sarah Clark, to tell her. Jane went home and Sarah drove us back in her buggy."

"And what did the prisoner do when he first saw Rosannah?" Alfred Frost asked.

Bridget sobbed at the question. She must have been thinking of how she had watched her sister die, Leonard thought. She repeated much of her mother's testimony. What Cook had done when he arrived at the Leppard place, and how he never asked what might have killed Rosannah.

Alfred Frost asked Bridget what else had happened that morning. She repeated that Cook had not asked any questions about what it was that killed Rosannah. Perhaps he already knew, Leonard reflected. He thought the question made for an effective conclusion to the prosecutor's examination.

James Masson began his cross-examination by asking Bridget if Cook had wanted to know whether anyone had sent for a doctor.

"Yes, he asked that question. No one had gone for a doctor."

"And did Cook Teets at any time say to you that he had killed his wife? Did he confess?"

"No, but like my mother said …"

"Never mind what your mother said, Bridget, we're interested in what you have to say."

James Masson paced back and forth before asking his next question.

"Bridget, did your sister have many boy friends?"

"A few, but only one at a time. She didn't really trust men."

"What do you mean? Didn't she like having men around her?"

From the corner of his eye, Leonard caught a look of exasperation on Molly's face. She was motioning to Bridget, muttering, "No, no." Molly shut up when people seated close by began to shush her.

Bridget hesitated before answering James Masson.

"She liked men, but she was always on her guard. Perhaps because of what happened with the priest, she was never the same after that."

"Whatever do you mean, Bridget?"

Leonard saw a look of horror on Bridget's face. She seemed to shrink into herself as the meaning of what she'd said came over her.

"The priest, he had his way with her. When she was about twelve. And it happened more than once. Rosannah told me every time. She said she hated men."

Judge Armour slapped the dais in front of him. It was clear he had been angered by what Bridget had said.

"Miss Leppard, you're under oath. You've sworn to tell the truth. We'll have no slanderous fantasies against the Roman Catholic Church. The jury will disregard those remarks, obviously a tissue of lies. I could have you charged with perjury, or even criminal libel. Is counsel finished with this witness?"

"I am, your Lordship," James Masson said. He retreated hastily to his seat. He had no wish to risk anything that might further inflame the judge.

Leonard struggled to absorb the startling facts he had just heard. Bridget wasn't so timid after all, he thought. Her testimony explained so many things, no matter what the judge might believe. He remembered hearing rumours about Father Quinn and now he knew they'd been more than idle gossip. Leonard realized what a horrible mistake he'd made that time he'd forced himself on Rosannah. He never had a chance, after that. No wonder she wouldn't admit he was the father of Lenora. It was a miracle she could love the baby, considering how it had been conceived.

The swearing in of Constable John Field distracted Leonard from these thoughts. Why were policemen always so thickset and brawny? Field sat heavily in the witness chair, his weight warping its slight wooden frame. He couldn't have gotten that way on his constable's pay. Probably picked up more than his salary from other, more devious pursuits.

"Please tell the jury," Alfred Frost began, "how it came about that you arrested Cook Teets."

Constable Field explained that when the inquest jury returned a true bill against Cook a year ago, he was sent to his house to arrest him for murder.

"All right now, John. In what condition did you find Cook Teets? Did he resist?"

"His mother answered the door. She said Cook was sick in bed. I went to his bedroom and told him he was under arrest. He didn't resist. I told him I had to search the house."

"What did you find?"

"I asked Cook if he had any strychnine. He said he did. He got out of bed and went to a chest that he kept in his bedroom. He took out a tin box and showed me a bottle he had inside it. It was marked strychnine."

Alfred Frost reached for a small green bottle that sat on a table beside the witness stand.

"Is this the bottle you took from Cook Teets's house?" He held up the bottle, no more than four inches tall and perhaps an inch across. It was about three-quarters full of a white crystal, the color of strychnine. The powder stood out clearly against the green glass.

"That is it."

"What else did you retrieve?"

"I asked Cook for any paper connected with his marriage. He gave me a marriage license and a life insurance policy. He got the papers from his trunk. Said he paid eleven dollars for the life insurance. He handed everything to me and said he had nothing to hide."

James Masson asked only a few questions in cross-examination.

"Constable Field, did Cook Teets attempt to conceal anything from you?" Field admitted he did not.

"Did the prisoner confess to you he had killed his wife?"

"He said nothing of that sort to me."

When Masson was finished with Constable Field, Alfred Frost told Judge

Armour his next witness would be Dr. Richard Ellis of the Toronto School of Medicine. He made a show of thumbing through the file in front of him as the doctor made his way to the witness box to be sworn in. Dr. Ellis was tall, bald, and wore thick glasses that were the result, one could assume, of long hours of study of medical texts by the feeble light of coal oil lamps.

"Dr. Ellis, do you remember the last witness bringing two jars to you?"

"Yes, he brought a large glass jar and a stone jar."

"Can you tell the jury what those jars contained?"

Dr. Ellis said both jars bore Township seals that identified them as containing body parts from Rosannah Teets.

"One held the stomach and parts of the liver and kidney," he said. "The other contained part of the intestines."

"Did you make an analysis of those parts?"

"I made an analysis of them all. I found a very small quantity of strychnine. A fraction of a grain, but quite sufficient to confirm a presence in the viscera."

"Did you find sufficient to have caused death?"

"You never find all the strychnine because four fifths is absorbed in about half an hour and is scattered throughout the whole body. From the symptoms that have been described, I would say it was strychnine that killed her."

James Masson wanted to know how the analysis of Rosannah's organs had been conducted. Dr. Ellis said he immersed them in a mix of sulphuric acid, alcohol, ether and ammonia. The process produced a yellow residue that turned out what he took to be strychnine when he tested it.

"What test did you apply?"

"I tested it on two frogs. It produced convulsions in both of them. Exactly the same convulsions known to be caused by strychnine."

Leonard held his breath as he watched Alfred Frost rise to his feet and prepare to speak.

"Your Lordship, if I may be permitted, can the witness tell us what is in the bottle Constable Field removed from Cook Teets's trunk?" He picked up the bottle from the table beside him and made to give it to Dr. Ellis.

Judge Armour held up his hand, as if to signal the transfer should not take place.

"Mr. Masson, do you have any objection to the witness answering this question?"

"No objection, your Lordship."

"The witness may proceed."

Dr. Ellis held the bottle up to the light. He withdrew its cork and sniffed the contents. Carefully, he tilted the bottle so the crystals slid toward its open end. Bringing it to his mouth, he hesitated and looked directly at Alfred Frost. After a moment, he closed his eyes and touched his tongue against the crystals. Leonard heard gasps throughout the courtroom. When Dr. Ellis opened his eyes he replaced the cork and stared again at the prosecutor. The courtroom had fallen silent.

"It has the taste and physical properties of strychnine. I have no doubt it is strychnine."

A tremor of excitement spread through the courtroom. Dr. Ellis had given dramatic evidence that Cook Teets had been in possession of strychnine. Leonard knew this was something the jury would remember. When the court rose for its midday break, he hurried to the washroom.

Leonard relieved himself standing in front of the tin sheet that covered the wall above the urinal trough. The sound bounced off the tin, announcing his presence. As he buttoned up his pants and turned away, he saw Nelson Teets come into the room. He remembered seeing him the day before. He'd heard he was paying for Cook's lawyer.

"You're Leonard Babington," Nelson said. "You've been printing funny stories about Cook. You don't know the half of it."

"Suppose you tell me," Leonard replied.

"You have no idea what Cook has had to put up with," Nelson said. "And that girl Rosannah! Everybody around here has had her in bed. That priest really started something. I can vouch for that, personally."

What was Nelson saying? That he'd been a lover of Rosannah, too? Had he too resented her easy ways with men? A resentment that could have been a motivation for murder? If that were the case, why would Nelson Teets put himself under suspicion? Perhaps he meant to shift attention from his brother, even at the risk of implicating himself. Leonard knew only that Cook had both the means and the motivation to take Rosannah's life.

"You seem to know an awful lot about Rosannah Leppard," Leonard said. He couldn't bring himself to call her by her married name. "Are you sure you're not just making assumptions? Because the girl had a poor reputation, that doesn't mean everything that people say about her is true."

Leonard remembered a conversation he'd had with Rosannah a long time ago. It was something about men who called out to her and made rude remarks when they saw her in the village. He was sure she had mentioned Nelson Teets as one of the men who had badgered her. Perhaps there'd been more to her relationship with Nelson than she'd let on. If he felt so vindictive toward her now, it was likely he'd felt that way when Rosannah was alive.

Leonard left Nelson Teets in the washroom and went out the side exit of the Court Building. Doubts about Cook's guilt nagged at him. Alone now, watching fresh snowflakes fall to the ground, Leonard reached into a jacket pocket and withdrew an envelope. It contained his notes on the trial and material about Rosannah's death. He found the clipping he was seeking. It was the article he had written shortly after Cook had married Rosannah. Leonard had filled it with invective. He was sure now it would have convinced some that Cook was capable of murder.

## Cook Teets' Exploits! Shoots at Some Children and Draws His Revolver on a Fellow Imbiber

Cook Teets is a blind man who has figured rather conspicuously in columns of The Chronicle. He is not one of those people who go around led by the hand or is the subject of such sentiments as "pity, pity the blind."

On Tuesday, Cook accompanied by his paramour, a lady who shall remain nameless, arrived home from an extended trip to Michigan. On the road leading to Vandeleur he involved himself in an incident that clearly showed the desperate character of the man. As he was passing a house some small boys offered up certain jocular remarks and tossed a few snowballs in his direction, there having been an early arrival of inclement weather in the district.

Only one other person noticed this confrontation with the boys. According to this witness, the language emanating from the mouths of the boys was so insulting to Cook Teets, to say nothing of what feeling it might have engendered in his companion, that he drew his revolver and fired two shots in succession in their direction. Fortunately his aim was not good; nobody got hurt. The witness, who just happened to be passing by demanded of Teets what on earth was he doing.

Cook Teets has had things too much "all to himself" for quite long enough. He must be made to understand that the people in this county will not tolerate such uncivilized and heathenish "cowboy" pranks.

Leonard had no need to read the entire clipping; he remembered exactly what he had written. Nelson had said he didn't know the half of it. There was only one person who could tell Leonard the truth – Cook Teets. He had to see him – right away.

The entrance to the Owen Sound jail was at the north end of the County Court Building. Leonard asked to see the governor, John Miller, and was admitted to a small, dark office. A window looked out onto a courtyard covered with grass now white with frost. Beyond it, sheltered by twenty-five foot walls, was the two-storey limestone cellblock where Cook was being held. Miller was spooning soup from a bowl.

"Babington of the *Vandeleur Chronicle*," Leonard told him. "I need to talk to Cook Teets. Appreciate if I can see him before the afternoon sitting."

"I've read your paper. Always glad to oblige the press. If he's willing, I've no objection. You've got an hour and a half. Maybe he'll confess!" Miller shouted to the guard who had shown Leonard in. "Tell Teets he has a visitor."

# Chapter 16

## THE VISITOR

### Noon, November 4, 1884

Cook Teets lifted the cup of cold broth he found in his cell when he was brought back from the courtroom for the noon break. A layer of grease had formed on the offal that floated in the mix. It coated the roof of his mouth when he tried to swallow. He spat the mess onto the stone floor; he had no appetite and his eye was hurting again. Cook heard footsteps in the stairwell leading to the narrow landing outside his cell.

"Visitor for you, Cook," the guard said. He stood at the cell door. "It's Mr. Babington, the reporter. Says he wants to interview you."

Cook shifted uneasily on the cot that hung from an iron frame bolted to the wall. It held a thin mattress of padded straw covered by two grey blankets. The cell was more comfortable than the tiny cubicle where he'd spent his first six months. His lawyer had complained to Governor Miller that it was inhumane to hold a man not yet convicted of any crime in a cell just three feet wide. His new space, atop the second floor of the jail, held a table that served as a combination washstand and resting place for his lunch dish. A toilet pail was lodged on the floor beside it.

A window set high in one wall cast a narrow shaft of light into Cook's small world. He was barely aware of the difference between night and day. His head ached from the fever of the flu that had sent sweat and chills through his body for a week. His eyes watered and his nose ran. One eye, especially, hurt and he held his handkerchief against it to catch tears that oozed onto his cheek. His stomach ached. He wondered whether he would have the strength to endure another afternoon of testimony. Now this man Babington was standing at his cell door, no doubt planning to write more vile stuff that would turn the public still further against him.

"If you're going to write more lies I don't think I want to talk to you," Cook told Leonard Babington.

"I'm not here to write lies," Leonard said. "I'm only interested in the truth."

Cook calculated his chances with Babington. He knew all about him and Rosannah. She'd told him how Leonard had tried to make a lady of her, and how she had resisted his efforts to get her off patent medicines. He was forever after her to take an interest in good literature. She'd called him "the professor."

Cook struggled to his feet. He stood at his cell door, leaning on its bars. "I'm not sure I should tell you anything," he said. "But if you want to know the truth you'll have to let me start at the beginning."

"Once we got to Vandeleur," Cook began, "my father started making furniture. I got to be a master craftsman. We did pretty well, and I was able to put aside most of what my father paid me. I remember when my bank account had five hundred dollars. I was really proud."

"How did people treat you?"

Cook gripped the bars with his hands. He told Leonard people taunted him as he went about the countryside. "That blind fool should stay at home," he heard neighbours say. Children were especially hurtful. "Suck my teats, Teets," boys would shout. They'd take turns trying to trip him, often succeeding. Some threw stones at him.

"They say you went to the school for the blind. How did you find it?"

Cook remembered when he first heard that an Institution for the Blind had opened in Brantford. He was forty-four then. "I made up my mind right away I wanted to go there. I was determined to learn anything to make me more normal. They took a dozen of us grown men. I slept in a dormitory with about four-dozen other boys and men. We were segregated from the girls.

"The principal was Mr. Hunter. He said us men were there as a special favour. Officially, he represented the Department of Prisons. That's where the school gets its money. He told me that because of my lack of sight, I might find it difficult to learn what they were teaching, but that I had to do my best. What a laugh."

"What did you say when he told you that?"

"I told him I knew how to make furniture. I offered to teach others to work with wood. He told me that wouldn't be necessary. He said they had programs that would make good workers of the kids. Weaving baskets, if you can believe it."

"Why did you stay?"

"They had these dogs, German Shepherds and Labrador Retrievers. They were being trained as guide dogs. I wanted to learn how to handle them, to give commands and get the knack of following their lead."

Cook said that once he got to be pretty good with the dogs, he decided to go back to Vandeleur. "I think they were glad to see me go. They let me take one of the dogs. I chose Cromwell, and I've had him ever since."

"That gave you a lot more freedom," Leonard said.

"It sure did. I started going to Munshaw's Hotel, I became a regular in the saloon there. That was where I met Ann Jane Sargent. I married her. I think her parents were willing to overlook me being blind on account of I had a bit of money."

"But that didn't work out, did it?"

"I guess I relied too much on her to do little things for me – bring me my clothes, clean up after me, and open doors wherever we went. We'd been married only a few months when she began to sleep in her own bed. That was when we started quarreling."

"It must have been hard for both of you."

Cook said his wife complained that he couldn't do anything for himself. "It never entered my head that she would leave me. My mother said I was too much trouble for a wife."

Cook moved away from his cell door and sat down on his cot.

"I don't understand why these things happen to me," he said. "First I'm blind, and then my wife leaves me, now I've lost Rosannah and I'm charged with her murder. I wish somebody could explain why God has done this to me."

There was nothing Leonard could say about that. Instead, he said he'd like to hear how Cook and Rosannah came to get married. "Molly Leppard testified that you hired her to keep house for you and your mother."

Cook remembered his mother was cool to Rosannah from the day he had hired her. Rosannah was a good housekeeper, he told Leonard. "She put in a nice garden and used to come back to the barn where I was looking after the animals. She was amazed I was able to care for the livestock. I told her I could make out shapes, and of course I knew my way around there pretty well."

Sounds are so important to a blind person, Cook reminded Leonard. He used to tell Rosannah that sounds made pictures in his head. He would listen for the wind to get an idea of what kind of day it would be. And smells. Every place smelled a little different. The furniture shed of maple and sawdust. His bedroom smelled of the feathers in the pillows.

"We used to talk about all kinds of things," Cook said. "About what it would be like to live in the city, or how the Negroes were doing over at Priceville. We had good, intelligent discussions. And we talked about you sometimes, Leonard."

Cook remembered the time Rosannah told him most men had treated her as if she knew nothing, while Leonard was always trying to get her interested in things she couldn't fathom and didn't care about. She wasn't sure which was worse. She called him The Professor. Cook saw no point in telling Leonard.

Rosannah wanted to marry someone she felt equal to, Cook said. "She found it easy to feel that way with me. She said I needed someone like her to be my eyes. I used to tell her I thought she was wonderful. I wasn't lying. We were getting pretty chummy together. You know what I mean."

Cook thought of how it had been with Rosannah that time in the barn. It was as if they were in a world of bliss, freed of all their problems. His blindness was of no account, and he had a woman in his arms.

Cook paced once around his cell. He didn't want to tell Leonard what had actually happened. That his mother had caught them together, making love. "Is this what I'm paying you for?" his mother had asked Rosannah. Cook felt lost when Rosannah had to leave. That was when he made up his mind to ask her to marry him.

When Cook and Rosannah told her parents they were going to get married, he remembered he was surprised at how quickly her father agreed. Even Rosannah's mother seemed to go along without too much protest, provided a priest married them. But the more he thought about Molly's insistence on a Catholic wedding, the more nervous he became. He'd have to learn Catholic rites, and it would take some time to arrange the wedding.

"I said to Rosie," – and here he used his pet name for her – "are you really sure we need to have a Catholic wedding? What difference does it make as long as we're married? Let's go down to Toronto where nobody's ever heard of us. I told her I knew of a minister who'll marry us."

Because Rosannah needed new clothes, Cook remembered, he had taken her to Eliza Carson, the dressmaker. They needed a marriage license and for this they went to Mr. Purdy, the postmaster in Eugenia. It was safe to see him because he knew nothing of each of them having already been married. Mr. Purdy also sold life insurance. He charged Cook eleven dollars for the first year's premium for a policy on Rosannah's life. Mr. Purdy sent Rosannah to a doctor in Meaford for a medical examination. Cook recalled that the long drive took most of the day but the examination lasted only a few minutes.

"Rosannah passed the exam just fine, but the doctor said she was pregnant. Well, I wasn't surprised!"

Leonard interrupted Cook to ask why he had not purchased life insurance on himself.

"I'd thought about it, but I wasn't sure I could pass the medical. My stomach had been bothering me a lot. One of my eyes hurt so much it drove me crazy. Dr. Griffin gave me morphine, he told me there was no law against it. He charged me ten dollars for a bag of morphine crystals. I used to pour out a few crystals onto the kitchen table, and mash them up with my fingertips. Then I'd wet my fingers and put the powder on my tongue. It was bitter, but it stopped the pain. I decided not to bother about insurance."

The trip to Toronto went off smoothly, Cook told Leonard. They'd said nothing to his mother or Rosannah's parents. He'd called for her in a hansom before dawn, in time to catch the morning train to Toronto. That afternoon they walked from Union Station to St. Andrew's Presbyterian Church on Simcoe Street. The Rev. Macdonnell had preached at the school for the blind, and he remembered Cook. He married them in the manse, with the minister's brother and a woman from the church as witnesses. Cook gave Rosannah a wedding ring he'd bought in Meaford.

"The minister warned Rosannah that her people would say she's not married and that she'd be living in sin. Rosannah said she didn't care. She said she was a Methodist now."

Cook remembered how excited and happy he'd been. He'd never expected Rosannah to marry him, yet there they were, walking down the street in Toronto arm in arm, husband and wife. "Every man will envy me," he'd said to her. Cook had felt important, a successful man; life was going to give him everything he wanted.

At the Rossin House Hotel, Rosannah booked their room. She'd shown their wedding certificate and had explained their situation. Cook remembered her words: "My husband's blind and he'd like to rent a room, we're just married."

"That room cost me a dollar and a half,' Cook said. "That's because the hotel had an elevator, the only one in Canada. We took the train back the next day and walked to my house from Flesherton Station. It was a beautiful September evening, everything smelled so sweet.

"Mother was none too happy when we told her what we'd done. She said she didn't want Rosannah in the house and that even if we were married, our wedding certificate didn't mean a thing. She said there are no seats for Catholics at the Methodist church. I tried to tell her Rosannah was a Methodist now but she wouldn't listen to me."

Cook remembered they began the long walk back down the Beaver Valley Road and took the footpath across the river to the Leppard place. It was dark when they got there.

"I waited at the fence while Rosannah went inside. When she came back she was really upset. She said her mother was angry and she didn't think I should come in. I was sorry I hadn't gotten a place for us before we were married. So we decided Rosannah would stay with her mother, and I went back home.

"While I was looking around for a place I decided we should make a trip to Michigan to see my relatives in Grand Rapids. They all made furniture there. We stayed a week, had a nice time. When we got back I ran into Joseph Pedlar at the post office and he said he was moving in with his daughter and he'd rent us his house. It was near Eugenia Falls, not far from Rosannah's place."

Tired of pacing his cell, Cook sat down on his cot. The springs squeaked as he shifted his weight.

"The last time I saw Rosie alive, I asked her to go with me to Eugenia to see our new home. She didn't feel up to it, so we sat on that big rock by the fence and talked. It was starting to rain. I gave Rosannah some tobacco and she lit a pipe and smoked it. I could tell by the smell that she was still smoking when she got up to go back inside. It was the last time I saw her alive."

Leonard asked Cook if Rosannah had ever told him about bring raped by a priest.

"She told me when we were in Michigan. I would have killed the asshole but by then, nobody knew where he was."

"I understand your feelings," Leonard said. "But you still haven't told me if you gave Rosannah strychnine."

"You know I didn't," Cook answered.

"But you had some. What did you do with it?"

"I scattered some in the bush, to kill the foxes that were raiding our chicken pen. I used their pelts to make a cape for my mother. I never got to give it to her. I never let anyone else have any strychnine."

Before Leonard could ask another question, the door to the corridor opened and the guard brought in James Masson.

"Now your lawyer's here I may as well tell you," Cook heard Leonard say. "That piece I wrote about you. It wasn't entirely fair. I'm sorry. I'm going to publish a clarification." Cook thought, What good will that do me now?

The guard rattled his keys against the bars of Cook's cell. "Time to go back to court, Cook, visiting hour's done."

# Chapter 17
## A QUESTION OF INSURANCE

### Afternoon, November 4, 1884

Outside the Grey County Court Buidling, people were going about the essential acts of daily life -- activities of little importance on their own, but when tallied up become the glue that binds a community together. At the Toronto, Bruce and Grey Railway station, caretaker Josiah Ralston swept cigarette butts from the floor of the waiting room. Instead of depositing them in a trash can as usual, he swept them out a door and into the alley, perhaps because he was feeling rankled by a breakfast time argument with his wife. At the Owen Sound High School, vice principal Emma Cartwright finished her lunch of salad and a sausage, put on a sweater, and went outside to ring the bell that called students back to classes. At John Fry's butcher shop on Front Street, Adele Ross, who lived in the largest house in Owen Sound on the town's West Hill, was buying a fat turkey for Thanksgiving dinner. At Damnation Corners, a few stragglers huddled against a chill breeze as they headed into the Bucket of Blood, the most popular tavern at that intersection. On the hill behind the Grey County Court Building, the early snowfall had attracted a few adventurous tobaggoners.

The mayor of Owen Sound, Duncan Morrison, sat in the study of his home and made notes for a speech he would give that night to the Grand Lodge of the Masonic Order: "There are no more firm believers in a bright and prosperous future for our own magnificent Dominion, this Canada of ours, than among those whose names are enrolled in the register of the Grand Lodge of Canada."

The Owen Sound harbour was emptied of shipping when the Canadian

Pacific steamer Algoma became the last ship to depart for the season. It set out in early afternoon for Port Arthur, with a crew of nine and thirty-seven passengers. It would encounter a blinding snowstorm and run aground on an islet in Lake Superior. Most aboard would be lost.

When Leonard Babington returned to his seat after the lunchtime adjournment, he found the courtroom warm and stuffy and filled with the scent of damp scarves and sweaty parkas. On his way to his seat at the newspaper table, he encountered James Masson. "We'll see the last of Mr. Frost's witnesses today," Masson told Leonard. "Then I'll put Cook Teets's sister and mother on the stand." Leonard thought Masson was showing a friendlier tone since hearing his apology.

In the few minutes Leonard had with Masson, he gained considerable insight into the probems the lawyer was having in building Cook's defence. Masson recounted how he and Cook had argued vigorously about their legal strategy. The lawyer had told Cook that he must have shared his strychnine with somone – Molly Leppard, Scarth Tackaberry or maybe even his brother, Nelson Teets. Cook denied it. Masson said he'd told Cook bluntly: "How can I defend you if you won't cooperate? You'll end up swinging if we can't shift suspicion away from you."

The lawyer hooked his thumbs in his vest as he leaned over Leonard. He spoke barely above a whisper. "Cook insisted they couldn't convict him for something that happened when he wasn't there. He told me that if I thought differently, he'd have to get another lawyer." Masson added that when he threatened to quit, Cook backed down. "It would have been impossible for him to find another lawyer and the judge wouldn't have allowed an adjournment."

The two continued to whisper while the guards brought Cook in through the door opposite the jury. In a moment, Judge Armour entered and Alfred Frost called his first witness of the afternoon. He was Roger Purdy, an emaciated-looking man who ran the post office and general store in Eugenia. He'd spent years cultivating his political connections and the postmaster job was his reward, along with his appointment to issue marriage licenses. Between those jobs and the commissions he earned as an agent for the Canadian Mutual Life Association, he'd been able to put up a handsome brick house on a choice property upstream on the Beaver River.

Alfred Frost ambled to the witness box, folded his arms on his chest, and brushed a loose lock of hair from his forehead. The questioning began.

"Did the prisoner apply to you for a marriage license?"

"Yes, he did."

"Is he able to write his name?"

"He just signed with an X."

"Did he make an application for life insurance on Rosannah Leppard?"

"He came to me for such – he and her together. I sent them to Meaford for her medical examination. When they got back I wrote a policy for four thousand and four hundred dollars on Rosannah's life. Teets spoke of getting some insurance on himself, in her favour. But he never did. I've always wondered why not."

Leonard underlined his notes about the insurance. The fact there was a witness to Cook having taken out a policy on Rosannah's life was important. He was not surprised when James Masson began his cross-examination on that very point.

"Mr. Purdy," Masson started, "you will recall Cook told you he was in poor health, and the doctor in Meaford had said he should go to the company's chief surgeon in Toronto for an examination."

"I don't remember anything of that kind," Purdy declared.

"But you knew him as being blind a great many years?"

"I know he had the appearance of it."

Judge Armour interrupted to ask a question. "Has the witness ever seen the prisoner without his guide dog?"

Purdy seemed to be embarrassed for having questioned Cook's blindness. He didn't answer the question but instead talked about how Cook learned to use other skills.

"I know boys used to put things in front of him to tell the colour. He said he could tell between light and dark. He would tell the colour of their clothing and caps partly by feeling."

James Masson took four steps, putting him less than an arm's length from Purdy. Hands on his hips, he resumed his cross-examination.

"So Cook Teets can do his own business and go about the country? He's a pretty smart man in doing his own business?"

"I believe he is so," the witness answered.

The exchange seemed to Leonard to have ended in a standoff. But there was hard evidence now about the insurance, and that could be taken to implicate Cook.

The next two witnesses were neighbours of the Leppards. They were sure to have known something about what had gone on during Rosannah's last day.

Moses Sherwood testified to having seen Rosannah and Cook together outside the Leppard house between four and five o'clock that afternoon.

"What were they doing?" Alfred Frost asked.

"They were sitting on a stone together, talking. Rosannah had a piece of paper in her hand and she looked very steady at it. She looked up into his face and whispered and he made an answer. I cannot say what was said."

"What was in the paper?"

"I couldn't tell, looked like some kind of a powder, maybe medicine. She was folding it over and over, as if she was trying to get what was in it into a heap. I walked past lightly. I did not want to disturb them, I did not want to get into a conversation with Cook, he's none too friendly. I just wanted to go on about my business."

"And after that she went home?"

"Yes, and he went toward his mother's house."

James Masson told Judge Armour he had no questions for Sherwood.

The next witness was Scarth Tackaberry. He strode to the witness box, all legs and arms, and sat down with a flourish. Leonard thought he had an impudent look that showed contempt for Cook Teets and disdain for everyone else in the courtroom. On second thought, perhaps he was being unfair.

"You live opposite the prisoner, I believe," Alfred Frost began. Tackaberrry said he'd been born right there, in the house on the Beaver Valley Road. He said it boastfully, as if the act of birthing had made him a real son of Vandeleur.

"As a neighbour, were you aware at any time of the prisoner having strychnine in his possession?"

"I was. He showed it to me one day in July of last year, 1883, on a visit to his house."

"Where was he keeping it?"

"He took it out of his trunk. He showed me a revolver, too. The strychnine was in a small bottle, something like the one we've seen in evidence. That looks like the bottle."

Leonard watched as Scarth Tackaberry pointed to the bottle on the evidence table.

"And Mr. Tackaberry, can you say, at the time you saw the bottle, how much strychnine there was in it?"

"I think it was pretty nearly full when he showed it to me. I asked him where he got it and he told me first in Canada. I told him he could not get it here and then he said he got it in the United States."

"And is there as much in the bottle now as when you saw it?"

"There was more then than there is now. Yes, I am quite satisfied as to that."

James Masson was up immediately to face Scarth Tackaberry. He put his hands behind his back, looked from the witness to the jury, and then back at the witness. Leonard thought he was signaling that he had a critical point to make.

"Mr. Tackaberry, I put it to you that you were a suitor for the hand of Rosannah Leppard."

"I never was!"

"But you wanted her to marry you?"

"I never did. Never a word of that kind was said between us."

"Did not you and the prisoner have words about your relationship with Rosannah?"

"He told me Rosannah said I wanted to marry her. I told him he lied, that I knew Rosannah couldn't have said any such thing."

"Admit it now, you had some hot words with each other, didn't you?"

"We had some hot words."

Before James Masson could pursue this admission, His Lordship broke in with a question.

"How long was this before her death?"

"It was before her marriage," Tackaberry said. "I guess it would be a month before."

It looked to Leonard as if Scarth was getting a bit frazzled. He kept running his hand through his hair and making as if he was brushing lint off his jacket.

"Now Mr. Tackaberry, were you in the habit of visiting Rosannah?"

"I saw her at her house two or three times."

"And did you call on the Leppards the night before Rosannah's death?"

"I stopped by there for a bit. I was on my way back from Flesherton. I heard Cook had offered Mrs. Leppard some strychnine to control varmints. I'd been having trouble with raccoons and rabbits and I calculated I might get some from her."

"And did you?"

"As a fact, no. She said it was too late and I should come back another time."

Leonard thought it sounded rehearsed, the way Tackaberry had answered that question. So, apparently, did James Masson.

"I put it to you," Cook's lawyer argued, "that you'd gotten some strychnine from Cook Teets, and you'd gone to Rosannah's house because you wanted revenge for her having spurned you. You went there to kill her."

"If I did, I didn't succeed. She was still alive when I left. Ask Mrs. Leppard."

"But for how long, Mr. Tackaberry?"

Judge Armour cleared his throat. "Where is counsel going with this line of questioning?"

"I'm trying to point out, Your Lordship, that Cook Teets was not the only person who may have had the means to carry out this crime. There were other people in the house that night. We should not forget that. The defence has no further questions."

When Alfred Frost told Judge Armour he was finished presenting the Crown's case, the judge called on James Masson to began the case for the defence. Masson's first witness was Cook's sister Sarah Ann Clark. Leonard wondered how Cook felt about her being dragged into this mess. No matter what she said, everyone would think it a lie, a cover-up for her brother.

"When did you first see your brother on the morning of Rosannah's death?" Masson asked.

"It was when Mrs. Tackaberry and Bridget stopped at my house. They'd gone to mother's place to get him. He'd been there all night."

"Bridget has testified you drove her and Cook to the Leppard place that morning. Can you tell the jury what you found when you got there?"

"One of the girls, I think it was Mrs. Leppard's daughter-in-law, was scrubbing the floor. She rose up to let us pass. I led Cook by the arm. The place is very small, just room to walk between the stove and the table. We passed through that space and Cook went and knelt by the head of the bed. He said to me, 'Sarah, is she dead?' I said she was. He said, 'Poor Rosannah, just speak one word so I will know you are not dead.' I said she will never speak any more. I turned around and Mrs. Leppard came and shook hands with Cook. I said, 'How in the world has this happened, what is the cause of this sudden death?'"

Masson asked the witness if anyone had sent for a doctor.

"Nobody had," Sarah Ann Clark replied. "I said to Mrs. Leppard, 'When you first saw Rosannah was ill, didn't you send for a doctor?' She said no."

Alfred Frost declined to cross-examine.

James Masson called Margaret Teets to the stand. Leonard considered it cruel to force such an old lady to testify in court. She'd raised her family and lived through a great piece of history, all the way from the War of 1812 to the Civil War and the Confederation of Canada in 1867. A woman her age, around ninety, deserved to finish out her life unmolested, Leonard thought.

Margaret Teets rose slowly from her seat and leaning on a cane, made her way forward. Leonard looked at Cook and saw he was dabbing both eyes with his handkerchief. At least he hasn't had to watch his mother age, Leonard thought. He probably still thinks of her as she looked when he last had his sight, when he was a boy of twelve. Mrs. Teets was old now, her face wrinkled and worn. The one good thing about Cook being blind, Leonard thought, was that he didn't have to watch his mother grow old.

Cook's lawyer led Margaret Teets through Scarth Tackaberry's visit to her home, the time he claimed Cook had shown him a bottle of strychnine.

"Do your recollect your son showing Mr. Tackaberry the bottle?"

"Mr. Tackaberry never saw that bottle to my knowledge," Margaret Teets said. She spoke in a high-pitched but clear voice, and showed no hesitation in her answer. She waved her hand to one side, as if to dismiss both Tackaberry and the question.

"Did you ever give Cook the keys to the trunk to show the bottle to Mr. Tackaberry?"

"No, I never did."

"Do you remember him having a little wooden box about the colour of that box?" He pointed to the one on the evidence table.

"Yes, he had a box. There wasn't much in it. Just a little glass tube and a magnifying glass. It had a couple of pieces of glass with a flea between them. People could look at it and see what the flea looked like from real close."

"One more question, Mrs. Teets. Was Cook at home with you the night Rosannah fell ill and died?"

Mrs. Teets gripped the sides of the witness box and looked directly at Masson when she answered.

"Yes, he was with me all night. We were just getting breakfast when Bridget and Mrs. Tackaberry came for him."

Leonard wasn't surprised that Mrs. Teets had stood up for her son. He was impressed with the firmness of her answers. Old people are often forgetful, he thought, but she knew what she was doing and saying.

Alfred Frost's cross-examination took only a moment. "Did you know your son kept strychnine in his trunk?"

"I knew he did."

"Is that the bottle?"

"It looks very much like it."

"What did he keep the bottle in when he had it in the chest?"

"I don't know as he had it in anything. Whenever I saw it, it was loose."

Silence enveloped the courtroom when Margaret Teets stepped from the witness box. Leonard felt immense respect for this tired woman, faced with the burden of having to testify at her son's murder trial.

"Are my learned friends finished with their presentations?" Judge Armour asked. James Masson and Alfred Frost agreed they had completed their cases. "In that event, I will adjourn for today. Be prepared to sum up your arguments for the court in the morning."

# Chapter 18

## THE VERDICT

### Morning, November 5, 1884

By the third morning of the Cooks Teets trial, those gathered in the Grey County courtroom had become accustomed to the routine of the proceedings. Most felt they shared a common bond that allowed them to comfortably exchange opinions on the evidence and speculate knowingly on the trial's likely outcome. Summations by Alfred Frost and James Masson, and the charge to the jury by Judge Armour, took until noon. Leonard Babington listened carefully to each man's arguments, knowing that a life was at stake with the words he was hearing.

James Masson was up first and he spoke for almost an hour. He made an emotional but well-reasoned argument, Leonard thought. You could tell from the quaver in his voice that Masson believed strongly in his client's innocence. He reminded the jury that Rosannah was not the only tragic figure in the case. "There is the unborn child that died in her womb and two helpless children left without a mother. And there is Cook Teets, a man weighed down with a grievous handicap for much of his life, confined to a small, dark cell for the past twelve months, accused of a horrendous crime. A crime which the Crown has failed completely and utterly to lay at his feet."

Masson argued that the circumstantial evidence against his client did not warrant a conviction. As long as there was reasonable doubt of Cook's guilt, he deserved to be acquitted. He finished by reminding the jurors they were intelligent men. "I know you are determined to give the prisoner a fair and square deal. You must allow him the benefit of your reasonable doubt. Gentlemen, do your duty. The Crown has not proven its case. Going strictly on the evidence you have heard, you must find Cook Teets not guilty."

Alfred Frost took only half the time James Masson had used. His tone, Leonard thought, was one of vengeful retribution. It was calculated to arouse in the jury a Biblical sense of righteousness. He said the acts of Cook Teets were those of a devilishly depraved man, carried out in deceit and deception. "His methods were fraudulently conceived and cunningly executed," Alfred Frost proclaimed in a voice that echoed to every corner of the courtroom.

"Whether Cook Teets administered strychnine to his wife during his last visit, or whether he left her with a supply of the poison on the pretext that it was medicine of some sort, knowing she would innocently follow his direction, is of little import. Rosannah Leppard died by the hand of Cook Teets. It matters not whether his hand was present at the crucial moment of ingestion. He is as guilty as if his own hand had placed the poison in her mouth. "

In his charge to the jury, Judge Armour conceded that the evidence against Cook was entirely circumstantial. But he said that need not prevent the jury from convicting him. "As long as you are satisfied the facts of the matter are such as to be inconsistent with any other conclusion than that the accused committed the crime, you may find him guilty."

He then reminded the jury of the words of a notable American barrister: "As Daniel Webster has wisely remarked, 'Every unpunished murder takes away something from the security of every man's life.'"

Leonard Babington thought Judge Armour might be using those words to signal his belief that Cook Teets was guilty of the murder of Rosannah Leppard. He thought the judge was showing his bias by reminding the jury that the guilty needed to be punished.

Judge Armour concluded by remarking that the next day, Thursday, would be Thanksgiving Day, the sixth of November having been set aside by Parliament for observance of this rite of autumn. If the jury didn't reach a decision tonight, they'd have to be sequestered until Friday.

The twelve men knotted up in twos and threes as they made their way along the narrow hallway leading to the jury room. Leonard, sitting at the newspaper table, was making notes when he saw that Henry Johnson was being careful to hold himself toward the end of the pack. The black man was the ninth or tenth man into the jury room.

Spectators collected in groups of three or four. There was much discussion as to how long the jury would be out, as well as vigorous speculation on the verdict. "It shouldn't take but a few minutes," a big man in a checkered red coat told his neighbour. "The sooner the jury's back, the more likely Teets will hang." Another thought that because no one had been able to put Cook Teets at the Leppard house when Rosannah died, it would be diffiult to find him guilty. One of the few women in the courtroom, Agnes McNair, elbowed her husband in the ribs at this. "He'll hang, as sure as God made little apples," she said.

Leonard watched as Cook's mother and his sister Sarah put their hands on his shoulders. They seemed to be trying to comfort him and prepare him for the outcome. After a few words, they walked sedately from the courtroom. "My guess is they're too frightened to stay for the verdict," the *Telegram* man said. Cook bobbed about in his seat and nervously ran his hands through his hair. A stir at the back of the courtroom caused him to leap to his feet. At James Masson's urging, Cook sat down, only to get up again a moment later when the guards came to take him away.

After twenty minutes of mingling with the crowd, Leonard went to the washroom. Coming out, he decided to explore the hallways back of the courtroom. The walls were none too thick, he knew, and if he just happened to overhear something, who was to say anything about it?

The hallway he was in made a jog to the left and ended in a small alcove. A window looked out on the wall of the jail and Leonard was able to see where Cook would be waiting in his cell.

Once he reached the alcove, Leonard heard a murmur of voices. A heating grate had been left open and by listening carefully, he could make out what was being said. As long as no one came along, Leonard thought, he might as well stay here.

The discussion that Leonard heard appeared to have begun in an orderly fashion. He didn't recognize the voices, but from time to time men would be referred to by name. Leonard was able to match the names with the faces he'd seen in the jury box. It sounded as if the jurors had chosen Captain Copeland, the retired shipmaster, as their foreman.

"Maybe we don't need a lot of time to discuss this," he heard Captain Copeland say. "We better just get a feel for where we all stand. We've heard the evidence. I'm going to ask everyone right out, guilty or no? We'll start here on my right, Mr. Wilson, I believe?"

"Yessir, Captain, but maybe you could tell me something first. How did an old blind man get a young good-looking girl like that? I'd like to know his secret." He must have smirked as he said it, because Leonard heard guffaws all around.

"I'd say she was a chippy," came a voice from the end of the table. "Two little kids by different men. Cook must have looked pretty good to her." Leonard thought he'd like to get that man alone, he'd show him a thing or two about chippy. Then he heard another voice chime in. "He lost a good bed-warmer when he did away with that girl."

"So why did he do it?" another juror asked.

"For the insurance money," someone said.

"But what's a blind man want with that kind of money?" the first man responded.

Leonard had no difficulty recognizing the next voice. Henry Johnson spoke with the lilt of the typical black, a legacy of a long history in the South.

"Gentlemen, that's what bothers me." Johnson said. "Seems to me Rosannah was worth more to Cook alive than dead."

"You mean a good lay's worth four thousand dollars?" somebody asked.

At this rate, Leonard thought, Captain Copeland would soon lose control of the jury.

"Now gentlemen," he heard the Captain say, "we can speculate all we want on why she married him, or what a good bed partner she might have been, but we have to decide on a murder charge here. I ask again, how do we feel about that?" There were mutterings of guilt from several jurors. Henry Johnson's voice came through the grate: "I'm not sure, I think we should talk about it."

Leonard worried about someone seeing him here, listening to the deliberations. He wasn't sure if what he was doing was legal. He slipped down the hallway and returned to the courtroom. No one had noticed his absence. He took his seat at the newspaper table, uncertain whether what he'd heard meant what he most feared.

The appearance of Angus McMorrin, the clerk, signaled to the courtroom that something was about to happen. An hour and a half had passed. A click marked the lifting of the latch on the jury room door and the twelve men filed into their seats. Cook Teets was brought in and Judge Armour mounted his dais.

Leonard's eyes surveyed the jury. None of them looked too happy, he thought. The verdict might have gone either way. He wished the judge would get on with it.

"Who will speak for the jury?" Judge Armour asked.

Captain Copeland hesitated, coughed and stood up. "I will your Lord-ship."

"Has the jury reached a decision – and if so, what is it?"

"We have, unanimously," Captain Copeland said.

"We find the prisoner ... guilty."

He added, almost as an afterthought, "With a recommendation for mercy."

Leonard saw Cook Teets lean forward in his seat and whisper to James Masson. It seemed he needed confirmation of the awful judgment. Cook's shoulders sagged and his head fell to his chest. A deathly still hung over the courtroom. So this is what it's come to. Leonard felt disheartened – any sense of triumph he might have had at Cook being found guilty had long since vanished.

Judge Armour broke the silence. "Cook Teets, have you anything to say why the sentence of this court should not be passed upon you?"

The words, in deep measured tones, heightened the tension in the court-room. It seemed to Leonard as if everyone had stopped breathing.

"Your Lordship," James Masson called out, rising to his feet. "This deci-sion cannot be ..."

He was shushed by Cook Teets. With a wave of his arm, he motioned his lawyer to be seated.

Now standing, Cook took hold of the gate to the prisoner's dock. His heavy breathing could be heard throughout the room. Leonard saw one hand rise and pull away the handkerchief that had covered an inflamed eye. Straightening himself, Cook began to speak. His voice was firm and clear.

"Lies have been told about me in this courtroom," he began. "Wilful and malicious lies.

"Mrs. Leppard has lied. That sonofabitch Scarth Tackaberry has lied. I have been persecuted and misrepresented. I have been treated badly by the public press."

Leonard cringed when Cook railed against articles about him in the *Vandeleur Chronicle*. He felt the stares of the newspapermen sitting alongside him. Rather than meet their gaze, he bent his head to his notes.

"A man should not be hanged first and tried after," Cook said. "But that's what the press has done to me."

"If I never leave this dock alive," he declared, his voice rising, "so help me God, I did not kill Rosannah."

"This man Tackaberry," Cook spit out his name as if it was snake's venom, "he is not a reliable man. Never was. I can't recollect ever having any conversation with him about strychnine."

Cook's outburst had left him momentarily breathless.

"There is something wrong with the law," he began again, his voice now sounding raw, "when a man is not permitted to speak in his own defence before the jury decides his fate."

That was true, Leonard had to concede. While Cook had been called to testify at the coroner's inquest, he'd not been allowed to speak in his own behalf at his trial. Leonard scribbled furiously to catch all that Cook was saying. The words were flowing more rapidly now, and Leonard marvelled at the man's ability to speak so well under such strain.

Cook said neither he nor Rosannah had wanted to be married by a priest. This was why they eloped to Toronto. The Sunday before her death, he said, she had met him on the road near his mother's house and had told him her mother was treating her badly. She pleaded for a place of their own.

"I went over there the next afternoon. I had tea and left the Leppard place about five o'clock. Rosannah went part of the way with me. We stopped to light our pipes when Moses Sherwood passed. She told me, 'I don't want to let him see me smoking.' I said you are my wife, not his servant. We then parted. She went back to her mother's and I went home. It was the last time I saw her alive."

Cook trembled, passed his hand over his face, and paused.

"I never knew anything about what happened to Rosannah until they came and told me the next morning. I don't know what I said. I was so full of grief. I went to her bedside and asked her to speak and tell me what was the matter. My sister said Rosie will never speak again. I never said I was the cause of it or that I knew anything about it.

"I do not know where the poison was got or who got it. Mrs. Leppard asked me for some to poison dogs. She said there were dogs that bothered her cattle in the bush. I never gave her any."

The longer Cook talked, the more disconnected his words became. He claimed again that Scarth Tackaberry had sworn falsely against him and denied ever having shown him any bottle of strychnine. He had no idea as to who might have killed Rosannah. He wondered if it was actually strychnine that caused her death. He complained about the months he'd been kept in his tiny cell in the Owen Sound jail, having to put up with the ridicule of other prisoners, men charged with such crimes as incest, assault, abusive language, forgery, or bigamy. After an hour, Cook sounded hoarse and tired. Finally, he said, "Now that you've convicted me, hang me, hang me right away. I don't want to spend my life in some cell."

Leonard could hear sobs from women in the courtroom. Men coughed, crossed and uncrossed their legs, and shuffled their feet as Cook sat down.

Judge Armour had let Cook speak without interruption. Now it was his turn.

"Gentlemen of the jury, I concur entirely in your verdict," he said. "You could have come to no other conclusion. You have discharged a difficult task with honour."

He looked at Cook, now slumped in the prisoner's dock.

"Cook Teets, the jury has recommended mercy, a plea that will be forwarded to the proper authorities. But I cannot hold out any hope for you. You have but a short time to prepare to meet your God. Make good use of the time you have left."

He then pronounced the fateful decree:

"It is the sentence of this court that you be taken from the place whence you came and that you there remain until the fifth day of December next, when you are to be taken to the place of execution and there hanged by the neck until you are dead. May God have mercy on your soul."

Two guards moved to Cook's side. They seized his arms and escorted him through the side door of the courtroom, down the stairwell toward his cell.

"You've condemned an innocent man," Leonard heard Cook Teets say on the way out.

Members of the jury dispersed quickly. They had orders to speak to no one. Leonard tried to catch a few words as they passed the newspaper table. He heard Henry Johnson throw a caustic remark to Captain Copeland "You tricked me with your talk of mercy."

December fifth, Leonard thought. A month from today. So that's what it's come to. And what about mercy? He realized, with a pang, he'd shown none when he'd written about how Cook had fired his gun at the boys who had thrown snowballs at him. Leonard remembered his days at the *Globe* and reminded himself what it was like to be wrongly accused. He could not forget how his thoughtless treatment of Rosannah had caused him to lose her. How much of what happened today, he wondered, had been set in motion by his own actions?

But was all hope really gone? On the steps of the courthouse he caught up to James Masson. Leonard needed to know whether the lawyer would make an appeal for a new trial.

"Will you be going to the court of appeal?" Leonard asked.

"Not an easy course," Masson said. "It's a matter left to the discretion of the trial judge. Judge Armour would have to agree the case involves a contentious point of law where he might have made a mistake. Then a panel of judges would decide whether the court of appeal should hear the case.

"That's not going to happen. There's no time, there's no money, and there's no chance of Judge Armour ever permitting an appeal."

Leonard added the lawyer's comments to the running account of the trial that he'd been writing since Monday morning. Every night he had put copy in an envelope and sent it to Tyler Thompson, who met the train at Flesherton Station. Leonard had left space at the top of his final report for a headline. He now penciled in:

### TO BE HANGED

By the neck till he is dead!

### COOK TEETS!

Found guilty of murder & sentenced to be hung

Leonard folded the copy into an envelope and addressed it to the *Chronicle* It was a story every reader would devour.

# Chapter 19

## THE PETITION

### November 6, 1884

Leonard Babington stumbled into a gale that whipped his cheeks, blew snow against the Grey County Court Building, and rattled its windows. He went first to the railway station to put his copy on the ovcernight train. After, he visited the bar of Coulson's British Hotel, ate an egg and a sausage, and went to his room. He had no desire to debate the trial, which was being heatedly picked over at the bar downstairs. The decision of the jury was final. There would be no appeal; Cook's only hope lay in the jury's recommendation for clemency.

When Leonard awoke the next morning his first thought was that it was Thanksgiving Day, and Cook Teets was in his cell at the Owen Sound jail. What did Cook have to give thanks for, Leonard wondered. He had awakened to a thankless day. He dressed, went to the dining room, and ate a quick breakfast of bacon and eggs. The storm had abated during the night and Leonard decided to go for a walk while waiting for the one o'clock train.

The air was clear and Leonard noticed a small crowd trailing off toward the Methodist Church. Leonard fell in with a couple on their way to Thanksgiving service. The man was big and bearded and the woman wore a thin cloth coat. When Leonard brought up the Cook Teets trial, the man snorted, "I was there, what a farce! That lawyer did a poor job of it. How could a blind man poison somebody? Not my idea of justice." The remarks irritated his wife. "You men! Worried about Cook Teets. What about his wife? What kind of justice did she get?"

The notice board at the church door said the Rev. James Howell would preach at ten o'clock. Leonard followed the couple inside.

Nearly every pew was filled. Leonard felt warmed by the heat of the bodies and the friendly recognition of those he sat beside. The congregation sang lustily, prayed fervently, and sat quietly as the Rev. Howell looked out onto his flock. His sermon included the usual Methodist repetition of John Wesley's three precepts – shun evil, perform acts of kindness, abide by God's edicts. The minister took note of Thanksgiving Day and likened the good fortune of his flock to the parable of how Jesus had transformed a few loaves and two fish into a feast for a crowd. All this Leonard expected from a Methodist minister; what he had not expected was what came next.

"In our age we have wandered far from Biblical truth," the Rev. Howell proclaimed. "We are diverted and distracted by the inconsequential and the irrelevant. We are immersed in an outpouring of putrefaction from the press. Their words tempt us to immorality and invite us to mimic the lives of the sad souls whose sinful and degrading actions they glorify in their pages."

Leonard cringed. Putrifying – a good word for that story he'd written on Cook Teets. He couldn't leave without speaking to the minister. He had to explain himself. He lingered at the door of the church as the Rev. Howell blessed departing worshippers. The warmth of the minister's smile made Leonard wonder if his heart was as stern as the words he had spoken.

"My paper is the *Vandeleur Chronicle,*" Leonard told him. "I'm here for the Cook Teets trial. I'm not proud of everything we've published but I hope we're not the cause of your sermon."

"Goodness no," the Rev. Howell answered. "It's those dreadful Toronto papers with their scandalous stories of actors and their nonsensical discussions of evolution. I'm sure they could find more uplifting subjects to write about."

Leonard intimated there were unpleasant truths of which the public had to be made aware.

"A man sits in Owen Sound jail, sentenced to hang. It's more than possible he's innocent. Would you be willing to go and comfort him?"

Leonard saw a sparkle in the minister's eyes.

"Innocent or guilty, it's my duty to bring the comfort of Jesus to all sinners. We'll go and see him now."

A half hour later, Leonard and the Rev. Howell stood outside Cook's cell.

For a condemned man, Leonard thought, Cook gave off an air of complacent disregard. He talked with the minister for several minutes. "I'll never hang," Leonard heard Cook say. "I'll be out of here by Christmas."

Rev. Howell told Cook he would visit him every day. "You don't have to pray unless you want to," he said. "In any event, I'll pray for you."

A sound signalled the opening of the door to the upstairs landing. A guard allowed James Masson to enter. He carried a bag of biscuits his wife had baked that morning. He reached through the bars to give them to Cook and turned to face Leonard. "We need to send petitions to Ottawa," he said in a tired voice. "Try to get the sentence commuted to life. Will you help?"

Leonard weighed James Masson's plea while the train carried him south to Flesherton Station. He thought Cook's trial had been a farce, just as the man outside the Methodist Church had said. Nothing but circumstantial evidence, burdened by a weak defence – Cook could well be innocent. Leonard's resentment of Cook's marriage to Rosannah had evaporated as the likelihood of this sunk in. He couldn't forget the article he'd written about Cook before his arrest; there was no doubt it had inflamed public opinion. Everything told Leonard he should do whatever he could to save Cook from the rope, even at the cost of stirring up his subscribers. What would it matter if he lost a few readers here or there?

Leonard was at the *Chronicle* early the next morning. Tyler and the new printer, Virgil Bannerman, had done their jobs. The paper had been printed and was ready for the post office. He settled behind his desk to review his account of the trial. It took up the front page. Inside, Virgil had played up Leonard's story about the life of Rosannah. He had to admit he had been a little maudlin – especially the part about the "innocent girl deceived by a succession of iniquitous suitors."

The air over Vandeleur was clear and cold with hardly a cloud in the sky. Leonard decided to walk to Munshaw's Hotel. It felt good to be home. He was going to take a meal at the hotel, then make a call on a gentleman who could be of great help in organizing a petition to save Cook. Before leaving Tyler and Virgil to strip the week's pages, he addressed a note to the editor of the *Weekly Globe*, a new man who had replaced Melvin James. He hoped the man's news sense would override any prejudice he might have about receiving information from someone who had left the paper under questionable circumstances.

"This is a case that warrants closer examination," Leonard scrawled. He tucked the note into a copy of the *Chronicle* and asked Tyler to get it on the night train.

Leonard found Aaron Munshaw presiding over a saloon filled with noisy customers. They were enjoying their freedom to buy strong drink again after the enforced abstinence of Thanksgiving Day.

"You've been at the trial," Munshaw told Leonard when he took the last vacant seat at the bar. "Do you think they'll hang him?"

Leonard drew a copy of the *Chronicle* from his satchel. "Save you a trip to the post office, read all about it. Yes, I think they will hang him, unless folks do something."

The innkeeper served Leonard a meat pie and a glass of beer. He passed the paper down the bar and as it went from hand to hand Leonard heard a variety of opinions.

"Folks feel strongly about what's happened," Munshaw said. "You know I had to get out of this country after the Rebellion back in '37. I had ten years exile in the States, with William Lyon Mackenzie. Took that long to get an amnesty. That tells you what I think of the justice that's served up in Canada."

Leonard ate quickly and an hour later he was in Robert Trimble's dry goods store. He told Trimble that Cook Teets's trial had been a questionable affair and that James Masson was looking for someone to start a petition.

"I remember very well when Cook and Rosannah came in to buy things before their wedding," Trimble said. "They sure looked to me like they were in love. I can't imagine Cook murdering that poor girl."

Leonard was sure he had come to the right man. They talked about getting up a petition. Trimble would be the first to sign, and he'd pass it around to his customers and other merchants. He agreed Leonard should not sign; a newspaperman should appear neutral. "But how will we word it?" Trimble asked.

Leonard had brought a pad of lined paper. He laid the pad on the counter and asked for pen and ink. He told Trimble the petition should express surprise at the verdict – it should stress that Rosannah could have been poisoned by some person other than Cook.

The chief evidence, such as it was, came from members of the Leppard family who were not known for their reliability. The petition should ask that the death sentence be commuted to life imprisonment, as the jury recommended.

"Put in that he's been blind for years," Robert Trimble interjected. "They shouldn't overlook that."

Leonard addressed the petition to the Minister of Justice, Sir Alexander Campbell. Robert Trimble borrowed Leonard's pen to sign it.

"Come with me," he told Leonard. He led the way across the road and in a few minutes two more merchants had signed: Robert J. Sproule and Matthew Richardson. Sproule said his uncle Dr. Sproule, who had conducted the autopsy on Rosannah, was going to write to Ottawa to request clemency. He'd heard that the coroner, Dr. Christoe, was doing the same.

People came and went as they talked. One of them was a solicitor in Owen Sound. Sam Platt had come down to deal with a property dispute.

"People seem to feel a little different about Cook Teets now that he's been convicted," the lawyer told Leonard.

"When this petition gets to Ottawa they'll have to show mercy," Robert Trimble said. "Sir John A. won't want the hanging of an innocent blind man on his conscience."

Sam Platt removed a silver plated watch from the pocket of his vest and checked the time.

"I have to be on my way but I can tell you a couple of things about petitions," he said. "The government generally doesn't give a hoot about them, so don't expect too much. Just the same, I agree with what you're doing. Two other lawyers besides me are sending in their own letters. You shouldn't hang a dog on the evidence against that man."

When Robert Trimble's petition reached Ottawa a few days before Cook was to hang, it had 168 names on it. It went before the cabinet at the end of a long day, when Sir John A. Macdonald and his ministers were tired from hours of acrimonious discussion.

Leonard Tilley sat across from Macdonald in the cabinet room, another "Father of Confederation." Now the minister of finance, he'd spent two hours talking tariffs. The talk droned on until Sir Alexander Campbell, Macdonald's old law partner in Kingston, plopped the Cook Teets petition on the table.

Sir John A. Macdonald was accustomed to the consequences of violence. He'd seen as a child how sudden and unpredictedly it could come about. A family caretaker, in his parents' absence, had beaten young John's little brother to death in a drunken rage. He'd lost three men to the gallows while practicing criminal law. One of the first things he did, as Prime Minister, was to speak out against public hangings. He'd commuted as many death sentences as he dared. But of course he'd allowed the hanging of Paddy Whelan, the assassin of Darcy McGee, one of the Fathers of Confederation.

"Sir Alex," he said, turning to Campbell, "what are the circumstances of this case?"

The justice minister told the cabinet the case had been tried by one of the best men on the bench, Mr. Justice Armour. The Department had ordered up notes from the trial, fifty-two pages of them, all done up on one of the new typing machines. The case was largely circumstantial, but was brilliantly presented by Alfred Frost, the crown attorney for the county. A recommendation for mercy from the jury.

"Now, here is a rather remarkable thing," Sir Alex said. "An outburst of support for the prisoner; people no doubt feeling sorry for him, blind for thirty years, something about a snowball fight. Our member for Grey East, Dr. Sproule, has written me. Says he knows Cook, man's never been in serious trouble, only support of his aged mother, et cetera, et cetera, and says he thinks the evidence is not wholly to be relied on. The coroner, Dr. Christo, concedes Teets is guilty but he supports commutation. Three lawyers from Owen Sound have sent notes, same thing. On top of that, there's a merchant out there, Robert Trimble, who's gotten up this petition. Signed by all sorts of substantial men."

"And the judge," the prime minister inquired of Sir Alex, "have you determined his sentiments?"

"I have his telegram to hand. Ah yes, here it is. Says, and I quote, 'I am satisfied with the verdict.'"

"And your recommendation, Minister?"

# Chapter 20

## THE PENALTY

### December 5, 1884

A
t about the time the cabinet meeting was breaking up, Leonard Babington stepped aboard a train of the Toronto, Grey, and Bruce Railway for its run to Owen Sound. He'd put the *Chronicle* to bed that afternoon, its front page asking the question ESCAPE FROM THE ROPE? He'd also added an item under the heading CLARIFICATION. No newspaperman ever likes to publish an apology, but Leonard was faced with having to admit he'd been less than fair to Cook in the story about him shooting at a gang of schoolboys who had hurled snowballs at him. Leonard's note, which appeared with a box around it, took pains to point out the story was based on an unverified report, and therefore could not be accepted as absolute fact.

His conscience somewhat pacified, Leonard began to focus on Cook's chances of finding mercy in Ottawa. By now, he felt the prospect of a reprieve was driven by more than just blind hope or mere faith. He had expected no more than twenty or thirty to sign Robert Trimble's petition, and was surprised that 167 men had added their names. He was even more surprised by a sympathetic editorial in the *Globe;* it was clear it was based on his report in the *Chronicle*. Other appeals that had gone to Ottawa each made an equally compelling case for the sparing of Cook's life. Leonard was beginning to believe he was on the verge of accomplishing something truly worthwhile. He was feeling better about himself than he had in years.

There'd been arguments, of course. He'd encountered Moses Sherwood, the neighbour who'd testified to Rosannah having that slip of paper filled with something that looked like medicine when he saw her with Cook the afternoon before her death. "Remember what Judge Armour said," Moses told him. "He didn't hold out any hope. Told Teets to prepare to meet his maker. Couldn't be any clearer than that." At the Eugenia post office, James Rowe figured the jury's recommendation was just a harmless gesture. "They found him guilty, didn't they? Intelligent men, all of them."

Leonard shrugged off these remarks. He was convinced Ottawa would have to consider public opinion, as evidenced in the petition and letters that had been sent in. In Owen Sound, Leonard went to the jail to call on Governor Miller. He thought the Governor looked frazzled, bearing the demeanor of a man who would be glad when he no longer had to contend with having Cook Teets as one of his prisoners. Dozens of people were demanding to see the hanging and there were reports half the town would watch it from the hill behind the jail.

"I've got my men in the yard now," Miller said. "I'm putting the gallows at the south end. And I've told them to build a screen over it. I'm not going to entertain people on the street." He called a guard to escort Leonard upstairs.

Leonard found two clergymen sitting outside Cook's cell. The Rev. James Howell was there, along with an older man. The man was introduced to Leonard as Hugh Scott, the minister from Knox Presbyterian Church. He was urging Cook to confess.

"You have told us you were taught the name of Jesus," the Rev. Scott said. "You were warned against evil and advised towards good. Remember the words of Scripture, 'as a man soweth so shall he also reap.' You only have twenty-four hours, Cook. You need to make your peace with God."

Leonard was surprised by the harsh way Mr. Scott was speaking to Cook. He thought a man with the prospect of hanging in his immediate future deserved kinder words.

Cook sat quietly on his cot, his head down, showing no reaction.

"Let's just pray for a reprieve," the Rev. Howell said. "Dear Lord, we beseech thee to allow mercy to be visited on this humble subject …"

The arrival of James Masson interrupted the prayer. Gripping a bar of the cell with his right hand, the lawyer muttered an apology. In his left hand he held a sheath of paper. Leonard could tell from the look on his face that he was unhappy.

"I've been at the telegraph office," Masson said. "Now this." As he spoke he flourished the paper in midair. "Cook, I have to tell you it doesn't look good."

The lawyer read a telegram he had just received from the deputy minister of justice.

"'The Governor General in Council' – that's fancy language for the cabinet," James Masson interjected – 'has not informed me of his conclusions but I can hold out no hope of execution interference. Will telegraph decision.'"

It took a moment for Leonard to absorb the lawyer's message. He wondered if Cook realized its significance. "Are you sure they're not just being cautious?" he asked. "Afraid to say anything definite, so they put things in a bad light, knowing we'll forget it soon enough when the commutation comes through."

"Perhaps, but it's not encouraging," James Masson said.

Leonard stayed with Cook most of the day. He took a break at noon to spend an hour walking the streets, growing more nervous as the minutes went by. He marvelled at Cook's composure. Nothing seemed to upset him, not the importuning of the ministers, the frantic last-minute exchange of wires by his lawyer, or the worries of unexpected visitors, all unhelpful and unwanted. Leonard imagined he would be frantic if he was in Cook's shoes, knowing it was likely he would be mounting the gallows in less than twenty-four hours.

When Leonard returned to Cook's cell, he heard further stories of Cook's boyhood and tales of his life in Vandeleur. Cook raised his voice whenever the sound of hammering in the jail yard threatened to interfere with his recital.

"Leonard, I'd just as soon hang as spend my life in jail," Cook said when they were alone. "I've been locked up for a year, a year too long. How many more would I have to spend like this?"

Before Leonard could answer, a guard appeared with a tray covered with a white towel.

"You'll enjoy this," he told Cook, removing the cloth. "Look, a steak, a roast potato, and a big piece of apple pie."

"If they'd fed me like this before I would have liked it here," Cook answered. "Better than that awful bean cake they kept pushing at me."

The guard's keys rattled as he opened the door of Cook's cell long enough to place the tray on the table next to the cot.

Cook lifted the cloth off the tray. "I may as well get started," he said, slicing a large piece from the slab of beef. He chewed vigorously, a dribble of juice running into his beard.

Cook had cleaned the plate and Leonard was about to leave when James Masson returned. He looked even more shaken than he had this morning, his eyes blood-shot and two days of beard on his face.

"We've received word," he told Cook. "A decision has been made. The law is to be allowed to take its course. There's no commutation, Cook. You have until tomorrow morning."

Leonard watched Cook as he slumped on his cot. His chin dropped to his chest and he swept a hand across his face, as if to brush away what he had heard. It reminded Leonard of when his friend Tom Winship had been struck by the barrel of steal rods that fell from the deck of the Australasia. Leonard felt there was no longer enough air in the room to allow him to breathe. He hurried to the stairwell and almost fell into the arms of Governor Miller. Leonard apologized, calmed himself, and returned with the Governor to Cook's cell.

"We'll try to make your night as comfortable as possible," Governor Miller told Cook. "You can have as many visitors as you wish. I'll send for Mr. Howell and Mr. Scott. I'm sure they'll bring you comfort. We'll go at eight in the morning."

Cook Teets had wondered for a year what it would be like to endure these last hours. Now he knew. His body was numb, his mind was in turmoil, and the pain too great to bear. He was unable to settle on what he should do or think. The agony of a dying man, he realized. Babington was gone, the Governor had left, and he was alone to confront the spectre of his hanging.

There was one thing he could do, he decided. Leave something to testify to his innocence. A last statement. That was it. Tell the world exactly what had happened, how an innocent man was going to his death. But how to get it down on paper? He could barely write and even if he could master the mystery of forming letters and words he wouldn't be able to see whatever he might get down on paper. Where's that Mr. Howell? He could write it down for me.

More footsteps in the stairwell. The voice was by now familiar. The Rev. Howell was settling himself on a chair just outside the cell.

"Cook, have you any last wish?" he asked.

"My wish is to find a way out of here other than feet first," Cook said. "But as that's not going to happen, I'd like you to take down a statement for me." Cook and the minister spent the next hour on Cook's last message, Cook talking constantly as the Rev. Howell struggled to copy down every word.

Cook began by reciting how he and Rosannah had gotten married. "Her mother consented, and was anxious for me to marry her. After all, she said, it would cost no more now than afterwards. She went with Rosannah and me to Robert Trimble's store to purchase things for the marriage.

"As far as the death of Rosannah is concerned, I know nothing about it. Thank God I do not die with a load of guilt on my shoulders. I am ready to die. I feel my Saviour say, 'It is all right, Cook.' I bid all my friends goodbye and die an innocent man."

There were more people arriving to say goodbye to Cook. Soon, the landing in front of his cell was crowded; Cook noted that Leonard Babington was back, as well as James Masson. Nelson Teets was there, along with Robert Trimble and other men he had known. Jokes were made, laughter rang out, and there was a good deal of bantering back and forth. Cook felt the tension inside him ease. He began to tell stories as if he was back at Munshaw's and was vying with friends to see who could impart the most outrageous tale of encounters with women, survival in the bush, or accomplishments in shooting and fighting. When Trimble said it was unfair that Cook had to hang, he cut him off. "We're not talking about that," he said.

Just as the last visitor was leaving, Dr. Sproule arrived. "I thought I should come in and have a word with you," he told Cook.

"I'll speak to you as if I were your doctor," he said. "One of the saddest jobs I ever had to do was conduct that autopsy on your wife. She was a beautiful woman, and too young to die. I'm sure you had nothing to do with it. But that's not why I'm here."

Cook looked at Dr. Sproule, a slight smile on his lips. "You have it right as far as Rosie was concerned," he said. "She sure was beautiful."

Dr. Sproule drew a vial from his coat pocket.

"I've brought you something to help you through these last hours," he said. "I think you've seen morphine crystals before. I had these ground up for you. Don't take it all now. Save some for the morning."

With that, Dr. Sroule departed. The prison guard, who had retreated to the end of the hall, returned to remind Cook the night was half over. "It's near three o'clock Cook, time you got some sleep."

"Sleep? I'll have no fucking shortage of that where I'm going."

Cook lay down on his cot, exhausted from talk and from frayed nerves. He licked a fingertip, put it in the vial, and sucked in morphine. One leg twitched a few times, then quieted. He turned on his side and closed his eyes. He knew he would soon be with Rosannah. Then he saw her, in front of him, and reached out to her.

Leonard slipped out the front door of Coulson's British Hotel a few minutes past six o'clock on the morning of the fifth of December, 1884. He was groggy from lack of sleep. He stepped over the thin layer of ice that had collected on the doorstep. In the darkness he set off for the Grey County Court Building, encountering other men bound for the same place. A guard checked the passes of the men waiting to enter. Leonard noticed the line-up had no shortage of doctors and lawyers. He surrendered his ticket, nodded to James Masson who was in line ahead of him, and shuffled past Governor Miller's office into the snow-covered courtyard. Another guard waited at the cellblock entrance. He was directing the witnesses down a corridor and through a door that opened onto the jail yard.

The gallows stood in the corner, a construction of raw lumber, ominous in its shape and dreadful in its meaning. A roof had been thrown over it, obscuring any view of the hanging by the crowd gathered on the ridge above the jail. The fact they wouldn't see anything hadn't stopped the curious from collecting there.

Leonard tried to imagine how it had been for Cook Teets this fateful morning. Had the howling wind kept him awake through the night or had a guard needed to rouse him from sleep? Perhaps the guard helped Cook put on the black broadcloth suit Nelson had left him. There'd have been prayers in his cell, led by Mr. Howell and Mr. Scott. Cook might have taken a morsel of food. Then, Leonard knew, Governor Miller and Sheriff Moore would have made their way up the stairs and onto the landing outside Cook's cell. "It's time to go," the Governor might have said. And so the death parade would have begun, down the stairwell, along the corridor, and through a back door into the jail yard.

A commotion in the crowd interrupted Leonard's thoughts. "They're coming," someone said. He recognized the voice of Scarth Tackaberry. Trust him to show up, doubtless to gloat at the hanging of the man who had bested all Rosannah's younger suitors. How did he come by a pass? Leonard thought of the time he had seen Scarth behave badly at a country dance when a girl scorned his approach. A knowing smile on Tackaberry's face bore a hint of delight at the prospect of watching a man die.

Sheriff Moore and Governor Miller led the cheerless parade. Cook followed, with the two ministers, one on either side, each holding an arm. No one faltered in their steps – especially not Cook. The line moved resolutely across the jail yard, stopping only when it reached the stairs at the foot of the gallows.

Leonard wondered about the hangman. Where was he? He'd seen a stranger in the hotel last night and wondered if it was him. Leonard thought the man had mobile eyes, his glance darting about nervously as if he were being pursued. The hangman's last deed had been botched, Leonard had heard. The rope had been too long and the condemned man had to be hanged twice.

Then Leonard saw him. It was the man he had seen last night. He'd come out from behind the gallows. It seemed as if he was skipping about, first on one foot and then the other. Leonard thought he looked to be the most nervous man in the yard. The crowd became aware of church bells ringing and Leonard looked at his watch. It was exactly eight o'clock, the time set for the hanging. It was barely light now and someone pointed to the jail's flagpole, just visible over the wall. A black flag had been run up, signaling the deed about to take place.

No sound, not even the intake of breath of the nearly sixty men in the jail yard, could be heard. Leonard stood not more than ten feet from the gallows. The hangman ascended the stairs first, taking care to see the rope was free of any interference. When it was Cook's turn to take the stairs, Leonard watched him move steadily from one step to the next. Were there thirteen? Leonard wasn't sure. A few words were spoken. Someone said the Governor had asked Cook if he had any last words. He did not. He said he just wanted to get it over with; he would die an innocent man. When the hangman bent to tie Cook's legs, the Rev. Howell recited the Lord's Prayer. That done, the hangman put a black hood on Cook's head and made a final adjustment to the rope. He nudged Cook forward onto the trap door. Leonard saw Cook turn to one side and he detected a shudder pass through his body.

"Well gentlemen," Leonard heard Cook say, "this is the fatal board." Mr. Scott began to read the twenty-third psalm: "The Lord is my shepherd; I shall not want." The sky darkened, its blackness matching that of the spirit of the crowd. Leonard detected a blurred movement as the hangman reached to pull the bolt on the trapdoor. The bolt slipped free and the trapdoor opened, followed by a sickening thud.

That was when Leonard remembered that today was Cook Teets's birthday. No mention had been made of it last night. His fifty-fifth birthday, December 5, 1884. His last.

A fluttering of wings sounded from atop the prison wall. Dozens of passenger pigeons roosting there had taken flight, disturbed by the noise from the prison yard. Leonard saw the birds, majestic in their blue crowns and wine red breasts, rise and wheel off in the direction of the ridge above the jail. Cook's drop had ended with the thick knot of the noose lodged against his neck, breaking it. His body quivered as he hung a few feet from the ground, swaying slightly as he died.

As Leonard watched, he heard gunshots in the distance. Men out on the ridge, denied the chance to see Cook hang, were taking out their frustrations on the birds.

It's done, Leonard thought, how will we ever know the truth? The men in the jail yard began to wander out but Leonard felt rooted to the ground. Cook's body continued to hang; fifteen minutes passed before a guard, supervised by the hangman, cut the rope and allowed him to slump to the ground. Leonard heard a large double door in the prison's outer wall creak open. A man drove a horse and wagon into the jail yard. The wagon contained a coffin.

Nelson Teets waited outside to claim his brother's body. "We'll bury him in the Greenview Cemetery," he told Leonard. "They won't be able to get at him there, he'll rest in peace. Mother and Sarah couldn't bear to be here. They're waiting at the cemetery."

Across the street, Leonard saw James Leppard talking with another man. When Leonard approached him he heard Leppard say, "Good thing they hung the son of a bitch." Leonard asked him whether he had seen the hanging. "That I did. A terrible sight. But the poor fool's just as well off dead. He was screwed well and proper from the age of twelve, blind and all."

A cruel comment, Leonard thought, but true. It wasn't as if Cook was some dumb farm animal. There'd probably been a lot of joy in his life, as least when he was with Rosannah. But James Leppard walked away before Leonard could say anything further.

Leonard turned his attention to James Masson who had just come out of the prison, his hands thrust into his overcoat pockets and his head down.

"I should have been able to save him," he told Leonard. "I don't understand why they wouldn't commute his sentence."

Leonard was about to return to his hotel when Dr. Sproule spoke to him.

"This has been an unhappy affair," he said. "I wrote to the Minister of Justice but he chose to ignore me, a Member of Parliament. I'm saddened."

Leonard, already feeling dejected, found himself overcome by despair. Everything that had happened was wrong, Rosannah's death, Cook's arrest, the one-sided trial, and now this hanging. If they would not listen to Dr. Sproule, they would have listened to no one. Leonard looked at Dr. Sproule and took a deep breath before he spoke.

"Cook never had a chance," he said. "He was just too different from the rest of us. But that wasn't his fault, it was ours. We're all to blame for this act of injustice. None of us know the truth. I've made up my mind to find it, no matter how long it takes." For a moment, Leonard regretted his choice of words, spoken hastily and without much thought. He'd been reckless in asserting his determination to prove an innocent man had been hanged. Then he thought, just as well, he had left himself no choice. He had made his commitment, and there would be no going back on it.

# PART II
## A NEW WORLD AWAITS US

It is in literature that true life can be found. Under the mask of fiction you can tell the truth.

Gao Xingjian

What are facts but compromises? A fact merely marks the point where we have agreed to let investigation cease.

Bliss Carman

# Chapter 21

## REMEMBERING ROSANNAH

### December 24/25, 1884

It was time for Leonard Babington to put the death of Rosannah Leppard and the hanging of Cook Teets behind him. The day before Christmas, he walked into the woods behind Vandeleur Hall, selected a suitable pine tree and severed a dozen limbs, each with a single careful swipe of his hatchet. His mother had always decorated the house with pine boughs at Christmas and he intended to do the same. Their fragrance would remind him of happier days.

While Leonard was collecting pine cuttings others went about their preparations for Christmas. James Leppard beheaded a goose. John Brodie, the cheesemaker, wrapped cloth around new rounds of cheddar cheese. There was a heavy call at James Henderson's store for raisins and holiday candies. When Leonard went there on Christmas Eve he felt warmed by the smiles of shoppers who crowded around the Chrusrtmas delacies set out on the store's counters. Children laughed as they played tag between barrels of pickles and molasses. Their games reminded Leonard of the happy Christmases he'd enjoyed as a child. He was thinking of those days when he felt a touch on his arm. It was Amanda Brodie, the cheesemaker's wife. Leonard knew her from his schoolteaching days. She was shopping for Christmas dinner.

"Come and join us, Mr. Babington," she said. "No need to spend Christmas on your lonesome. The children would love to see you."

Amanda Brodie had grown into a handsome young woman and her husband was known to serve a tolerably good home brew. Leonard didn't even mind the children. Why not get a good meal into himself, on Christmas of all days?

It was dark when Leonard reached the Brodie house just after four o'clock on Christmas Day. The house gave off a cheerful glow from coal oil lamps at each of its two front windows. Inside, Amanda Brodie hurried from the kitchen to welcome him. The house was filled with the smells of Christmas. Leonard absorbed the pungent scent of spiced gravy and the aroma of a cooked bird and mincemeat pie. He was glad he had come.

Leonard brought with him a gift for each of the children – paper cutouts and a doll – and Amanda placed them beside the stockings set out at the hearth. They contained the remnants of treats which had been excitedly extracted early Christmas Day. Small candles burned on the mantle of the hearth and pine boughs had been set out in windows, over doors, and on the stairway. In a moment John came clattering down the stairs, a bottle of whisky in hand.

"Just in time for a nip afore supper," he chortled. "Nothing better to raise up an appetite."

The conversation during the meal was about the joys of Christmas, the weather, and the likelihood of trouble with the Indians in the North West. Nothing was said of the Cook Teets trial. John Brodie refilled Leonard's glass several times and then brought a tankard of ale from the kitchen. The room grew warmer as the meal proceeded, and Leonard felt himself sweating. He was finding it difficult to grasp what his host was telling him. Long after Mrs. Brodie had shooed the children from the table, John rose, staggered, and clumped away down the hall.

"He's gone for the night," Amanda Brodie told Leonard. "Let's sit in the parlour. We can have a visit and all."

It didn't surprise Leonard that Brodie had gotten himself so drunk that he had to go to bed. Strong drink in large amounts was common among the people with whom Leonard had grown up. He wondered what Amanda meant by her invitation to move into the parlour.

"If you're feeling warm you can take off your jacket and loosen your collar," Amanda told him. She helped him shuck his coat and when he put his hands up to free his collar, she pulled them to her breast. Her breath was hot and inviting. Feeling a little dizzy, Leonard kissed her and let his hands explore her breasts. She offered no resistance. Leonard worried that Brodie might reappear at any moment, and silently cursed his host for getting him into a condition where he was losing control of himself.

"Don't worry, he's gone for the night," Amanda whispered. She reached into Leonard's pants and caressed him. Then he was inside her and all thought of restraint was now far from his mind.

After, he clung to this woman he hardly knew. Amanda was kissing his neck and ears and Leonard wanted her caresses to go on forever. His mind moved to thoughts of Rosannah, and he felt guilty for the pleasure he was taking from this embrace. The guilt told him it was time to leave. Besides, it was always possible Brodie might wake up and find them still together.

"You're wonderful, Mrs. Brodie, but I think I had better go."

"Must you?" she asked. "It'll be hours before he wakes up."

Later, outside with the snow drifting down in large, soft flakes, Leonard had to concentrate on finding his way home. He knew of people who had passed out on the roadside, to be found later frozen to death. That mustn't happen to him. When he reached the crossing at the Beaver Valley Road he knew he was nearly at Vandeleur Hall.

Relieved, and now mostly sober, Leonard thought of all that had happened: his loss of Rosannah, his time at the *Globe*, Rosannah's death, the inquest, the trial, the petitions, and the hanging of Cook Teets. His memories leapt from one incident to another in a confused jumble of haphazard recollections.

He never knew what he was getting in for, when he'd first met Rosannah. That's not so strange. No one can tell what the future might reveal. Except those who live such narrow lives they can safely predict how the sameness of one day will be followed by another. He'd seen enough of that. Nothing ever new in their lives, no chances taken, no rewards sought or attained. What did he want from life then? His insides squirmed with remembrance of all the stupid things he'd done and said. He seemed to be forever starting over. And lonely – he was always lonely. What had he learned from where life had taken him? Perhaps he needed to write it all down.

At home, his wet clothes shed at the front door, Leonard wrapped himself in a robe and stocked the fireplace with fresh wood. It was long past midnight. He went to his father's stand-up desk, lifted the lid, and took out paper and a pen. I need to write it in a book, he thought. Put everything about Rosannah and Cook down on paper, so everybody can understand what happened to them, and what I had to do with it. But where to begin?

With Rosannah as the beautiful young girl she was? With Cook Teets and his blindness? Or with the inquest, or the trial? Standing at the desk, and writing in a fluid and clerkly hand, Leonard began *Rosannah's Story:*

There was no sweeter girl in the entire Queen's Bush than Rosannah Leppard. Her affectionate personality and warm, inviting eyes foretold an enduring friendship for those she invited into her life. It was these qualities, by unhappy circumstance, that would lead her into difficulty. Perhaps it is true she was not sufficiently discriminating in her choices. The better elements of the Beaver Valley, where Rosannah lived with her parents and her twelve brothers and sisters, were unforgiving in their criticism.

Rosannah's short life brought her more of both the pain and pleasure than is our usual allotment. She grew up in a family that was desperately poor. She had seen enough of the outside world to know there was a better life than the one bestowed on her. The choices she made were made in hopes of attaining that better life.

I remember Rosannah for her bright eyes and dark hair, in which she often wore a white daisy. Also for her joyful teasing, which sometimes amused and other times exasperated me. I never saw her more aglow than the time she danced at a village social in the Vandeleur school. She wore a calico dress and a necklace of shells that she said came from the shore of Georgian Bay. There was a fine band that night of Negro musicians from Priceville, the little community started by fugitive slaves. Two fiddles, a banjo and an accordion. How they played! Rosannah, just sixteen, kicked off her shoes to dance. Her favourite tune that night was Going to the East, Going to the West, a song brought from the slave plantations of the South. I think she liked it because one of the steps called for a kiss. I was lucky enough to twirl her in my arms at that point in the dance.

Rosannah loved her children. This I know, although I saw her rarely after Lorena was born and not at all after the birth of her second, Elizabeth. Rosannah's disposition would not allow her to be anything but kind and caring. I remember how she nursed a thrush with a broken wing, and the care she took with the kittens that were born behind her barn.

Rosannah was always helpful to her mother, although her failure as an obedient Catholic gave rise to much disagreement and distress. I remember the two of them making wild plum preserves, and apple pies from the sack of Mackintoshes that Rosannah's father had brought home from a carpentering job at Meaford. The preserves were served with roast goose and pie that Christmas. People in the Beaver Valley may have been poor, but between what they could grow on their stony acres and what they could capture in the woods or streams, they were seldom hungry.

Leonard slept late the day after Christmas. Toward evening, with a fire burning in the parlour he stood, again wrapped in a robe, at his father's desk. He returned to the desk many times in the weeks that followed. One Sunday afternoon, Leonard stared at his watch that lay beside his writing paper. His glance shifted to the stack of notes he had collected. He'd gone over them time and again, recalling every detail of what had happened. He had studied the depositions Cook and others had given at the inquest and he read and re-read the report of Dr. Sproule's autopsy. He looked again at his watch.

It was then it came to him. The trial had heard that the amount of strychnine found in Rosannah's body was insufficient to prove the cause of death. Dr. Ellis, the public analyst who had examined Rosannah's organs, admitted he'd only been surmising, based on the symptoms she'd shown, as to the composition of the fatal dose. Why, he'd even swallowed a bit of strychnine right there in the courtroom, without suffering any harm. Leonard had it all in his notes; he now saw it was even possible she'd died from another cause. It was too late to save Cook or bring back Rosannah, but not too late to find the truth. If he was ever going to redeem himself – in his own mind at least – for the mistakes he'd made, he'd have to produce evidence – new evidence – that would exonerate Cook. He needed time to think about this.

Leonard put out the *Chronicle* every week, recording the small happenings of Vandeleur. Winter gave way to a sudden spring that greened the fields of the Beaver Valley, and finally summer settled on the land. Writing sessions at his father's desk became a rare thing. He could go no further, Leonard decided, until he was more certain about the cause of Rosannah's death. He'd have to learn the secrets of strychnine – how the poison worked, what it could do to a person, and exactly how long it took to do it. There was only one place he could find that out: at the School of Medicine in Toronto.

# Chapter 22

## SECRETS OF THE DEAD HOUSE

### September 8, 1885

Once out of Union Station, Leonard Babington found the streets of Toronto clogged with horses and carriages, with new buildings having risen all around him. It was a much busier place than he remembered from five years ago, when he'd been caught up in the excitement of being a real reporter, working for the *Globe*. He checked into the Queen's Hotel, took dinner in the dining room, and after a foray into the fringes of The Ward – an immigrant district more congested and louder than he ever remembered it – he returned to his room and slept like a brick. In the morning he set out for the School of Medicine.

At the corner of Church and Front Streets Leonard admired the magnificent new branch of the Bank of Montreal. Further east, he passed the St. Lawrence Hall and the City Hall, buildings he knew well from his days as a reporter. But those were not his destination this morning. He continued east until he reached Sherbourne Street. There, he turned north.

The Toronto School of Medicine was identified by a small sign tacked onto its front porch. The two-storey brick house was little different from its neighbours; other than the sign it bore no indication that wonderful experiments were conducted here on the human body, a place where the future doctors of Canada were being trained.

"I am a journalist," Leonard told the man who stood over a desk in the foyer. "I want to inquire about certain medical practices." Leonard made mention of the *Globe*, without as much as saying he was from that paper.

"Then you'll need to see Dr. Barrett, the principal," he was told. "He's giving a lecture now. Perhaps he can see you when he's free."

An hour later, Leonard was admitted to a small back room. Dr. Barrett sat behind an oak desk. Two chairs stood at angles to the desk. Bookcases lined the walls, filled with texts and files of medical journals. A sofa, covered with a fabric in a red rose design, occupied what little space remained. Leonard was surprised to see that on it sat a young woman.

"I am glad to meet you, Mr. Babington," Dr. Barrett said. "The School wishes to educate the public as well as its students. There is so much we need to do in public health."

Dr. Barrett went on:

"This is my niece, Miss Kaitlin Tisdall. She's studying medicine here at the School. Unlike certain institutions, we welcome women students. Kaitlin will see you meet our demonstrator in anatomy. We call her Dr. Ann. Maybe you've heard of her. Ann Stowe-Gullen, the first woman to graduate as a doctor in Canada."

Leonard thought Dr. Barrett a little pompous. The presence of the pretty young woman slightly intimidated him. He decided to be quick about explaining his mission.

"I'm interested in the case of a man accused of poisoning his wife with strychnine. I would like to know more about how the drug affects the body. If it could be mistaken for some other poison. Perhaps see how an autopsy is conducted. Whatever would illuminate the reaction of the human body to a foreign substance."

Dr. Barrett listened intently. "You're well spoken for a reporter. We've had some in here who didn't have the foggiest idea of what they were about. Glad to see the *Globe* is hiring a better type."

Leonard ignored the reference to the *Globe*.

Kaitlin sat quietly as Dr. Barrett spoke. She wore a long checkered skirt, a white blouse and a cape, and her hair was in a bob. Leonard thought her very attractive.

"Let me take you around, Mr. Babington," Kaitlin said.

The classroom where Dr. Barrett had lectured was now empty. Its dozen desks, similar to those that had furnished Leonard's school in Vandeleur, were piled with papers and textbooks.

"I'll show you the dead house," Kaitlin offered. She saw the puzzled look on Leonard's face and quickly added:

"That's what we call the dissection room. Don't let it bother you."

The room she led him to might once have served as a dining room. It contained two tables and a few chairs. Hooks on the wall held old coats and aprons. There was a pile of sawdust in the corner. Someone had laid a shovel, much used and rusty, beside it.

Kaitlin pointed to a trapdoor that opened to the cellar. Lifting the door, she motioned below.

"We students go down there to retrieve the cadavers. Don't worry, there are none there right now." She chuckled, her laugh like the tinkling of a bell.

Kaitlin led Leonard down a flight of narrow stairs. At the bottom, she pointed to two large vats in a corner of the cellar.

"They're filled with wood alcohol and other chemicals," she said. "You get used to the smell after awhile."

Leonard had begun to feel queasy. He told Kaitlin he didn't have much time today, but would come back another day. He left hastily, making apologies. Once outside, he gulped fresh air and felt his head clear.

Leonard returned three times to the School of Medicine that week. He had tea twice with Kaitlin. He told her about the trial of Cook Teets and confided that while he had once worked for the *Globe*, he now had his own newspaper.

They talked about whether Leonard could witness a dissection.

"Are you sure you want to?" Kaitlin asked. "We've been told never to divulge the secrets of the dissecting room. We can be expelled for that. In the popular mind, dissection is an abomination."

When Leonard met Dr. Ann, he was surprised at how young and attractive she was. She had graduated just that year. Perhaps she owed her appointment to the fact her mother had been educated in the United States as a doctor. Then he realized he was being unfair.

"Kaitlin tells me you're a newspaperman and that you wish to see a dissection," she said. "They're always done in private, but it's time the public realized we can't treat people without understanding the body's organs. That's the purpose of dissection."

"Where do you get the bodies?" Leonard asked.

"That is the problem. You'd think they'd let us have unclaimed cadavers from the morgue. But no. Unless we get a rare donation, we have to go all over for them. There's a man in Buffalo who supplies us. He's been accused of stealing from the graveyards. You're a journalist. You could explain we need a legal source. But you must never let it be known your presence was something I allowed."

"Leonard can take the place of the janitor," Kaitlin suggested. "Old George is always there to wipe things up. The girls never pay any attention to him. We can send him off for the day."

Leonard arrived a few minutes early for the demonstration. There was very little light in the dead house when Kaitlin led Leonard into the room. He felt uncomfortable, wearing a tattered coat belonging to the janitor. Kaitlin directed him to the end of the room to stand near the sawdust pile. "Just look bored, pretend you're ready to sweep up," Kaitlin said.

Several girls entered the room. They paid no attention to him.

When the cadaver was placed onto the table, Leonard was stunned at what next unfolded.

"You will observe the skin has been removed from the body." Dr. Ann told the students. Leonard felt almost overcome by the subtle, sweet smell of phenol and the other chemical preservatives used to cure the body.

"De-skinning is part of the necessary preparation," he heard the anatomist say. "Now we can begin the dissection. Watch carefully. You will have a close look at the organs that will be the object of your care and attention for the rest of your medical lives."

The cadaver was that of a male. Working fastidiously, the anatomist cut out the heart, liver, and kidneys. She held each up in turn, commenting on its condition. An engorged heart valve pointed to respiratory difficulties. A blackened liver indicated a diseased organ. A small towel covered the cadaver's waist. Nothing was said of its genitals.

Leonard struggled to stay on his feet. Kaitlin sensed his discomfort and edged toward him. Taking care no one was looking, she held his hand and squeezed it twice. A sense of momentary blur passed over him. He found himself looking at the flesh on the table, now with no more abhorrence than if he were viewing a slaughtered animal. It looked like raw chicken.

Leonard was amazed by Dr. Ann's ability to pluck organs from the body.

There was no blood and scarcely a fragment of flesh fell astray. He imagined Rosannah's body as it must have lain on the autopsy table. And he understood now a lot of what had seemed puzzling in the medical testimony at the trial. He could see how the examination of an organ could lead to the solution of a crime. He was glad he'd come, although he wouldn't want to watch a second time.

"I can understand how a doctor must know these things," Leonard later told Kaitlin. "Now I need to learn more about strychnine."

"You could start with the pharmaceutical journals," Kaitlin said. "We keep them in the book room. Later, you can ask Dr. Ann about anything you don't understand."

Kaitlin left Leonard to riffle through the magazines piled up on a shelf along one wall. He read about children who had died after being given strychnine by mistake, and of experiments on dogs that died a half hour after being poisoned. He found an article about strychnine's effects on humans in *The Practitioner's Handbook of Treatment*. "In toxic doses this drug produces severe and prolonged spasms, in which the body is arched, resting upon the head and heels. Death commonly occurs in an hour or so."

They're all in agreement, Leonard thought, that strychnine is quickly fatal. And in the manner witnesses had said Rosannah died. But there were other points he had to clear up. He raised them with Dr. Ann that afternoon.

"There was evidence at the trial." Leonard told her, "that the body can withstand a minor amount of strychnine. How much does it take to kill?"

"Not very much, about fifty milligrams, just a tiny bit in a teaspoon."

Leonard leafed through the notes he'd made at the trial, looking for the testimony of Dr. Ellis.

"This is the defence lawyer questioning Dr. Ellis:

```
Defence - Did you find enough strychnine in the body to prove
          conclusively it was from strychnine that she had
          died?
Dr. Ellis - Most of whatever was there had dissipated.
Defence - So you didn't find enough to kill her?
Dr. Ellis - No.
```

"What do you think of that?" Leonard asked Dr. Ann.

"I think it means there was a lack of forensic evidence to show the woman died of strychnine poisoning." An important technical point, Leonard thought. That fact could have been useful to Cook's defence, had it been raised at the trial.

"I understand it now," he said. "Rosannah's death bore the symptoms of strychnine, but there wasn't enough in her body to prove it. It dissipates too fast. But if strychnine did cause her death, she must have consumed it sometime that night, not the previous afternoon. However you look at it, the jury had no evidence on which to convict Cook Teets."

By now, Leonard had been in Toronto for more than a week. He decided he had learned all he was going to about the effects of strychnine. It was time to get home to Vandeleur. The next morning, he sought out Kaitlin and told her of his decision.

"Do you really have to leave?" she asked. Leonard was tempted to stay in the city. Kaitlin obviously liked him, just as he liked her. He would be sure to see a lot of her if he remained. He thought of the secret pleasures he night enjoy with Kaitlin if he stayed in Toronto. Then he remembered why he had come to the city, and what he had to do with what he had learned.

"It's been wonderful to meet you," Leonard said, "but I must get back to Vandeleur. I've a paper to get out. I'll call on you when I'm next in Toronto." When they shook hands to say goodbye Leonard saw sadness in her eyes.

Tyler Thompson was wiping down the press when Leonard arrived at the *Chronicle*. His new tramp printer, Willie Babcock, was cleaning out a form that held last week's type.

"We're going to upset a few people," Leonard told them. "With what I've learned at the medical school, the case against Cook Teets just doesn't hold up. I want the front page for the story. Move the ads inside."

Willie set the type for the headline that ran across the top of the front page:

**LEGAL MURDER** – Cook Teets Was Innocent

Leonard's story challenged the decision of the jury and the acceptance by Judge Armour of its verdict. He cited the fact strychnine kills quickly, but there was insufficient evidence of the poison in Rosannah's body to prove the cause of death. If she had died of strychnine, it must have been administered well after the time that Cook Teets had left the Leppard household.

"We are inclined to think an innocent man was doomed to death," Leonard wrote. "Should a man have been hanged on purely circumstance evidence? Granted that he had strychnine in his possession, granted further that he held an insurance policy on his wife. Both these facts were known to a number of persons before Rosannah's death. How easy it would have been, with such knowledge, for someone with malice and murderous intent to administer the poison. Yet no one granted Cook Teets the benefit of reasonable doubt. The powers that be in Ottawa insisted on proceeding with what, on any fair examination, can now be revealed as nothing less than a merciless act of unwarranted retribution."

Reports of how certain people reacted to the *Chronicle* story soon began to reach Leonard's ears. In Owen Sound, the prosecuting attorney, Alfred Frost, read the *Chronicle* in outrage and disbelief. The governor of the jail, John Miller, slammed the paper onto his desk in anger. Even James Masson, Cook's lawyer, thought Leonard had gone too far.

"Everybody connected with this trial shares responsibility for what has happened," Masson told his law clerk. The clerk, dozing over his study of a boring account of a long ago legal action in the courts of England, perked up.

"Then they won't like what Babington's written, will they?"

# Chapter 23

## THE WARNING

### October 20, 1885

Leonard Babington scrawled his name on the last cheque he would ever write to the Toronto Paper Manufacturing Co. It paid off his debt and he vowed he'd never again do business with the company. He returned the chequebook to the top drawer of his desk. It was then that John Miller, the governor of the Owen Sound jail, stormed into the *Chronicle* office.

"Babington, God damn it, I've come to straighten you out on this Cook Teets business. These contemptuous articles you've been writing – you've got to stop spreading that manure. You're causing all kinds of talk, getting folks worked up. Destroying faith in the courts, the police, all of us in authority."

Leonard had written about the case in his last three issues. He'd published half a dozen letters, including two that were critical of what he'd written. More worrisome, four merchants withdrew their ads. "Don't like all this controversy," he was told by Joe Greene, the butcher.

"Mr. Miller, have a seat," Leonard said. "You've come down from Owen Sound just to tell me that?"

"Yes, and I'll tell you more. Teets was guilty as hell. He even confessed to me."

"What do you mean, he confessed?"

"Just that. He told me he did it. He said he thought it would be a good piece of business, collecting that insurance money. Rehearsed his confession speech, right in front of me."

"Mr. Miller, why have you never said anything of this? Never told the court?"

"No need to. I knew he'd be found guilty."

"You mean you knew he'd be railroaded!"

Leonard reared back in his captain's chair. What Miller was telling him flew in the face of common sense. If Cook had wanted to confess, he wouldn't have confessed to his jailer. He'd have confessed to those preachers, Howell or Scott. He wouldn't still have claimed he was innocent, there on the gallows.

"Governor," Leonard said – being careful to address Miller by his title – "what you say doesn't ring true. It looks to me you're trying to put a false face on things, so it won't seem that injustice has been done. You want to look good in Alfred Frost's eyes, and in the eyes of the government. I don't believe Teets ever confessed to you."

Leonard and Miller argued for another twenty minutes. Miller grew red in the face, raised his voice, and shook his fist at Leonard.

"We won't stand for it, Babington," he warned as he stomped from the *Chronicle*. "If you won't cease and desist, we'll see that you are shut down. The law has its ways."

A few days later, Scarth Tackaberry hailed Leonard as he walked along the Beaver Valley Road. Tackaberry looked worried, Leonard thought, not quite so sure of himself as he'd put on at Cook's hanging.

"You're making quite a fuss in your paper," Tackaberry said. "Trying to make out somebody else did in Rosannah. Some folks are dreaming up all kinds of possibilities. Mentioning different names. Some even think it might have been me."

"I never said anything about you."

"You didn't have to. Folks know I was interested in Rosannah That's the way it's been for me. People blame me for things that's their fault, like what happened to her. Maybe she was asking for it."

That didn't make sense to Leonard. "Nobody asks to die. If you didn't do something you can't be blamed. If you did, someday you'll have to own up to it. Clear your conscience." This wasn't what Tackaberry wanted to hear, Leonard could see. Tackaberry walked away, muttering to himself.

That night, as Leonard was locking the door to the *Chronicle* office, he noticed a shadow on the ground. That was when he saw the Runt. It was the only name by which the little man crouched beside him was ever known. The

Runt had lost both legs when, drunk on a day that was well below zero, he'd fallen under the wheels of a Toronto, Grey and Bruce freight train he'd been trying to board. When he was picked up, he was nearly frozen to death. The blood running from his wound had congealed, preventing infection from entering his legs. After a month in the hospital, he'd been outfitted with a small, square board fitted with four casters taken from a discarded bed. He learned to squat on the board and propel himself along the wooden sidewalks of the village. He spent most of his time hanging around the general store where he made generous use of the bucket of free whisky that always sat on the counter.

"Runt, what are you doing today?" Leonard asked.

"Hearing bad news about you."

"What have you heard?"

"I heard it's time for you to wise up." The Runt paused, allowing a blank look to come over his face. He farted, then resumed his warning. "Or somebody's gonna fix you. Lay off the Cook Teets case."

Leonard handed the Runt a quarter.

"Get yourself some more of whatever's been making you crazy."

The next morning Leonard found the front window at the *Chronicle* smashed by a rock. A note tied to it had fallen loose. "Shut up Babington," it read. The day after, Leonard spotted a soggy paper bag on the doorstep of his office. When he lifted it, the sack broke. Shit slithered down his pant leg and onto his shoes.

That night Leonard heard a gunshot as he stepped into the road. Involuntarily, he ducked. He crouched in the darkness for a few minutes before he made his way into the forest and found a path that led him home. He wondered who could be behind the attacks. A rock, or even a bag of shit, he could slough off. But being shot at? Either he'd upset the authorities more than he'd realized or the killer of Rosannah was still out there, wanting the world to forget about her and Cook Teets. No one in Grey County was going to help him. He didn't feel safe in Vandeleur now. He had to either give up his campaign to find justice for Rosannah, or accept the liklihood of further assaults. He would have to look elsewhere for help. The Dominion Police, perhaps, or even the Minister of Justice. He had to talk to somebody. He'd have to go to Ottawa.

Ottawa was dirty and dusty. Leaves were falling from the elm and maple trees that grew along Wellington Street as Leonard made his way from the railway station to the Russell Hotel. The hotel was directly across the street from the Parliament Buildings. Leonard asked for one of the cheaper rooms, and he was given one that looked over an alley at the back of the building. He had planned to rest for awhile, but the room was so stuffy that he decided to go out and have a look at the Parliament Buildings.

So this is the seat of Canada's government, Leonard thought, standing near the crest of the hill that rose above the Ottawa River. The three great sandstone structures, topped with towers covered with gargoyles and gro-tesques, seemed part of a different world than the one Leonard had encoun-tered on his walk from the railway station. He'd smelled rancid garbage in the gutters, seen men behind push carts filled with old clothes and sticks of used furniture, and watched ladies who carefully raised their skirts as they stepped into the road.

Leonard noticed that the Parliament Buildings were protected by nothing more than a waist-high wrought iron fence that ran along Wellington Street. He heard the big clock in the main tower chime eleven times. A gate had been left open and Leonard went through it, heading for the main door of the biggest building. The doorman at the hotel had called it the Centre Block. Under a stairway he found a sign directing him to the office of the Dominion Police. He opened a door into a room barely large enough to contain a bench, a counter, and two small desks fitted under a pair of low windows. One desk was occupied by a short man wearing khaki breeches. They were held up by wide, brown suspenders. Leonard asked to see the officer in charge.

"Mr. McMicken's on his walkabout. Should be back soon."

Leonard wondered what a commanding officer of the Dominion Police would find on a walkabout of Parliament Hill. He would have to ask about that.

"Intelligence, don't you know," Mr. McMicken told him an hour later when he'd returned and Leonard had been granted a hearing. "Our job is to guard these buildings, and gather information that will help protect the government people. A murder case over in Grey County?

"Nothing we can do about that, I'm afraid. Out of our jurisdiction. You'd be better off talking to the Justice Department. Go to the other place," Mr. McMicken said, waving vaguely toward what Leonard took to be the building he had heard referred to as the East Block. "Get in to see Richard Langley. Chief clerk to the Minister of Justice. But I warn you, all they care about right now is that Riel business."

The Riel business? Leonard had almost forgotten about the rebellion on the Northwestern plains. Led by the half-breed, Louis Riel. Captured, and sentenced to hang. Everyone in Ontario was keen to see him drop from the gallows. But not Quebec, Leonard had heard. The French were in an uproar; Riel was half French, half Indian, a Metis as people of that mix were known, and the Quebec newspapers were full of demands that his life be spared. Leonard decided his best chance of getting to see the Minister of Justice would be to ask to interview him about the Riel affair.

Leonard found the Department of Justice in a row of rooms on the second floor. The door to the main office was covered with pebbled glass, and when Leonard entered he found himself in a small waiting room where two men occupied its only chairs. There was no one else about. Leonard stood near the door, wondering what he should do. In a minute, an elderly man carrying a bundle of files came in, spoke to the waiting men, and took them inside. He returned in a few minutes and asked Leonard to state his business.

"I'm here to see the Minister of Justice, press business," Leonard said.

"You'll have to talk to the chief clerk, Mr. Langley. I can't just send you into the Minister. Take a seat."

It took Leonard two visits before he was admitted to the office of Richard Langley. Sitting in the cramped waiting room, he thought about what kind of man Langley might be. He assumed he'd be stuffy and formal. He wondered whether such a man would show any interest in the murder of an innocent young bride, or in helping to find the person responsible for her death.

# Chapter 24

## THE TRANSCRIPT

### November 5, 1885

R ichard Langley fingered a letter opener on his desk and shifted a stack of files as Leonard took a seat. The chief clerk's striped dark coat and white shirt, with its massive celluloid collar, gave him a stern countenance. He appeared to be about Leonard's age, thirty-five at the most. He was cleanly shaved and Leonard suspected he was a man who fussed over his clothes and cared about the impression he made on visitors.

"The Minister's in cabinet," Richard Langley said. "There is much deliberation on matters related to the North West."

"That's just it," Leonard said. "We're very interested in Ontario to know the Minister's views on the matter of Riel. Anything I write for my paper will be shared with other newspapers."

"That would be good of you," Richard Langley replied. "What to do about Riel is much on the minister's mind. John Thompson has only recently taken on the justice portfolio. We have to schedule his time carefully. He resigned from the Supreme Court to run in a by-election in Nova Scotia. Successfully, thank God. Now he's got a bit of stomach trouble – the doctors say it's kidney stones – so it may take a few days to arrange something. But tell me about yourself and your paper. I've always wanted to get up there to the Queen's Bush. Enjoy a bit of pheasant hunting."

Richard Langley listened avidly to Leonard's account of experiences at the *Chronicle*, at the *Globe*, and on the lake boats. These were fascinating new topics for the chief clerk. He compared Leonard's adventures with his own life in England. "Rather tame compared to what you've seen," he told Leonard.

"A bit of fox hunting – dogs and all – and an occasional week of fly fishing in Scotland." It was clear to Leonard that Richard Langley came from the upper class. Still, they shared a common love of nature. The two men talked for nearly an hour. By the end of it, Leonard felt he had a new friend in the making, despite their different backgrounds.

"Look, it's four o'clock," Richard Langley finally told Leonard. "This is Thursday, and the wives of the cabinet ministers will be arriving for their weekly tea. We senior staff usually join them. Come along as my guest."

"I've no wish to intrude," Leonard answered. He was surprised to be invited to such an exclusive gathering.

"Not an intrusion, a pleasure," Richard Langley answered.

The room where Langley took Leonard was decorated with vases of fall flowers set on serving tables. A thick rug covered the floor and rich paneling embellished every wall. There was no need of a fire in the hearth. A large painting of General Wolfe, the conqueror of Quebec, hung over it, his bright red jacket a contrast to the heavy clouds behind him. Chairs set out along each wall filled up as the wives of cabinet ministers, led by Mrs. Thomas White, wife of the Indian Affairs minister, and Annie Thompson, the new Justice minister's wife, came into the room. He dutifully bowed his head and offered his hand in response to the gloved hands of each of the ladies. Leonard thought them dowdy compared to the woman who sat a little apart, on a Queen Anne chair. She had on a fancy tea gown and Leonard suspected she wore no corset. Langley introduced her as Miss Janette Robertson. He added, under his breath, that she was the latest mistress of that old goat from Nova Scotia, Sir Leonard Tilley. Leonard watched as she daintily balanced a cup of Earl Grey tea with a saucer of tiny sandwiches. Miss Robertson smiled warmly, arched her eyebrows and told Leonard, "I do hope this will not be your only visit with us."

After an hour spent circling the room and meeting other government people, Richard Langley nudged Leonard and suggested it was time to leave. On the way out Leonard caught snatches of whispers about "that handsome young man with Mr. Langley."

"Staying in the city?" Langley asked Leonard. "Drop in and see me Monday afternoon."

Leonard went to a branch of the Bank of Commerce on Saturday morning and drew fifty dollars from the two thousand dollar inheritance his father had left him. He slept late on Sunday and in the afternoon walked out to Rockcliffe Park where the best families of Ottawa had their mansions. He was at Richard Langley's office at three o'clock on Monday. The occasion marked the first of what would become almost daily meetings between Leonard and the chief clerk. They took beer at the Russell Hotel. They had long discussions on the responsibilities of a citizen to help build his country.

"We've got to get in there and stir things up, especially in a new country like Canada," Richard Langley said.

Leonard said he agreed wholeheartedly, and if his services were ever needed, he could be counted on. After a week, Leonard felt he had known the chief clerk for ages. He decided to tell Richard that if he ever got to interview John Thompson, he would ask about the trial of Cook Teets.

"In that case, I'll have to brief the minister."

Leonard spent fifteen minutes sketching the highlights of Cook Teets's trial. He spoke of what he'd learned at the Toronto Medical School and his belief that the killer of Rosannah Leppard was still at large.

The next day, Richard Langley told Leonard about the trial transcript.

"It's all there, word for word," he said. "But we're supposed to keep stuff like that confidential. If I let you see the transcript, you must never divulge how you got it."

The Department of Justice filled several rooms on the second floor of the East Block. The chief clerk led Leonard to the smallest, a cramped room containing rows of filing cabinets separated by narrow aisles. "No one ever comes here but me. You shouldn't be interrupted. The file you want is up there, on the top shelf. Put it back just the way you found it."

Leonard took down a box marked Ta-Th and set it on the floor. There was one chair in the room and he moved it next to a window. He dragged over the box and from it selected a thick file on which had been written in large letters, "Queen v Cook Teets." Nervous, fearful of being found in the room, but excited at the prospect of what the file might reveal, Leonard began to read.

The first page bore an imprint in fancy lettering of the Department of the Secretary of State, Deputy Minister of Justice. It was dated 22/23 November, 1884, file #13588. "A transcription or copy of the notes of Evidence in re Cook Teets a Convict under sentence of death." Below, someone had written, "File away."

Several notes were tucked into the bundle. One, addressed to Mr. Justice Armour on 22 November 1884, requested "as early as circumstances will permit, for the information of His Excellency the Governor General in Council, a copy of the notes of evidence." Leonard knew that was government talk for the cabinet, Prime Minister Macdonald and his ministers, who had held Cook's fate in their hands. Justice Armour, replying five days later from Osgoode Hall in Toronto, had sent a hand-written note advising he was enclosing fifty-two pages of typewritten script.

So this is what the cabinet would have made its decision on, Leonard thought. He began to read. He tried to see the words through the eyes of Sir Alexander Campbell, the justice minister at the time. He tried to imagine how he might have reacted to what he would have read. Would any of the other ministers, or even Prime Minister Macdonald, have read the transcript? Or would they have left it to Sir Alexander to say what he thought of it?

No matter, it began in straight enough fashion. Molly's evidence, drawn from her by Alfred Frost, just as Leonard remembered it. Her cross-examination, the interjections by the judge, they were all there. Dr. Sproule's testimony, his hand-written autopsy report, now typed up. The defence witnesses, Cook's mother and sister, the thrust of what they had said. But look! Something's missing. No mention of the summations by James Masson and Alfred Frost. Gone. Nothing of Justice Armour's charge to the jury – the charge that even the *Flesherton Advance* admitted was "strongly against the prisoner." Not a word of what Cook Teets had said after the jury's verdict, when he pleaded for an hour that he was innocent.

Now Leonard understood it all. The cabinet had been given only half the picture. Nothing but "evidence" but where was the truth? Something to balance the faulty logic of the prosecutor? Or the biased interpretation of Justice Armour, one that led the jury straight to Cook's guilt? All the wasted hours, all the petition signing, the letters from the Owen Sound lawyers, from Dr. Sproule, their own Member of Parliament, none of it meant anything.

The pages on his lap made Leonard seethe. He'd have something to tell John Thompson if he ever got to see him. He remembered his promise to Richard Langley; he could say nothing of this transcript. Leonard's head began to hurt. At first, he barely noticed the noise from the other side of the room. The click of a door latch, the scrape of wood against floor. A footstep. Someone was coming. Alarmed now, Leonard froze in his chair. He saw the shadow of a man as he moved from aisle to aisle. He heard a groan. The man turned and faced Leonard. He stared at him, full in the face. The man's lips twitched. He was short, but thick and heavy. Leonard recognized the new Minister of Justice. He'd seen a picture of John Thompson in the outer office. What was he doing here? Leonard felt ill. Suddenly, the man turned away. Leonard heard the noise of the scraping door. He was alone again with the Cook Teets file.

Leonard worried about how he would explain his presence in the file room. Research, he would say, research on the rule of law in Ontario. He couldn't afford to stay in Ottawa much longer, and it bothered him that Richard Langley was in no rush to arrange an interview. Finally, after a week in the capital, on the morning of his next to last day, he received a message inviting him to present himself at the minister's office at two o'clock. It was almost a year to the day since Cook had been convicted; two years since Rosannah had died.

Richard Langley escorted him into a room with large windows and a high ceiling decorated with plaster cherubs. Rich wood paneling covered the walls and a marble mantle set off a large fireplace. A thick rug lay on the floor.

"Sir, may I present Leonard Babington," Richard Langley said. "The journalist with many readers in Ontario."

John Thompson grunted and motioned Leonard to a seat.

"You want to talk about Riel, I'm told," he said. "That's all the newspapermen care about. His Excellency might decide otherwise, but to me he's a paltry hero. He's struggled long and hard for the privilege of hanging. Once he's in his grave, all this fuss will go quiet." Thompson had apparently forgotten their meeting in the storage room. There'd be no need for the fancy excuses Leonard had invented. It was safe now to move on to another subject.

Leonard raised the case of Cook Teets. He described how a man had been convicted on a paucity of evidence. Petitions in support of the jury's plea for clemency had been ignored. There was a strong suggestion an injustice had been done, and that the guilty party was still at large.

"It seems to me the justice system doesn't always work that well," Leonard said. "Teets was given no opportunity to tell his side of the story. The appeal procedure was so complicated that it left Teets's lawyer with no way to continue the case."

Leonard saw a look of pain cross over John Thompson's face. He didn't know whether it was in response to what he'd said, or to some other cause. In a moment, the face cleared.

"Some modification of procedures is warranted," John Thompson conceded. "Canada is in need of a codified criminal law. I intend to bring that in. We are going to amplify the right of appeal. As for an accused testifying on his own behalf, I thank you for raisng an interesting point. I'll ask the legal people to see if they can do something on that. Of course, we'll have to permit the Crown to cross-examine."

Leonard was surprised by how readily the Minister conceded the point. He wondered if he'd be as quick to agree to a review of Cook Teets's trial.

"But I've no time now to look into a case where a man's already dead." The finality of what Leonard was hearing came as a shock.

"Perhaps after this Riel business …" the Minister added, pausing.

John Thompson never finished the sentence. Instead, he stood and squeezed his stomach, pressing his hands into his gut as blood drained from his face. He let out a feeble groan and fell forward onto his desk.

The next day, Leonard was told the Minister had suffered a severe attack of kidney stones. He wondered if he'd ever be allowed to complete his interview. He waited another week, but when Richard Langley still had no idea when John Thompson would be back, Leonard told him he could stay no longer in Ottawa.

"Quite understand, you've been more than patient," the chief clerk said. "But look here, there's something else. We've talked about the responsibility of British subjects to give their all to their country. Let's talk about Canada. Sir John and his party are committed to keeping Canada British. None of this creeping Yankeeism that the Liberals promote. Where do you stand on that subject?"

Leonard wasn't sure what to make of the question. Of course, he stood by the Union Jack, why it was only natural to see it hanging in the courtroom back in Owen Sound. "To the extent I've thought about it," he said, "of course we want to stay British."

"Good, good, that's what I wanted to hear. Now, I've been given certain political responsibilities. I'm to advise the government on suitable new candidates. Sir John feels it's time for fresh blood. You must be well known in Grey County. There'll be openings there in the next election. How would you feel about being a Member of Parliament?"

Leonard sucked in his breath. He'd never thought of such a thing. He liked what he'd seen of Ottawa. But become a politician? How would he go about getting elected? Wouldn't people think it too grand an idea for a simple editor? Mind you, Dr. Sproule was just a country doctor, but of course everybody in the County knew and respected him.

"I've always had an interest in politics," Leonard claimed. "My father campaigned for Dr. Sproule. So maybe it runs in the blood."

"Think it over," Richard Langley urged. "If you're interested, I can put you in touch with some party people out there. Try the idea out on them. See how they react. Write me when you get back to Vandeleur."

"Of course," Leonard answered. "But it seems you've rather quickly formed a good opinion of me. I'm not sure you know me well enough to recommend me for Parliament."

"Let me worry about that. If it turns out you've character flaws I've not detected, our people up in the County will put me wise soon enough."

A larger than usual number of passengers crowded the concourse of the Grand Trunk Railway station on the morning of November 17, 1885. Leonard bought a ticket for Toronto, making sure it would allow him a stopover in Cobourg where he hoped to meet with Justice Armour. He noticed the *Toronto Mail* was being hawked in the station and that people were lined up to buy it.

He paid two cents and unfurled the front page:

### EXECUTION OF RIEL
#### The Rebel Chief Meets His Doom Stoically

As the train snaked through the shantytown outskirts of Ottawa on in its run south to Kingston where it would turn west and head along Lake Ontario toward Cobourg and Toronto, Leonard read the long report on Riel. The main story was from Regina, in the North West Territory. It covered almost all the front page and continued on to inside pages. "Riel met his fate bravely, and displayed more fortitude than had been thought possible." He had died as stubbornly as Cook Teets, Leonard thought. Both had been powerless. Is that why they were unable to save themselves? What would old Wahbudick, the Indian chief Leonard had known in the forest of the Beaver Valley so many years ago, have made of it?

Leonard sighed and thought about his last conversation with Richard Langley. Was the man really serious about involving him in politics? The idea excited Leonard. He could imagine joining the Thursday tea sessions in the cabinet rooms as a Member of Parliament. He decided he had better put aside such thoughts, at least for now. He opened his satchel and withdrew a sheath filled with paper. The pages were covered with his scrawls, some in ink and some in pencil. He'd have time before the train reached Cobourg to read everything he'd written about Rosannah Leppard.

# Chapter 25
## A QUESTION OF JUSTICE

### November 17, 1885

Leonard Babington ate a mutton sandwich and took water from his flask as the train steamed over the Great Cataraqui River on its approach to Kingston. He'd heard it was a sleepy town little known for industry or any purpose other than its Queen's College, a place undistinguished for Presbyterian learning, and Fort Henry, from which no shot had ever been fired in anger. Twenty minutes later, the train eased to a stop at the Grand Trunk Railway station, a two-storey building of almost-white limestone blocks. Leonard poked through a shop while the train took on water. Back in his coach, he dropped his manuscript onto the seat beside him. His eye caught mention of Rosannah's sister Elizabeth. He remembered how he had struggled with that passage from *Roseannah's Story:*

You will want to know about Rosannah's brothers and sisters and I will begin with her favourite, Elizabeth. She was just a year older than Rosannah, so close they were almost twins. Rosannah named one of her children after her. Elizabeth attended school for only a few years but all who knew her insisted she was well versed in reading and arithmetic. She possessed an independent mind and when she was only sixteen she traveled up to Collingwood to help Mrs. Wycliffe, who sorely needed assistance with her five young children. It was there that Elizabeth would become acquainted with William Wonch, the son of a farmer. They fell in love and were married in the Collingwood Methodist Church by the Rev. Edwin Clement. She declared herself a Presbyterian for the occasion. Elizabeth was nineteen and Will twenty-four.

Many young people in these modern times possess an indomitable urge to be away from their parents. So it was with Will as well as Elizabeth. He had relatives in the Barrie area and through a cousin he secured work at farms around Vespra, one of the outlying villages. It was not difficult for Will to gain a reputation as an industrious young man. The small house and acreage he rented on the Mill Road was one of the best kept habitations in the district. Elizabeth became known as a kind-hearted Irish woman and a good mother to her children, which eventually numbered four.

One day in July of this year, Elizabeth had words with Will when he arrived home. She'd smelled smoke during the day and had discovered a smouldering coat he'd left hanging on a hook. She'd found sparks in the lining. She doused them with a pail of water.

"You've got to stop dropping your pipe in your pocket when it's still lit," I could imagine her saying. "You'll burn us all up." One could picture Will lifting the coat off the peg where Elizabeth had hung it. It wouldn't have looked to him as if it had been on fire. After taking tea, Will went about his evening chores, feeding the pigs and attending to other small jobs. He'd have checked the coat again when he'd come back in. "Looks fine to me," he might have said.

As Will later told the story, around ten o'clock, after Elizabeth had finally gotten the four children settled down, the two went to bed. He awoke to find their bedroom and the bed they were lying on a mass of flames, burning like fury. He would tell neighbours he had tried to get Elizabeth up but she was unconscious. He found flames bursting out of the bed. When he went to pull off the mattress, it fell apart and all the straw caught fire. There was nothing he could do but jump through the window. His hands and face were badly burned. The children were beyond rescue.

The next morning, neighbours found the remains of Elizabeth and the children in the cellar. Lillian was seven; little William, four; Peter, two; and the baby, just a few months old. They'd fallen there when the floor had collapsed. Farmers who lived nearby had seen the blaze but they'd thought it was logs or stumps burning. They'd paid no attention.

I heard of the deaths when the telegrapher at the railway station copied down a news report meant for a Toronto paper. He brought it to me a few nights later. Rosannah never knew of her sister's death, of course; she'd been dead herself for going on a year and a half or more. What had happened to Rosannah must have been heart breaking to Elizabeth. Will would have felt guilty about his family's fate, but I never got to ask him about that. I had to wonder how Molly would take the news. One daughter poisoned, another burned up. Four little children lost. She'll think the wrath of God is on her family, I figured. I don't think Molly ever got over losing a second daughter that way.

The late afternoon luminescence of a fall day was settling over Cobourg when Leonard got off the train. If he hurried, there might still be time to catch Justice Armour in his chambers at Victoria Hall. By the time he reached the Kingston Road, gas lamps had been lit and his shadow kept pace with him on the walk to the Hall, home of both the courthouse and the town council. Inside, he found large double doors that opened onto a courtroom configured as a deep well, like a theatre pit. Pale light filtered through windows at either side. The well contained a prisoner's box, a clerk's table and two witness boxes. An elevated judge's bench filled the end of the room.

"Just like Old Bailey," he heard a voice beside him. "Only one of its kind in Canada. The Prince of Wales sat down there, the day he opened it, back in 'sixty."

"Not as a prisoner, I hope," Leonard answered. He caught himself, realizing it was injudicious to make the Prince the subject of bantering remarks. "I'm here to see Judge Armour. I wonder if he's still about?"

When Leonard reached the judge's chambers on the second floor, Judge Armour's clerk was putting on his coat. He had thin, dry lips that could have been painted on in chalk. Barely opening his mouth, he asked Leonard's name and business, motioned him to a chair, and disappeared into another room. He was back in a moment, pointing inside. "You can go in," he said, and left.

"Ah Babington, come in, I'm always glad to meet a newspaperman, though it's late." He peered more closely at Leonard, picking up the contours of his face revealed by the oil lamp on his desk.

"Oh," he said as he realized who it was. "I remember you from the Cook Teets trial. A poor sod, that man."

Justice Armour spoke affably of his time in Owen Sound. "A sad event, but a good place. Been in a lot worse. They expect a lot of a judge for six thousand dollars a year."

Leonard figured he'd go just about anywhere for that amount of money. He said it was a lot more than he'd ever make as a newspaperman.

"But the responsibility," Justice Armour replied. "You've not held people's lives in your hands. At least I have my independence. Not like the politicians, always having to curry favour through corruption. Bribery, that's all it is. I sometimes think bribery's the cornerstone of party government in this country."

Leonard wondered if the bribery of politicians had interfered in the rendering of justice. What Justice Armour was saying seemed remote from what went on in a courtroom. Did he mean government was founded on bribery? Surely not.

"I'd like to ask you about the Cook Teets trial," Leonard said. "I've never understood why the jury convicted him. So little evidence. And why his sentence was never commuted. Some think there was reasonable doubt as to his guilt."

Justice Armour began to stuff files into a travel bag. He frowned, flicked his eyelids, and looked directly at Leonard.

"Twelve of the most intelligent men in Grey County made the correct decision," he said. "I have no doubt Teets was guilty. You should not question the outcome of a judicial process."

Leonard wondered whether Judge Armour knew of the articles he'd written in the *Chronicle*. There was no reason to think he would have seen them.

"But surely mistakes are sometimes made," Leonard countered.

The judge rolled his tongue in his mouth as he pondered the point.

"All the more reason not to challenge an outcome. The public must have confidence in the justice system. Otherwise there's no law and order. Start undermining the courts and the whole apparatus of justice falls apart. Public order is built on a trusting public. Trusting citizens don't question figures of authority.

"Anyway, it's getting late and I must say good night. I'll walk you to your hotel. Come again and I'll have you out to Calcutt House."

Leonard thanked Judge Armour and said goodnight as they reached the steps of the Lake Ontario Arms. He'd chosen the hotel because it looked cheap and his money was running low. Its ground floor was filled with a reception room, a combination saloon and dining room, and a dry goods store that sold men's clothing, harnesses, and bolts of wool and linen. He took supper at the common table in the dining room. Two people were seated there – an aged, bearded man and a younger woman. Leonard judged her to be about thirty years old. He assumed they were together, perhaps father and daughter.

The old man ate untidily, dropping scraps of food onto the table and the floor as gravy collected on his beard. His conversation was limited to muttered comments about the weather and the state of the hotel's food, both of which he considered unsatisfactory. He wiped up the last of his supper with a crust of bread, belched, and got up and left.

Leonard looked at the woman. "Your father is a man of few words," he said.

"Oh, he's not my father. I've not seen him before."

Leonard had no previous experience of women travelling alone. He noticed she wore a wedding ring.

"Were you on the train, Mrs....?"

"It's Mrs. Birch and I've come in from my husband's farm on Rice Lake," she said. "I'll be going to Toronto tomorrow."

Leonard introduced himself and spoke of his stay in Ottawa. He told her he was on his way to Toronto and that they might travel on the same train. When the barmaid brought Leonard a second glass of ale he invited the woman to accept a glass.

"Perhaps just one," she said. "I never drink."

They talked for an hour. Mrs. Birch took a second glass of ale. Leonard never found out her first name but he learned a lot about the rigours of harvesting wild rice and surviving springtime floods. He saw she was a bit tipsy when she stood and he offered to escort her to her room. It was across the hall from his.

"I can see you are a gentleman," she said, standing at her door. She offered a hand and Leonard shook it.

"Good night," she said, and disappeared into the room.

Leonard was about to get into bed when he heard a tap on his door. It was Mrs. Birch.

"I am sorry to bother you Mr. Babington, but I am having trouble with the lock on my trunk. Could you assist me?"

The trunk was a tin object painted blue, two feet wide and three feet long, with brass strapping and an impressive brass lock. The key he was handed refused to fit.

"Gracious, silly me, it's the wrong key," the woman said. "Here, try this." The new key easily opened the trunk.

"Oh, I'm feeling dizzy," Mrs. Birch said. She leaned on Leonard's shoulder. "I just need to get off my feet for a bit."

Mrs. Birch sank to the bed, pulling Leonard with her. He felt her hot breath on his ear. It was followed by a tongue that explored his ear lobe before traveling to his mouth. He could taste the scent of lavender and beer in her kiss. Leonard let himself fit into the curves of her body. He unbuttoned his pants, drew her hand to him, and put from his mind all thought of why he was on this trip.

After, he fell asleep in her arms. He awoke hours later, feeling panic in the darkened room. The overnight train from Montreal would be in Cobourg at six o'clock. He had to get to the station. He dressed quickly and silently, crossed to his room for his things, and went downstairs.

In the lobby, Leonard saw a large, swarthy man awaken a sleeping clerk behind the counter.

"Where is she, where's Mrs. Birch?" he demanded. "My wife's run away from me and I've tried every place in Cobourg. She must be here."

"Upstairs, first room on the right," the terrified clerk replied.

The man looked at Leonard, his eyes filled with anger. He brushed past him and leapt up the stairs two steps at a time, cursing as he went. Leonard left the Lake Ontario Arms quickly, convinced he had escaped a fatal beating, or at least a serious bruising. He stepped aboard the last coach of the train as it gathered speed for the run into Toronto.

# Chapter 26

## A MEETING AT ST. ANDREW'S

### November 18, 1885

Dampness hung in the morning air when Leonard Babington left the train at Union Station in Toronto. He was glad he'd brought his overcoat. As he slung it about his shoulders he thought of the task he had set for himself. St. Andrew's Presbyterian Church was only a few blocks away. He intended to see the Rev. Daniel Macdonnell; Leonard had never understood why his testimony at Cook's trial had been so brief. There must have been much more he could have said about how Cook and Rosannah had turned up at his church, asking to be married.

Leonard found the Rev. Macdonnell in the manse. He'd just finished breakfast and his wife was still clearing away the morning's dishes when Leonard was admitted into a small sitting room. A bouquet of flowers sat in a vase on a stand beside a small chesterfield. When the Rev. Macdonnell came into the sitting room, Leonard was struck by the heavy eyebrows and sad eyes that dominated his face. The pain of troubled parishioners was plainly evident in his bearing.

Rev. Macdonnell dropped his napkin on the table and called to his wife to bring Leonard a cup of coffee.

"Strange case, that one," he said, when Leonard raised the matter of Cook Teets's trial. "I didn't stay for the whole thing. They just wanted me to confirm I'd married them. Wasn't on the stand more than three minutes. I could have told the jury a whole lot more."

"What could you have told the jurors?"

"That Rosannah and Cook gave every appearance of being a devoted

203

couple. Anyone could have seen that. Otherwise, I wouldn't have married them, just in off the street, without any notice. My brother gained the same impression. 'Those two are mated for life,' he said."

"It would seem they were," Leonard replied.

"Still, we must accept God's will in all things," the Rev. Macdonnell added. "Everything has a purpose even if we don't understand it."

The conversation turned to other reasons for Leonard's visit to Toronto, as if he had any other purpose than to inquire into the minister's impressions of the couple for whom he had conducted a hurried marriage ceremony. Leonard felt the old sadness coming back. What he was hearing today convinced him more than ever that Rosannah had not died at her husband's hands. Cook Teets had not deserved to hang. Perhaps a few moments alone in the church will help settle my mind, Leonard thought. Thanking the minister for his time, he moved into the church and took a seat near the chancel. He looked up at the stained glass windows that filtered light onto the altar, bowed his head, and closed his eyes. He did not pray, but he wished fervently for the survival of the souls of Rosannah and Cook in a happier place than they had found on earth.

When he rose to leave Leonard saw a figure standing near the front door of the church. As Leonard drew close, he realized it was that of a man, scarcely more than a youth, drawing in a sketchbook. Leonard watched him sketch uninterruptedly, creating lines and slashes. The pews, aisles and glass windows of the nave came alive on the page as Leonard watched.

"It looks even more real in your picture," Leonard said. "Where did you learn to draw like that?"

The young man held his charcoal pencil in the air. "I was taught to etch engravings but I prefer to draw," he said. "Mr. Robertson wants me to draw every church in Toronto."

"Then you've a job ahead of you."

The young man laughed. "And who are you?" he asked.

Leonard gave his name. He learned that Owen Staples was nineteen years old and that he had been given a commission by John Ross Robertson, the proprietor of the *Evening Telegram*. He was to do a picture of a different church every week: St. Paul's, the Church of Holy Trinity, Jarvis Street Baptist, even the Jewish synagogue, Holy Blossom. After being printed in the paper, his drawings were to be put in a book that Mr. Robertson planned to call *Landmarks of Toronto.*

"It'll keep me going for years," Owen said.

Owen's eyes sparkled as he spoke. Leonard remembered the enthusiasm he had felt during his first days at the *Globe.* The youth before him reminded Leonard of himself. In truth, they looked not alike; Owen's higher forehead and leaner face was set off by a straggly mustache that held promise of better days ahead.

"So you're a newspaperman," Leonard said. "So am I." He told Owen Staples of the *Vandeleur Chronicle* and said he'd just come from Ottawa.

"I've just started at the *Evening Telegram,*" Owen said, "but I've already had one good assignment. I went up to Manitoulin Island for the Indians' feast for the dead. What a time! The Indians build a huge bonfire – just like Hell, the Catholic missionaries say – and they fire off their guns all night to protect the departed. The priests let them do it – they call it 'shooting the devil.' I was able to make some really good pictures."

Owen's story about the Indians set Leonard to telling of his days with the old Indian of the Beaver Valley, Wahbudick. The two traded tales for most of an hour before Owen suddenly announced, "I'm hungry." He invited Leonard to dinner at his boarding house on Ann Street. "Mrs. Coles won't mind."

When they arrived at Owen's boarding house, Leonard thought he might have been dropped into some make-believe fairyland set amid a grimy neighbourhood of foundries, tanneries, harness makers and rendering plants. The house was altogether too neat and clean. Its white clapboard siding, recently painted, gleamed in the midday light. In front of the bungalow was a well-tended garden of flowers and vegetables. A wooden fence protected the property. The house wouldn't be so white in a few months, Leonard told himself. The coal smoke that drifted north from the factories below Gerrard Street would see to that.

Leonard ate every morsel of the meal put before him – potatoes, sausage, and turnips, followed by bread pudding and tea. He exchanged stories with Owen and the two *Evening Telegram* reporters who had come in while they were eating. Tom White had hilarious tales of bankers he'd caught carrying on with lady tellers – women were now being hired for such jobs – and Tim Healey told of drunken escapades involving men of the city council. Leonard chimed in with an account of the Cook Teets trial. He had found an audience that was keen to hear his story of heartbreak and injustice.

"It's a sad tale, but we're all having a gay time," Mrs. Coles said, "I've never seen the like of it. Mr. Babington. If we had you living here there'd never be a dull moment."

"Yes, why don't you move in?" Owen said.

A sense of foreboding darkened Leonard's eyes as he heard these encouraging words. He'd not told his new friends of his disastrous experience at the *Globe*. They might not be so welcoming once they knew of that episode. Besides, he had responsibilities back in Vandeleur. And to Rosannah and Cook. Who would keep the *Chronicle* going if he stayed in Toronto? There would be crops to think about come spring, and he had to make arrangements for the upkeep of Vandeleur Hall. Too many things were cluttering up his head.

"I'm sure Mrs. Coles can put you up for the night," Owen said. "Come out with me when I go sketching tomorrow. Maybe we'll run into Mr. Robertson."

The next morning, Owen led Leonard down Church Street to the docks below The Esplanade. "I need a break from drawing churches," he said. "There's still a few ships in the harbour and I want to sketch them before things close down for the winter."

Owen's skill with his stick of charcoal fascinated Leonard. He learned the young artist had been born in England and had grown up in Hamilton, where his father had been head groundskeeper to Lady MacNab, the mistress of Dundurn Castle. But something ominous had occurred when Owen was ten. His father had suddenly moved the family to Toronto. Fired or quit, Owen never knew. When word came that Grandfather Staples had died in England, Owen's father returned to the Old Country, only to die there a year later. His mother struggled to raise eight children, partly on the proceeds of a kindergarten she ran from their cottage on Berkeley Street. There was never enough money, and Owen contributed his earnings from delivering papers and his work as an office boy for a police magistrate. A lawyer who took a liking to Owen arranged for him to go to art school at night. That got him a job in an engraving plant. It was there he had met John Ross Robertson, the proprietor of the *Evening Telegram*.

"I like drawing for the newspaper," Owen said, "but what I really want to do is paint, I mean real painting, and for that I need training. I've saved almost enough money for art school. There's an Academy of Fine Art, in Philadelphia. I sent them my portfolio and they said they would take me. I'll need a leave of absence. Mr. Robertson is going to let me know when he can spare me."

Owen was one of those fortunate young men, Leonard reflected, who were given breaks by successful men in the conviction they might make something of themselves. He saw many similarities between himself and Owen, even though Leonard was older, had grown up in the country, and had enjoyed an easier boyhood. The fact they were both English in a city that was filling up with Scots immigrants and Irish Protestants – Toronto was becoming known as the "Belfast of North America" – drew the two more closely together.

By noon, Owen had sketched a freighter at anchor and drawn a picture of workmen unloading sacks of sugar. He and Leonard sat at the edge of the dock and shared a sandwich. Leonard's appetite vanshed in the stench of sewage and the acrid smell of factory smoke. He preferred to talk rather than eat.

"I was at the *Globe* when George Brown was shot," Leonard announced.

For the first time since he had shared that secret with his boyhood friend Tom Winship, Leonard found himself talking about the shooting of George Brown. Although he barely knew Owen, he was comfortable in the presence of the younger man. He described how he had won a reporter's job, the exciting assignments he'd been given, and how he'd been blamed for encouraging the man who had fired the fatal bullet at Mr. Brown.

"If it wasn't your fault, you've nothing to be ashamed of," Owen told him. "But I can understand how something like that could give you a black mark with the Toronto papers. That's why you're up there in the Queen's Bush, publishing that little sheet."

"It's where I'm from," Leonard said. He felt he had to defend his "little sheet."

"Besides, there's this big story I'm working on." He told Owen more of his own history – his friendship with Rosannah Leppard and his guilt over stories he'd written about Cook Teets before his trial.

Owen folded up the cloth sack that had held their lunch. Leonard looked out over the harbour, pointing to a departing vessel that was racing to beat the incoming ice before reaching its winter port of Kingston. Leonard thought about how Owen's father, rather than staying in Toronto to look after his children, had chased some illusion back in England.

Owen turned to face Leonard. "You're like a ship going from port to port, never knowing where you'll end up. I think you'd best forget about where you've been, and drop anchor for awhile."

# Chapter 27

## AT THE EVENING TELEGRAM

### November 19, 1885

Leonard Babington and Owen Staples made their way past a tangle of warehouses, sheds and grain elevators. A spider's web of railway tracks lay between them and Union Station. Its three domed towers rose like sentinels while trains shunted nosily, their wheels squealing against the rails. Steam belched from locomotives, signalmen waved flags, and high-pitched whistles warned of oncoming traffic. The two waited for the crossing to clear, then turned to walk up Bay Street. They picked their way through an intersection paved with cedar blocks rotted from years of rain, frosts, and thaws. "We're making them pave the streets with asphalt," Owen said proudly. "We sent reporters out with picks and they brought back sacks of rotted blocks. Mr. Robertson put them on display in our lobby. There was so much fuss the council voted money for asphalt paving."

At the corner of King Street, Owen led the way into a two-storey building that was the home of the *Evening Telegram*. It looked to Leonard like nothing more than a large farmhouse. Its peaked roof and whitewashed walls were set off by a small balcony on the upper floor used, according to Owen, for political speeches on election nights. Owen stopped to talk to one of the girls who sat behind a counter taking small ads from the public. The ads filled the front page every day. For a penny a line, people could list their wants – rooms for rent, furniture for sale, domestic help wanted. Thousands did so, giving the *Telegram* the largest circulation of the city's five daily newspapers.

"Mr. Robertson wants his paper to be a local sheet," Owen said. "He says that if Montreal burned down, the *Telegram* wouldn't bother to report it. We're all about Toronto: politics, crime, church news – and of course my drawings." He didn't mention that the paper also specialized in serial novels and Christian sermons, and short, pithy editorials in support of Canada's imperial connection to Britain.

The editorial rooms were on the second floor. Owen led Leonard up a back stairway into cloistered quarters where, from a corner office filled with a roll-top desk and four leather chairs jammed against a small table, John Ross Robertson directed the affairs of the paper. Owen knocked on the glass door and awaited a sign of recognition. When John Ross Robertson looked up Leonard saw a man with an intense gaze, clad in a dark coat set off by a Prince Albert collar and a striped tie. He had a short, neat beard. A gold watch was suspended between the pockets of his waistcoat. He nodded brusquely and Owen opened the door.

"Good afternoon, sir, I've brought you this morning's sketches. I thought they might suit the financial page, seeing as we print so much shipping news."

"You're always going off on your own, young man. I want more church pictures." He stopped to peer at what Owen had drawn. "I like these. Take them over to Mr. Lund in the engraving department. Tell him to run them Saturday. Huh, and who's this you've got with you?"

Owen introduced Leonard as the publisher of the *Vandeleur Chronicle*. He said they'd met while he was sketching at St. Andrew's Church. Robertson stood and extended a hand.

"Always glad to meet a fellow publisher," he said, laughing at his little joke, as if it was amusing to put Leonard's paper, which Robertson had never heard of, on the same level as the *Evening Telegram*.

"Babington, you say? Ever worked in Toronto?"

Leonard admitted he had. "Five years ago, but I left the *Globe* after Mr. Brown died."

"Now I remember," Robertson said. "You're the fellow they fired." He looked closely at Babington, clearly intrigued that this man had surfaced so long after the scandal, showing up at the *Telegram*.

"I had nothing to do with Mr. Brown's death, but leaving Toronto seemed the best thing at the time. I went home to Grey County and when the *Chronicle* came up for sale I bought it."

"That shows you've spine, taking on a small paper. I like that. I never put stock in those rumours about your being connected with that drunkard Bennett. Typical of their high and mighty airs at the *Globe*. Crucify a man for no good reason. Now tell me about this *Chronicle* of yours."

Leonard said he'd expected that putting out a country weekly would be a humdrum affair. But something had happened in Vandeleur that had changed everything. It wasn't just the terrible murder that had taken place, but that an innocent man, Leonard was convinced, had been hanged. He was doing everything he could to find whoever was guilty.

"I'm convinced the jury railroaded Cook Teets," Leonard said. "His wife, Rosannah, was given poison. Strychnine. But Teets was nowhere around. Couldn't have done it. I knew both of them. I've been working on the case, trying to figure out exactly how Rosannah died. And who poisoned her."

"Admirable, I'm sure," Robertson answered. "Unfortunately, it does Teets no good now to have you worrying your head about him. My advice is to leave that behind you. You've got perseverance, that's obvious. That counts for a lot in this business. Perhaps I can find something for you at the *Evening Telegram*."

For the second time today Leonard had been told to put aside the cause that had become the focus of his life. It was not an idea he was ready to grasp.

"That's kind of you, sir, but I have things to do in Vandeleur."

"If you change your mind come and see me," John Ross Robertson said.

Leonard spent Saturday and Sunday at Mrs. Coles's boarding house. On Monday morning, as he was preparing to pack his satchel and take a train north, there was a knock on the door.

"Mr. Robertson would like you to come along to the *Telegram*," a messenger boy told Leonard. "He needs you in the next half hour."

Close to an hour had passed by the time Leonard stood in John Ross Robertson's office. The publisher, clearly agitated, wondered what had taken him so long. "I came directly that I got your message," Leonard said.

"Good, good," Robertson answered, apparently mollified. "There's been a terrible murder. Awful crime, woman beaten to death. Seems like your kind of story. If you hurry you can get there before they remove the body. Find out who's done it and work up the whole thing in a major piece – maybe a series of articles."

Leonard stiffened as he listened to the publisher's terse accounting of the crime. He had no wish to write about the gory death of a helpless woman, a task certain to plague him with memories of Rosannah's fate.

"Your reporters must be on it, Mr. Robertson. I was going home today. Why do you need me?"

"I've been reading your stuff, Mr. Babington. Had your paper sent over from the Provincial Library. Anybody can put together bare facts. But you write with insight and understanding. You could give the *Telegram* something different."

Leonard had heard of Robertson's persuasive powers. How, after the failure of his first publishing venture, he had raised a hundred thousand dollars to start the *Evening Telegram*. Leonard held back his answer. He needed time to choose his words.

Impatient, Robertson babbled on.

"There's a lot of people in this city who grovel for a living in the gutter. Like fleas on a carcass. We see the consequences in crimes of this type. You can help the public understand the awful inevitability of it all. It's your duty, a man of your talents."

If flattery didn't work, a call to duty would, Leonard thought. He could see it now. He had no choice.

"All right, but just this one story. Then I have to get back to Vandeleur."

"Good man. Mr. Holmes will put you on the payroll. Now get over to Dafoe Street, Number 150. Take this police pass."

Leonard found a uniformed policeman on duty in front of the house, one of a row filled with tenement flats on the street behind Thompson's Silverplate factory. Word of the crime had spread through the neighbourhood and the curious were parading in the road, careful to dodge puddles left by last night's rainstorm while stepping over fresh dog dirt and manure.

Leonard showed his press pass.

"Second floor, Sir," the policeman told Leonard. "We've had quite a few pressmen already. Chief Grassett's come and gone. Inspector Archibald's taken charge."

Voices guided Leonard to a flat at the end of a dark, grim hallway. The door was open. He tapped on the doorframe, stepped inside, and stopped suddenly.

A kitchen opened off the entrance to the flat. Leonard saw a body on the floor, angled between the stove and a table. The long hair and clothes confirmed it was that of a woman. Her head rested on a bread pan where blood had trickled and had now congealed. She was of substantial size, and she had been badly beaten.  An eye had been gouged out and her cheeks had been crushed. Splatters of blood covered one wall and Leonard could see a trail of blood along a hallway. Ashes were scattered over most of the kitchen floor. It looked as if someone had tried to clean up the mess.

"Careful where you step," a voice told Leonard. He retreated to the doorway and waited. In a moment, a large man wearing a heavy overcoat and a grey derby came out of the bedroom. A uniformed policeman followed him.

"More press, I suppose," Inspector Archibald said when Leonard proffered his pass. "You'll want to know what's happened.

"The crime took place Saturday night," the Inspector began. He sounded tired from repeating the story. "The neighbours heard noises but they figured it was just another drunken brawl. Goes on all the time in these places. We weren't notified until Sunday evening. The man in the next flat, Robert Stirling, came by the police station. He said the occupant of this flat had invited him in. Drunk, the man was. Stirling saw what had happened, fled, and came straight to us.

"This here's Constable Rutherford, he caught the killer. Found him wandering on Chestnut Street just before daybreak. Drunk as a sot. Covered in blood. Brought him in for questioning. He's in the Don Jail now. Name of Thomas Kane, a plasterer. He was plastered, all right."

"And the woman?" Leonard asked.

"Mary Kane. Not his wife, but lived as man and wife. She was the widow of Kane's brother."

Inspector Archibald pointed to the ashes strewn on the floor. A mop, wrapped in a piece of old carpet, lay on the floor in a corner.

"We think the quarrel started in the bedroom. Kane, drunk, probably tried to force himself on the poor woman. She must have tried to get away. Blood all down the hallway. Kane caught up to her in the kitchen, beat her something awful."

The walls, floors and furniture were stained with Mary Kane's blood. Her assailant must have tried to clean up the mess with the bit of carpet and the mop. The work of a drunk or a madman, likely both, Leonard thought.

"What do you think of this?" Inspector Archibald asked. He held out a plasterer's trowel, covered in blood.

"This is what did her in. This and the hammer over here," the Inspector said, pointing to a claw hammer that rested, covered in blood, on a kitchen counter.

Leonard had seen enough. He thought of how Rosannah had died. He was glad she had not had to defend herself against a brutal physical assault. What could have brought this couple to such a violent end? He decided to tour the neighbourhood. He intended to give Mr. Robertson's readers what he wanted them to have – some insight into the struggle for existence that went on in Toronto's slums, and some understanding of how that struggle could result in terrible consequences.

Two days later, after the *Telegram*'s reporters had hashed out the facts of the killing in half a dozen stories, Leonard's special report appeared atop page five. It was the first page that was clear of classified ads:

## HER LAST HOURS
### Life of Despair for Penniless Widow
### Prison Cell a Refuge for Mary Kane

Struck down in the night in her bedroom. Attacked by the man with whom she lived. Died in a pool of blood on the kitchen floor. Such was the sad demise of Mary Kane, her fate not dissimilar from that of others of Toronto's poor, who die at the hands of drunken assailants, all too often either their husbands or another man known to them.

Leonard's story revealed that Mary Kane had suffered from a mental impairment of some kind. Her husband's death had left her penniless and incapable of supporting herself. Leonard wrote of how even the able bodied were suffering in the hard times that gripped the city in the 1880s. Beggars besieged the homes of the well off, and on some nights hundreds of people sought refuge in the police stations. Leonard had learned that Mary had spent several nights in a jail cell last winter. Feeling sorry for her, Thomas Kane reluctantly assumed responsibility for Mary's support. His drunken sprees grew increasingly frequent. He lost his job after repeatedly missing work. His frustration and anger vented itself in the explosive outburst that ended in Mary's killing. There was no excuse for Kane's actions. But it was time, Leonard's article concluded, for the City of Toronto to come to the assistance of citizens in distress before they suffered the awful fate of Mary Kane. Warehousing the homeless and indigent in the city's police cells must come to an end.

A parade of distinguished citizens, singly and in pairs, made their way to John Ross Robertson's office the next day. All were indignant that the *Evening Telegram* had stirred up sympathy for the shiftless, irresponsible, and drink-ridden denizens of the city's most deplorable neighbourhoods. The guilt or innocence of Thomas Kane and the fate of Mary were lost in the outrage at the paper's coddling of the craven, immoral poor. With the six o'clock edition ready to go to press, John Ross Robertson called Babington to his office.

"You've stirred things up!" Robertson told him. "Well, it's about time. I've wanted to do that ever since I started this paper, nine years ago. Now they'll know what the *Evening Telegram* stands for. Mr. Babington, you've rendered a great service, not just to this newspaper, but to everyone in this city."

The praise made Leonard apprehensive. He knew some of the reporters were jealous of the free rein he'd been given. There'd been remarks passed in the newsroom. One leathery veteran of the court reporting ranks, Angus McIntosh, had spat on the floor in front of him when he'd come in that morning. Besides, Leonard planned to be back in Vandeleur before Christmas. What else did Robertson want from him?

"You'll stay to the end of the case," Robertson said. "See the thing through, acquittal or hanging, whichever it is."

The idea of seeing the case to the finish had a certain appeal. Leonard had missed several issues of the *Chronicle* and he might as well wait for the New Year. "All right." He acquiesced without argument.

Leonard's tiny room on Ann Street held space for only a cot and a night table, but he was comfortable. That night, he undressed and reached into his satchel for his papers. He took a blank sheet and wrote a letter to Richard Langley. He told him how honoured he had been by the chief clerk's suggestion that he might consider standing for Parliament.

"I am spending a few weeks in Toronto at the request of Mr. Robertson of the *Evening Telegram*," he wrote, "but will be returning to Vandeleur in the New Year. The prospect of a political involvement I find most appealing. I believe I could make a contribution in that regard. If you have any instructions as to what I should do in preparation for having my name go before the leaders of the party, please write to me at my temporary Toronto address." Leonard looked at the letter, and added a PS: "My interest in standing for a Grey County seat would be to support the government in bringing about much needed changes in the justice and legal system of Canada." And solve the murder of Rosannah Leppard, he thought.

A few days before Christmas, Leonard found himself in the courtroom where Thomas Kane was on trial before Judge Street. The trial began with Kane's lawyer, an ambitious young solicitor bearing the name of James A. Macdonald – no relation to the Prime Minister, he told anyone who asked – making peremptory challenges to every man called to jury duty. "We must know you are unbiased and not affected in any sense by anything you may have heard or have read in the press about this case," he told each prospect. It was only after Sheriff Mowat had picked a dozen more men from the courtroom that a jury was finally impanelled.

The witnesses were clear and convincing about what they'd seen. Robert Simpson testified to Thomas Kane having called him to his flat where he found Mary Kane dead. Constable Rutherford described his arrest of Kane on Chesnut street, drunken and bloody. Inspector Archibald testified to finding the murder weapons, the trowel and the hammer, in the kitchen. The jury took twenty minutes to find Kane guilty, adding a recommendation for mercy. He was sentenced to hang on February 12, 1886.

That night, Leonard was again the centre of attention as Mrs. Coles's boarders sat down for supper. He took turns with Owen Staples, who had spent the day sketching scenes in the courtroom, in telling stories of the trial. Owen's drawings were being engraved as they ate, ready for tomorrow's paper. Leonard was asked to compare the Kane trial with the trial of Cook Teets in the death of Rosannah Leppard. "There's no comparison," he said. "Nobody saw Kane do Mary in, but the condition of his rooms and the man's state of mind at the time of his arrest left the jury no choice but to convict."

The day of Kane's hanging dawned cloudless and cold. Between the trial and the hanging, Leonard had a free rein to roam the city as he wished, picking up story ideas as he spoke with merchants, workers, police constables, and men of the cloth. He arrived at the Don Jail early, just as he had been among the first at the Owen Sound jail the morning Cook Teets was hanged. Leonard was surprised to see two priests going into the jail. Up to now, Leonard knew, Kane had been attended by Protestant ministers.

"He changed his mind and asked for Catholic clergy," a guard told Leonard. "Said he was really a Catholic. He'd only pretended to be a Protestant. Thought that way he was more likely to be shown mercy. Didn't help much, did it?"

There were rumours among the reporters that some new type of hanging device was to be used. The governor of the Don Jail, Mr. Green, had refused comment. Leonard had been asking questions of lawyers he'd met, but it was James A. Macdonald who finally confirmed the speculation. "I know who's going to do it, and how," he told Leonard. "John Radclive will do the job. He was an apprentice to England's hangman. Thinks Canada's the place to try out his new ideas." But no matter how hard Leonard pressed, Macdonald would reveal nothing of the manner in which Thomas Kane would meet his fate behind the high wall of the Don Jail.

When Leonard and the other witnesses, mostly newspapermen and medical students were admitted to the yard, they saw an astonishing sight. Instead of the usual gallows, a weird collection of timbers had been assembled. Two upright beams, set seven or eight feet apart, rose some fourteen feet above the ground. On them sat a crossbar from which hung the rope, its noose dangling about five feet off the ground. It swayed in the breeze. A heavy weight, attached by a slender cord, hung a few inches below the crossbar.

Leonard looked at his watch. At precisely twelve minutes past eight a side door opened and Sheriff Mowat emerged, followed by Governor Green. Behind them came two priests, a pair of policemen, the jail surgeon, and the coroner. Between the policemen, Thomas Kane walked in a steady pace. He wore a brown suit and a black wool cap and his arms were fastened to his sides. Lagging behind the death march came the hangman. A black mask covered his face. He had on a soft felt hat and a brown rubber coat.

Kane was led to the swaying rope. The hangman fixed the noose around his neck. In a quick movement, using a hammer and chisel, he cut the cord holding back the weight that hung from the crossbar. As it descended, Kane's body shot into the air, doing a pirouette before it settled back to dangle a few feet above the ground. Leonard felt his heart thud. He thought Kane had died instantly but then he saw the doomed man lift his right hand, as if in a final parting wave. A doctor stepped forward to check Kane's pulse. He pronounced him dead.

Leonard hurried to the *Evening Telegram*. His orders were to have a story for the eleven o'clock edition. He couldn't free his mind of the image of Kane being jerked to his death. He'd died by a newfangled method of hanging but he was no deader than Cook Teets had been when they'd finished with him. It was then the idea struck Leonard. When the presses churned out an extra ten thousand copies that day, the headline he'd put atop his story read:

**JERKED TO JESUS**
**Thomas Kane Hanged This Morning**
**The Doomed Man Meets His Fate in New Device**

Leonard headed directly to the Queen's Hotel after the paper came out. He'd seen two hangings now. He realized that what had happened to Cook Teets hadn't been all that unusual. Should he be upset about what was after all a common occurrence? Leonard decided that death sentences and hangings were something he could do nothing about. Society was determined to wreak vengeance on its transgressors. Still, nothing could justifty the hanging of an innocent man.

A few days after the execution of Thomas Kane, Leonard received a reply to his letter to Richard Langley. A friendly note, it expressed the hope that Leonard was enjoying a profitable time in Toronto. The letter complimented him on his willingness to offer himself in service to the electors of Grey County. "However, any such plans must be deferred for the present. The government has decided that James Masson, the man who had defended Cook Teets, will be the party's candidate in Grey North in 1877." So that's it, Leonard thought. I was just a loose fish to lure in a bigger catch. He finished reading the letter. "It is possible other opportunities might arise," it told him, in which case Leonard would be contacted. The chief clerk had signed off, "Your most obedient servant."

Leonard tucked the letter into a book he was reading. He was not entirely surprised. It had been far-fetched to think the Liberal-Conservative party would want him as a candidate. The whole business of getting into politics depressed him. He fretted about how he would explain this latest misadventure back in Vandeleur. That led to his wondering how practical it was to think he could ever find Rosannah's killer. Before turning down the lamp on his night table, he wrote two letters. The first was to James Henderson, Vandeleur's storekeeper, postmaster, and all-round paramount citizen. He asked him to try to find a new tenant for the *Chronicle*'s weathered little edifice, and to forward any mail. The second letter went to Sam Bowles, the neighbour who was looking after Vandeleur Hall and the Babington farm. Leonard said he had decided to stay in Toronto and would not be returning for some time. "Plant the crops you believe will do the best, and keep an eye on the house," he wrote. "I have the utmost confidence that your prudent management will yield the most positive results." Leonard wasn't sure whether Sam could read but he knew that if he could not, he would have one of his children read the letter to him. He could see it clearly now – he would never forget Rosannah, but for now, he would stay on with the *Evening Telegram*.

# Chapter 28

## A GIRL OF THE ORANGE ORDER

### July 17, 1887

Aday for Leonard Babington at the *Evening Telegram* began with visits to the city's three police stations. He got to know the constables who had the responsibility of logging the names and offences of citizens who had run afoul of the law. He tracked down detectives such as Amos Dewart, also known as "the Wart" for the ever-present growth on his neck, and asked questions about their cases. Collecting the names and details of offenders arrested overnight, Leonard was amazed at the myriad of charges that brought wayward Torontonians into the hands of the police. Most offences were petty – small-scale burglaries, assaults, drunkenness, or cases of homeless men and women picked up on vagrancy charges. Brothels were raided regularly, with predictable results: small fines to the madams and orders to the girls to get out of town. Street whores were treated more harshly, receiving sentences of sixty to ninety days in the Mercer Reformatory for Women. Even that failed to satisfy the city's crusading mayor, William Howland. He wanted his city to be known as "Toronto the Good." In pursuit of that goal, he set up a special morals squad with instructions to root out gambling and drug dens, and to stop the "desecration" of the Sabbath.

The *Evening Telegram* duly recorded the mayor's orders that Toronto's streets be carefully patrolled on Sundays; the day was not to be marred by games or other levity. The mayor pushed to have bars in the city shut down, or failing that, to force them to close at nine o'clock. Leonard wrote that this would "get the working man home at a reasonable hour, and make sure of his fitness for work the next day." In two years, Leonard reported only two killings, a trifling number for a city of almost two hundred thousand.

One day, Owen Staples came to Leonard with exciting news. "Mr. Robertson has given me a leave of absence. I got his letter from London this morning. At last, I can go down to Philadelphia to study. You know it's what I've wanted." Drawing Toronto streetscapes and sketching the interiors of city churches for the *Evening Telegram* was one thing. But Owen had spoken often of his need for formal training if he was ever to become a serious painter.

The Toronto Art Students' League kept clubrooms above the Imperial Bank and whenever Owen could afford it, he invited Leonard there for a noonday meal. "I come here because I meet older, more experienced artists," Owen said. "That's how I came to get the idea of going down to Philadelphia," he added. On their first visit, Owen pointed out the famous J.W. Bengough, the political cartoonist for the *Grip* paper, who was dining at a nearby table. "He gave me good advice," Owen said. "Told me that if I wanted to amount to anything as a painter, I'd have to give up cartooning. Rubbish drawing, he called it."

When Owen got his ticket-of-leave from Mr. Robertson, Leonard decided to make an occasion of his departure. He joined the Art Students' League expressly to give Owen a going-away dinner. They met at Owen's boarding house and together walked down to Gerrard Street. Leonard had not told Owen the true purpose of the evening. When they entered the clubrooms, a dozen young men began singing "For he's a jolly good fellow." To Owen's delight and embarrassment, they one after another gave short, satirical talks about their guest of honour. Especially telling were the stories told of Owen's school days. No one could top the tale told by Owen's schoolmate Roger Easton. "Why, I'll never forget how you jumped out the window to escape a birching from old Tompkins! Didn't do you much good, he gave you twice as many as usual the next day." The stories were accompanied by much drinking of ale and whisky and toasts were proffered all around.

The next morning, nursing a headache, Leonard escorted Owen and another art student to Union Station. He envied the two young men. Up till now he hadn't given much thought to how Owen's absence would affect his life. He'd often felt alone but as he stood with Owen on the station platform, he knew the loneliness that would move into him would be as sharp, almost, as when he had lost Rosannah. He was going to be lonely, damn lonely. Leonard tacked several of Owen's sketches to his bedroom wall and wondered how he would fill his days during the two years he would be away.

Owen's departure was painful to Leonard Babington in many ways. He had become accustomed to the good fellowship and camaraderie that his young friend's presence had always brought him. But more than that, Leonard realized he was now almost forty years old and still a bachelor. He had not solved the murder of Rosannah Leppard. He preferred to turn his mind to the advice Owen had given him on the subject of marriage: "Get a wife. Live a full life. That's what I intend to do when I get back."

Leonard had seen Kaitlin Tisdall a few times and had even had tea with her and Dr. Barrett at the Toronto Medical School. But he hadn't pressed his chances and he'd recently heard she had married a doctor who had a flourishing practice in Hamilton. He was tiring of the life of a bachelor and realized he'd have to become a serious suitor if he was to find a wife.

Leonard didn't belong to a church nor did he wish to become a regular churchgoer. His job as a crime reporter put him in contact with many people, but most were only slightly respectable at best, and few had sisters or daughters. You couldn't find a wife by taking supper in some dining room or attending a recital – respectable girls didn't go out alone, and if they did they took care to ignore uninvited overtures. Occasionally, he visited one of the houses on York Street that he'd written about for the *Globe*. He'd never find a wife that way, he realized. Leonard decided to wangle introductions through men at the *Telegram* who had the social connections he lacked. He went first to his editor, John Robinson. He was known at the paper as "Black Jack" and was considered a good fellow, if strict in his ways.

"This is something that I'll have to think about," Robinson told Leonard. "You're asking me to put you in a position of trust by introducing you about. I'll have to talk it over with the Misssus."

The next day, Robinson called Leonard to his office.

"There are a few families I know with marriageable daughters," he said. "I could probably fix you up an introduction to Mr. Hughes and his wife. You know, he's the Superintendent of Roads. Lives over on Beverley Street. Their Rebecca is a bright girl. He's grand master of the Orange Order for Ontario West. Get into their circle and you'll meet lots of fine people."

Leonard had not paid much attention to the Orange Order back in Vandeleur. He knew it mostly for the parades it put on every 12th of July, celebrating King William of Orange and his victory over the Catholic, James II, at the Battle of the Boyne River. That saved Ireland for the Crown and made it a certainty that Catholics would never get the upper hand on British soil. He remembered as a boy watching parades led by a man who played the role of King Billy. He rode a great white horse, just as the king was said to have done. Since coming to Toronto, he'd acquired a better appreciation for the power and influence of the Orange Order. If you were Protestant and you wanted to succeed in politics or business, Irish or not you had better belong. The news he'd had from Richard Langley made it unlikely Leonard would go into politics, so he hadn't given any thought to falling in with the pack.

On a pleasant Sunday afternoon, "Black Jack" and his wife Martha escorted Leonard to the Hughes residence. The house was large, with steeply pitched rooflines, a profusion of gables, and a three-storey square tower capped by a widow's walk. The house was painted white and was surrounded by a generous lawn. The three visitors made their way to the garden where a harpist played classical tunes. Couples strolled about munching on sandwiches while drinking ginger ale and lemonade. About twenty people were in the garden.

Robinson headed directly to the hosts. "Ah, good afternoon, Mr. and Mrs. Hughes, and Rebecca. Your garden looks dazzling, as always. As does Mrs. Hughes and Rebecca. May I present Mr. Leonard Babington, one of our key men at the *Evening Telegram*."

Leonard noted that Emmett Hughes bore his substantial girth and mutton chop whiskers with a dignified air, acquired no doubt from his years of leadership in civic government and the Orange Order. Mrs. Hughes, a stout but dainty woman, fluttered her fan and pronounced herself delighted to meet Leonard. It was Rebecca's presence that made the visit memorable. Leonard was struck immediately with her beauty – the graceful lines of her chin and nose, her clear eyes, and her long dark hair that fell in curls to her shoulders.

"A man of the press," Emmett Hughes commented, "must be a man well read. What books have you been into recently, Mr. Babington?"

Leonard hesitated. Truth to tell, he'd been too busy for much book reading beyond the few cheap novels he'd borrowed from the rental library. No need to mention those.

"I've been taken with a work of catastrophe," Leonard confessed. "The new Zola book, *The Flood*. His depiction of the terrible inundation from the Garonne River is positively shattering. A small book, but nonetheless one hard to forget."

Rebecca caught her breath. "Did you read it in French, Mr. Babington?" She said French had been her favourite subject before enrolling in the Normal School in St. James Square. She'd received her teaching certificate only a month before.

"If only I could," Leonard answered with a sigh. "I'd need to spend at least a year in Quebec if I were to take on that challenge."

The mention of Quebec brought a grimace to Emmett Hughes's face. He was none too disposed to his daughter having learned a language spoken almost exclusively by Catholics.

"It's English for me, Mr. Babington. The Queen's English, if I may say so. Not the shoddy English those Irish Catholics speak, nor the foreign tongue of Catholic France."

"Oh, I've never had any problem with Catholics," Leonard said. The words had tumbled out before he'd stopped to think that an influential member of the Orange Order might have had a different experience.

Emmett Hughes forced a smile to his face.

"You'll have to excuse us, we must see to the needs of our other guests."

Once out of earshot, Rebecca turned to her father.

"You were rude to Mr. Babington, father. I should like you to invite him to supper."

Emmett Hughes had long ago come to the realization that he could never say no to his daughter. Before the afternoon was out, Leonard had his invitation to supper Friday night next, a summons he accepted graciously.

Assisted by Mrs. Coles, Leonard dressed with care for the engagement. He'd polished his boots and his landlady had pressed his blue wool suit. He arrived at the Hughes residence at a quarter past five and when he raised the brass knocker on the front door a footman bid him enter. Emmett Hughes greeted him warmly. He seemed ready to overlook Leonard's thoughtless comment of last Sunday. Rebecca inquired after his health. Mrs. Hughes, once the formalities of Leonard's arrival had been completed, excused herself from the parlour, confessing the need to check on the serving staff.

At supper, Leonard sat opposite Rebecca, allowing him ample opportunity to study her face as well as her chest and shoulders. He could not keep his eyes from her. Several courses were served – quail, roast beef and salmon – each accompanied by a different wine. Leonard wondered how Emmett Hughes could maintain such an extravagant table on the salary of a civic office holder. The man must have private wealth, he told himself. Or perhaps he was the recipient of favours.

The conversation turned to politics once an appetizer of pigeon hearts had been disposed of.

"Toronto's an English city and must remain one." Emmett Hughes declared. "We've been inundated by Irish Catholics these past twenty years. Those Irish fill the hovels of Corktown and Cabbagetown. They'll get no road improvements, I can assure you. City money's best spent elsewhere."

"Yes, we must be prudent with Crown revenues," Mrs. Hughes sniffed. Rebecca looked uncertain as to whether she should be part of this conversation. After a moment, she turned to her father.

"I hope you'll use your influence," she told him, "to do something about that horrid Dr. MacMurchy at Jarvis Collegiate. He absolutely refuses to engage female teachers. I think he's been there too long."

"He'll go in his own good time. A great disciplinarian. Runs what must be the best school in Toronto."

Leonard thought it would be wise to inquire into the affairs of the Orange Order. He commented that this year's parade had gone off smoothly. There'd been few hecklers compared with past years, when the Greens, the tag taken by Catholic protestors, had created a fuss over the parade's passing through Catholic neighbourhoods.

"We've never been so strong or enjoyed such influence," Hughes replied. "All but one of the council men are of the Order. We've never had more staunch an Orangeman than Mayor Howland. Three of the four Toronto men in Parliament wear the sash. Doesn't matter, Conservative or Reform."

"Then you see prospects for harmony in the city, Mr. Hughes?"

"Harmony? Who said anything about harmony? It's quiet that we want." He paused to swallow a morsel of trout. "Quiet from those Corktown Irish. We see Irish beggars everywhere, as ignorant and vicious as they are poor.

Lazy, improvident, and unappreciative of all we do for them. They fill up our poorhouses and our prisons. What money the Irish have they give to their priests, spouting an alien religion. Or spend it on booze. Bent on violence, like those Fenians that tried to invade Canada."[*]

Leonard was well aware of the fundamental differences that divided Protestants and Catholics. It had all come out at the Cook Teets trial. But he was unprepared for the venom issuing from the mouth of this man. He thought of Rosannah Leppard's family, half Irish and at their mother's behest, Catholic, and what Emmett Hughes would have had to say about them. Rosannah and her like would have been kept in their proper place.

"Don't you think education's the answer, Mr. Hughes? I taught school for a time and thought it a worthwhile vocation. Perhaps Rebecca would like to teach the Irish children. Despite the law requiring it, many receive no schooling whatever."

Leonard qjuickly realized his words were, to put it mildly, not well received.

"No daughter of mine will waste her talents on Catholic children," he declared.

Leonard had to respond, to say something to amplify what he'd already told his host.

"Yet Rebecca is hurt by the fact Dr. MacMurchy will not engage female teachers. Are not Irish children equally hurt if we decline to engage them in a proper education? We all know most of the Irish live in poverty – it's as if we put up a fence and told them they could never cross over to a better life."

Leonard realized he was challenging the Superintendent of Roads. He couldn't help himself. Everything he'd seen and learned in Vandeleur convinced him the Irish were no better or worse than English and Scottish riff raff he'd encountered. He often regretted having been schooled at home where he had little opportunity to mix with others. Now, he realized, that solitary upbringing had spared him from the worst prejudices of his community. Leonard suspected Rebecca held a kinder view of the world than her father, but he knew that if he were to court her he would have to accept her family's

---

[*] In 1866, a contingent of an Irish Republican Brotherhood crossed the Niagara River with the intention of seizing Canada as a base to attack Britain's control of Ireland. The invaders were beaten back and the U.S. cracked down on the movement.

intolerance and prejudice.

Emmett Hughes pushed his plate away and laughed. "I'm glad to see you have a sense of humour, Mr. Babington."

The supper went on with no further disagreement, much to Leonard's relief. He wondered how a Christian who believed in the Kingdom of God – where the Gospels say there are neither Jews nor Gentiles – could hold such enmity against other human beings. There was a lot of judging and weighing going on here on earth, but how would these same people be judged and weighed when they were called to the final accounting? He didn't know much about the Jews. There were none in Vandeleur and he'd seen only a few on the street in Toronto. Old men, mostly, with long beards, sometimes pushing carts of workmen's clothing. They'd stand outside factories and try to sell to workers as they came off shift. People spoke of the Jews gathering up the riches of the world, but that seemed to him an unlikely possibility.

When Leonard bid the Hughes's good evening a little after nine o'clock, he had the sense that Rebecca had been embarrassed by the mealtime conversation. Still, he thought later, he could never be comfortable in their house. He did not expect to dine there again.

On the way home, Leonard thought he saw a familiar face in the shadows of the elm trees that grew on Church Street. With a start, he realized it was Angus McIntosh. "What do you think you're on to?" Leonard demanded. As he spoke, McIntosh rushed at him and shoved him to the ground. Leonard scrambled to his feet and struck McIntosh in the face. The blow sent McIntosh reeling backward. He turned and ran into the dark. Leonard debated whether he should go to the police station and report the incident, but decided against it. The next morning, when Leonard confronted McIntosh at work, he denied the encounter. Leonard noticed a bruise on his face, but said nothing more. Unaccountably, several strange incidents occurred over the next few days. Leonard's name was forged to a note supporting American annexation of Canada. A dead rat was found in his drawer at the reporter's table. He made up his mind to ignore such occurrences.

The 1887 general election put the *Evening Telegram* in a great struggle against its Liberal rival, the *Globe*, for the loyalty of Toronto voters. Leonard was sent to cover several rallies for Conservative candidates, with orders to "always put our man in a good light." All three Toronto seats returned

Conservatives – as did Grey North, which elected James Masson. Leonard wondered how his life might have changed if he had been given the chance to carry the Conservative flag in the Beaver Valley.

Leonard had put such things as elections out of his mind by the time he remembered that an important anniversary was almost upon him. The last day of October, 1888, would mark five years from the day that Rosannah had died. He felt guilty that he had almost forgotten this. He'd been back to Vandeleur a few times on short visits. But almost everything that had happened there had been pushed to the back of his mind by his new life. It had been ages since he had written anything for *Rosannah's Story*. He was relieved when he found he could still bring Rosannah's face to mind. He wished he had her picture, but no one he knew in Vandeleur had a camera. He thought on this for a while and then took a sheaf of paper from a drawer and began to write:

Five years and what have I accomplished? Five years after Rosannah's death and I am no closer to finding out the truth. My work at the *Evening Telegram* has distracted me from pursuing the matter of who killed Rosannah and why. Yet, my memory of her has in no wise faded. She remains in my mind the delightful, puzzling, exciting and beautiful girl that I knew in Vandeleur. A girl of dark, wavy hair and amber eyes. Even stronger in my mind than the image of her face is my recollection of her scent. Sometimes she smelled of fresh-cut clover, and other times after we'd been together in the woods, of pine boughs and resin.

Most of all, I remember the tangy odour of her sweat. That was the smell I loved. In the city, ladies try to hide this with soap and perfume. I don't know why. I would not want a girl who did not carry with her the smell of womanhood. Perhaps this is because I love the essence of the country. The fragrance of wild flowers in the meadow. The mustiness of the barn, a mix of cattle odour, dung and hay. Of newly turned soil, ready for the seed. The breath of a fresh breeze through the trees. All these things are absent in the city.

I do not think the doctors who attended Rosannah helped her any. Opium and alcohol, the main ingredients of modern women's medicines, hardly make a healthy mix. Add to that tobacco and you have a dastardly combination. If a person is sad some days and happy another, then it seems logical that one must try to multiply the circumstances that prevail on their days of contentment, and minimize the conditions that induce days of bleakness and pity. I regret I did not have the wisdom and experience, during the time I knew Rosannah, to help her find solutions to the problems that confounded her.

At the trial, we learned from Bridget Leppard that Rosannah had been interfered with as a child. How innocent she must have been when that depraved man satisfied his lust at her expense! And a priest, of all things. Had her father ever learned of this, I am sure he would have killed him. I never heard James Leppard speak against the Church, although it is well known he has become a staunch Orangeman after having quitted Rome. He had only become a Catholic in order to marry Rosannah's mother. One wonders what events might have transpired to lead him to break off from the Church.

While Owen Staples was in Philadelphia, Leonard filled his time by seeking out new pursuits. He bought one of the new bicycles with air-filled tires that made it easier to ride over the city's rough streets. He spent more time with other boarders at Mrs. Coles's and tagged along on excursions to nearby beauty spots – one time to Niagara Falls and another to Lake Simcoe. On summer days he cycled out to Victoria Park and swam beneath the Scarborough Bluffs. He kept his visits to Vandeleur to a minimum as he was receiving regular reports on the farm and house from Sam Bowles's granddaughter. A small but satisfactory sum was deposited in his bank account every fall, representing his share of proceeds from oats and barley crops.

Owen and Leonard had promised to write each other often. In one letter Owen described the "most valued lesson" he had learned from his instructors. "It's to know and understand anatomy, that's the basis of true art. We are forever sketching models, or modelling for each other. They make us paint direct from the model to the canvas. We're not to sketch an outline or make a drawing of the subject first. Now I have learned to go straight to the picture without those time-wasting and distracting preliminaries."

Owen returned to Toronto in possession of a diploma from the Academy of Fine Art and a portfolio of work that gained him much praise in the city's art circles. A picture Owen called "In Captivity" depicted a tiger prowling in its cage during a snowstorm at the Philadelphia Zoo. "I'd gone out there one winter morning and before I knew it, a blizzard struck," he told Leonard. "The keepers thought I was crazy when I set up my easel. But I think it's my best work." At Leonard's urging, Owen submitted the painting to the annual exhibition of the Royal Canadian Academy. When it was accepted, "In Captivity" became the first Owen Staples work to be publicly shown in Canada.

By now, Leonard was the only one of the old gang still at Mrs. Coles's boardinghouse. He expected Owen would join him there and he was surprised that on his return to Toronto Owen took a room with the Coopers on Henry Street.

"Isn't the old place good enough for you?" Leonard asked.

It took a fair bit of digging and jabbing before he found out the reason for Owen's move. He had met a girl at a church event. Her name was Lillian Hewitt and she was musically accomplished. When Owen discovered that Lillian's aunt, Mrs. Cooper, had rooms to let, he arranged to stay there. Lillian visited often to play her aunt's spinet. Soon, Owen was taking singing lessons from her. Within a few months they were engaged to be married.

It was so simple for Owen, Leonard thought, but so difficult for him.

# Chapter 29

## RETURN TO VANDELEUR

### September 20, 1889

The Grange was a gracious place, the most famous of all the fine residences in Toronto. Leonard Babington's first sight of it came one Sunday when he managed to extract Owen Staples from Lillian Hewitt's embrace long enough to have an afternoon walk together. The Grange stood like a fortress on high ground on McCaul Street, surrounded by terraced gardens. "It's like a Georgian manor house," Owen told Leonard. "Made of bricks, but you can hardly see them under all those vines. Belonged to Mayor Boulton until he died, then his wife up and married Goldwin Smith. They still live there."

In Leonard's view, Goldwin Smith, a writer of often contentious opinions, was one of the great intellectual and political minds of the nineteenth century. He'd read about Smith's work with the Canada First movement and he agreed wholeheartedly with the idea of being for Canada as long as you were for the Imperial connection as well. He'd heard Smith had put money into the *Evening Telegram* but pulled out over John Ross Robertson's insistence on backing the Conservative party.

"A fine house for a great man," Leonard said.

"I guess, but how is it that some people come off with so much, while the rest of us have to scratch and scrounge for crumbs?" Owen asked. "Especially folks like your friends the Leppards and the Teets's up in Grey County."

"I've often wondered that myself," Leonard said. "Some do it by hard work, others by conniving and stealing, and some people just get it handed to them." He winced as he said that, realizing he'd been favoured with the legacy of Vandeleur Hall. Recovering, he added: "Rosannah Leppard wouldn't have dreamt such a place as The Grange could exist." Just the saying of her name brought a catch to Leonard's throat. Rosannah could have been nothing but a scullery maid in the mansion they strood before. Leonard had a troubling dream that night. Rosannah appeared before him, reminding him he hadn't yet found out who was responsible for her death. He awoke with a start, and it took him a long time to get back to sleep.

Leonard thought no more of Goldwin Smith or his great house until one day when John Ross Robertson brought up Smith's name. Leonard was in the publisher's office taking notes for a speech Robertson would be making to the opening of the Industrial Exhibition. He wanted to talk about Toronto's reputation for law and order. Leonard's knowledge of the courts and the pro-clivity of the denizens of The Ward to flout the law made him just the man, Robertson told Leonard, to help him with his speech.

"That man's the greatest thinker of our time," Robertson said of Goldwin Smith, "but I disagree with his every thought. Would you like to meet him?"

The occasion was the publication of Smith's new book, *Canada and the Canadian Question*. He was holding the celebration in the library that Harri-ette had built for him at The Grange. With Mr. Robertson guiding the way, Leonard found himself among thirty men who were crowded into the room to hear Smith talk of his latest project. Leonard thought it a jocular crowd, good-natured from the flow of fine liquor and eager to hear the latest quips that might fall from the lips of this notoriously free wheeling observer. Af-ter a half hour's reading from his book, Smith retired to a sideboard cabinet where a waiter was serving whisky and gin. Smith was a handsome man, clean-shaven, and on this occasion he wore an ascot necktie that added a splash of colour to a white shirt, a dark vest, and a brown coat. Leonard edged to the front long enough to introduce himself and pose a question: What is the greatest problem facing Canada?

"What is wanting in this country is unity," Smith answered. "Quebec's a theocracy, like an antediluvian animal preserved in ice. Ontario is a world unto itself. If the North West ever fills up, Old Canada will be dwarfed and the centre of power will shift westward. The disappearance of your Indians, of course, will be of little loss to humanity. I explain all this in my book."

Leonard had hastily scanned a few pages back at the office. He was left with the impression that Smith was writing off Canada, suggesting its destiny lay in union with the United States.

"Do you really believe our future is to be an American state?" Leonard asked. "I know some think it a grand idea but it hardly seems practical to me."

Smith swirled the gin in his glass before answering. "The idea of a United Continent of North America is both grand and practical," he said. "It would secure free trade and intercourse over a vast area, with external safety and internal peace."

"But what of our manufactures? The National Policy?"

"Babington, remember this: the great industry of Ontario is farming, despite the efforts of protectionists to make it a manufacturing country. Let's concentrate on what we do best – grow food."

Leonard had one more question.

"Growing food, that's right, we're good at that. But many of our farmers are in abject poverty. Where I come from, Grey County, some folks, the Irish especially, are hard up. What can be done to help them?" As he asked the question, a vision of Rosannah scrubbing clothes in the Leppard shack filled his mind.

"Ah, the Irish," Goldwin Smith answered. "Amiable but thriftless, a saint-worshipping, priest-ridden race."

Leonard saw he wouldn't get much sympathy from this man for the struggles of a few no-account Irish hidden away in the Queen's Bush. Other men were coming forward to demand the attention of the great thinker. Leonard heard more of Smith's ideas as he fended off questions from his guests. For all his dismay at Goldwin Smith's slurs toward the Irish and the Indians, Leonard thought his other insights dazzling. Through the chatter of the guests, he picked up bits and pieces of his remarks: "The sapling of Canadian literature cannot grow beneath the shadow of the parent tree … The merit of Ontario landscape painters will someday be recognized in England … Farm cookery is vile – fried pork, bread ill-baked, heavy pies coarse and strong, that account for the advertisements of pills which everywhere meet the eye."

It was bewildering. What Leonard heard impressed him but gave him no new insight into what still remained the unfulfilled mission of his life – solving the mystery of Rosannah Leppard's death. Nor did it prepare him for the news he received when he got home. A note had arrived from Owen Staples.

Angus McIntosh had jumped from the Queen Street bridge into the Don River. He'd left a letter accusing Leonard of hounding him to his death.

Astonishing news. Trembling, Leonard dropped Owen's letter to the floor. Blamed again for something not his fault – was this to be his fate? Angry now, he picked up the note and ripped it to shreds.

Leonard felt his stomach tighten and his head throb when he walked into the editorial department at the *Telegram* the morning after the suicide. He had shivered in bed during the night and his heart had raced at an alarming rate. He awoke determined not to take the blame for the old reporter's tragic end. People weren't always rational when they wrote suicide notes, he told himself. McIntosh had been on the edge for a long time and nothing Leonard had done could have pushed him over.

"Are we printing the suicide note?" Leonard asked the men around the reporter's table. He let the question hang in the air.

Tom White, who was searching through a pile of newspapers for stories missed by the *Evening Telegram*, finally answered. "Mr. Robinson says to make no mention of it. Nothing about how McIntosh has been dispirited and gloomy. Just a paragraph that the poor sod fell into the river. All a misadventure."

Hearing this, Leonard's heart slowed its pace. He went to Black Jack Robinson's office where he found him scrawling an editorial on a piece of brown wrapping paper that he'd found lying on his desk.

"Ah, Babington, let me read you a line of what I've written about Goldwin Smith's book. Listen to this:"

> Professor Goldwin Smith's book is distinctively a great effort. It will charm all by the power of its style without, let us hope, enforcing acceptance of its conclusions. For the hopes of Young Canada outrun his beliefs. Its heart craves a destiny nobler than that which he assigns to this Dominion.

"A backhanded compliment, I'd say," Leonard answered. "And one I'd agree with. But I want to talk to you about McIntosh. I'll not let him reach back from the grave and blame me for his death."

Black Jack Robinson was used to dealing with the frequent disputes between men at the *Evening Telegram*. A hotheaded, conceited bunch, he often called them. Always trying to impose their wills on those around them. Leonard had been different, he had to admit.

"I spoke to Mr. Robertson this morning. You'll have to see what he thinks. He's at church meetings today and he'll be out of town for a week or so, down to New York. Just carry on until he gets back. Who knows what he's thinking? A man of very strict morals, you know."

Black Jack's remarks left Leonard with a hollow feeling in his chest. He tried to put McIntosh out of his mind and carry on as if nothing had happened. If the *Evening Telegram* thought he bore a shred of guilt over McIntosh, he'd have it out with the proprietor. He wasn't going to live again through what happened at the *Globe*. He avoided his usual beer sessions at the Queen's Hotel and went straight to Mrs. Coles's boardng house every night. Owen Staples did his best to help Leonard keep up his spirits. "Everybody knows you did McIntosh no harm," he told him over and over. A week went by.

Leonard had just returned from his police rounds when he found a note telling him to go to Mr. Robertson's office. He saw the proprietor at his desk. He knocked on the glass door and went in.

"This McIntosh business," Robertson began. "How do you feel about it?"

"I feel damn put upon," Leonard answered. He was growing agitated. "Everybody's been going around as if nothing had happened. I'd like to get it cleared up. I hardly ever spoke to the man."

"We know you had nothing to do with what happened to McIntosh," the proprietor told Leonard. "He'd been acting crazy for months. But I was worried how you'd react. Thought it best to just let things play out, see how you handled the situation."

"You've been testing me," Leonard challenged John Ross Robertson.

"In a manner of speaking."

"But why?"

"To satisfy myself you're fit for a higher position."

"What higher position?"

"In the service of the people — as a Member of Parliament."

"I had that idea once, but I've given up on it,' Leonard said.

"I know all about that. Richard Langley is an old friend of mine. Speaks very highly of you. Too bad they couldn't use you in '87, but their loss has been the *Telegram*'s gain. Now, we've got to get ready for an election in 1891.

It could be difficult, the Liberals have that young Frenchie, Wilfrid Laurier. He'll have Quebec behind him. I'm tempted to run myself, but I've got my hands full here at the paper."

Leonard felt a flicker of excitement. He'd never gotten over having his hopes raised, and then dashed, that time he went to Ottawa. If he could get into the governent, he might be able to force a re-examination of Rosannah's murder and Cook's trial. "What did you have in mind?" he asked.

"Richard Langley is scouting out Liberal seats he thinks we could pick off. Grey South, that's near where you're from, has a Liberal member. Some doctor by the name of George Landerkin. From some little town, Hanover. Langley will be in Toronto tomorrow. He'd like you to go with him up to Grey County to get a feel for things on the ground. That's if you're interested. I told him it would be all right with me."

A return to politics was the last thing Leonard had expected. Richard Langley hadn't forgotten him, after all. And the publisher was willing to free him from his work. Of course, he'd have to move back to Vandeleur Hall. He could see himself traipsing around the County, appealing for votes. With Langley's backing, he'd no doubt have the support of influential Conservatives like Dr. Sproule and James Masson. And out of it all, he'd work for a better justice system that would put an end to the hanging of victims such as Cook Teets. Leonard was no lawyer, but for that very reason he could speak for the common man, let the powers in Ottawa know what the people wanted.

Leonard told the publisher he would be very glad to accompany Langley to Grey County. If the party felt he would be a suitable candidate, and with Mr. Robertson's backing, he would take it on.

The arrival of Richard Langley at the *Telegram* was celebrated in Mr. Robertson's office with sandwiches and tea. Leonard and the chief clerk were soon in deep discussion of the details of their coming foray. It seemed as if the past five years had vanished – everything that was happening fit into the picture Leonard had built in his mind when it had first been suggested that he get into politics. That night, Mr. Robertson hosted a dinner party attended by some of the leading men in the party. Only a few had brought their wives. There was much optimistic talk about the next election, in which it was assumed Leonard would play an important part.

"I hope you didn't think I was putting you off when I wrote that letter," Langley told Leonard. "I promised we'd look for another opportunity. We've just had to wait for the right moment."

Two days later, after the chief clerk's meetings with key party men in the three Toronto ridings, the two took the train north. They got off at Flesherton Station and went straight to Munshaw's Hotel where they rented rooms. Leonard had decided not to go to Vandeleur Hall, or to say anything more to Langley about Rosannah's murder. There'd be time for that later. Tomorrow, they would visit the Vandeleur Fall Fair. It would be a good chance for Leonard to meet people he hadn't seen in years. He would let it be known he might stand for election in 1891.

At the hotel, Aaron Munshaw gave Leonard a loud welcome and set the two up in the best corner rooms in the house. "It's not every day that one of our finest comes home," he said on hearing that Leonard might be taking up residence again at Vandeleur Hall. He insisted on providing scotch and ale on the house at supper, and passed in and out of the dining room every few minutes to check on the progress of their meal. The next morning, groggy and not a little hung over, Leonard and Langley got up in time to make their way to the Orange Hall where a crowd had gathered to watch the parade that would launch the Fall Fair. Assorted farmers drove their prize cattle down the Beaver Valley Road. Then came the marchers, a ragtag bunch of Orangemen supported by a few veterans of General Middleton's Royal Canadian Dragoons, the men who had put down the Riel Rebellion. The march past brought lusty cheers at the reviewing stand where a special guest took the salute. He was Colonel Patrick Galloway, Adjutant-General of the Canadian Miltia. He had been lured to Vandeleur by promise of a wild turkey hunt.

"Damn, it's dusty here," Leonard heard Colonel Galloway complain. The marchers had stirred up clouds of dust and Colonel Galloway beat at his pants with his riding crop in a vain attempt to keep his uniform clean.

Tents and booths had been erected in a field across the road from the Orange Hall. Farmwives offered their best craft work and baked goods while children pranced around the pony rides. Leonard and Langley wandered among the exhibits. Leonard waved to old acquaintances and stopped to chat with past neighbours. Scarth Tackaberry was there with his wife and children. When he saw Leonard, he backed off and pushed the children toward the pony rides. He wouldn't want to chance Rosannah's name being raised in front of his wife, Leonard thought. Amanda Brodie motioned Leonard aside, eager to engage him in a private conversation. He was relieved when they were distracted by a sudden commotion in front of a nearby tent.

"Gad, what a beastly little animal." It was Richard Langley, holding his arm against his chest, blood on his sleeve. He had wandered off while Leonard had been talking to Amanda. "He's bitten me, anybody got a tourniquet?" Young Tom Couey was pulling on the leash that restrained his pet fox, Red, from a second attack. "Get Dr. Sproule," Leonard shouted. "And in the meantime get that fox out of here. He could be rabid, drooling the way he is." A cry went up for the doctor, who was judging cattle in a field a hundred yards away. Fifteen minutes passed before Dr. Sproule arrived, collected his medical bag from the booth behind him, and bandaged Langley's arm.

"A most unfortunate incident," Dr. Sproule told Leonard. "I didn't expect this kind of welcome for our guest. Glad to hear you're considering jumping in, by the way. With Langley behind you, the party men in Grey County shouldn't be hard to convince." Encouraged as he was by these words, Leonard worried about the fox bite. There was to be a dinner that night in the community hall. Richard Langley was to introduce him as an up and coming journalist who was giving up his trade and returning home to serve the party. Leonard had prepared some remarks.

"We'll get you back to the hotel and let you rest up for tonight," Leonard said. "A few hours in bed and you'll be shipshape again."

When Leonard went to rouse Langley at five o'clock, he found a man who was confused about where he was and what he was doing. He drank two glasses of water and fell back on his pillow. It was obvious he was in no condition to attend the dinner. Leonard went downstairs, asked Aaron Munshaw to look in on his guest throughout the evening, and got into a buggy for the drive to Vandeleur.

Leonard's arrival alone at the dinner caused consternation among the party men who had come expecting to meet an important official from Ottawa, in Vandeleur on behalf of Sir John A. Macdonald. They had been told it was time to hatch plans for the next election.

"Oh, it's just you, Leonard, where's that Langley fellow?" asked Emmett Cartwright. He had managed Dr. Sproule's campaigns in Grey East and had looked forward to expanding his fiefdom to the adjoining riding of Grey South. Other men chatted among themselves while sipping whisky or beer. When dinner was announced, Dr. Sproule took the seat at the end of the table. He said grace, proposed a toast to Queen Victoria, and expressed regrets at the absence of Richard Langley. Leonard was growing more nervous by the moment. Without Langley present to endorse him, he wondered how he would convince these men he could carry the party flag against a well-regarded Liberal incumbent.

Small talk dwindled after a serving of coffee and apple pie and Dr. Sproule tapped a knife against his cup to gain the attention of the dozen men in the room.

"Gentlemen, we expected to meet a distinguished official of Sir John A's government here tonight. I am truly sorry that a most unfortunate accident has deterred our guest, Mr. Richard Langley. As you know, he was the subject of an unprovoked attack by a fox at the Fair this afternoon. He is resting quietly tonight, at Munshaw's Hotel."

"As if that's possible in that den of iniquity," somebody called out. The men all laughed. Dr. Sproule continued, tapping his cup again for order. "I understand it had been Mr. Langley's intention to speak on behalf of Leonard Babington, who has evinced an interest in standing on behalf of our party in Grey South." He went on to recall Leonard's presence at the Cook Teets trial, and his spirited campaign in the *Vandeleur Chronicle* ("a now defunct journal") in support of clemency for the condemned man. "I show no favour for whoever the party might wish as our standard-bearer in our neighbour riding, but I am glad to ask Leonard to say a few words in his own behalf."

For a moment, Leonard felt an intruder in his own hometown. He looked at the men around the table. Two of them, he recalled, had been advertisers in the *Chronicle*. Others he had vague memory of from his teaching days. He knew he was in unchartered waters, and he thought of his time on the lake boats when he knew he could rely on the captain to make port safely. This was different. None of the men here tonight looked especially friendly, and they were not going to hear the glowing recommendation he had counted on from Richard Langley. Still, he was determined to deliver his message of needful reform.

When he got to his feet, Leonard found he had forgotten the words he had carefully rehearsed. He had to say something, so he began with a tribute to Richard Langley. "I too am sorry Mr. Langley cannot be with us, because it is he who has encouraged me to offer myself in the cause of our party. I met Mr. Langley when I went to Ottawa to make further investigations into the death of Rosannah Leppard." Hardly had he got those words out, than Leonard realized he had made a mistake. The men here did not want to hear about Rosannah or Cook Teets. They did not wish to entertain thoughts on how the justice system could be improved. They were interested, as Langley had hinted to him more than once, in better prices for their crops, how they might secure a government contract, or have the Owen Sound harbour deepened so bigger ships could bring in more cargo, at lower cost.

Having raised the Teets trial, Leonard felt compelled to state his thoughts on the changes in criminal law that he would support as a Member of Parliament. A man must be allowed to testify on his own behalf – something that had been denied Cook Teets. Judges need to remind jurors they should acquit if the Crown has not proven the guilt of an accused beyond a reasonable doubt. As he spoke he remembered other things he had planned to talk about – the appeal to British loyalty against Liberal annexationism, the benefits of Sir John's National Policy, and the need to bring more settlers into Grey County. Murmurs of approval went around the table as he touched on these topics. He spoke of the dilemma of the village of Hanover – the hometown of the Liberal MP – split, as it was, half in Grey County and half in Bruce County. "Roads on one side are gravel, the other dirt. Our Liberal friend seems content to remain mired in the muck." Laughter. A bit of humour would help win these fellows over, Langley had told Leonard. He spoke hurriedly, wanting the ordeal to be done. He paid his respects to Dr. Sproule, and assured the men he would keep their best interests at heart in all matters concerning the party and the government. Richard Langley would be up and about in a few days, he was sure, and he looked forward to meeting privately with every man present. There was a flurry of applause when he sat down.

"I'm not sure I'm going to be able to carry it off," Leonard said later to Dr. Sproule. "You were fine, considering it was your first speech," the doctor told him. He left unsaid whether he thought Leonard had won the approval of the men at the dinner.

The next day, Richard Langley and Leonard took the train back to Toronto. Leonard understood that the chief clerk didn't feel up to going about the countryside while recovering from a fox bite. Leonard wanted to stay on, thinking he would look up Scarth Tackaberry and others who might, at long last, reveal more of what they knew about Rosannah's death. Dr. Sproule discouraged Leonard's remaining in Grey County. He told him that without Langley at his side, it would be difficult to gain the support of the party's influential men. "You're better off waiting until you can get back up here together."

# Chapter 30

## THE CITY EDITOR

### September 24, 1890

**W**hen Leonard and Richard Langley arrived at Toronto's Union Station, they found it crowded with passengers bidding farewell to their friends while others rushed to retrieve their baggage. Leonard hurried to put Langley aboard the overnight train to Ottawa. They agreed to make another effort to get his candidacy off the ground – the election was still at least a year away. Leonard felt spent, exhausted by the trip and upset at what had happened to Langley. The next morning, John Ross Robertson lifted Leonard's spirits when he welcomed him back to the *Telegram*. "Don't give up hope yet," he said. "Langley's an influential man and with him behind you, you have a good chance."

A few days after Langley's return to Ottawa, Dr. Sproule made an unannounced visit to the *Telegram*. The MP was on his way to the capital for a new session of Parliament. Dr. Sproule said he wanted to discuss how, if Leonard were the Conservative candidate, he would finance his campaign.

This was the first time Leonard had heard a mention of money. "I really haven't given that any thought," he declared.

"Perhaps it's time you did," Dr. Sproule told him. He tapped his coat pocket, indicating the location of his wallet. "We'll need a couple of thousand dollars, at least," he said. "Votes in the next election will be worth five dollars a head, or a bottle of Scotch. Depending on whether our blighters are prone to enjoy a drink."

Leonard was a little stunned. Did Dr. Sproule mean the party bought votes at election time? "We all do it," the answer came back. "I know the party has more subtle methods of encouraging supporters in Toronto, but in Grey County we're still stuck in the old ways. I'll leave it with you, think it over and let us know how you

245

can contribute to the needful."

A month passed. The eleven o'clock edition had gone to press when Tom White brought Leonard a telegraph dispatch from the paper's Ottawa correspondent.

"The capital is saddened today by the death of an official in the department of Justice, Mr. Richard Langley, brought on by the bite of a rabid fox while visiting a country fair …"

Leonard read the words on the telegraph paper. "Oh, Christ," he said as he handed the sheet back to Tom. Leonard feared his prospects of a life in politics had come crashing down again. He had little chance of gaining the Conservative nomination in Grey South without support from the top.

The envelope that arrived on Leonard's desk a few days later bore the return address of Dr. Thomas Sproule. Leonard eagerly torn it open. The note inside was written in an elegant, flowing script. The words were blunt and to the point. The Conservative committee would be putting up John Blyth, the member of the legislature for the provincial riding, for the federal seat in the 1891 election. "A good Conservative and a farmer, and in a position to raise his share of the campaign fund." Sproule's note added: "That should help us swing over the farmers who think Macdonald's National Policy has put them at the mercy of the manufacturing interests." And swing me out of politics for good, Leonard thought.

For the first time, Leonard had to admit he had desperately hoped to enter the new world that would open up to him as a politician. It was more than a desire to meet women like Janette Robertson, the paramour of Sir Leonard Tilley. He'd become tired of writing what he thought of as routine stories about the denizens of the Toronto police cells. As an MP, he'd be in a position to do something about Rosannah's murder. Leonard wondered if this latest failure was a sign there were certain things that were simply beyond him. Like Rosannah's death, and the possibility that he might never find out who had murdered her.

The noise in front of the *Evening Telegram* building began as newsboys gathered outside the pressroom to await the eleven o'clock edition. A dozen women were shouting suffragette slogans. Their signs demanded "Votes for Women in all Elections." A city council that prided itself as progressive allowed women to vote for Toronto's school trustees and councilors, but women had no say in provincial or Dominion elections. Leonard had just returned from his court beat when Black Jack Robinson accosted him. The *Telegram* editor was upset that no one was making notes of the demonstration occurring under their noses. "Leonard, see if you can find out what's going on down there."

When he got to the street, Leonard Babington was surprised to see Dr. Ann, as he affectionately remembered her, the anatomist he'd met at the Toronto School of Medicine. She was holding a banner bearing the words, "Canadian Women's Suffrage Association."

"What's this all about?" he asked. "Why are you parading here?"

Dr. Ann Stowe-Gullen smiled at Leonard's question. "You know very well, Mr. Babington. It's those dreadful editorials your paper has been printing. Have a little respect for women, please. We're just as able to understand politics as any man."

Leonard spent an hour with the women. As they walked up Bay Street, he reminded Dr. Ann of the times he'd gone to the Medical School to quiz her about Rosannah's death. Workers on their lunch breaks gathered at street corners, some hurling catcalls and others politely doffing their hats as the women went by. Leonard returned to the editorial room with enough notes to write a long article about "the newest dilemma to face Toronto men – the women's vote." He knew that John Ross Robertson detested the idea of votes for women, but Leonard enjoyed preparing the story. He thought about what he would have said if he'd been a candidate in Grey County. He secretly liked the idea, but wasn't sure he would have been brave enough to suppprt the suffragette cause.

The winter had come and gone since Leonard's visit to to Grey County with Richard Langley. After Langley's death and Dr. Sproule's disheartening letter, he'd given up on going back – neither to engage in politics nor to search for clues to who had killed Rosannah. Too many things had happened, too many obstacles had been thrown in his path.

John Ross Robertson, despite his long-standing opposition to giving women the vote, liked Leonard's suffragette article, and told him so. "Sometimes it's more satisfying to write about politics than to practice it," he said. "Have you decided if you'll try again for a nomination?"

Leonard put his hands on his hips and looked out the window. He knew that his answer had to satisfy his publisher. "No, I'm done with politics. I'm staying right here at the *Telegram*," Leonard answered. "I had a certain itch, but it's been well scratched."

"Their loss is our gain," Robertson told him. "If you're definite about that, we must go ahead with other plans."

"What other plans, Mr. Robertson? What do you have in mind?"

The publisher swerved in his chair, tossed a copy of that morning's *Globe* into a waste bin, and smiled before answering.

"Mr. Babington, it's time you took on more responsibility," he said. "I'm going to make you city editor of the *Evening Telegram*."

The declaration surprised Leonard. He felt his mouth go dry and he licked his lips. He still had a lot of doubts about himself. The job of city editor would require that he learn to manage men as well as the news. It would take a lot of organizing, and involve a good deal of politicking with the reporters. If he could pull it off, he might have a good future in newspapering, after all. But he was uncertain if he could do it.

"Are you sure you want to give me that position, sir? Are you sure I can handle it?"

"Of course you can. The way you've handled this political business has proven it. Steady and sober, you've been. Besides, the men like and respect you. You're a first-class journalist. I'll never forget that quote in your story on the Thomas Kane hanging, 'Jerked to Jesus,' greatest line we've ever published."

Leonard cringed. He'd always felt foolish for having passed on that remark by a witness to Kane's hanging. Robertson continued:

"Your crime reporting has acquainted you with the city. You know all the police, the lawyers and the judges. Now you'll get to know the bankers and businessmen, and the church ministers, to say nothing of the politicians. But you'll have to stop consorting with that riff raff you've been seen with at the Queen's Hotel. The city editor of the *Evening Telegram* has better use for his time."

The old Robertson approach, Leonard thought. All compliments in one breath, derision in the next.

That afternoon, a memo was sent around the editorial department, signed by John Ross Robertson.

Mr. Leonard Babington is appointed city editor. He has shown a great sense of duty and responsibility. His supervision will include the sporting, legal, financial, police, and municipal news. When not otherwise engaged, he will review the exchange papers for news items and give at least a column a day from that source. All religious, financial and medical weeklies will be scalped by Mr. Babington.

Mr. White will act as news editor. He will rewrite all A.P. dispatches and attend to the scalping of outside news in the Toronto morning papers. He will fill out special cables from the London office.

Mr. C.H.J. Snider will, as usual, have charge of City Hall work. Major L. Anthes will attend to church, Ministerial Alliance, Lord's Day Alliance, hotels and small conventions. Mr. Fitzgerald will be responsible for all the real estate news. Mr. David Carey has charge of all railway stations, wharves, steamers, labour unions and cemetery returns. Mr. Thomas Champion will do the East End news, the hospitals, and get all the accidents that have been brought in. Mr. Charles H. Fowler's duties will cover all financial news, Board of Trade, Customs, manufacturers associations, Harbour Commissioners, and insurance matters.

Reporters are reminded they are not to allow themselves to be pressured for free ads. Mr. Robinson is to be the sole dispenser of free theatre tickets.

Leonard Babington eased himself into the city editor's chair. He felt good about how he'd handled the Grey County episode and the suicide of Angus McIntosh. He was feeling a lot more self-confident. Reporters stopped by to shake his hand. Owen Staples found it hard to restrain his pleasure at Leonard's promotion. "Now we'll see the Old Lady get ahead right smartly," he said. That was his favourite name for the *Telegram*, the "Old Lady," sometimes expanded to "the Old Lady of Melinda Street," for the little street that ran beside the paper's office.

Since his return from Philadelphia, Owen had been drawing a cartoon every day for the front page – the only thing there besides the small ads. The day Leonard was named city editor, he chastised Owen for the way he signed the cartoons as "Rostap," a combination of Black Jack Robinson, and Staples.

"It's your cartoon, only your name should be on it," Leonard argued. Owen said Black Jack often gave him ideas, and he was reluctant to say anything to upset "the boss." The signature never changed.

Two months after becoming City Editor, Leonard found himself organizing coverage of the city's three ridings for the federal election of 1891. He felt distanced from any desire to be part of the campaign, and was content to be one of the *Telegram*'s loyal supporters of Sir John A. Macdonald. "This is your first big test," Owen told Leonard. "The *Telegram* always makes a grand fuss on election night. People will come down by the thousands to stand outside the building and watch as the returns are posted. We put placards up on the windows."

"I've a better idea," Leonard said. "I was at a magic lantern show last week and I got to thinking we could do the same thing. Flash results onto the building opposite."

Even before the polls had closed on election night, the street in front of the Evening *Telegram* was dense with a mass of people jostling for the best positions. At a quarter after eight, a sudden stream of light shot from a window of the Telegram onto a canvas that had been hung on a building across the street. As if by magic, result after result began to flash onto the cloth, each giving the latest vote count in Toronto ridings. Then came news from outside the city. The pro-Macdonald crowd, at least twenty thousand in number, roared in exultation when the most important result of all was flashed into the darkness:

## KINGSTON
## SIR JOHN A. LATEST
## MAJORITY 400

Men cheered, old men were seen to weep, and a woman screamed, "I knowed it!" The next day, Leonard's account of the government's re-election included this paragraph:

> The soul of a great people was photographed on The Telegram canvas
> last night. The magic of projection brought the people from every con-
> stituency in Canada ▯ the people from along the seashore, the people
> from the woods, the ranches, the farms, the quaint cities and towns,
> the prairies and plains, the mountains and the big islands, and made
> them shake the people of Toronto by the hand. For the people had
> spoken.

Sir John was back for another term, and nothing was said in the *Telegram* about the success of the Liberal member for Grey South, Dr. George Landerkin, re-elected by a margin of forty-six votes over the Tory candidate, John Blyth. Perhaps I could have won, Leonard thought.

Three months later, everyone at the *Evening Telegram* was overcome, as if possessed of a common soul and mind, by the devastating news of the death of the Old Chieftain. Sir John A. Macdonald was gone. Leonard sent *Telegram* reporters into the streets to record the city's reaction. The Standard Bank, the Traders Bank, and the favourite hangout of Macdonald's supporters, the Albany Club, were draped in black cloth. The Toronto Board of Trade closed its doors for a week of mourning and the City Council adjourned on hearing the news. "It is only a few times in a century that the death of a man is felt as widely all over the world," Black Jack Robinson wrote, "as for the statesman for whom the nation now mourns and has passed away in the zenith of his power and popularity."

An impromptu wake got underway at the Queen's Hotel around five o'clock. The last edition of the paper had been cancelled and reporters, pressmen, printers and men from the business office made their way to the saloon in the basement of the hotel. By six o'clock, every seat was filled and men stood at the bar and along the walls. The room was smoky, noisy, and smelled of sweat, beer farts and tobacco. Anyone who had ever met Sir John A. had a story to tell. Leonard remembered his visit to Ottawa when he'd seen the great man at his seat in the House of Commons. "There was no one in the place to match him," Leonard said. "I can't believe he's dead." Somebody called out, "He'll never die! Three cheers for Sir John A." The barroom exploded, "Hip, hip hurrah, to the great John A." After the cheer, silence descended on the room. Every man, Leonard thought, should ponder how his life would be affected by the death of the first Prime Minister of the Dominion of Canada. He nudged Owen Staples and the two edged their way from the room and walked slowly along King Street. They said good night quietly, each deep in his own thoughts.

Leonard gave himself over so completely to his job that he barely noticed the passage of time. He realized he was getting older, and worried sometimes that he was still a bachelor. Still, better to be single than be carried off by passion and marry some woman who might make a poor wife. His years, he realized, had been marked by events rather than dates. Of these, the blackest was the day of Rosannah's death. Another occasion he would not forget was the dinner for Arthur Conan Doyle at The Grange. Leonard's invitation had come from Goldwin Smith, for a dinner to take place the night before the author's lecture at Massey Hall. "The interest excited in the public mind is very intense," the *Telegram* had noted of Doyle's visit.

Leonard enjoyed the Sherlock Holmes stories. He knew that Doyle had allowed the detective's sidekick, Dr. Watson, to diagnose death by strychnine in a case where a victim "twisted and turned in the most fantastic fashion."

He'd thought of Rosannah when he'd read the story. Who better to ask about strychnine poisoning than this famous writer, himself a medical doctor? Leonard waited for a lull in the chatter over another crime, the shooting death of young Frank Westwood, heir to a Toronto fortune. He had been caught up in an affair with a mulatto seamstress, Clara Ford. Doyle didn't think much of the fact Toronto police had grilled the woman for hours to force a confession from her. "It savours more of French than English justice," he said.

As Arthur Conan Doyle fingered his walrus mustache, Leonard thought him a well-fed man, with his large head, high forehead, and cold, clear eyes that betrayed a sense of insolence. A break in the conversation gave Leonard a chance to speak up.

"Dr. Doyle, did you have occasion in your medical career to attend a victim of strychnine poisoning?"

"As a matter of fact, I did," Doyle said. "A sad case of suicide, a young woman with child, abandoned by her lover." Doyle spoke in a high-pitched voice that carried a strong Scottish brogue, something he had been unable to put aside despite his many years in London. His words held the attention of everyone in the room. Leonard's heart thumped as he listened to the description of the girl's death and the autopsy that followed. How similar to Rosannah!

"It took her some time to die because she had just consumed a large meal – a last meal – which slowed the effects of the poison. My autopsy showed trace amounts of strychnine, evidence of the very large dose she had taken."

Leonard spoke of the death of Rosannah – "a sad event in one of our outlying villages" – and of his belief that an innocent man had been hanged when her husband went to the gallows.

"The husband is always the first suspect when a woman is killed," Doyle answered. "We call it spousal murder. So common, I've not often written about it. Our divorce law encourages murder, I sometimes think. But I prefer more tangled mysteries."

Still, there was an exception or two, Leonard knew. "What about your story, 'The Cardboard Box?'" he interjected. "Your character, Browner, has killed his wife Mary and her boy friend in a jealous rage. He severs an ear from each and sends them to Mary's sister. A gruesome touch but effective," Leonard allowed.

Doyle smiled at Leonard. "It's likely, Mr. Babington, that your jury just assumed your man was guilty." He paused to chuckle. "That's why I demonstrate impeccable evidence of guilt in my villains!" Everyone laughed but Leonard could only reflect that Doyle might have put his finger on the reason for Cook's conviction. Leonard also thought it much simpler to write of an imaginary crime than solve a real one. Later, when an all-male jury acquitted Clara Ford of the murder of Frank Westwood, he thought about how men can be forgiving of the crimes of women, but seldom of other men – whether they were guilty or innocent.

# Chapter 31

## VANDELEUR, AGAIN

### June 23, 1896

Great change can arrive with suddenness, as Leonard Babington and countless others learned when the federal election of 1896 brought to an end the long era of Conservative party rule in Canada. The election proved a great test for John Ross Robertson, the Conservative Party, and the *Evening Telegram*. There had been been a succession of Conservative leaders since the death of Sir John A. Macdonald in 1891. The party seemed to wander aimlessly. John Thompson, who Leonard remembered watching as he collapsed at his desk, had been a promising prime minister until he chose to die while on a visit to Queen Victoria. Even more tragic than Thompson's death, Leonard thought, was the way he had been vilified for his conversion to Catholicism. Fanatical Orangemen called him a pervert. The prejudices of religion were beyond belief, Leonard told himself.

Now, the government was caught up in a great controversy over Catholic schools and the use of French in the classrooms of Manitoba. The provincial government was against both the schools and French, but the Conservatives in Ottawa argued that publicly funded Catholic schools were a right guaranteed to Manitoba when it joined Confederarion. Black Jack Robinson groused to Leonard that the Liberal party's new Catholic leader Wilfrid Laurier "has danced all over this business, making the government look bad without taking a stand himself"

John Ross Robertson was in Kingston, staying at the British-American Hotel, when he received a telegram that would force him to do something he had always resisted: run for Parliament. A breakaway wing of the Conservative party, opposed to Ottawa's efforts to force Manitoba to stand by the deal that brought it into Confederation, wanted him as a candidate. The wire told him that twenty men had been nominated in Toronto East, but all had withdrawn. They wanted Robertson, whose *Telegram* was read in virtually every home in the east end.

When Robertson returned to Toronto, he called in Black Jack Robinson and Leonard Babington and told them of his decision. He would run. "It's not the duty of the federal government to stretch out a hand to help the French minority," the publisher thundered. He accepted nomination just a week before election day. Robertson's readers loyally supported him, and he easily beat the sitting Conservative. "We had a short season for sowing, but we reaped a quick and bountiful harvest," he said on election night. But Robertson found himself in the House of Commons as a member of the Opposition, not the government. In the election of June 23rd, the Liberal party under its Catholic leader Wilfrid Laurier, took power.

On Robertson's instructions, Leonard had played down his publisher's role in the election. He dropped the news of his chief's election into a wrapup story headlined, **BATTLE IN THREE TORONTOS.** The *Telegram* chief spoke rarely in Parliament. When he did, it was to berate the new government. "Sympathy with minority is a weakening disease," he told the House of Commons. No voices were raised against him. Leonard knew Robertson was speaking of the French in Quebec, but his words could apply equally to the Irish, Jews, or Negroes, or the country's natives, still referred to as Indians. The people who ran Canada had more important things to deal with than the problems of those who were not white, Protestant, and British. They cared little about such things as the murder of an Irish girl in Grey County or the hanging of an innocent man.

The pages Leonard had written for *Rosannah's Story* by now filled most of a small drawer in his bedroom cabinet. Riffling through them, he made a sudden decision. Too long had passed without an answer to the puzzle of Rosannah's death. In September of 1897, Leonard made up his mind to return to Vandeleur once more. It was time, finally, to come to terms with his obsession.

Summer in Toronto had been cool and wet. The skies cleared finally and the city looked forward to glorious autumn days, brisk nights and the changing colours of the leaves. Leonard invited Owen Staples to go to Vandeleur with him, where he could paint the fall scenery. Owen had never been north of the city and he welcomed the opportunity. The two arranged a week's leave and on the last Friday of the month they boarded the noon train. By seven o'clock they were at Flesherton Station where they hailed a hansom and set off for Vandeleur Hall. The driver took the short route to the Beaver Valley Road. The trail had been widened and covered with gravel and Leonard saw new houses in the fields along the way.

When Leonard first sighted his old house, he was appalled by what he saw. It was smaller than he'd remembered and it gave off an air of despair and neglect, from the weeds around the porch to the paint peeling from the doors and window ledges. The remnants of a rose garden — a single bush bearing two fading blooms — reminded him how carefully his mother had tended those plants, and of the time he had cut a bouquet for Rosannah. The glass in one of the front windows was cracked. The river stone embedded into the brick around the windows looked ridiculous. Leonard realized his father had designed a house that was more a rural monstrosity than the palatial mansion he'd once imagined. He didn't want to admit this to Owen. "Seems a bit old and tired," he conceded. "Maybe I should get you to paint the house instead of pictures." Owen had a quick answer: "Paint the place yourself. I'm here in the cause of art!"

Leonard withdrew a large key from his jacket and unlocked the front door. The rays of a late evening sun reflected off a shiny floor, evidence that Sam Bowles's granddaughter Maggie had received his letter and had made an effort to have the place ready for them. The parlour had been dusted and in the kitchen Leonard found a plate of roast beef, a pumpkin pie, a jug of milk and a loaf of bread.

"A veritable feast awaits us," Leonard laughed. Owen took a bottle of whisky from his trunk and while Leonard primed the pump, he poured generous helpings into two glasses. They spent the evening telling stories of their boyhood. Owen recalled his early life in England. Leonard remembered Tom Winship who had lost his life on the docks — either a murder or an accident — and he thought of his father, dead from an errant dynamite blast. The whisky bottle was nearly empty by the time the coal oil lamp on the kitchen table ran dry. Leonard was feeling teary as he told Owen of that long ago picnic on the banks of the Beaver River when he fell in love with Rosannah Leppard.

"It's a damn shame what happened to you two," Owen offered. "You'd have been happy together. But all that's behind you, Leonard. I hope this visit to Vandeleur doesn't get your mind off where your life is today."

Leonard took Owen into the countryside almost every day. Sometimes it was to fish in the Beaver River and others times to wander about the hills above the valley. Owen carried his paints with him and on most days he produced two or three watercolor pictures. No matter the weather he dressed in the clothes he'd worn at the *Evening Telegram* – solid shoes, a suit and a vest, with a tie around his neck and a fedora on his head.

Whenever the mood struck him, Owen would open up his campstool and set it down. Leonard watched fascinated as Owen reached into his paint box, took out his brushes and paints, and set about mixing his watercolors. "I like to use the colours of the Impressionists," Owen said. "My favourites are Cadmium yellow, Alizarin crimson, Ultramarine blue. Add a nice touch to a picture. Before I start, I like to soak my paint blocks in water." He poured from a small bottle, making little puddles of colour on his palette. Then he unfolded his easel, propped a board on it, and tacked on a sheet of paper.

Leonard noticed that Owen would pause to take in a scene, as if he were drinking it up. They were in an open meadow atop a hillside on Bowles's Bluff, property that had once belonged to Jacob Teets. A path bordered with maple and beech trees ran down the hillside. You could see crops planted up and down the valley. Hills on the other side faded away into the purple distance, revealing a high ridge of the Escarpment.

"The Impressionists have changed everything about art," Owen told Leonard. "Their pictures reveal their conception of what they see, rather than what's merely there. I like to stop and get a feeling for the scene. Get an impression of it. Take a moment to measure the light – you have to watch that in plein-air painting. There, I've got it now."

With a few quick strokes, Owen set the horizon, the route of a path running up from the river, and the foliage on the hillside. Then he began to paint the sky, capturing the warm sunshine that filtered through a thin cloud. He painted in the lower reaches of the valley, purposely blurring the detail. Next he dabbed at the trees and flowers in the foreground, using strong colours to contrast with the lighter shades of distant slopes. No more than twenty minutes had passed.

"You have to decide when a painting's finished," Owen said.

Leonard stood behind Owen looking at the picture. He thought it more striking and its colours more vivid than anything he'd seen in nature. "It's the most beautiful thing you've done," he said. "Do you like it?" Owen asked. "Here, you can have it."

"Are you back to stay, boy?" It was Rosannah's father, James Leppard. Leonard had thought of looking him up, but hadn't been able to bring himself to doing so. "Folks say they still miss that paper of yours, after all these years." James was standing on the steps of the Methodist church after Sunday morning's service. Owen had insisted on going.

"Only here for a visit," Leonard said. He introduced Owen and they talked about what they'd done during the past week. Leonard wanted to bring up Rosannah's name, but he wasn't sure how to go about it. Too many years had gone by, there was really no reason to talk about her, and he had no wish to return to those dark days in the life of the Leppard family. He decided instead to ask about how James and the other Leppards were faring.

"Oh, good as can be expected, I calculate," James answered. "Family's all scattered. Tom's got a farm in the North West. Joe and Jimmy are still around Vandeleur, Jimmy had a bad marriage and come home. Young Billy's my biggest help, he always stuck by me. The girls are all married, and away."

James stopped talking. He stared across the road, over Leonard's shoulder. "Guess you've heard what's become of Molly," he added, as if in afterthought.

The remark caught Leonard off guard. "No, what about Mrs. Leppard?"

"Why, they've got her in jail. Sent down to Toronto for arson. Tried to poison the cattle and burn up the barn over to Peter Campbell's. They had a feud going. She was upset about one of Peter's bulls loose in our yard. I told her it weren't worth it, making trouble like that."

All the old apprehension Leonard had felt about Rosannah came back on him. A chill came into his chest and his mouth tasted chalky. Would this news of Molly Leppard be likely to help him in his search for Rosannah's killer?

"You never can tell what will set someone off," Leonard said. "How long did they give her?"

"Six months, and that was last February. She still hasn't come back. I had someone write a letter to the Mercer prison, but I've never had an answer. In some ways, I think she's maybe more comfortable down there than she's ever been around here."

Leonard wanted to get away, to clear his mind, and think out what this meant and what he might do about it.

"I'm sorry to hear about Molly," he answered. "When I get back to Toronto I'll see what I can find out. I'll let you know. But we have to go. Owen wants to finish up a painting he's started."

Leonard nudged Owen to get him moving. He couldn't imagine Molly locked up in a cell. She might hold the clue he'd almost given up ever finding. The thought of seeing her was foremost in Leonard's mind, and by the time they boarded the Sunday afternoon train to return to Toronto he'd made up his mind. He would go to the Mercer Reformatory on Monday. He had to find out what had become of Molly Leppard.

Black Jack Robinson was waiting on the second floor landing of the *Evening Telegram* when Leonard came up the stairs. It was seven o'clock, an hour when few reporters had arrived at work. Leonard carried a black umbrella in the crook of his arm and on his head he wore a black Bowler hat. He imagined his outfit gave him the appearance of a proper Victorian gentleman, a fact that did not entirely displease him. "Why are our reporters never around when we need them, Babington?" Robinson demanded. "A damn fool horseless carriage has run amuck on Queen Street, rammed a streetcar, several people injured." Robinson's insistence on calling automobiles horseless carriages irritated Leonard. He thought it was time to call an automobile by its name; they'd been on Toronto streets since 1893. "I'll go myself," Leonard said.

He found a policeman interviewing the owner of the automobile while onlookers inspected the damage. The driver said his passage had frightened a horse just as the streetcar approached him. It was one of the new electric models. He swerved to avoid the horse and skidded into the streetcar. No one had been seriously hurt. Leonard returned to the paper and wrote a one-paragraph account of Toronto's first automobile accident.

All day, Leonard thought about Molly Leppard and wondered how she was dealing with her imprisonment. He left the *Telegram* at four o'clock, caught the streetcar going west on King Street, and twenty minutes later stood outside the Andrew Mercer Reformatory for Women. He wondered if she would remember him, or if he'd recognize her. It had been how long – thirteen years since Cook Teets's trial? She'd be embarrassed at his finding her in jail. A visit could bring him closer to learning the perpetrator of Rosannah's death. That was the important thing.

# Chapter 32

## LOOKING FOR MOLLY

### October 4, 1897

The Mercer Reformatory, like all prisons, had a forbidding look about it. Leonard Babington lifted the knocker on the front door and banged to make his presence known. A small panel at shoulder height slid open. "State your business," a voice demanded.

"Babington of the *Evening Telegram*," Leonard answered. "Inquiring about Molly Leppard. I want to know if she is at this institution."

The door opened to allow Leonard entry. The guard escorted him to an office where a man sat behind a stack of ledgers. "Do we have a Molly Leppard, Jocko," the guard asked. "Newspaperman here wants to know."

"If we've got her, she's in here," the man named Jocko said, referring to the ledgers. He bent over a large journal and ran his finger down lines of black script. He flipped over several pages before stopping. "Ah, here it is," he said. "Molly Leppard, six months for arson, assigned to kitchen work. I remember her. We have to keep these wretched women busy. Of all wretched women, the idle are the most wretched. We teach them the importance of labour. One of the great means of their reformation."

Leonard had to laugh at the man's oafish arrogance. He'd never known anyone who had worked harder than Molly Leppard. Raising thirteen kids on a stone farm takes a lot more effort than sitting in some dismal room writing entries in a ledger. "Can I see her?" he asked.

"Not visiting hours," the man named Jocko answered. "But it doesn't make any difference – she's not here. Transferred to the Asylum for the Insane, 28th of August. Go over to 999 Queen Street. Doubt they'll let you in today."

Molly in the Insane Asylum? Leonard found this hard to believe. He'd always thought her a little strange, but insane? Should he still try to see her? Rather than visit the Asylum now, he decided to go home and think about what he should do. At the office the next day, he sent a copy boy to the *Telegram*'s morgue to collect clippings on the Insane Asylum. There were stories about the rehabilitation of its inmates and flattering accounts of the work of its doctors. One article invited the public to enjoy the grounds and wander through the Asylum to see "the favourable consequences of treatment as it is effected on the inmates." There were several articles quoting the Superintendent, Dr. Daniel Clark. Leonard decided to telephone him. A device that should be used more often in gathering news, he thought as he put in his call. He was connected at once. Dr. Clark agreed to see Leonard at four o'clock the next afternoon.

The stone walls loomed large around the Asylum when Leonard stood in front of it in the afternoon sunshine. A dome set atop the highest tower in Toronto rose over the middle of the building. Wings four storeys high, windows barred, extended left and right for several hundred feet. The only door was at the foot of a stone stairway that descended to the basement, creating a dismal and forbidding entrance even on a day as bright as this.

How frightening these surroundings must be for new arrivals, Leonard thought. He hesitated at the top of the stairway. He was curious to see Molly. And if a visit could lead to him finding out more about how Rosannah had died, it would be worthwhile, no natter how uninviting this place. He had pictured in his head so many times how Rosannah's last hours might have unfolded. How was she given the strychnine that killed her? In some food, or in a drink? Mixed in with her tobacco, perhaps? And who had brought the poison into the Leppard house that night? Someone the Leppards must have known. Not a stranger assuredly. Thinking through all the possibilities, for the thousandth or the ten thousandth time, made him dizzy.

Leonard rang the bell at the bottom of the stairs. An attendant ushered him inside. Everything about the building was grey. The concrete floors and walls were soiled and dingy with the accumulation of years of grime. The white gowns worn by male and female staff alike provided a sharp contrast. Leonard saw Dr. Clark emerge from his office leading an elderly man by the hand. "Lie down when you're taken back to your ward," he told the man. "Someone will be along soon with your tot of rum." He sent him off with an affectionate pat on his shoulder.

Seeing Leonard, Dr. Clark whirled suddenly. A brief flash of pink traveled up his cheek. He seemed embarrassed at what Leonard had just witnessed.

"Pay him no mind," Dr. Clark said. "Many of our patients respond favourably to a tittle of alcohol once or twice a day. Better than giving them opium. Helps them to relax and eases their minds. But you don't have to print that, do you?"

"I've come only to inquire of an inmate," Leonard said.

"Patient, you mean," Dr. Clark interjected. "All our guests are patients."

"Of course," Leonard acknowledged. He was seeking a middle-aged woman named Molly Leppard. He knew her family back in Vandeleur and they were concerned for her welfare. Would it be possible to visit her?

"That might be arranged," Dr. Clark said. Leonard thought the Superintendent sounded a little defensive, perhaps worried about having let it be known patients were given alcohol.

"Mrs. Leppard came to us suffering manic depression," Dr. Clark added. "She experiences delusions and threatens violence to herself and those around her. Just yesterday, she claimed Napoleon was her uncle and she raved about a pit with buried gold and explosives. Poor woman, we're doing our best to help her."

Fanning his arms as if to brush off some unwanted presence, Dr. Clark declared that no matter how unruly a patient might become, no physicial force was ever used at the Asylum.

"You'll find none of the physically corrective forms of confinement here. No crib-beds, restraining waistcoats, or tethering to chairs. We emphasize moral enlightenment and firm guidance. We prefer fresh air, generous diet, and cleanliness to drugs."

Leonard listened carefully. He barely noticed the arrival of a burly man in a white gown. He stood a few feet from Leonard, glowering as he waited to speak.

"You buzzed for me, Dr. Clark?"

"Ah, yes, Wainwright. This is Mr. Babington. He's here to see Molly Leppard. Take him to her, please. But for no more than half an hour."

Wainwright escorted Leonard to a ward at the far end of the Asylum basement. The occasional bare electric light bulb cast a dim light on this dak corridor. Not long ago, Leonard thought, candles would have been used down here.

A female attendant guarded a door at the end of the corridor. She was of medium height but thick, with an expression suggesting she had no time for levity.

"Bring out Mrs. Leppard," Wainwright told her. "She has a visitor."

Wainwright motioned Leonard to a bench. He sat down and waited. There was no conversation. In a few minutes, the door opened and the attendant emerged, followed by a woman clad in a grey nightgown. She had torn slippers on her feet. Leonard stared. It took him a moment to recognize the woman he had known as Molly Leppard. Her hair fell in knotted strands to her shoulders and her wrinkled face bore evidence of strain and worry. Nonetheless, she carried herself with a certain dignity. At the age of sixry-one, she still bore the bones of a good-looking woman.

The attendant sat Molly beside him. They looked at each other.

"Do you remember me?" Leonard asked.

Molly searched his face for a clue to his identity.

"Now I do," she said. She spoke in a soft, throaty voice. "You're Leonard, Leonard Babington. I wouldn't forget you." She looked around quickly. "Too bad you have to see me like this." She let out a nervous laugh.

Molly told Leonard she would be going home soon. "My sentence is just about up."

She must think she's still in the prison, Leonard thought. The attendant offered to take Molly and Leonard to the verandah where they could enjoy the view and the fresh air. The day had warmed and he saw women sitting about in light dresses. The men had the sleeves of their shirts rolled up. Leonard soon realized the veranda was not just a place for dormitory patients to take fresh air. It also served as a ward for the tubercular sick, who ate and slept here. Molly was given a chair near a screened door. As they talked, a tall, red-haired girl approached. Leonard judged she was in her mid-twenties. She had brown eyes and a clear, unblemished face and he wondered if she was a nurse. Then he realized she wore the same grey nightdress as Molly.

"Who is your friend, Molly?" the girl asked. "I think I'd like to meet him."

The attendant interjected. "You shouldn't be trying to flirt with the visitors," she said.

"Gosh, that's just Kathleen's way," Molly said.

Leonard learned a lot about the red-haired girl: that her name was Kathleen Fitzgerald and that she had been committed on the complaint of her stepfather. "They told me I was bad but I could never see why," Kathleen said. Leonard found her easy to talk with. She answered his questions in a forthright way and expressed a keen curiosity about newspapers and their doings.

To Leonard, Kathleen seemed quite normal. Still, he thought, there must be a good reason for her being in the Asylum. She was attractive, yes, he had to admit that. She seemed bright enough, too. But he had learned from Rosannah that the mood of a high-spirited girl could shift in a flash from exuberance to despondency. Be careful with this one, he told himself. He said goodbye to Molly and promised to come back on Saturday. That night, he wrote to James Leppard to tell him of Molly's confinement. He suggested James visit her but as far as Leonard could learn, he never did.

All that week, Leonard fretted as he tried to concentrate on his work. One day, he went with Owen Staples to the Queen's Hotel after the five o'clock edition had been put to bed. He went over everything he could remember about finding Molly Leppard and of his encounter with a girl called Kathleen.

"You have to go back," Owen said. "You'll never rest until you find out what happened to Rosannah. You're still in love."

Leonard became a weekly visitor to the Asylum that fall and winter. In good weather, he bicycled there. Bicycling was all the rage in Toronto, encouraged by the Ministerial Association in its fight to keep streetcars in their barns on Sundays. His paper had opposed Sunday streetcars, but in a referendum the citizens had voted by a margin of a few hundred to let them run on the Sabbath. On Sundays, he sometimes joined Owen and hundreds of others cyclists to ride out to High Park.

Leonard told himself that if he saw Molly often enough he would find out everything she remembered about how Rosannah had met her death. He was less willing to admit it was Kathleen who had become the lure that led him to the Asylum with such regularity.

On one visit, Leonard found Molly at dinner in the first floor dining room. She jumped up when she saw him. "You've come back," she said. Leonard looked around for Kathleen. The room contained a half dozen tables, all filled by patients. He could see the remnants of their meal – crumbs of crackers and leftover corned beef and sauerkraut – scattered on the table and the floor. He was disappointed there was no sign of the girl.

"I've been feeling better this week," Molly said. "But they won't tell me why I'm here. Anyway, they gave me tobacco and I had a good smoke. Would you like some?" Leonard declined. They spoke of how Molly's husband James, all alone now except for Billy, would be getting on. This seemed like a good time to discuss what had happened to Rosannah.

"I still miss Rosannah," Leonard told her. "How much do you remember of the night she died? I wonder if we'll ever know what took her life?"

Molly turned her head away and then snapped back. Leonard could see pain on her face.

"Rosannah? Rosannah was going to Hell. I pray she's been spared."

Suddenly, Molly burst into tears. The attendant rushed over. "You've upset her," she said. "You'll have to leave now." She led Molly away.

The next time Leonard went to the Asylum he decided to look first for Kathleen. By now, the attendants were familiar with him and paid him little attention. He found Kathleen in the west veranda. There was no one nearby and she seemed to be moving about freely. Kathleen smiled and waved when she saw him. "I'm on an hour's inside parole," she said. "I can go wherever I wish as long as I'm back in the ward by two o'clock. But they won't let me outside. Come sit with me."

Kathleen pointed to two chairs by a window. Leonard told her of his last visit with Molly. He was sorry he'd asked a question that had upset her.

"Molly gets upset easily," Kathleen said. "She's my friend, but I worry that she'll never get out of here. I hope I'll have better luck."

Kathleen peered at Leonard and smiled. She reminded him of Rosannah and for a minute it seemed as if he was back with her in Vandeleur.

"So, Mr. Babington, where did you get that name?"

"From my father, of course. Where else would I have gotten it?"

"I mean, how did your family get it? Are you descended from Babington the Catholic? The one who plotted to assassinate Queen Elizabeth?"

Leonard was surprised Kathleen would know of this episode from British history. "Quite possibly," he said. "I really don't know. I'm not a Catholic."

"Neither am I," Kathleen answered. "My people were all Quakers, from Waterford, in Ireland. I was born in Toronto."

Kathleen looked around the room as they talked. "I'm just keeping an eye out for old Meggity McLean," she said. "She likes to keep watch on me but she's wandered off again. I know a nicer place where we can talk. We might even be alone."

Kathleen led Leonard to a small storeroom. Wooden crates held spare blankets and mattress ticking. "This is a good place to talk," she whispered. "No one ever comes here. Do you have any tobacco?"

Leonard told her he never used the stuff and he didn't think she should, either.

"I don't understand why you're here," he told her. "You seem perfectly normal to me."

"I'll be honest with you," Kathleen said. "They think they're making me better but I'm no different than the day I got here."

"What did they say was wrong with you?"

"It's what my stepfather said. He told them I was running wild. Said I had committed acts of the most immoral kind. He signed a paper saying I had no control over my sexual desires."

Leonard blushed on hearing this. "Why ever would he do such a thing?" Leonard wasn't used to discussing sexual matters with young women. But there would be no more talk of such things that day. Instead, Kathleen told Leonard of an incident that had happened in the ward that morning. An old woman had come up to her and waved a finger under her nose. "You should be ashamed of yourself," she'd shouted. "You and your gang of murderers. You've killed my husband. You'll never get to heaven!"

"People like her are here for life," Kathleen said. "They have all kinds of delusions. That woman's incurable."

On his next visit, Leonard went straight to Molly's bedside. His reward was a frustrating hour spent trying to coax her into conversation. He had never seen Molly so dispirited and depressed. She shut up every time he tried to get her to talk about Rosannah. Relieved to be away from her, he looked forward to Kathleen's usual cheerfulness. She smiled when she saw him and led him to the storeroom where they'd spent his last visit. Her lighthearted mood fell away when Leonard asked to know more about why she was in the Asylum.

"It's a long story Leonard, and not a pretty one. Let's not talk about it right now. Would you like to kiss me?"

Leonard had wanted to kiss Kathleen since he'd first set eyes on her. He leaned toward her and brushed his lips against her forehead. She raised her face and gave him a small smile before she closed her eyes. He kissed her on the mouth and pressed himself against her. Kathleen made no effort to move away and he put his palms on her breasts and began to caress her. With one knee, he gently nudged her legs apart. She unfastened his pants and took him in her hands. In a moment, he was inside her. She moaned and clung to him. It was over quickly. After, they talked about the unfairness of Kathleen's detention. Leonard thought he had never been with a girl as exciting and willing as Kathleen. It was unfair for her to be locked away with a lot of crazy people. There's nothing wrong with her, I'm sure of it, he told himself. He had to admit he'd heard only her side of the story. He pushed aside the thought he might have taken advantage of a sick woman.

That night, Leonard dreamt of Kathleen and Rosannah, but he was unable to separate the two visions that haunted his sleep. He awoke troubled, disturbed by the apparition of a woman dead a dozen years. Rosannah was the reminder of a promise not yet fulfilled, a failure that crowned all the other failures of his life.

Leonard was careful to seek out both Molly and Kathleen on his later visits. One time, he went with Molly to the Asylum chapel. It was in a garret under the great dome of the tower. "The different faiths take turns," the attendant said. "The Catholic Mass is at eleven o'clock."

Leonard had expected something resembling an ordinary church. Instead, they entered an oval room with a deep pit that held four rows of seats. He thought it no more cheerful than the foulest ward. A Catholic priest was readying his vestments. He stood in a pulpit built high into the wall, well out of reach of the half dozen patients who sat below. A faint light filtered through windows near the top of the dome.

Molly went to the bottom row, knelt and made the Sign of the Cross, and waited for the start of the mass. Leonard thought how strange we Christians are to celebrate the Cross, the symbol of Christ's agony. If Jesus had been hanged like Cook Teets, would nooses of silver and gold adorn women's necks? Would a rope dangle from each church steeple? He stood with the attendant as the priest droned on in Latin. Molly was as religious as ever, he realized. *That's the only thing she has to hold on to.*

As spring approached and Leonard continued to visit the Asylum, he found himself becoming more entranced with Kathleen. Their trysts took up most of his visits. He marvelled that they hadn't been found out. He wondered if the attendants knew what they were doing. It was information that could be used against Kathleen, an excuse to keep her confined. One time, as they clung together on the packing cases, Leonard asked Kathleen to tell him more of the events that had brought her to this place.

"It was my stepfather's fault, the rotten bastard. Any time a girl gets into difficulty with her family, she can be put away. All that's needed is a complaint from the family, signed by two doctors. If they think you're immoral, they say you're mentally deficient."

Kathleen told Leonard that her stepfather "had his way with me" ever since she was fifteen. When he found her kissing a delivery boy, he ordered her out of the house. Kathleen took work as a servant to a doctor's wife. When Kathleen rebuked the doctor for his sexual advances, he made his wife dismiss her. She stole the family's silver but was arrested when she tried to pawn it. She was given six months in the Industrial Refuge for Girls.

"My stepfather came for me. I wouldn't go home so he complained to the police. He had me charged with sexual promiscuity. They said I showed all the symptoms of erotomania. What bunk! I've been here nearly two years. They put me in a straitjacket and spoon-fed me. Then they put me in a bath for hours at a time. First hot water, then cold. They were going to fix me so I could never have children. The matron said a woman's mental problems start in her womb. But Dr. Clark wouldn't allow them to operate."

It amazed Leonard that Kathleen could unfold a story of such rejection and despair and yet still smile and laugh, like a girl without a care in the world. He told her about Rosannah and what had happened to her. He confessed she'd had a child by him. It seemed to Leonard that Kathleen's life had been as difficult as Rosannah's, if on a different path. Talking about Rosannah still troubled him, and he wondered if he would ever be free of remorse. He looked at Kathleen and for a moment, he thought he saw redemption in her eyes.

# Chapter 33

## LEONARD IN LOVE

### September 15, 1898

Leonard Babington shuffled absent-mindedly through the stack of fresh stories that had collected on his desk. They were about Toronto's new City Hall at Queen and Bay Streets, nearly finished after almost ten years of construction. He picked up a batch of copy and began to read. The story boasted that the hall, built at a cost of two and a half million dollars, was the largest municipal building in North America. Leonard corrected some errors of grammar, changed the lead in one piece, and thrust the five pages onto his copy spike. His mind was not on his work. He'd been seeing Kathleen Fitzgerald for nearly a year and his thoughts were on her, not the tasks he faced. He had to admit it: he was in love.

Leonard left his desk and went to the corner of the newsroom where Owen Staples sat at his drawing board. He was inking in the smug face of Mayor John Shaw for tomorrow's cartoon. "A nice bit of work, but I'm having trouble concentrating today," Leonard said. He told Owen he'd finally made up his mind. "I'm going to marry Kathleen."

"Are you sure you want to do that?" Owen asked. "Having a wife in the insane asylum might not be a good thing for the city editor of the *Evening Telegram*. Anyway, I don't think they allow weddings there."

Leonard studied the face of his best friend. Was he joking or was he serious?

"You've been working too hard," Owen said. "And I suspect there's more to your wanting to marry Kathleen than her pretty face. I think you see her as a substitute for Rosannah. Maybe it's Rosannah you're really in love with, not Kathleen."

Leonard bristled at Owen's honesty. He had to concede he'd sometimes thought of Rosannah as he held Kathleen in his arms. But it was Kathleen who was alive, not Rosannah. Vowing to keep such thoughts from his mind, Leonard assured himself he was in love with the girl from the Asylum.

"Rosannah's dead, it's Kathleen I love," he said.

Owen said he was not so sure about that.

"Maybe I should take you down to Philadelphia and introduce you to my old artist friends."

If Owen thought some fresh acquaintances would make Leonard forget Kathleen, he was badly mistaken.

"I mean it," Leonard said. "There's nothing wrong with Kathleen. I'm going to find some way to get her out of that place and marry her. We love each other. I'm going to have a doctor from outside the Asylum look at her. Someone who will give her a fair examination."

"Why don't you see a lawyer?"

Leonard had seen lawyers at work in the courtroom, and he had no desire to put Kathleen's future in the hands of some man whose interest would run more to money than to justice.

"No, I'd sooner rely on a doctor."

"And if you find someone who says she's sane, will they ever let her go?"

"That's what I've got to settle with Dr. Clark. I'm going to see him after work."

Leonard finished marking up the last of the city hall stories about three o'clock. He knew all the Toronto papers were making a big fuss. The *Globe* would have a page or two but Leonard was more concerned about competition from the new evening paper, the *Star*. It was gaining readers among the trade unions and the working class where the *Evening Telegram* had always been strong. He walked up to Queen Street and spent ten minutes watching workmen clear away the last of the City Hall construction debris. He boarded the first streetcar that came in sight.

When Leonard reached the Asylum he rang the new electric doorbell. No one answered. He rang again, this time pressing the buzzer three times. The door finally opened. Leonard recognized the guard, a man he'd always chatted with when he'd come to see Kathleen or Molly. But today, the guard blocked him from entering.

"I'm sorry, Mr. Babington, I can't let you in. Orders of Dr. Clark."

"What do you mean? I've never had trouble before. You'd better let me see the Superintendent."

"I can't do that. I have the note right here. 'Mr. Babington is not to be admitted under any circumstances.'"

"That's nonsense. I insist on seeing Dr. Clark."

The door banged shut.

Leonard stood at the bottom of the stairway, puzzled and upset. Whatever could be going on? Nothing out of the ordinary had happened on his last visit. He'd spent most of his time with Molly. He decided to wait. Perhaps he'd see someone who could tell him why he was being kept out.

A few people came and went as the afternoon dragged into evening. He recognized some as attendants but none spoke to him. Finally, he saw Meggity McLean who gathered her cloak about her ample frame as she puffed up the stone stairway. Leonard called to her when she cleared the last step.

"Oh, Mr. Babington. I'm not sure I can speak to you."

"Why ever not? They've barred me from the Asylum. I can't understand why."

Meggity pursed her lips and frowned.

"You should know why, Mr. Babington."

"Whatever do you mean?"

"You and that girl. You know what I mean. The place is full of talk. You were found out having improper relations. That sort of thing can't be permitted."

Leonard's stomach churned and his heart began to thump.

"I'm not sure what you mean, Mrs. McLean. But Kathleen and I love each other. I want to marry her."

"You should have thought of that before you started carrying on. Wainwright was suspicious all along. He heard the two of you in there, and saw how you looked when you came out of the storeroom."

"Wainwright? Dr. Clark's man? He always was a sour type. Why'd he want to get me into trouble?"

"I have no idea, Mr. Babington. It seems to me you've gotten yourself into trouble. To say nothing of poor Kathleen. They've put her in isolation.

For moral rehabilitation, Dr. Clark says."

Leonard was outraged. Kathleen could teach the lot of them about morals, he thought. A sweet girl, never been given a chance, always been taken advantage of. It was horrible to know they'd been found out. It was what he'd feared all along, but nothing could have dissuaded him from falling in love with Kathleen. He could only stare at Meggity. She turned and hurried into the darkness.

Leonard stumbled home, uncertain what to do. He poured himself three fingers of whisky and sat on the edge of his bed. He thought of how he had lost Rosannah, and he berated himself for having taken stupid risks with Kathleen. After an hour, Leonard began to compose a letter to Dr. Clark. He considered denying everything, but decided that might not be wise. He was certainly not ready to admit what he'd done. Instead, he wrote of his love for Kathleen and of his hope to marry her. Finished, he copied the letter to a fresh sheet, folded it in an envelope and put it on the dresser beside his bed. The next morning he spoke to Tom Cornell, his favourite among the copy boys at the *Telegram*. He sent him to the Asylum with urgent instructions to deliver the envelope to Dr. Clark.

A week later – a week of nerves, sleepless nights and worry – Leonard received his answer.

"I cannot meet with you in the foreseeable future," Dr. Clark had written. "I leave this week for a medical conference in London, after which Mrs. Clark and I will spend three months touring Europe and the Holy Land. You may contact me on my return. However, I must inform you that your transgression represents a serious breach of trust. It is only out of concern for your professional future that I have refrained from advising your employer. I suggest you give careful thought to this indiscretion and learn to accept the consequences of your actions."

Three months! How could he bear to go so long without Kathleen? What would Molly think had happened to him? Or would she know, too? The questions filled his head but he had answers to none of them. He could only write letters to Kathleen. He did, but never got an answer. She'd likely never been allowed to read them, he thought.

The sweltering heat of a humid summer had settled over Toronto by the time Leonard got word that Dr. Clark had returned to the city. He tried to reach him by phone but was frustrated at every attempt. The ever-present Wainwright exercised control over the Superintendent's public contacts. For almost a year after Dr. Clark's return from Europe, Leonard's calls and letters went unanswered. That was when the lonliness gripped him hardest, and he knew it was going to be bad. He'd lived through so many lost years after Rosannah had left his life. Now he was enduring another empty year, one filled with spurned appeals and days of desolation and nights of despair. Finally, a message was left for him at the *Telegram* giving the hour and day for which an appointment had been set.

A new guard stood at the main door of the Asylum when Leonard arrived. He made him wait ten minutes before being admitted. A white-cloaked attendant took him to Dr. Clark's office.

"I trust you've been well, Mr. Babington," Dr. Clark said. Bowing his head slightly, he indicated Leonard should take a seat. He neither stood nor offered to shake hands. Leonard wondered if the coolness of his reception was an ominous sign of what he should expect. He told Dr. Clark he was worried about Kathleen and he hoped he might see her.

"I can assure you, Sir, there will be nothing improper take place if I am permitted to visit Kathleen," Leonard added.

"There are some matters to be cleared up before any visit can be considered," Dr. Clark said. "We've been deeply troubled by your behaviour."

"I don't think anything I did has directly hurt Kathleen," Leonard answered. "We are in love and we hope to be married." Leonard was not prepared to admit any transgression; better that he leave unspoken what may have happened in the storeroom.

"The rules of this institution forbid sexual contact among the patients, between the patients and the staff, and particularly between patients and their visitors," Dr. Clark answered. He recited other rules and regulations governing the treatment of patients and their relationships with people from the outside.

"Don't you realize, man, we could have had you charged with rape?"

"There was no rape."

"You may not think so, but in law, Kathleen was incapable of providing consent. Good God, Mr. Babington, people have been hanged for rape in this country." The outburst staggered Leonard. He felt swept away, as if he had been tossed into the flotsam that surged over Eugenia Falls. He'd given no thought to Kathleen's legal status. He wondered how to respond. He decided to challenge the Superintendent.

"I repeat there was no rape, Dr. Clark. Charge me if you wish. If Kathleen's mental capability was ever to be put to the test in a court of law, I have no doubt of the outcome. She has a fine mind and is in full possession of her faculties. She should not be in this institution."

Leonard feared he might have gone too far. Dr. Clark frowned, put his hands on his desk, clenched his fists, and stared directly at him.

"That may be your opinion, Sir. It has taken great care on my part to prevent this matter from becoming public knowledge. Had word leaked out, it would have destroyed your reputation and damaged the *Telegram*. A scandal of such magnitude would also have done great harm to this institution." He paused before adding:

"I could only permit you to see Kathleen in the presence of an attendant. And only very briefly."

Leonard's stomach heaved. He was going to see Kathleen after all.

"And what of her release?" Leonard asked. He decided to press whatever advantage he may have gained. "I'd like to have an outside doctor examine Kathleen."

"I would willingly consider any medical assessment that might be brought before me."

Fine, Leonard thought, I'll hold you to that promise. He pressed Dr. Clark on the details of bringing in an independent doctor.

"I'll permit an examination by a qualified medical practitioner of your choice," Dr. Clark said.

That afternoon, Leonard returned to the Asylum for his visit with Kathleen. He was taken to a nursing station where an attendant escorted him to a small ward on the second floor. There were four beds in the room. Three were occupied. Kathleen was sitting on the bed closest to the door. She glanced up at him, a look of shock on her face. Then she smiled and held out her arms. Leonard pulled her from the bed and embraced her. He let her go only when the attendant ordered them apart.

Kathleen seemed to Leonard a bit thinner, perhaps, but in other ways the same girl he had not seen for more than a year. Her eyes sparkled with the delight of their meeting. They discussed small things – how warm it was in the ward, what she'd had for dinner, how Leonard was getting on at the *Evening Telegram*.

"I'm sorry about what's happened," Leonard said. "It was my fault."

"No, I wanted it to happen, I wanted us to be together," Kathleen said.

"I want to marry you, if you'll have me."

"Of course I'll marry you."

"First, we've got to get you out of here."

"They kept me alone in a tiny room for weeks. They shoved my food in through a crack in the door. I thought I'd actually go mad. Since I was moved back into the ward they've lectured. They said me my illness is the result of my poor morals."

Leonard glanced at the attendant and decided he had to speak the truth.

"That's all nonsense. There's nothing wrong with you. Dr. Clark has agreed to have you examined by an outside doctor. Now it's up to me to find someone who would be qualified to see you. And he might as well see Molly, too."

It was time to go. Leonard hugged Kathleen and left the ward. He was thrilled with finding her again. Now he had to get to work on his scheme for Kathleen's release. Where to start? He wanted to find the best doctor in Toronto. Among all the men he knew, he considered Goldwin Smith to be the best connected and the best informed. He decided to stop in at The Grange tomorrow.

Leonard found Goldwin Smith in his vegetable garden behind the great house. The sun shone warmly as he tended his tomato vines. A basket partly filled with fresh tomatoes lay at his feet.

"Look at this, Babington. Have you ever seen the like of it?"

Goldwin Smith held a large tomato in his hand. "A Big Rainbow," he said. "Must weigh over two pounds. These and my Lemon Boys are the best I've ever raised. It's been so hot they're two weeks ahead this year."

Leonard duly praised the fruits of Goldwin Smith's labour. Then he brought up the matter of finding a doctor in possession of a keen understanding of mental diseases. His inquiry, he said, was on behalf of someone in the Asylum who Leonard thought should have the benefit of an independent assessment.

"There's only one choice," Goldwin Smith said. "That's Dr. Creighton. Horace Creighton, I've known him for years. One of the outstanding alienists in North America."

"Alienist?" Leonard muttered. He tried to recall the meaning of the word, which he remembered hearing in his days of covering the courts in Toronto.

"Yes, alienist, a doctor who's been accepted by the courts as an expert in mental disease. One who understands how you can become alienated from your normal faculties. Deranged, in other words."

Kathleen was hardly deranged, Leonard thought. Goldwin Smith took Leonard into the house and had him wait while he wrote a note for Dr. Creighton.

"Take this along and I'm sure he'll see you."

The next day, Leonard excused himself as soon as the eleven o'clock edition had been put to bed. He slipped out of the office without speaking to Black Jack Robinson. There was no need to make his departure obvious. He'd been out of the editorial room too often lately.

Dr. Creighton had his office in a large house on Sherbourne Street. It was close to where John Ross Robertson lived and not far from the house once occupied by the Toronto School of Medicine. Leonard presented Goldwin Smith's note to a young man who sat at a small desk in the foyer. He would have to wait. After half an hour, a buzzer sounded and the young man disappeared down a hallway. When he emerged he told Leonard the doctor would see him.

Dr. Creighton smiled benignly when Leonard entered his office. He was tall, with a neatly trimmed beard. A pince-nez rested on the bridge of his nose. Its presence made Leonard wonder whether the doctor suffered from fading eyesight, or if he had just taken on European airs. Perhaps the glasses were a way of putting himself in the company of the famous Dr. Freud.

"How is my old friend?" Dr. Creighton asked of Goldwin Smith. His voice boomed across the room. "You are seeking a consultation, according to Mr. Smith's note."

"Not for myself," Leonard said quietly. The door had been left open and Leonard had seen a cleaning woman at work in the hallway. He did not wish anyone to hear what he had to say. "It's for a young woman confined to the Toronto Insane Asylum. I have reason to believe she is entirely normal. If you would agree to assess her, your report could go to Dr. Clark. He's willing to permit an independent assessment."

Dr. Creighton looked at Goldwin Smith's note and back at Leonard. His face became a mantle of suspicion. He would need to know more before he could agree to see the subject. What were the circumstances of the young lady's confinement? Leonard spoke briefly of how Kathleen had been committed. He emphasized the mistreatment by her stepfather and the fact she had been falsely accused of immorality and degeneracy. Under questioning, Leonard admitted that he had become a close friend of the girl.

"My advice is to leave that girl well enough alone," Dr. Creighton said. He spoke for several minutes about similar cases he had dealt with. He had been called upon to give testimony in both civil and criminal trials. The cases had ranged from murder to disputes over the mental soundness of persons who had bestowed great wealth on virtual strangers.

"From what you've told me, there's no hope for this girl. Immorality will always out. It drives purity from the soul. I see no point in putting you to the inconvenience and cost of a consultation." Dr. Creighton stood and offered his hand.

Leonard left discouraged by what he had been told. He would have to look elsewhere for someone to examine Kathleen. He stood on the wooden sidewalk outside Dr. Creighton's house and thought about where he might seek help. He had gone only a few steps when he heard a voice call to him. It was the cleaning woman.

"I heard what the doctor said to you," the woman said. She spoke in a thick European accent.

"I learned something of mental diseases when I worked in Vienna," she added. "I have known Dr. Creighton to be in error. You need a good honest doctor for your girl. Go to Dr. Samuel Lavine on John Street. Tell him Devorah sends you."

The woman's abrupt approach flustered Leonard. He muttered a few words of thanks and strode away. Did the cleaning woman truly know of what she spoke? He had better get back to the office. But first he'd try to see Goldwin Smith.

Goldwin Smith was in his study when Leonard arrived at The Grange. He invited Leonard to sit down and asked if he'd seen Dr. Creighton.

"I did," Leonard admitted. "Without result. He does not feel the case warrants his intervention. But I have been given a recommendation for another doctor. A Dr. Samuel Lavine. Do you know of him?"

Goldwin Smith closed the book he has been holding and gave Leonard a look of exasperation. He smiled and shook his head. "You've picked a horrible Jew," Goldwin Smith said. "The only Jewish doctor in Toronto, thank God. But not a man you can put your trust in. These accursed Jews. Responsible for all the wars of the world. Plotting the downfall of Christianity. It's not for nothing they're known as Christ-killers. Their presence in Canada is a misfortune, dangerous parasites, all of them."

Leonard tried to decipher the spiteful words that tumbled from Goldwin Smith's mouth. He had become accustomed to the casual put-downs of Jews heard every day on the streets of Toronto. But this was an incoherent litany of hate, all but incomprehensible to one not immersed in the gibberish of anti-Semitism.

"I don't see much sign of any damage they've done to Canada," Leonard protested.

"Wherever they go, they're a parasitic race," Goldwin Smith thundered back at him. "Eating out the core of our British nationality."

If he could not turn to Dr. Lavine, who was there? Leonard left The Grange with the chill of fear seeping into his veins – fear that he was about to fail the most important test of his life.

# Chapter 34

## THE DIAGNOSIS

### November 18, 1899

After thinking for two days on Goldwin Smith's lurid denunciation of the Jews, Leonard Babington decided he still wanted to talk to Dr. Lavine. He quickly discovered this was not easily accomplished. The telephone operator said she had no listing for him, nor could Leonard find a Dr. Lavine in the 1899 issue of *Might's City Directory*. He remembered Devorah's mention of John Street and decided to check out the street house by house. Walking up from Front Steet, Leonard wondered if he was not on a ridiculous mission. Surely there were many doctors in Toronto who would be able to examine Kathleen and Molly for signs of mental instability. But where could he find one that would be sympatic to their plight?

As Leonard reached Adelaide Street he caught sight of a cottage set well back from the roadside. He knew he had found Dr. Lavine when he saw his name on a small sign tacked to its porch. Paint peeled from the window frames and the cedar shingles on the roof were weatherworn. A bicycle lay sprawled on the porch floor. Pots of flowers showed wilted buds, evidence of a lack of watering. Leonard followed the gravel path to the front door. He did not intend to stay long. A short visit would tell him if he was wasting his time.

Leonard banged the brass knocker on the front door and waited. In a moment, a woman wearing a scarf invited him in. "Do you have an appointment with Dr. Lavine?" Leonard was surprised to recognize her. It was Devorah, the woman from Dr. Creighton's office.

"I thought I would follow your advice," Leonard told her.

"Sit, please sir," the woman said, pointing to a chair. She disappeared into the back of the house.

When Dr. Lavine came into the room, Leonard was struck by his efficient air and neat appearance. He had a closely cropped beard and his head of dark hair was parted in the middle. He wore a black and white hound's tooth suit, complete with vest and a neatly knotted grey tie. His brown eyes glittered in the shaft of sunshine that entered through the parlour window. He was young, Leonard thought, probably not more than thirty-five. They shook hands and he followed the doctor into a small office crowded with a desk, a couch and a single visitor's chair.

"I won't take much time," Leonard said. "I was at Dr. Creighton's office and when I was leaving Devorah suggested I see you."

Dr. Lavine smiled. "Yes, she cleans for me also. I have time to see you. My patients will allow me a moment." He arched his eyebrows, as if to acknowledge he was not overworked.

"I work for the *Evening Telegram,*" Leonard began. "I am interested in a young woman who has been confined to the Insane Asylum for the past three years. Dr. Clark, the superintendent, has agreed that I might have someone not connected with the Asylum examine her."

Dr. Lavine frowned, pondering what Leonard had said.

"That may be difficult to arrange. What makes you think they would let a doctor new to Toronto assess one of their patients? I am sure I don't need to say anything more. Besides, I have only a general practice."

"But you've treated all sorts of patients." Leonard hesitated to make any reference to mental illness.

Dr. Lavine explained he'd graduated from Trinity Medical School and had tried to set up a practice in Chicago where he believed a Jewish doctor would be welcome.

"I found Chicago quite unfriendly," he said. "The Jewish doctors there resented my arrival. And of course I would never get any Gentile patients. I knew Toronto had a few thousand Jews but no Hebrew doctor, so I decided to set up my practice here. It's been slow going. Did you see the bicycle on the porch? That's how I get around. My patients see me ride up to their house. They call me 'the bicycle doctor.'" As he talked, he spun a small top on his desk, grabbing it just before it toppled over. A nervous habit of a man who seemed a bit eccentric, Leonard thought.

It was time to steer the conversation back to treatment of the mentally ill. Leonard observed that a lot of people were confined to insane asylums. Had Dr. Lavine treated any insane patients? Did science hold out any promise of new methods of treatment? Was there hope for people who had been locked up as a danger to themselves and to others? Or morally degenerate? And most important, did Dr. Lavine think there might be people in the asylums who did not belong there?

"You ask a lot of questions, Mr. Babington," Dr. Lavine said. "As do we all when we think about such things. I have studied mental sickness. It is more challenging to the intellect than splinting a broken arm. The real work is being done in Europe. Charcot has looked deeply into the causes of hysteria. Breuer has had success with his 'talking cure.' Freud sees the involuntary repression of 'unconscious memories' as a cause of hysteria and other problems. Especially when the memories relate to sexual experiences from a tender age. Dr. Creighton knows nothing of this work. He's still warning of the dangers of masturbation. Canadian doctors have hardly begun to understand how to deal with matters of sex, or issues of the mind."

Dr. Lavine's mention of sexual memories jolted Leonard. There was no doubt Kathleen remembered the abuse by her stepfather.

"And when one has clear memory of past abuse?" Leonard asked.

"Childhood experience shapes the adult in ways we do not entirely understand. One may seek escape through transferance, which leads to treating others in like manner. Or we may rebel and disregard the moral code of society. Defy what society has set up as a barrier against behaviour offensive to the majority."

"And can that behaviour lead to confinement in an asylum?"

"Promiscuous behaviour of females from the lower classes may indeed lead to a diagnosis of mental deficiency," Dr. Lavine said. "Such is often equated with moral degeneracy."

"So you're saying there may be women who are perfectly sane in the asylums?"

"That is possible."

It was time to tell Dr. Lavine everything. Leonard revealed how he had met Kathleen Fitzgerald, and the fact that he intended to marry her if he could obtain her freedom. He had a promise from Dr. Clark to allow an independent assessment of Kathleen as well as of Molly Leppard. He explained that Molly might be able to lead him to the killer of her daughter Rosannah, and that the man who was hanged for her murder was assuredly innocent. About Molly's sanity, he was not so sure. Was Dr. Lavine willing to examine both?

"You must understand I am not recognized as an alienist," Dr. Lavine said.

"But you would be willing?"

"It's a field of great interest to me. Some of my patients exhibit characteristics commonly associated with the mentally unsound. Who is not a little crazy at some time or other? Does that mean we should be confined? I have no doubt there are many in the Asylum who should not be there. I'll see these ladies, if you can arrange it. We can discuss the matter of my fee."

The October sun shone brightly and the day was beautiful for Leonard when he left Dr. Lavine's office. He hurried to *The Telegram* to tell Owen Staples the good news.

Owen bent to his sketch board where he was drawing a cartoon hailing the departure of volunteers for the South African War. He'd just gotten back from festive ceremonies at Union Station. At last, Canada would be at the side of the Old Country in putting down the Boers, despite the foot-dragging of Prime Minister Laurier.

Leonard shared the news that Dr. Lavine had agreed to see Kathleen. "Huh, don't be sure it will do you much good," Owen said. "Even if he does give her a clean bill of health, what makes you think Dr. Clark will let her go?"

Leonard was far ahead of that challenge. His mind had turned already to the time when Kathleen would be free and he'd be able to marry her.

"There's one thing you must promise, Owen," Leonard said.

"No one but you knows about me and Kathleen. When I marry her, I won't want anyone to know she's been in the Asylum. Promise me you'll never speak of it."

"Of course I promise," Owen said. Leonard wasn't sure why he had felt the need to ask for such a commitment. He told himself he had to get everything exactly right.

Leonard drummed his fingers on the arm of the chair as he waited to see Dr. Clark. Wainwright had brought him in and had said the Superintendent would return shortly from his morning rounds. After all the trouble Wainwright had caused, Leonard was surprised he acted so unperturbed. I might as well be a toad on a log, he thought. He wondered whether Dr. Clark had told Wainwright the reason for Leonard's visit. He stood when the doctor came into the room.

"As you were," Dr. Clark said. "I've just looked in on Kathleen. She's cheerful this morning. We believe our moral therapy is producing beneficial results. Dr. Stafford is trying to determine her psychiatric classification. Of course, it's a relatively new science and there are few standards."

"You're still agreeable to her being looked at by someone from outside?" Leonard

"I've said I would be willing to consider any qualified medical assessment. Who do you have in mind?"

Leonard told Dr. Clark about Dr. Lavine. He mentioned the doctor's interest in problems of the mind. Leonard had interviewed him and he was willing to do the assessments.

Dr. Clark listened without interruption. "Have Dr. Lavine contact me," he said. He showed Leonard to his door, shook his hand, and went back to his office. At his desk, he pressed a buzzer to summon Wainwright. "Make a note," he told him. "There'll be a Dr. Lavine to examine Molly Leppard and Kathleen Fitzgerald. Some Jewish meddler butting in. Have him see Dr. Stafford. And make sure I get the report."

Two weeks after Leonard's meeting with Dr. Clark, the phone on Leonard's desk rang just as the six o'clock edition was going to press. It was Dr. Lavine, calling to invite him to his office the next day.

Leonard arrived a little after four o'clock and was met by Devorah. She brought him a cup of tea and a cookie, and said Dr. Lavine would be with him as soon as he finished reviewing his report. Leonard glanced over that afternoon's *Star* and twenty minutes later was sitting across the desk from the doctor.

"I can't tell you exactly what I say in my report," Dr. Lavine began. "That would be a violation of medical confidence. I've written my report for the

Asylum, you understand. But in view of the circumstances, I have no hesitation in summing up my general impressions. Just between the two of us, of course."

Dr. Lavine said that on the whole, Kathleen had impressed him favourably. Molly was another matter. He recounted how he had arrived at the Asylum early for the consultation, and had been taken by Dr. Stafford to a small room on the fourth floor.

"I think he was a little annoyed with my being there," Dr. Lavine said.

When Molly was brought in, Dr. Lavine began by asking if she knew why he was there. "She just stared straight ahead at first. I told her I wanted to know how she was getting on. She was confused and uncertain."

Dr. Lavine told Leonard he'd read in her case history that she prayed for hours at a time and talked incessantly, but not to other people. Instead, to objects like a chair or the inkwell on the matron's desk.

"Unusual behaviour," Dr. Lavine said, "but not necessarily evidence of deviance. Deviance, that's the thing to look for. Alcoholism, drug addition, mental illness, each lead to deviant behavior, each rob their victim of the ability to act rationally and responsibly. That's what psychiatry is about, finding the cause of one's deviance, and understanding it, prescribing methods of treatment – opiates to alleviate distress, prolonged baths to calm the patient and when feasible, occupational activities such as laundering or kitchen work."

Dr. Lavine said it was when Molly began to talk of the buried gold she had at home that he concluded she was in no condition to be released.

"'Home, I've got to get home for my gold,' she kept telling me," Dr. Lavine said. "Then she stood and began to shake violently. The matron rushed over. They had to take her away."

Dr. Lavine paused, as if to give Leonard time to absorb what he'd told him.

"Now, let me tell you about Kathleen," Dr. Lavine began. "I was a little worried when she was first brought in to me. Her hair was rather unkempt and there were circles under her eyes. I asked her if you had told her I would be in to see her.

"Kathleen said you had, but she had forgotten. She said you could only see her for fifteen minutes a week. She apologized for my having to observe her, in that condition. She said she'd been having a difficult time and that sometimes her mind was on fire with all sorts of ideas. She said she just wanted to get out and be with you."

Dr. Lavine thumbed through the copy of Kathleen's case history that he had on his desk. "This file is full of references to melancholia and immoral behavior. It speaks of a preoccupation with sexual thoughts. It hardly seems to me to give a true picture of this young woman's character and condition. "

Leonard brightened when Dr. Lavine told him this. It was the first good thing he'd heard that morning.

Dr. Lavine said he recognized the symptoms — shared by so many women, he thought — of people who drift aimlessly through life. Kathleen had tried to put aside memories of her stepfather's mistreatment and other unpleasantness that had caused her life to spiral out of control.

"Her demeanor changed as we talked," Dr. Lavine said. "She said she tried not to think of what brought her there. She said it was all so unfair. She couldn't stay at home, and she had no place to go. She admitted she liked men, except for her stepfather, that is. I asked her if she thought she could manage on the outside."

The most important question, Leonard thought.

"She told me she didn't think she should ever have been inside. Said she thought she was just as sane as anybody. I told her she was probably right. Mind you, who among us isn't a bit crazy in some corner of our mind?" Dr. Lavine chuckled at the thought.

"But don't think it will be easy," he said he told Kathleen. "She has to know the stigma of what's happened to her will never go away. It's a cross she'll always have to bear. And you too, if you marry her."

Three men sat in the office of the Superintendent of the Toronto Insane Asylum. Dr. Clark told Leonard he had reviewed the report from Dr. Lavine and had gone over it with Dr. Stafford, who was at his side. He didn't tell Leonard of the disparaging comments he'd made about some of what Dr. Lavine had written or that he had concurred, reluctantly it was true, with certain of his observations. Leonard waited for them to deliver their verdicts on Molly and Kathleen.

"You understand, Mr. Babington, that we are bound by nothing that Dr.

Lavine has said in his report."

Dr. Clark flourished the blue sheets of lined paper he held in his hand.

"I told you we would consider any qualified medical assessment that might be put before us. This we have done."

Leonard wished Dr. Clark would stop reminding him of his authority, and just get on with it.

"Let's deal first with Mrs. Leppard." Dr. Clark said. "That should take but a few minutes."

He folded over the first page of the papers on his desk.

"Dr. Lavine's diagnosis is in accord with our findings," he said. "Dementia praecox. A debilitating illness. Mrs. Leppard's cognitive faculties are seriously impaired. The deterioration of her mind will continue until her death. There is no hope. Dr. Lavine recommends she remain here at the Asylum."

Leonard listened with alarm as Dr. Clark enumerated the main causes of insanity among women. First came grief, followed by religious excitement, and finally poverty. Molly suffered from all three, so her present status should be no surprise. Nevertheless, Leonard resented the Superintendent's facile explanation. He would have had no idea of the turbulence that his words, spoken in such an assured voice, held for him. But why should he? He doesn't care whether Molly will ever be able to help him find Rosannah's killer.

"So are we all agreed on Mrs. Leppard?" Dr. Clark took the silence that followed as assent.

"Now, the situation as to Miss Fitzgerald is somewhat more complex," he said. He reached again for Dr. Lavine's report. "Dr. Stafford and I agree that we face a rather large conundrum. We are going to have to talk this out."

A conundrum? Some excuse to keep Kathleen in this awful place, Leonard feared. His nerves tightened as he realized the next few moments could determine the direction of his life. He told himself to think quickly, and get it right, no matter what Dr. Clark might say.

"I'm sorry I have but one copy of the report," Dr. Clark began. "Let me summarize what Dr. Lavine has told us. I'll ask Dr. Stafford to help explain anything you don't understand.

"Kathleen experiences frequent changes in her mood, ranging from feelings of despair to optimism and cheerfulness," Dr. Clark read. "It is this change in mood that is at the root of Kathleen's condition." Looking up from the report, he added, "Dr Lavine has diagnosed Kathleen as being in a partial state of melancholia."

"We've known that all along, of course," Dr. Stafford interjected.

"That is correct," Dr. Clark said. "But Dr. Lavine brings an interesting perspective to his assessment. He says that Kathleen's deviance, her sexual misbehaviour and her disregard of rules, both before and during her time here at the Asylum, should not be seen as a sin or a crime. Rather, he argues it is an outgrowth of her depression. He also theorizes that she has used her sexuality to compensate for her unsatisfactory state of life since falling out with her stepfather."

"Falling out?" Leonard gasped. "What happened to her was no falling out. She was brutally abused."

"That may be your opinion, Mr. Babington, but here we can only deal with objective fact." Dr. Clark straightened in his chair, as if to stiffen his back against further protest. He picked up the report and counted off its three recommendations.

"First, Dr. Lavine sees no reason for Kathleen's continued confinement. He claims her condition may have worsened here. We can hardly agree with that observation, Mr. Babington. But let me go through what else our friend has to say.

"Dr. Lavine recommends that Kathleen be released into the protective custody of family members or others who would assume responsibility for her, such as a husband. I can tell you, Mr. Babington, we are not sure we can accept that recommendation.

"And his third recommendation is that Kathleen should continue to undergo medical observation. That of course could be most easily provided if she were to stay where she is, right here at the Asylum. Quite candidly, that is the course Dr. Stafford and I would prefer."

Leonard felt he had been on a high swing that caused his spirits to rise and fall. The Superintendent must be twisting Dr. Lavine's report. He raised Leonard's hopes with its findings only to dash them by disagreeing with its recommendations. Was Dr. Clark just playing a game?

It's not worth arguing about, Leonard thought, as to whether Kathleen has gotten better or worse at the Asylum. All that's in the past. As to Kathleen being under care of a doctor after she got out, that too was not to be debated. He'd agree to anything to have her released. He'd been waiting to put forth an idea that had come to him weeks ago and that he'd worked on ever since. It was an idea, he thought, that should win Kathleen her freedom if anything ever would. He took a breath and looked squarely at Dr. Clark.

"Sir, I know that in all that you've done for Kathleen, you've acted in what you saw as her best interest. You've provided protective custody. I'm not yet Kathleen's husband and so it's not right to ask that she be released to my care. But what about an eminent and respectable family that could assure Kathleen of a calm life? See that she receives medical attention. Until such time as we could be married, of course. I have a letter from Mr. and Mrs. Owen Staples. They are willing to take her into their home."

Leonard thought he saw a look of relief pass over the face of Dr. Clark. "What do you think, Dr. Staffrord?"

"I am not sure it would be the right thing," he answered.

"Now, now," Dr. Clark replied, "let's not set up too many obstacles to Kathleen's future. Let's just talk this out a bit."

Talk they did, and as Leonard suspected would be the case, agreement followed. Kathleen could be released come Monday, on one condition.

"You will understand, Mr. Babington, that the way in which we have arrived at this decision must remain confidential. Do you know what I mean?"

"I'm not sure I do."

"Let me spell it out for you. We have permitted Dr. Lavine to do his assessment. It must never be revealed that we have accepted his advice. There are reasons. Among them, the fact the medical society would not approve. Do I have your word on this?"

"Of course, Dr. Clark. I'll never let it be known."

Leonard felt his spirit soaring. He could not wait to get to the *Telegram* to share the news with Owen Staples.

After Leonard left the sylum, Dr. Clark turned to Dr. Stafford. "Well, what do you think?" the superintendant asked his colleague.

"I think you had already decided to release Kathleen."

"That I had, Dr. Stafford. With the knowledge we possess today, correct classification of our patients is impossible. Some we classify as insane could be sane. In Kathleen Fitzgerald's case, we lack justification for her continued confinement. However, I want you to keep Dr. Lavine's report in your active file. If any difficulty should arise following her release we'll know where to fix responsibility."

On a crisp fall morning, with the breeze scudding leaves across the sidewalks, Owen and Lillian Staples, accompanied by Leonard Babington, arrived at the Toronto Insane Asylum. They entered through the basement doorway and were escorted into the room normally used to receive new patients. Owen and Lillian "signed out" Kathleen at twenty-eight minutes past nine o'clock on November 18, 1899. She had been brought to the room by Mrs. Wilson, the attendant who had been present for Dr. Lavine's assessment. Kathleen smiled nervously as she added her signature to the sign out register. When she put down the pen Leonard took her hand and squeezed it.

"At last you're free, and we're together," he whispered.

The guilt about Rosannah Leppard that had been buried deep in Leonard's heart was less painful this morning. For once, he had achieved something worthwhile.

# Chapter 35

## A WEDDING AT ST. ANDREW'S

### June 16, 1900

Kathleen chuckled as she watched a Northern Flicker bob and bow through the garden, its tail stiffly spread, bent on outdoing a rival for the attentions of an intended mate. Oblivious to the display, a robin was building a nest in the overhang of a back roof. Hummingbirds fluttered over a wild Canada Lily, a splash of orange against green grass and red roses. She was in the garden of Owen and Lilian Staples on Maitland Place. Leonard relaxed in a wooden rocking chair, allowing himself a smoke from his pipe – a habit he'd recently acquired. Throughout the winter following Kathleen's release, she and Leonard had filled their hours together in front of the hearth, or in walks on Cabbagetown streets. They became familiar with every block of this Irish immigrant district. On Christmas Day they'd tobogganed down the slope of Riverdale Park above the Don River. Some evenings, they'd gone to concerts of the Mendelssohn Choir, where Owen was the lead tenor.

It was clear to Leonard that the lassitude that had gripped Kathleen at the Asylum had vanished. His mind was filled with thoughts of marriage. Kathleen told him she was convinced they loved each other, but she worried if it was right to bring such an unhappy past into his life. How might it affect them once the bloom of romance had worn off? Would he be able to withstand the cruel gossip that her past, once it became known, would swrl around them?

"I'm afraid I'll not be worthy of you," she told Leonard.

"I am the one who's not worthy," he answered.

"But will you still love me when people say you're married to a crazy woman? Will Mr. Robertson still want you at the *Telegram*?"

"Nobody's going to say anything like that."

"But if they did, what would you do?"

"I would thrash them to within an inch of their life. And I'd love you more than ever."

"Oh, Leonard, I hope you would. Love me, that is. Not thrash somebody." They laughed.

A few days after this conversation, Leonard turned up at the Staples house a little before four o'clock – a good two hours before his usual arrival. Kathleen put down the dress she was hemming and held her face up for a kiss. "I've brought you something," Leonard said. "I hope you like it." He handed her a small box and invited her to open it. In it, she found an engagement ring whose tiny diamond glittered in the afternoon light. "It's so beautiful Leonard, I love it," Kathleen said. He put the ring on her finger and together they set the day for their wedding – June 16, 1900.

Owen and Lillian wanted the wedding at their church but Leonard insisted on another choice. He had never forgotten his visit to St. Andrew's Presbyterian church on King Street where the Rev. Macdonnell had married Rosannah Leppard and Cook Teets. Macdonnell was dead now and his young successor, the Rev. Armstrong Black, was reaching out to more of Toronto's Scots population, hoping to enlarge the congregation. Leonard wasn't quite sure why he asked the Rev. Black to conduct their wedding. He'd become fed up with the raging Orangeism of the Jarvis Street Baptists and he looked on the Presbyterian faith as a reasonable compromise to the rivalries of Christian churches. Anyway, St. Andrew's made a nice fit with Klathleen's Ulster Protestant background. Leonard never admitted to himself that Rosannah Leeppard's connection there had any influence on him.

Kathleen had been taken with a wild rose bush she had seen in the Don valley. Its mass of flowers led her to her want a "wild rose" wedding. She had an arch set up over the church altar and covered it with clematis vines and wild roses. Kathleen wore a white wedding dress with puffy sleeves in the "Leg o'Mutton" style of the day and Owen took pictures with his new Kodak Brownie camera. It had cost him a dollar, which he considered a good investment. After the ceremony, the wedding party made its way along King

Street to the Hotel Falconer at Spadina Avenue, where the dozen guests – mostly *Telegram* men – toasted the bride and groom. Owen had hired a fiddler and every man insisted on a dance with Kathleen. After an extravagant supper – lobster, chicken, lamb and roast beef – washed down with ale and wine, Leonard and Kathleen escaped upstairs. They slept late the next day, a Sunday and it was afternoon before Leonard hired a taxi to take them to Parliament and Winchester streets where he had rented an apartment – parlour, kitchen, and bedroom – on the third floor of the grandest rooming house in the neighbourhood.

The newlyweds lived only for each other, oblivious to what went on around them. Kathleen spent her days with Lillian or with new friends she'd made in the neighbourhood. Leonard rushed up the stairs every night after work, swept Kathleen into his arms, and in a few minutes they were making love. After, they'd wander to the kitchen and eat the dinner, now cold, that Kathleen had prepared. Later, they'd creep into bed where they'd hold each close as they talked about the day when they'd have a house of their own and children to love.

Leonard became aware that Kathleen was tiring of her daily visits with Lillian and the gossip sessions with her neighbours. This caused him to worry about her. She made many trips to the Insane Asylum to see Molly Leppard and to inquire after former friends she'd left behind. Who knows what tidbit about Rosannah's death that Molly might share with Kathleen? Kathleen told Leonard she had felt nervous about returning to the place where she had suffered mistreatment and confinement. But slowly, her visits emboldened her to suggest changes the ward matrons could make to improve the lives of patients. "They need physical activity, exercise of some kind," Kathleen told Mrs. Wilson. They were discussing this when Dr. Clark happened upon them.

"He liked my suggestion and asked me to show the ladies what I meant," Kathleen told Leonard. "He said a healthy body leads to a healthy mind."

Dr. Clark's willingness to consider such an idea brought considerable change to Molly's ward. The women looked forward to Kathleen's weekly visit. They enjoyed stretching their arms and kicking their legs in impromptu exercises and after, they seemed more content and less complaining. They also slept better. Dr. Clark noted the difference in their behaviour. After the third week of exercises he invited Kathleen to his office. She told Leonard what he had said:

"I must congratulate you on what you've achieved. Would you like to do this regularly – as a volunteer of course – and wear a badge to show you're one of us?" Kathleen was thrilled to accept the invitation. Dr. Clark had told her they were doing "groundbreaking work" and congratulated Kathleen on being the first volunteer to assist in a mental institute in Canada.

Black Jack Robinson made a habit of meeting with Leonard every morning to discuss the day's news. A few months after the wedding he pointed out that Leonard had taken no time for a honeymoon. "Mr. Robertson thinks every young couple should get away for a bit. Why don't you take a week off?"

"A most generous offer," Leonard said. "We'll get around to it." He would have preferred to be invited again to supper at the Robinson house. Leonard had been there many times when he was single, but not once since he'd married Kathleen.

That night, Leonard told Kathleen they were going on a trip. To Vandeleur.

"You'll love it up there. There'll be lots of snow but it's not too cold yet. We'll cuddle up in Vandeleur Hall for a week. Let the world go to hell."

The train pulled out of Toronto on a grey winter morning. The snow in the fields deepened as they moved north and by the time they reached Flesherton Station, it was piled in drifts driven by a strong northwest wind. Leonard and Kathleen wore two layers of their warmest clothes but they shivered as they waited for a driver to maneuvre his horses and a sleigh up to the station platform. They piled their suitcases in the back seat along with supplies they'd brought – bread, coffee, tea, flour, butter, sugar, soap and the other essentials of a one-week stay. Leonard hadn't bothered to notify anyone of their coming. He wanted to be alone with Kathleen at Vandeleur Hall. They would get by on what they had brought and would go to the general store only to fill an urgent need.

The driver called out "Giddy-up" and whipped his horses as they galloped off toward Vandeleur. The sleigh rocked from side to side as the runners grappled with the icy road. Leonard threw his arms around Kathleen and she screamed with delight as they pitched from side to side, like a ship buffeted by a gale. When they drew up at Vandeleur Hall, a late afternoon sun was casting pale light on the snow, throwing long shadows across fields that stretched to the deep forest behind the farm.

Leonard stomped out a path in the snow and led Kathleen to the porch, where he extracted a key from his jacket and swung open the front door. He lifted Kathleen off her feet and with her cradled in his arms, they made their way into the house.

"I never carried you over the threshold on Parliament Street," he said. "Better that we do it now." Kathleen giggled as she clung tightly to Leonard.

It seemed even colder inside than out. Hoar frost covered the windows. Snow had penetrated the cracks in the window frames and lay in small piles on each sash. Firewood Leonard had collected during that long ago visit with Owen sat beside the kitchen stove. He got a fire going and then moved into the bedroom where his father had died. He opened the draught in the hearth and soon had a fire raging there, too. He closed off the door to the main hallway. "This is all the space we'll need," he said. "And I've got just what we'll want in the middle of the night." He laughed and held up a chamber pot that had sat for years under the bed. Kathleen packed away food in the kitchen and swept the floor and dusted the furniture. They'd brought a tankard of water and Leonard filled a brass tub with snow and put it on the stove.

They spent their days trekking in the woods and at night slept soundly under a pile of comforters. Leonard found some traps in the stable and decided to set them out, hoping to catch a lynx or a marten. After two days, they found only a hare, frozen stiff in the trap. Thawed, it made an excellent dinner that night.

Kathleen had spent not even a day in the wilderness. Leonard worried she would fear being away from the city. Instead, she relished the distance from other people, free of any need to answer to family, neighbour or authority. "Why can't we stay forever?" Kathleen asked. "The farm must produce a lot if you can share it with the Bowles family. We could live quite comfortably here." Leonard didn't want to tell her he'd spent his life trying to get away from Vandeleur. Now, his job as city editor meant everything to him and he had no desire to leave Toronto.

Both felt a need for a bath after three days at Vandeleur Hall. Leonard kept the brass boiler on the stove filled with snow and by now they had enough hot water to fill a tin bathtub he had dragged into the kitchen. While the fire crackled and sent heat waves across the room, Leonard poured the water into the basin, stripped off his clothes, and stepped in. Kathleen knelt beside him and soaped his back.

"I don't want to be in here all alone," he said. He began to unbutton Kathleen's dress and she quickly pulled it over her head, threw off a petticoat and underclothes, and slipped into the tub. There was just enough room for them to sit facing each other, their legs entangled. Leonard soaped Kathleen's breasts and drew her face to his. In a few minutes they clambered wet from the tub, wrapped themselves in towels, and ran straight to their big double bed. The mattress was filled with feathers and down and was still thick and comfortable. They huddled under an eiderdown quilt and in a few minutes, wrapped in each other's arms, they were very warm. Leonard lifted the quilt to look at Kathleen in the candlelight. Later, their laughter echoed through the house.

On the fourth day of their stay, Leonard began to feel restless. He thought about how his life had become so much better since he had met Kathleen. But he could not forget his promise to pursue whoever was responsible for Rosannah's death. He had long ago settled on the main suspects he thought most likely to have harmed her. Scarth Tackaberry, the late night visitor to the Leppard place, was still at the top of Leonard's list. Nelson Teets, Cook's brother, was another possibility but Leonard had no way of questioning him because he'd gone back to the States. Moses Sherwood had testified to seeing Rosannah with Cook on the afternoon before her death but Leonard had no evidence to link him with Rosannah's death. And what about that priest, Father Quinn? Maybe Rosannah had said something to the Rev. Macdonnell when they went to him for their wedding, and word had gotten back to the priest. But Presbyteran ministers don't talk to Catholic priests, do they? By process of elimination, that left only Scarth Tackaberry. He decided he must confront him.

Leonard's cheeks were red with the cold, each breath having turned to steam, by the time he'd walked the two miles to the Tackaberry house. He knocked on the door and waited. It edged open and Leonard could see Tackaberry's face take on a scowl when he recognized his visitor.

"I'd like to come in and talk to you, Scarth," Leonard said.

Tackaberry hesitated. "I wondered when you'd get here," he said. "There's been smoke from your chimney the last three nights. I see you're back to hound me some more. You can come in, but you're not welcome."

Tackaberry's coldness did not surprise Leonard. He was a little younger than Leonard, about forty, but taller and heavier. A shock of black hair tumbled over his brow. Leonard thought he wore a furtive look, made the more noticeable by Scarth's inability to lock eyes with anyone. His glances always darted sideways, as if he couldn't bring himself to deal with anyone face to face.

Leonard looked around the foyer and saw a peg for clothes near the door. "Do you mind if I hang up my coat? I'll freeze when I go out if I keep it on in here." He slung his fur onto the peg and rubbed his hands. "Can we sit down?" He caught a glimpse of Mrs. Tackaberry when Scarth led him into their parlour. She moved quickly out of sight. Scarth sat in his rocking chair, waiting for Leonard to speak.

"You know I've never given up on fixing the responsibility for Rosannah's death," Leonard began. "The jury's verdict doesn't hold water. You testified you saw Cook Teets with strychnine. But I don't think he ever had a chance to use it, even if he'd wanted to."

"Won't let up, will you?" Scarth stammered. "You think I killed her. But it's all over and done with. Everybody else has forgotten it. If you think you can come in here and accuse me of murder, you're out of your mind. You've always had it in for me."

"I don't give a damn about you Scarth, and I've never accused you of anything. But you're making me mighty suspicious. Why don't you tell me what you were doing at the Leppards the night Rosannah died?" Leonard was close to losing his temper. He had to calm down, keep quiet for a bit, if he expected to get anything out of this man.

Scarth looked away from Leonard, directing his gaze to the corner of the room. Finally, he spoke.

"Like I said at the trial, I was having trouble with rodents and foxes. You know that's a big problem around here. So I thought I'd find out what Molly was doing about the pests around her place."

"And you thought you'd use that as an excuse to slip some strychnine into Rosannah's food, did you?"

Leonard's question drew a look of rage from Tackaberry. He began to speak, apparently thought better of it, and stood up just as Mrs. Tackaberry returned to the parlour. "I think you'd better leave, Mr. Babington," she said.

"You'll answer to me one day, no matter how long it takes," Leonard said.

That night, Leonard awakened after midnight, feeling restless. He put on his clothes and went outside. The sky was cloudless. The glare of the moon on the snow created shadows as distinct as anything shaped by a painter's brush. The snow crunched under his feet and overhead a rare outburst of the Northern Lights framed the sky in dancing blues, reds and yellows. The night was silent but for the occasional yelp of a distant wolf.

When Leonard came back in he sat down at the kitchen table. He felt serene and confident in his love of Kathleen and secure in his place in life. Yet, Tackaberry's reaction to his visit had strengthened his conviction that the man knew more than he was admitting. Leonard lit a fresh candle, stoked the fire, and got some paper and a pencil from a box beside the table. It was time to write more of *Rosannah's Story*. His fingers became chilled while he waited for the words to form in his mind. After half an hour, he realized he had nothing to add to what he'd already written. How could he, Leonard asked himself, when he still didn't know who was responsible for her death?

Kathleen had entered the kitchen without making a sound. He stirred when she sat beside him. "I know you need to finish that book you're writing."

"I can't," Leonard told her. "Not until I know the ending."

Toronto was in full preparation for Christmas when Leonard and Kathleen returned to the city. The editorial room of the *Evening Telegram* had a festive air. The proprietor smiled as he handed around envelopes containing bonuses for the staff. Leonard and Kathleen slept in on Christmas morning and exchanged gifts before going to the Staples's for the day. Leonard gave Kathleen the engraved hand mirror he had bought for his mother at the first Toronto Exhibition. Her present to him was a pair of warm gloves and a muffler, paid with nickels saved from the household budget.

On New Year's Eve they ate an early supper with Owen and Lillian and danced at the Orange Hall before mingling with the thousands of people who gathered outside the new city hall to listen to the Grenadiers Band.

Rousing tunes like The Maple Leaf Forever and Roamin in the Glomin (aided by the presence of whisky flasks in the hip pockets of many of the men) brought the crowd to a fever pitch of enthusiasm and patiotism. Everyone sang Auld Lang Syne when the Hall's "Big Ben" chimed at midnight to usher in the first of January, 1901 and the twentieth century.

When the staff of the *Evening Telegram* returned to work after New Year's Day, Leonard looked askance at Owen's cartoon of a bloated Sir William Van Horne, the founder of the CPR. He had Van Horne grasping the Parliament Buildings to his bosom, a key to the Treasury Department in his hand. Owen's caption quoted the railway baron: "The old century may go and the new Liberals may come, but we remain forever."

By two o'clock on most days, with reporters and editors having finished their lunches, the editorial department would take on a busy hum as the staff made the final push to close the *Telegram*'s late editions. On the afternoon of the fourth Tuesday of January 1901, the 22nd of the month, Alex Carpenter, who for twenty years had deciphered the signals that came from the telegraph keys in his cubicle off the editorial department, collapsed to the floor as he finished taking down a dispatch. Leonard heard the thud and was the first to reach him.

"Help me up, Mr. Babington," Carpenter pleaded as he caught his breath. "I have awful news for you. The Queen is dead."

Queen Victoria had been on the throne more than sixty-three years. No one at the *Telegram*, and none but the oldest of her subjects anywhere, had known any other monarch. The clock in the editorial room showed a few minutes before two. Leonard called for assisstance, and ran to Black Jack Robinson's office. In a few minutes, the two men had mobilized the editorial staff to the all-consuming task of recording the passage of an era. Black Jack Robinson ordered all the small ads off the front page and told the pressroom to run fifty thousand copies of the three o'clock edition. An hour later, boys were selling it on the streets for five cents instead of the usual penny.

## QUEEN VICTORIA IS NO MORE.
## AND A GREAT EMPIRE IS BEREAVED

"I want every man to scour their beats for reaction," Leonard ordered his reporters. The bell at City Hall had begun to toll at a quarter past two. Flags dropped to half-mast. The bells of St. James's cathedral began to chime, followed by others throughout Toronto and all of Canada. Stores and offices brought out black draping and the council chamber was dressed in black. Civil servants were sent home. Mayor Howland dispatched a cable of condolence to Buckingham Palace.

Leonard arrived home late and exhausted. He had the last edition with him, and as he went through it with Kathleen, he told her how each story had been gathered and how the paper would be putting out a memorial edition in a few days.

"Everything is changing," Leonard told Kathleen when they finally settled into bed, a little before midnight. "We're in a new world, with a new king," he added. His voice rose with excitement. "An age of science. All these astonishing new things – moving pictures, the motorcar, those two brothers in the States working on a flying machine. Everything is out there for us, Kathleen. We just have to take it." And he wondered: Would there be any room for the memory of Rosannah in that new world?

# Chapter 36

## THE GREAT FIRE

### April 19, 1904

With the hanging of the painting of King Edward VII, on the throne for three years, all was in readiness for the grand opening of Toronto's most palatial hostel, the eight-storey King Edward Hotel. Leonard Babington watched a worker hastily remove a ladder from the lobby as George Gooderham, the whisky distiller who had raised two million dollars to build this splendid symbol of the city's wealth, sauntered through the front door. Bejewelled ladies applauded while reporters took notes of the ribbon cutting ceremony.

Leonard gazed with interest at the plush furniture in the lobby and the ornate oak counter where guests were being registered. Looking up, he saw an arched ceiling that rose over the mezzanine where tables had been set up for serving drink and food. He had more on his mind, however, than the celebration for the opening of this new hotel. He was meeting Dr. Thomas Sproule, one of the special guests invited for the occasion. Leonard hoped that Dr. Sproule, who had conducted the autopsy on Rosannah Leppard, might yet be able to tell him more about what had happened to Rosannah the night of her death. Perhaps he'd changed his opinion since that so long ago trial, or maybe there were facts he'd not told the court. Meeting Dr. Sproule tonight might be his final chance to learn the truth of Rosannah's last hours.

The crowd was beginning to fill up the lobby, chattering and laughing as they accepted drinks and canapés from hotel waiters. Leonard stood at the wall, next to the painting of King Edward and Queen Alexandra. When he spotted Dr. Sproule he moved to his side. He looked older and heavier than the last time Leonard had seen him, but his welcome was as warm as it had always been. Dr. Sproule spoke of the meeting of the Loyal Orange Order he would attend while in Toronto, and of the welfare work the Order was doing among poor Protestants.

"The Order is stronger now than ever and represents all the best interests of those who make up our British Canadian community," Dr. Sproule said. He always talked that way, Leonard thought, as if he was addressing a crowd. That's how he got to be a member of Parliament, and Grand Master of the Orange Order. Happily, there was no discussion of party politics. Leonard scribbled hasty notes that he would never use in a story – all he cared about was how Rosannah had met her fate. By now the two, drinks in hand, had wandered into the alcove between the hotel's front counter and the men's room. A pause in their conversation gave Leonard the opportunity to raise Rosannah's name.

"Have you ever given thought to the autopsy you performed on Rosannah Leppard?" Leonard asked.

"Cook Teets's wife, you mean?"

"That's right."

"I've never changed my conclusion, if that's what you're asking. She died of strychnine poisoning. Who did it, is another matter."

"Then you're not convinced it was Cook?"

"Never was. The poor devil didn't have a chance. He'd get a fairer trial these days, now they allow prisoners to testify in their own behalf."

"Do you have any idea who might have done it?"

Dr. Sproule drew his watch from a vest pocket and checked the time.

"Got to be going," he said. "Any number of people could have been involved in that foul deed. She had too many men friends. Vandeleur is full of incorrigible characters. Take that Scarth Tackaberry, he's jumped bail on assault charges. Beat up a man something terrible at Munshaw's hotel. If he dies, they'll be looking for a murderer."

Tackaberry? Jumped bail? So that explained it. Leonard thought he'd seen Scarth Tackaberry when he went to Allan Gardens on Christmas Eve to buy Kathleen a poinsettia. The man Leonard saw lifting Christmas trees off a wagon looked just like him. By the time he got close, the figure had disappeared. A ghost, or a figment of his imagination? He couldn't decide which.

Leonard left the King Edward and in less than three minutres was at his desk at the *Telegram*. He wrote a note and posted it on the reporters' bulletin board. "Information wanted – fugitive named Scarth Tackaberry. May be frequenting hiring halls or the docks, looking for work. Inquire at the saloons on Front st. and in The Ward. Let me know if you hear of his presence in Toronto. – LB, City Editor."

Toronto's poor still huddled in The Ward, the neighbourhood north of Queen Street that stretched drearily from Yonge Street to University Avenue. Immigrants crowded into shacks along its alleys while they struggled for a toe-hold in Canada. Leonard understood how The Ward embraced everything the most comfortable people of Toronto despised – the Irish who fled the potato famines, Jews driven from their homelands by pogroms, Chinese who made it their first home here, and before them, blacks who had found it a safe haven after escaping slavery via the Underground Railroad.

Leonard knew The Ward well from his forays there while covering crime stories; the robberies, shootings, and killings for which the district was notorious.

"I was terrified the first time I had to go in there," he had confessed to Kathleen. "I remember it was a cold, wintry day and I saw kids running in the alleys with no shoes. A girl who must have been no more than twelve said I could lie with her for a quarter. The men all seemed to be drunk. I thought to myself, I'd be drunk, too, if I had to live like that. Yet nobody ever seemed to care. There I was, raised in the clean fresh air of the country. I'd no idea such places exsted. Nor does anyone on the city council, if you believe what you hear."

For the Toronto that lived outside The Ward, the new century was shaping up to be all that Leonard had hoped for. The Art Gallery of Ontario was to get its own building, something Owen Staples was sure would make Toronto a city of culture. There were plans for a grand memorial on University Avenue to honour the volunteers of the South African War, while Sir John Eaton presided over meetings of Canada's first automobile club. At home, Leonard and Kathleen enjoyed their new gramophone machine. They liked the records of the Canadian tenor, Henry Burr, and their favourite song was Silver Threads Among the Gold. Kathleen was preoccupied with her volunteer work at the Asylum, and Leonard kept up his once-a-month visits to Molly Leppard. He was still hopeful that Molly would help him get to the bottom of what had happened to Rosannah, still convinced that Scarth Tackaberry was somehow involved in her death.

A little after eight o'clock, tired after a longer than usual day at the *Telegram*, Leonard was putting on his coat when he heard someone pounding up the stairs to the editorial floor. It was Tuesday, April 19, 1904. A few reporters and the night editor cocked quizzical eyes toward the stairway. Tom Cornell, the copy boy, rushed into the room.

"Fire, the whole place is on fire! The whole street is burning up. We're sure to be next. We better get out of here!" Tom couldn't stand still, so agitated was he at having witnessed flames burst through the roof of a warehouse a street away from the *Telegram*. Leonard watched him rush about the editorial floor. Alarmed that panic might set in, Leonard told one of the night men to take hold of the boy and calm him down. "I'll go out on the street and see what's happening."

The evening was cold and blustery and an unseasonable snowfall had begun. Leonard pulled his jacket closer as he stepped onto the sidewalk. He could hear noises of crackling and burning and when he reached Wellington Street, a block below the *Telegram*, he saw flames eating at the Currie Building. Leonard watched a horse-drawn fire wagon pull up in front of it, one of the largest buildings in the warehouse district. He recognized the fire chief, John Thompson, who led his men into a neighbouring building, and soon emerged on the roof. From there, they threw down lines to haul up hoses. A great roar sounded and the building across the street exploded, enveloping others on both sides of Wellington. The firemen, trapped and helpless as the blaze ate out the innards of the building on which they stood, scrambled to slide down their lines to the ground. Leonard saw chief Thompson fall the last six feet. He lay there until his men carried him off.

Elbowing aside bystanders, Leonard hurried back to the *Telegram*. He found the night staff clustered at the windows watching the fire. He dispatched Tom Cornell to the homes of his three best reporters, with instructions to come downtown right away. He gave Mary Dawson, the night telegraphist, orders to rouse Black Jack Robinson and every senior editor she could reach by phone or telegram. Then he turned to night editor Jerry Snider. "The fire will be here soon. We've got to try and save the building. Pray to God the sprinklers will work. We need to get a hose up on the roof." He remembered seeing a faucet on the roof and it was there that composing room foreman Charlie Crosby led his typesetters. They'd found a hose in the basement and lugged it to the top floor. Men stumbled as they struggled to connect the hose. Once hooked up, they began to spray water onto loose sparks that were landing on the roof. By now, the fire had burned its way up Bay Street and the Office Specialty Building, next door to the *Telegram*, was in flames. Its roof collapsed with a roar, setting fire to dozens of desks, chairs, and other furniture.

"Get back from the windows," Leonard ordered the night staff. Just as he did, one window blew out with a tremendous roar, sending glass across the editorial department. He picked shards from his jacket and watched water from firemen's hoses cascade onto desks and the floor. The noise and smells coming in through the windows told him that burning buildings along Wellington and Front streets had begun to collapse. Reporters arriving at the *Telegram* spoke of boats anchoring far out in Toronto Harbour to escape the flames. One told of how drinkers at the Queen's Hotel deserted the bar to man hoses and play water on the building. Guests were told to fill pots, pans, and pails while the staff tried to smother sparks with wet blankets.

Owen Staples and Lillian were enjoying dinner with their friends the Brigdens on Rose Avenue, close enough to the fire for them to hear the commotion of crowds shouting advice to the firemen. Owen raced first to the bridge at York Street, sketched the scene there, and made his way down Wellington Street before reaching the *Telegram*, a swatch of drawings under his arm. Sparks had landed on his jacket and smoke and dust had blown onto his face. "You look a sight," Leonard told him, "but we're glad to see you. Some of the boys are putting their stories together. We're going to lose everything in the wholesale district, maybe a hundred buildings are on fire."

For the next three hours, the fate of the *Telegram* — the last bastion preventing the spread of the blaze up Bay Street and into the city centre of King and Yonge — rested on fate and the wind. By eleven o'clock, the fire began to burn back into the structures it had demolished, leaving only outside walls and a few blackened storefronts. Banker William Cawthra's sandstone mansion at the corner of King and Bay Streets had been saved, the gold door-

308

RAY ARGYLE

knob on its front door having been removed and stored safely away. More firemen were on their way by train from Hamilton, Buffalo, and London.

It had taken Mary Dawson an hour to raise the Grand Trunk telegraph operator in Mimico, the western suburb where Black Jack Robinson lived. When a telegraph boy finally appeared at his door with Leonard's message, he hitched a horse and buggy and headed into town. He abandoned the buggy at Portland Street and walked the rest of the way. Barging onto the editorial floor, he called to Leonard: "Dammit, Babington, it looks like all Toronto's on fire. I want you to get out there and find out what started this infernal blaze."

Surveying the havoc on the editorial floor, Leonard considered how to answer his boss. He told Black Jack that putting out tomorrow's paper came first. "We've got our boys writing up the fire, and Owen's sketches are down with engraving. We'll find out the cause later."

As he spoke, Leonard looked around at upset wastebaskets and over-turned spittoons. There were puddles of water between the desks and a chill wind blew in through the broken window. It was then he saw three burly firefighters come onto the floor. Leonard recognized John Noble, the deputy chief. "We're doing everything we can to get things under control," Noble said. "The Queen's Hotel is saved, and you folks are safe. The fire's stopped short of the Customs House. Nobody's died, thank God, but poor Chief's in the hospital with a broken leg."

Leonard was anxious to send word to John Ross Robertson that the paper had survived the fire. The publisher was somewhere in Egypt, enjoying tours of the pyramids and no doubt feasting on Arab delicacies. He called Mary Dawson aside and dictated a telegram to Robertson's son Charles in London: "Big fire. *Telegram* saved. Publish tomorrow as usual."

More reporters had come in from the streets and Leonard by now had accumulated pages of their notes. He cleared off a section of the copy desk and put paper in a typewriter. His words came quickly as he typed:

The desolation wrought by the greatest fire in the history of Toronto, if not in Canada, cannot be described simply because, thank God, it does not occur often enough in the lives of men or of cities to have a descriptive term made for it.

Leonard looked up at the clock on the wall of the editorial room and saw it was about to strike one. He worried about Kathleen and realized he should have telephoned her long ago. Startled by a movement beside him, he saw she was standing at his desk. Her face was smeared and her shoes were sodden and smudged. Whatever had she been up to and where had she been?

"Kate, my God," – as he'd lately taken to calling her – "you should be at home instead of here in the middle of this terrible fire. What's happened to you?"

"I've been at the Asylum all evening. I had a terrible time getting here. The streetcars stopped running and I had to push my way through the crowds. Smoke and ashes all over the place. But that doesn't matter. There's something you have to know."

"All I know is I want to get you home."

"No, Leonard, now's not the time to be going home. I'll stay here with you. I don't care what you say." Kathleen looked for a chair, found one at the end of the copy table, and pulled it up to Leonard's desk. She was breathing rapidly as she struggled to hold back tears. Dabbing at her face with a handkerchief, she looked at Leonard as if in appeal for his understanding.

"We could hear the fire sirens at the Asylum, though we were never in danger. But that didn't make any difference to Molly. She was convinced the flames of Hell were about to consume her. She was almost hysterical. She absolutely has to talk to you, Leonard. Says she has something to tell you about Rosannah."

Kathleen reminded Leonard that Molly had befriended her when she was first sent to the Asylum. "She protected me from some pretty nasty people, and she taught me what I needed to know to get along there. It was awful to see her in such a state. She only calmed down when I promised you would see her tomorrow."

Leonard fidgeted with the pages of the story he'd pulled from his typewriter. "Of course I'll go and see her – whenever I can get away."

More reporters turned up over the next few hours, each with stories of havoc and heroism. Major Anthes laughed about how the Queen's Hotel was saved by its best customers – "saved by sentiment, they weren't going to lose their favourite watering hole." Chuck Fowler, the manufacturing reporter, read a list of buildings destroyed and goods lost.

"All that cloth stored in the Currie building, they won't be making neckties of it anymore," Fowler said. Leonard's favourite ties had come from Currie's, including the blue and white one he'd worn that day. Fowler said that Mayor Tommy Urquhart had even considered blowing up buildings to stop the fire. "The Highland Regiment was called from Stanley Barracks and they warned against it. Said explosions would just spread the flames. So the mayor put the soldier boys to work controlling the crowds."

Kathleen didn't speak until the reporters finished their accounts. "Those poor firemen, it's a miracle no one's died," she finally said. "A good thing it happened at night."

"Yes, the workers were safe at home," Leonard replied. "Could you get me a cup of tea, Kate? Kitchen's one floor up."

Kathleen was back in a few minutes with two cups of tea sweetened with sugar.

"No trouble?"

"I don't think anyone even noticed me." Leonard stirred his tea and crossed his legs. "I'm glad things are quieting down. Look, it's nearly six o'clock."

They were interrupted by the arrival of Leonard's deputy, Roland Cooper, who was wiping grime from his face and brushing ashes from his coat. "They've finally got the fire under control but you can still see flames in the burnt out buildings. There's debris all over the streets. The pavement's heaved and cracked and the telephone poles have burned and fallen down."

As Cooper finished his account, the first faint light of dawn was filtering into the room. "It's been a night we won't forget," he said, and fell silent. He crossed the floor to his desk and sat down after brushing shards of glass away from his chair. Leonard, Kathleen and Owen were left to contemplate the implications of his words.

"Some good has to come of this," Leonard said. For Kathleen and Owen, he thought, the fire would have different meanings than it had for him. Owen might have seen it through his artist's eyes, an opportunity to renew the city with buildings more grand than any that existed before. Kathleen, with her love of nature might have thought of the Phoenix, the mythical bird that builds its own funeral pyre but rises from the ashes to live again. He saw the fire as a metaphor for cleansing. Perhaps it would show him the way to examining the embers of his own dispirited life. And what would Molly Leppard or Rosannah, if she were still alive, think of the fire? Rosannah might see it as a comfort rather than, as Molly Leppard would be wont to think, a punishment for mankind's sins.

# Chapter 37

## AT THE ASYLUM

### April 20, 1904

Leonard Babington settled down on the floor beside his desk, using his jacket as a pillow, and hoped for an hour of sleep. Kathleen had left the *Telegram*, saying she would walk home. The presses were about to roll with the story of the Great Fire. A little after seven o'clock, Leonard roused himself and went to the composing room to make a final check of the news pages. That was when the trouble began. The pneumatic tube that carried copy to the composing room quit working. Leonard had to call for carbon copies of two missing stories that would fill the last page. The roll of newsprint on the press cylinder kept splitting and it took Ginty Harper, the head pressman, forty-five minutes to straighten that out.

Leonard moved the printing of the eleven o'clock edition up to nine o'clock, giving the circulation department a head start on getting the *Telegram* into the hands of readers anxious for news of the fire. Police and firemen stood outside the pressroom dock as the first bundles of papers were handed out to newsboys. Police were keeping anxious readers outside of the fire zone and it wasn't until the newsboys reached King street that they found their first customers.

Leonard scanned the eight-page issue, looking for errors that could be fixed in the next edition. At a quarter to twelve, hungry for some lunch, he picked up his jacket and took a last glance at the clutter on his desk. That was when he spotted a piece of paper he'd not noticed before. It was a note from David Carey, who covered the railway stations and labour unions. It had lain unnoticed in the chaos of the fire: "There's a 'Slim' Tackaberry at the

Colonial Rooms on Agnes st. One of the sleazier places in The Ward. Passes himself off as an ironmonger. He could be your man."

Leonard knew what he had to do. Get hold of Tackaberry and take him to the Asylum to confront Molly. It was the only way to get them both to tell the truth. He was more certain than ever that Scarth was implicated in Rosannah's death, and that Molly knew of his involvement. If only Rosannah could speak to him, she'd put all his doubts and questions aside. But that was stuff of midnight fantasies, not reality.

Leonard found a taxi idling on King Street and asked to be taken to the Colonial Rooms. His mind was filled with guilt about his failure to find a solution to Rosannah's death. In a small way, he resented Kathleen having brought him the message that Molly wanted to see him. He thought again about the vow he had made to Dr. Sproule the day Cook Teets was hanged. He might at last be able to coax from Tackaberry and Molly the truth of what had happened.

The Colonial Rooms turned out to be a grungy little hotel, three floors of squalid catacombs in one of the cheap wood frame and stucco buildings that had been thrown up in The Ward. It offered cheap rooms to immigrants. Leonard found a clerk behind a desk in the vestibule and demanded to know Tackaberry's room number. "Room 309, top floor at the back," he was told. Leonard kicked aside a pile of trash at the top of the stairs and made his way to the end of the hall. At the last door, he pounded on the thin frame and demanded to be let in. "I know you're there, Tackaberry, open up." He heard a movement behind the door, heaved against it, and the lock gave way. A figure backed against a dresser was reaching for a pair of pants draped over a chair. It was Scarth Tackaberry.

"What do you mean, busting in here?" Tackaberry asked. "I'll tell you what I mean," Leonard said. "Get yourself dressed and listen to me. You've some explaining to do."

Over the next fifteen minutes, Leonard heard denials, entreaties and finally pleas from Scarth Tackaberry. He hadn't meant to hurt that guy at Munshaw's, he was just too mouthy. He had a train ticket for the North West and was to leave that afternoon on the Canadian Pacific. Promise to let him go and he'd tell everything he knew about Rosannah's death.

"I'll need a better story than that," Leonard told him. "You're coming with me to the Asylum. We're going to talk to Molly. We'll get the truth out of you. If she clears you I won't tell the cops I've found you. But if she proves you're guilty you'll have to face the music. Otherwise I'll frog-march you down to the police station right now. They'll be glad to get their hands on a bail jumper."

"You've been bird-dogging me for years," Tackaberry complained. "You still think I killed Rosannah. You think Molly will say it was me."

"Or you'll admit it yourself."

"I ain't saying nothing. And who cares what Molly says? Who'd believe a crazy old woman? So why should I be afraid to go with you? Looks like I don't have no choice. I'd as soon stare down Molly as have you turn me into the bulls. But you've got to keep your promise. Let me get out of town this afternoon."

The stark lines of the Insane Asylum gave it an even more forbidding appearance on this cloudy spring afternoon. Leonard found the security precautions more stringent than in the days when he had been visiting Kathleen. He had to sign in at the basement office and wait for permission from Dr. Clark before he and Scarth were allowed to see Molly. Leonard said Tackaberry was her nephew. It was the only way he could get him in.

Escorted by an attendant, Leonard led Tackaberry to Molly's ward. Mrs. Wilson was still there, looking older and a little more harried than he remembered.

"Molly's been taken to the infirmary," she said. "Go up two flights and you'll find it at the east end of the building."

As they passed through the same dreary hallways Leonard had loitered in with Kathleen, he thought of how the patients looked as they always had, their faces vacant and their bearing dejected. It could have been just yesterday that he'd last seen them. Some slumped in chairs while others wandered about waving their arms and muttering oaths. They spoke in a variety of languages, or was it tongues? He heard a man declare his wife was God. "All who are here must obey her." An old man stepped into the corridor and asked Leonard if he had seen Jesus Christ. "I keep looking but I can't find him," he complained. A woman stood chanting outside the infirmary. "Get away, Devil," she muttered, sweeping her arms before her. Hearing such religious delusions disturbed Leonard. It troubled him that so many inmates were beset with such phantom beliefs.

The infirmary nurse examined the pass proffered by Leonard and motioned he and Scarth to the back of the room. "You must speak quietly and you'll have to leave if Molly becomes upset," she told them. Leonard heard groans from several patients. Others raised themselves to stare at the visitors. Tackaberry seemed overwhelmed at what he was witnessing. His face had lost its usual ruddy colour. He now looked grey and ashen as he sucked in sharp, quick breaths.

Molly appeared to be sleeping. Leonard sat beside her and focused his eyes on the iron grey linoleum on the floor. He heard Molly murmur and saw that she was waking up. When she turned on her side and opened her eyes, she was only inches away from him. How lined and waxen was her face, he thought. Her hair was completely white and one bare arm, exposed above the blanket, was wrinkled and fleshy. All old people get to look like that, he knew. He was almost glad his mother and father had not lived so long as to become but hulks of themselves, absent their natural vitality and familiar features.

"Is it you, Leonard?" Molly asked. "You've come to see me?"

"I have, Molly. How are you feeling?"

"All right, I guess. My head's not so mixed up anymore. But the consumption's got me bad." She began to cough and Leonard helped her sit up. She brought a handkerchief to her mouth and spat into it. Leonard could see a red stain darken the cloth.

"Kathleen told me you wanted to see me," Leonard said. "I'm sorry I haven't been around more often. There never seems time to do everything you want. But I've brought you a visitor. Look, here's Scarth Tackaberry."

Molly lay back on her pillow and stared at the ceiling. "Well, don't we make a pair, Scarth and me. How are you, Scarth?" Only then did she lift her head to look at him.

"All right, Molly. Haven't seen you for awhile."

"Can't say I've missed you, Scarth," Molly answered.

Leonard was anxious to learn why Molly had wanted to see him. He needed to find that out before challenging her to implicate Scarth in Rosannah's death.

"What was it you wanted to tell me, Molly?" he asked.

"Mebbe you don't have time to listen to me, an old woman. Not important anyway, what I have to say." She fell silent.

"We'd like to hear it, just the same."

If he could just get her talking, Leonard thought. He knew he had to be careful – a wrong word could send her off on some tirade and he'd never get to the bottom of what Molly might know.

"The fire got me to thinking, Leonard. About you and Rosannah. You always cared for her. Maybe if you two had gotten married, I mean a proper marriage in a Catholic church, things would have been different. You know her oldest girl, Lenora, is yours, don't you?"

So that was it. What he'd suspected all along. Leonard sucked in his breath and licked his dry lips. For an instant, he was on the verge of tears. The feeling passed.

"I always thought the child was mine, but Rosannah would never tell me. So I quit asking and decided to let her do as she wished. I couldn't have stopped her, anyway."

"There's something else," Molly said. "Something awful you need to know. Mebbe I'd better not tell you."

"Is it about Rosannah? About how she died? Did Scarth have anything to do with it?"

Leonard held his breath as he waited for Molly's answers.

"I used to think it a terrible sin what Rosannah did," Molly told him. "Going off and marrying that Protestant, Cook Teets. The priest told me she'd go to hell. I believed it. Maybe I still believe it. I had visions of demons dancing all around her. There were voices and wailing. They told me to find some way to wash away her sin. They never let me alone.

"I prayed and prayed and told God I would do anything to save Rosannah. I feared she'd spend eternity in the fires of hell, for marrying that blind man, in a Protestant church. It's all I thought about.

"One day, it came to me how to save her. A greater sin can wash away a lesser sin. Did you know that, Leonard?"

He said he didn't. Her voice was faint and he decided not to say anything more, just to let her talk as long as she had the strength to mouth the words.

"How I used to love making jam. Do you remember my jam, Leonard?"

What is this about jam, he wondered? What has that got to do with Rosannah's sins? He remembered Molly made jam from anything she could get her hands on, as long as she had a bit of sugar. Wild blueberries, alderberries, a few strawberries from the garden, apples, she'd boil them up and make jam. A pail usually sat on the kitchen table, the only thing sweet the Leppards ever ate.

"It was the jam, Leonard, crabapple jam. That's what killed Rosannah."

"How's that, Molly? What do you mean? Jam can't kill a person."

"It can if it's got strychnine in it."

"You mean Scarth put strychnine in the jam?" He watched Scarth out of the corner of his eye, half expecting him to try to flee from Molly's indictment.

"Tell us exactly what happened that night," Leonard said.

"Like I told the trial, Scarth come around, bothering us again. We finally got rid of him after about an hour.

"I was really tired, and Rosannah wasn't feeling well. So we went to bed early. I fell asleep right away. Later on, the noises woke me up. Rosannah woke up, too. So we both got up.

"Rosannah said she was hungry. I toasted some bread for her. That crabapple jam, so tart a body could hardly swallow it. I only made four jars of it, them little beggars' hard to cook up. Sour, that's for sure, but that covered up the taste of strychnine."

"You're saying Scarth put poison in it, Molly?" Leonard thought of other possible perpetrators – Rosannah's one-time lovers who might have allowed passion to snare them into an act of cold-blooded retribution. It must have been one of them. Rosannah's first husband, David Rogers, or perhaps Nelson Teets. But most likely it was Scarth. If Molly were to incriminate him now that would solve the puzzle.

Molly was sitting up and she brushed a strand of hair from her face. Leonard had never forgotten that Scarth Tackaberry had been the last visitor to the house the night Rosannah died.

"Then it was Scarth that put strychnine in the jam?" Leonard repeated.

Leonard heard Scarth shuffling his feet beside him. "God damn it Babington, no need of you to try to coach her. Just let her tell the truth."

Scarth Tackaberry's outburst produced laughter in Molly. It began as a gurgle and turned into a full-throated cackle. Her head bobbed and her eyes rolled. Leonard feared she'd pass out at any moment. Molly coughed and seemed to recover her senses.

"Ah, Leonard, you're pretty good at guessing the truth and I know you figure that Scarth had something to do with Rosannah's death. I let one man suffer for something he didn't do. I can't allow another man to go down the same way."

Her answer didn't make sense to Leonard. He didn't like the way this conversation was going.

"Sure, Scarth was at the house for awhile," Molly repeated. "But after he left, there wasn't nobody around but us family. I had such awful visions. And the wailing, it was the wailing of the banshee, it was terrible, it meant someone close was going to die."

Leonard had heard of the ancient Irish legend of the banshee, the fairy woman who comes around when a death is imminent, and wails for the soul to be released.

"That was no banshee, Molly. Don't you remember? It was Halloween night. What you heard was neighbourhood kids. Out for a bit of fun. Set up outside your house, singing and wailing."

Molly didn't seem to hear what Leonard had said.

"The wailing kept on and on. Even Rosannah heard it. I didn't want her to know what it was, that someone was going to die. I said it was just the dog. She went to the door and stuck a big knife in beside the lock. To stop someone from coming in.

"The wailing was driving me insane. Telling me over and over that someone was going to die. I knew it meant I had to sin against Rosannah. Do something to wash away her own sin."

Leonard caught his breath, astonished at what he had heard. "Whatever do you mean, Molly?"

"I mean it was me that fed Rosannah the poisoned jam."

"You couldn't have done that, Molly. Not on purpose, anyway. You're just imagining that. You didn't have any strychnine. Scarth must have put it in the jam."

"Oh, no, he didn't," Molly said. "I'd had the stuff for a long time. Cook Teets gave it to me. I told him I needed it to stop the wild dogs chasing the cattle." She shuddered and began to cry.

Leonard looked away, then found himself studying Scarth Tackaberry's face. There was a gleam of a smirk, followed by a look of contentment at what he had just heard.

Was it really possible, Leonard thought, that a Halloween prank could have triggered Rosannah's death? Halloween's a night for ghosts and goblins – and mischievous children. Molly must be leaving something out. He'd never heard of a mother killing her own offspring. He considered getting up and leaving. He wasn't going to listen to this ridiculous tale of visions and voices. He was half out of his chair when Molly put her hand on his arm.

"I thought it was the Devil's angel, that banshee I was hearing. Poor Cook Teets. Never was worse use made of a man than to hang him." Saying that, she turned her face away.

"If Cook gave you the strychnine, why didn't he say so?"

"I guess he thought the jury would never find him guilty," she said, turning back to Leonard. "Or if they did, they would never hang him. He was really a good man. It took his death to convince me."

Leonard found it hard to realize that so long after the trial, evidence of Cook's innocence had at last fallen into his hands. But there was so much more he needed to know. "What about that shot somebody took at me? They were trying to scare me off."

"That was Scarth Tackaberry." She raised her head to stare at him. "You're just a poor, dumb fool, Scarth. Not fit to mind mice. You were scairt, weren't you, Scarth, scairt you'd be blamed after testifying against Cook, and all?"

Looking at Scarth, Leonard saw that the smirk had left his face. He was shrinking within himself at the ferocity of Molly's remarks. It was time to interrupt her tirade.

"And you're not afraid, Molly?" Leonard asked. "Afraid of what you've told us? Afraid of what I might do?"

"I'm going to die soon, so it doesn't matter. You should put it in the paper. Nobody's going to do anything to a crazy old woman with one foot in the grave."

"You're not that close to the grave," Leonard answered. He wanted to know how Molly could have poisoned her daughter.

"What dd Rosannah say when she ate the jam?" Leonard asked.

"Just that it had a sharp taste."

"You didn't try to stop her?"

"It was too late then, even if I wanted to."

"So you didn't want to. Were you sorry for what you'd done."

"At first, I was. Then I decided it was really God's doing. That made me feel better.

"And there was no more of the banshee's wailing. So I went to sleep."

A feeling of loathing was beginning to take hold of Leonard. Not just loathing at what he was hearing, or of Molly, but loathing of himself, of everybody, but most of all of what had happened in that Vandeleur farm house twenty-one years ago.

Leonard stumbled up the stairwell from the Asylum, Scarth at his heels. He hardly heard Scarth's blabbering about how Molly had just vouched for his innocence.

"I knew it," Scarth said, "I knew she'd clear me, that's why I came with you. I kept my part of the bargain. Now you've got to keep yours. I'm leaving town today. You promised not to put the police onto me."

The words trailed off as Scarf hurried away, leaving Leonard staring into the haze of a dying afternoon. The air smelled of rain. It was too late to return to the office; he may as well go home. He walked the half block to the corner without noticing that a streetcar had stopped, taken on two women carrying umbrellas, and headed downtown. He waited for the next car. He tried to clear his head and think about what he was going to do.

Leonard waited outside the Asylum for so long it seemed as if time was standing still. Another streetcar car came by after twenty minutes. He dropped in his nickel and took a seat. His remembrance of past experiences had suddenly been overtaken by this new information. He gazed out the widows without seeing the buildings he was passing or the people on the sidewalks, hurrying home from their shifts. The conductor called out Parliament Street but Leonard was thinking only of the terrible consequences of Molly's delirium. The streetcar was turning around at the Don River Station before he realized he'd passed his stop. When he finally got off it was getting dark and the wind had stepped up. Rain that had been falling was turning to sleet as the temperature dropped.

By now, he had begun to put things in their proper perspective. He was terribly let down and once out of the streetcar he began to cry. Leonard was sorrowful that his long quest for truth had taken him where it had. His daughter Lenora had grown up without a father; he was nowhere around when she would have needed him most. Molly Leppard's life had unfolded as a journey of deprivation and tragedy. She was going to die alone and unmourned. Rosannah never had a chance and Cook had been marked in childhood for a lifetime of trouble.

Some of these things had nothing to do with Leonard but some of them were his fault. If he hadn't been so pig-headed he and Rosannah might have been married and most of this would never have happened. From the time of that trouble at the *Globe*, he'd felt overwhelmed. He had finally gotten his life under control after joining the *Evening Telegram*. He'd fought and won Kathleen's freedom and then he'd married her, and they were happy together.

Now he had answers to questions that had haunted him since the trial. Molly's attempt to control Bridget's testimony had been driven by fear her daughter might accuse her of murder, rather than by, as he'd thought, the shame of Rosannah's rape. He now saw Scarth Tackaberry as a pathetic and naïve figure who feared the suspicion his testimony would draw. Finally, his admiration for Cook Teets swept over him like torrents of rain. Cook had to have suspected Molly yet he had never spoken a word against her. His love for Rosannah had prevented him from accusing a mother of destroying her own child.

By the time Leonard reached the third floor landing and stood at the door of his flat, he realized he was not yet ready to tell Kathleen what he had learned. He needed to better understand how he felt and what he was going to do about it.

Kathleen was crimping the pastry of an apple pie she was about to put in the oven. "It'll be ready by the time you've had your dinner," she told him.

"I'm really not hungry," Leonard said. "I'm too tired to eat. I'll just pour a little whisky and rest awhile."

After two drinks, Leonard was feeling groggy. Kathleen sat across from him, darning a pair of socks. He saw her look at him strangely.

"Did you visit Molly?"

"I don't feel up to talking about it. I'm going to bed."

The effects of the whisky lulled Leonard to sleep. He awakened sometime after midnight. He'd dreamt of dancing with Rosannah at a party in the

Vandeleur school. She twirled away from him and he lost sight of her among the other dancers. It was the first time he'd dreamt of her since he'd met Kathleen. Rosannah would always be in his life.

Leonard had been convinced he would know what to do once he found out who had killed Rosannah. Now he was not so sure. He could divulge Molly's secret to *Telegram* readers, revealing Cook Teets as the innocent victim of a heartless justice system. The public would eagerly embrace the story of a man who had refused to implicate the mother of the girl he'd married, and had gambled with his own life and lost. Everyone would praise Leonard's enterprise in ferreting out such a dramatic story. But he dreaded the thought of indicting the mother of the girl he'd loved. Would exposing Molly deliver justice to a dead man? What could you do for someone who was dead? And if he published the story, would that help him overcome the sense of worthlessness that still dragged at his heels? He'd have to decide those things tomorrow. After a long time, he drifted back to sleep.

# Chapter 38

## LEONARD'S CHOICE

### April 21, 1904

T he piercing light of a clear spring morning roused Leonard Babington with a start. He turned on his side to reach for Kathleen, realized
she was not there, and saw by the bedside clock that it was after seven
and the alarm had not rung. It was then he remembered all that had happened: the fire, his visit with Molly Leppard, and her confession. He had to
get up and get going. He found Kathleen washing up dishes left unattended
from last night.

"I wanted you to have a little extra sleep," Kathleen said when she saw
Leonard. "You tossed and turned all night."

"I should be on my way by now. But there's something we need to talk
about before I leave."

Leonard washed and shaved quickly, dressed, and in ten minutes was ready
for the fried ham and boiled egg that Kathleen had prepared. He cracked
open his egg, dipped toast into the yolk, and swallowed a mouthful of tea.
As he ate he told Kathleen how Scarth Tackaberry had turned up in Toronto
after jumping bail, how he had confronted him at the Colonial Rooms, and
then made him to go with him to the Asylum.

When Leonard got to the part about how Rosannah had died from eating
jam poisoned with strychnine, Kathleen stopped him to ask if Molly said
Scarth had done it.

"It wasn't Scarth," Leonard answered. "Molly said he had nothing to do
with it. She admitted it was she who had killed Rosannah. Talked about visions and voices, all about a wailing banshee, and how she was told she could

325

wash away Rosannah's sins by sinning against her. Some crazy religious delusion. And the wails of the banshee – she'd forgotten it was Halloween, hadn't realized that what she heard was just kids making a noise.

"It's clear to me now. She straight out confessed to me. So do I keep quiet, or do I reveal the truth? My choice is to publish. It's only fair to Rosannah and Cook Teets. People have to know a mistake was made."

Kathleen poured Leonard more tea and refilled her own cup. "How do you know what Molly says is true? Maybe she's just hallucinating, acting out some lunatic fantasy. And you say you let Scarth go on his way? So you've lost your only witness."

"I don't need a witness, Kate. This is the second time Molly's confessed. I'd known about it for years. I just never could believe it. I always suspected Scarth of doing it."

"Whatever do you mean?"

"Rosannah had a brother, name of James. He was married to a girl called Jennie Wonch. I never told you, but a story Jennie told the police about Molly having confessed to her is in the files of the *Owen Sound Advertiser*. Nobody ever paid any attention to it. I never believed the story myself until I heard it confirmed by Molly yesterday."

"And you really think you need to put this in the *Telegram*?"

"I've no choice. I know she's told the truth. A newspaperman has to let out the truth, or he betrays everything he stands for. People have to know when the system goes wrong. How else are we going to stop the same mistake from happening again?"

"But think of what this will do to Molly."

"That's what's bothered me. She would never have confessed if the fire hadn't terrified her. I don't want to add to her pain, but I doubt she'll ever know her truth's been told. The police are not going to do anything. As Molly says, no one will care about a crazy old woman who's not got long to live."

The editorial department was at its peak of activity when Leonard arrived, a little before nine o'clock. Reporters hurried in and out, stories fell from their typewriters, and calls for copy boys rose above the din. Leonard's deputy, Roland Cooper, a recent recruit from Fleet Street's *London Transcript*, gave him a run-down of the day's main stories: more reports on the Great Fire; a debate on evolution at the Jarvis Street Baptist Church; arguments at Council over renewing the contract of the city's welfare officer (Goldwin Smith having decided he could no longer pay the man's salary); along with the usual collection of cases from the police blotter.

"I've something else for the one o'clock edition," Leonard said. "I've been working on it for awhile. We'll make it the top story on page five, first thing after the want ads. You can handle the desk while I write."

Turning his back, Leonard swung into a chair behind a vacant typewriter on the rim of the copy desk. He put in a sheet of paper and caught his breath. What he was about to write would bring to an end twenty years of pain and frustration. Yet it would not be a long story. And he knew just the headline he wanted on it:

## ACT OF INJUSTICE
## AN INNOCENT MAN HAS HANGED
## LAST EXECUTION IN OWEN SOUND WAS A LEGAL MURDER

It is twenty years since the last execution took place in Owen Sound. At that time, Cook Teets, a blind man, who resided in the village of Vandeleur, Grey County, charged with poisoning his wife, the former Rosannah Leppard, was tried and convicted on purely circumstantial evidence and hanged for the crime.

The execution of Teets was an act of injustice, carried out on the orders of Justice Department officials who disregarded the jury's appeal for clemency and ignored public petitions for commutation of the sentence to life imprisonment.

Information has come into possession of *The Evening Telegram*, in the form of a confession by the mother of the victim, that Cook Teets was innocent of the crime with which he was charged, and that she herself was the murderer of her daughter. The confession was delivered yesterday to a representative of this newspaper by Molly Leppard, sixty-seven years of age, who has been for a number of years a patient at the Toronto Insane Asylum.

In her confession, Mrs. Leppard explained that she was in a religious trance when she laced a quantity of crabapple jam

with strychnine and gave it to her daughter with bread. She la-
boured under the awful belief that Rossannah, reared a Roman
Catholic, had sinned by marrying Teets, a Protestant. The marriage took place in St. Andrew's Presbyterian Church in Toronto in 1883, a scant six weeks before the victim's death. Having
since recovered much of her sanity, Mrs. Leppard explained
to our representative, who has pursued the case since its in-
ception, that she heard voices and had visions of demons from
whom she received instructions that she could save Rosannah
only by committing an even greater sin, viz., the murder of her
own daughter.

The case warrants further investigation in that it sheds
light both on the failure of the judicial system to protect the
innocent among the accused, and on the prevalence of religious
delusion among the inmates of our asylums

Leonard paused in his typing. Those are the essential facts, enough to raise a
few eyebrows. He'd write more stories in the days ahead, giving added details
of Rosannah's life and how Cook was unjustly punished. He marked up the
copy for the typesetters, rolled the pages together, and slipped them into the
pneumatic tube to be carried to the composing floor. He shivered and felt
his heart race as he thought of what he'd done. Dear Rosannah, I am sorry
to have to tell the world of your mother's crime. Many crimes go unpunished
but the punishment for what Molly did has been visited on all of us – on
Cook through his wrongful hanging, on Molly by being thrust into a dement-
ed state, on myself for the doubts and despair I've suffered, but most of all
on you, dear Rosannah, for it is you who have paid with your life.

Leonard was jarred from his introspection by the realization that his editor, Black Jack Robinson, was standing over him. He looked up to see Robinson pawing through the pile of carbon sheets beside his typewriter.

"Cooper tells me you've something big you've been keeping to yourself,"
Robinson said. "I'm curious – can I have a look at your blacks?"

Robinson stood, swaying slightly, his ample stomach protruding around
the confines of his belt as he read Leonard's story. He wheezed and har-
rumphed as he went from page to page, his eyebrows permanently lifted as

if to hold his eyes wide open as he absorbed their content.

"You've sent this to the composing room?"

"Yes, a few minutes ago."

"Send down a note to call it back."

"Whatever for?"

"The *Evening Telegram* can't publish this. How do we know this isn't a figment of the woman's imagination? Her family could sue us. And the authorities. What will they think of these reckless charges of injustice? What will
the doctors at the Asylum say? Mr. Robertson is away, or I'd have him look
at this. In his absence, I have to decide. Let's take some time to think about
this."

Leonard was stunned by his editor's reaction. He had never given a
thought to the possibility the paper would not wish to run the story. He saw
years of frustration coming to a peak – printing Molly's confession had become the most important thing in his life. He was gripped by a sudden rage
that swept from his gut into his head, like a swarm of hornets bursting from
a nest that's been disturbed.

"God damn it, that does it," he told Black Jack, as he stood up. "If the
*Evening Telegram* doesn't want me, I can always go and see Joe Atkinson at the
*Star.* Maybe I'll find somebody with a conscience." He pushed away his chair,
reached for his coat, and headed toward the stairs.

"Wait a minute," Robinson called. He caught up to Leonard at the revolv-
ing door that marked the building's Bay Street entrance, and followed him
outside. "I don't understand why you're so touchy. It's my job to keep this
newspaper out of court and you're not making it any easier."

Robinson's admission surprised Leonard. He didn't think his editor should
behave as if he were a lawyer; his job was to bring the truth to readers. He
now felt even more angry, but still ready to try to explain the meaning of
Molly's confession. The two paced the sidewalk while Leonard went over the
history of Rosannah Leppard's murder. He left nothing out, not even the fact
he'd been in love with her, that at the beginning he had been sure of Cook's
guilt, and about his own contribution to the public prejudice against Teets.

"I've considered the case from all angles and it's clear Cook didn't do it,"
Leonard said. "That leaves Molly. I know her confession seems weird but it's
true. She's in no position to retract it, and the *Telegram* need have no fear in

publishing it."

"Mr. Babington, it's all very well for you to say that. I don't doubt your sincerity, but you have a personal interest in this. You have to consider the paper's position. We have to think of the attitude of the authorities."

"My God, Mr. Robinson what do you think the proprietor has been doing all his life? That was his whole intention in starting the *Telegram* – to hold the authorities to account. Would you have us abandon his principles?"

Black Jack paused before answering. Leonard hoped he might be looking for a way to settle their argument. "You put things in a difficult light, Mr. Babington. You're absolutely sure of your facts?" Leonard nodded. "All right, you don't leave us much choice – we'll go with your story. Now, let's get back to work. We've a paper to get out."

An hour later, Leonard stood beside the presses as the one o'clock edition sprang to life. Black Jack had alerted the circulation manager that something big was up and newsboys were standing in line for their copies. They made their way out of the burned out core of the city shouting "Innocent man hanged, read all about it!" A queue formed at the corner of Bay and King Streets where stockbrokers and office clerks vied with one another to pay their penny to read of this latest sensation.

When a bundle of papers came up to the editorial department, copy boys distributed them among the staff. Every man turned to page five to see Leonard's story. The room fell silent while they read, the quiet interrupted only by occasional gasps of disbelief or quiet curses of admiration for Leonard's ingenuity in ferreting out such an amazing scoop.

"This'll have the opposition curling their toes tonight," said Major Anthes, the church reporter.

Owen Staples slapped Leonard on the back and shook his hand, smiling conspiratorially.

Reporters asked Leonard how he'd secured the confession and how long it had taken. "About twenty years, if you want the truth," he told them. He heard their congratulatory remarks but he did not, fortunately, pick up what was being said at the far end of the office.

There, one reporter whispered to another, "Babington's at it again. Mixing with the crazies."

Leonard reflected on how John Ross Robertson might react to the news.

He was sure he would understand his City Editor's satisfaction at finally publishing the truth of the mystery they had discussed in their first meeting so many years ago. It would likely be weeks before today's paper would reach Robertson and Leonard considered clipping the article and sending it by special dispatch. He decided that would be boastful and dropped the idea. Around him, the low hum of voices told Leonard that his reporters were busy dissecting the hints of evidence yet to come that he had worked into his story.

Remembering the tears that had been shed in the making of today's headline, Leonard was filled with contentment over having at last laid responsibility for Rosannah's death. It was like after finishing any long and difficult job. Sometimes, you didn't want to start but you persevered, and when you were finished, you were pleased you had done the work and done it well. It was hard to compare everyday tasks to something that had drained his emotions for two decades. He'd lived so long with his guilt over Rosannah's fate and his complicity in Cook's hanging that it felt strange to have these feelings banished. His satisfacton would bring back neither of them but now he felt entitled to get on with his own life.

And what about Kathleen, who was so perfect and so deserving? She'd been uncomfortable when he first told her of Molly's confession. The fact he'd had corroboration from Jennie Wonch wouldn't have meant much to her. He'd be a better husband to Kathleen now that he could put away the ghosts of his Vandeleur past. He'd get that house he'd promised her; he'd see Mr. Robertson about a loan as soon as the proprietor got back. It was time to think about children. They had never talked seriously of having babies and he was a little surprised Kathleen had never gotten pregnant. They'd have to do something about that.

Later, walking toward St. Lawrence Hall and the Market, Leonard enjoyed the warmth of the spring sun on his face. The unseasonable snowfall that came with the fire was beginning to melt and the air was filled with the sounds of birds and the voices of children playing in the park. How wonderful it was to be alive and free. How good to have someone to love and be loved in return. How he had reproached himself for his past failings and how those failings now seemed unimportant. All he was sure of was that he had been given a new lease on life. Tears welled up in his eyes and he had to brush his cheeks with his coat cuff.

It was after three o'clock when Leonard returned to the *Evening Telegram*. He had been at his desk only a few minutes when the phone rang. It was Kathleen, who was calling from the Asylum. She had been worried about Molly and would be seeing her in a few minutes. Had his story been published?

"It went in the one-o'clock edition and the paper's a sell-out all over town," Leonard told her. "You don't have to tell Molly about it. There's really no need for her to know." He promised Kathleen he would be home by six o'clock.

Leonard declined offers to join his staff for after-work drinks. He didn't want to gloat about his story and there were a few tasks he needed to clean up, things he'd neglected since the fire. He half expected a telephone call from the police. He was relieved when the phone didn't ring again.

A little before six o'clock, Leonard made his way up the stairs to their rooms. He found Kathleen in the parlour, a look of distress on her face. "What's the matter?" he asked. "You look all pale and worried."

Kathleen dabbed at her eyes with a handkerchief. "I won't be going to the Asylum anymore, Leonard. It just won't be the same without Molly. She died this afternoon. They said she was content at the end."

Leonard felt an overwhelming sadness. He'd not forgiven Molly for what she'd done but neither was he prepared for her death. The strain of having confessed to him must have been too much. Or was he just looking once more for a way to put guilt on himself? He wondered if there really was a purgatory or a heaven and hell and whether Molly and Rosannah would be in one of those places together and would they get along better than they had on earth? "May both their souls rest in peace," he said.

"Poor Leonard, you've been through so much. Saving the *Telegram* from the fire, taking Molly's confession and writing about it, then having me tell you Molly's dead. All those sad memories from Vandeleur. Would you like to hear some good news for a change? At least, I hope you'll think it's good news." Leonard saw her lips tremble as she waited for his answer.

"That depends on what it is," Leonard replied.

"I may as well tell you right out. I'm pregnant. You're going to be a father."

"I knew it, I was sure of it!" Leonard answered, in triumph. "Why was I thinking that very thing a second ago?"

"Do you really want a baby, Leonard?"

"Of course I do. You know it's what we've both wanted. We'll have to make sure we get that house, now. Oh Kate, you make me so proud." He pulled her toward him and kissed her full on the lips.

The thought of again becoming a father – and this time, being able to acknowledge it – filled Leonard with exultation. He understood now that none of the events that had marred his life – the shooting of George Brown, the accident to his father, the death of Rosannah and the hanging of Cook Teets – were cause for him to bear guilt. He had nothing to gain by blaming himself. His discovery of the facts of Rosannah's death had served the truth, he knew. But it also came to him that truth could more often be found in the power of love and forgiveness, than in the possession of mere facts.

Kathleen put her hand on Leonard's shoulder. "Perhaps we should go home – home to Vandeleur," she said. "It will be quiet – you could write in peace there. You'd be able to finish *Rosannah's Story*, now that you know the ending. And perhaps you'd get to know your daughter."

Leonard thought about the turmoil and trauma that Rosannah and Cook and he and Kathleen had lived through. "Let's go for a walk," he said. They put their coats on, went downstairs and out through the big front garden and onto Parliament Street. All the shops were closed now and the streetlights were on. The last of the melting snow was making rivulets at the edge of the street The footprints they left in the slush became indistinct and blurred, and in a little while there was no trace of their passage.

THE END

# Afterword

A N ACT OF INJUSTICE is a novel inspired by the lives of Rosannah Leppard and Cook Teets – real people who lived and loved. Vandeleur is a real place, although Leonard Babington and Kathleen Fitzgerald bear no resemblance to any actual persons, and there never was a *Vandeleur Chronicle.*

I became aware of the tragic fates of Rosanah and Cook while researching wrongful hangings in Canada. An astonishing story turned up in the October 12, 1908, issue of the *Toronto Evening Telegram.* A single paragraph buried below the fold of an inside page, it bore the headline, HANGED AN INNOCENT MAN. The story carried neither attribution nor byline, but suggested a plot far deeper than the modest space it occupied might indicate. The actual murderer had confessed, leaving no doubt that Cook Teets was innocent of the crime for which he had been hanged.

As I delved into the lives of Rosannah and Cook, a missing link persisted – someone who might have been the source of that report in the *Telegram.* It was to fill this need that Leonard Babington, his *Chronicle,* and Kathleen Fiztgerald came into being. Their presence enabled me to set the story of Rosannah and Cook against the broader panorama of frontier Ontario and Victorian Canada at the approach of the twentieth century. I have jockeyed names, dates and places to fit the plot.

I was fortunate to find a descendant of Rosannah Leppard. April Bell lives in British Columbia and I thank her for giving me a connection to her great-great aunt. My historical sources include the Ontario Archives, the Grey Roots Museum, the South Grey Museum, and staff of the Owen Sound Provincial Jail (since closed). At Library and Archives Canada I found the official transcript of the trial. Public libraries in Owen Sound and Flesherton also held valuable information. I borrowed stories from the *Flesherton Advance* for the fictional *Vandeleur Chronicle,* and some pieces I have attributed to Leonard while at the *Evening Telegram* come from the files of that paper. The notice on the appointment of Leonard Babington as City Editor has been adapted from a memo by John Ross Robertson, cited in Ron Poulton's book, *The Paper Tyrant.*

Rosannah Leppard's mother was also named Rosannah, but to avoid confusion I have called her Molly, the Irish pet form of Mary. The Teets family, disgraced by the murder trial, sold up and left Vandeleur shortly after Cook was hanged.

The real Vandeleur thrived as a small community in Grey County well into the 1890s, when it began to decline in the face of a great migration of Grey and Bruce County settlers to the more fertile plains of Western Canada. Vandeleur's only remaining structures are an Orange Hall and the former Public School No. 11, a brick building erected in 1892 on the site of the original one-room school in which Leonard Babington would have taught.

Besides Rosannah and Cook, many historical characters have roles in this book. Mr. Justice John Douglas Armour returned to his home, Calcutt, in Cobourg, Ontario after the trial. He later served as Chief Justice of Ontario and, in the year before his death in 1903, was appointed to the Supreme Court of Canada. His portrait hangs in the Old Bailey-style courtroom of Victoria Hall in Cobourg. James Masson, who defended Cook Teets, represented Grey North in the House of Commons from 1887 to 1896. Dr. Thomas Sproule served in Parliament until 1915, the last four years as Speaker of the House under Prime Minister Robert Borden. Goldwin Smith produced a prodigious number of articles and books and died in Toronto in 1910. A well-known anti-Semite, he nevertheless coined a phrase, "Above all nations is humanity," that has been adopted as the motto of several universities around the world. Prosecutor Alfred Frost became mayor of Owen Sound and died from pneumonia after an ice fishing accident. His large house was converted into an orphanage. The County Court Building, erected in 1853, no longer serves that purpose and despite its historical and architectural significance, faces an uncertain future.

Dr. Daniel Clark headed the Toronto Asylum for the Insane until 1905, gaining a reputation as a free-thinking if quirky caretaker of the mentally ill. According to The Dictionary of Canadian Biography, "Clark participated in the debates of his time, notably on the relationship between insanity and masturbation, on the connection between gynecological problems and insanity in women, and on the use of physical restraint, which he claimed to have ended at Toronto in 1883." He testified at the trial of Louis Riel in 1885, declaring that he thought Riel was insane "for thinking he could come into the Saskatchewan and gather a force that would make him a monarch."

John Ross Robertson led a legendary life as proprietor of the *Evening Telegram*, dying in 1918. Owen Staples was an outstanding painter and an illustrator for Robertson's newspaper. He died in 1949. I had the privilege of knowing his daughter Madge Staples when we both worked at the *Telegram* before its demise in 1971.

I had the support of many people in writing this book. James Lockyer, founder of Innocence Canada -formerly the Association in Aid of the Wrongly Convicted (AIDWYC), encouraged me from the beginning. Genni Gunn and Jeanette Lynes read early drafts and gave me valuable suggestions. Barbara Kyle and Tom Taylor offered helpful advice. I appreciated the assistance of medical and legal experts: Dr. Margaret Thompson, Medical Director of the Ontario Poison Centre; Dr. Peter Kopplin of Toronto; and Judge Robert J. Sharpe of the Court of Appeal for Ontario. My Sherlockian friend, Hartley Nathan, gave me an expert's view of author Conan Doyle's approach to crime solving. I am grateful to my daughter, Sharon Argyle, for having created the map of Victorian Ontario at the front of the book.

My thanks go to Matthew Goody and his entire team at Mosaic Press who have so enthusiastically supported the publication of this book.

I also thank my partner Deborah Windsor for her everlasting support.

# Postcript: Another Thought

**C**ook Teets was the first but not the last man to be hanged in Owen Sound. That dubious honour goes to Frederick Bussey, who was executed in 1948. From Confederation in 1867 to the last hanging in Canada in 1962, some seven hundred men and thirteen women died on the gallows. Capital punishment was abolished by Parliament in 1976.

We have no idea how many Canadians may have been unjustly hanged. Since the abolition of hanging, numerous persons convicted of murder have later been found innocent. They range from David Milgaard who served twenty-three years in prison and won $10 million in compensation, to Guy Paul Morin who spent eighteen months behind bars and was awarded $1.25 million for his wrongful incarceration.

The fact innocent people continue to be convicted of serious offences does not, however, seem to have blunted Canadians' support for capital punishment. An Angus Reid survey in 2012 showed 62 per cent in favour of capital punishment for murder, although this figure drops to 50 per cent when life imprisonment is offered as an alternative. A 2016 Abacus Data survey reported 58 per cent of Canadians regard capital punishment as "morally right."

Approval of the death penalty had stood at a low of 44 per cent in 2005. The rise since then may be partially a consequence of the Stephen Harper government's insistent drum beating between 2006 and 2015 for harsher penalties against lawbreakers. Fortunately, there appears to be no political will in Canada to reopen the question of capital punishment.

A compliant media may also bear some responsibility. It is cheap and convenient to play up crime – even petty crime – creating an impression that wrongdoing is more prevalent than is actually the case. Violent crime in Canada has been on the decline for several decades. Statistics Canada reported that in 2014, the violent crime rate was five per cent lower than in 2013 and twenty-six per cent lower than a decade earlier.

On any given day there is an average of 36,845 adults housed in Canada's provincial or federal jails. This cost Canadian taxpayers $4.6 billion in 2013/14. About one in three have been convicted of no crime; they are on remand, awaiting trial. Most are younger adults, and one in four of those in provincial institutions is of aboriginal descent, a rate far in excess of their proportion of the population. Canada's federal penitentiaries, where offenders serve sentences of longer than two years, house some 15,000 prisoners.

But there are more grim conclusions. According to federal Correctional Investigator Howard Sapers in his 2013 report, changes that saw inmates serve longer sentences, together with cuts in prison pay and imposition of austere conditions did little to improve public safety; instead, he says it made it more difficult to rehabilitate and reintegrate prisoners back into society upon their release. The Supreme Court has set aside some of these laws as unconstitutional, and it is likely the federal government will repeal or amend others.

When Prime Minister Justin Trudeau took office in November, 2015, he issued a series of mandate letters to his cabinet ministers, setting out his expectations for each of them. The Justice Minister was mandated to reform use of solitary confinement and review changes made by the Harper government. The letter, however, was silent on whether we should continue to jail people who have not committed violent crimes. More than three-quarters of all criminal charges (360,000 in 2013/14) are for non-violent offences. About one-third of those found guilty end up serving jail terms. With so many alternatives to prison available – including fines, probation, and conditional sentences – is there really any reason so many of these non-violent offenders need to be behind bars, each at a cost to taxpayers of more than $100,000 per year? This warrants the urgent attention of Ottawa's committee of experts on justice reform.

Conditional sentences, allowing terms to be seved in the community rather than in jail, came into effect in 1996. They offer a process that many consider the best alternative to imprisonment. Judges cannot apply conditional sentences in cases requiring mandatory minimum sentences. As a result, their latitude was greatly reduced by the sixty new mandatory minimum prison terms enacted between 2006 and 2015 for drugs, guns, sex offences and many non-violent crimes. In most situations, these minimums are a barrier to the principle of making the penalty fit the circumstances of the individual offender. They should be repealed.

Governments can take these steps while recognizing the harm done to victims and the need to keep society safe. In fact, the best way of encouraging released prisoners to lead useful lives is not by extending their periods in jail or otherwise penalizing them, but through education, treatment of mental illness, and by offering assistance in their reintegration into society.

Some judges have declined to comply with minimum sentences, asserting they constitute "cruel and unusual punishment." In one case, a judge refused to apply the mninimum six months for possession of between six and two hundred marijuana plants for the purpose of trafficking. With legalization of marijuana in Canada, the high number of arrests on related charges – 75,000 in 2013 – will no longer occur.

If people are not sent to jail, will they not simply be encouraged to repeat their crimes? Unfortunately this is what is happening now, as seen in the statistics for rearrests of people for repeat offences. Nothing has been achieved by imprisoning them. The John Howard Society warns that prisoners are facing longer periods of incarceration and are receiving less support and supervision through parole as they return to their communities. "This approach," it concludes, "makes communities less safe."

The cost of providing counselling and moral and educational support to keep people out of jail need be no greater – probably less – than what is now spent to keep them in jail. The return to society in the form of rebuilt lives and reduced crime will be immeasurably greater.

# POISON

### The Cause of the Sudden death of Rosannah Leppard.

## Verdict of Coroner's Jury.

To-day (Thursday) the inquest into the death of Rosannah Leppard, which was adjourned two weeks ago in order to obtain an analysis of the contents of stomach. was resumed. It will be remembered by our readers that the circumstances attending the death of this woman indicated most strongly poison by strychnine. The jury requested that an analysis of the stomach and intestines might be had, and the Coroner having obtained the authority of the Attorney General, forwarded them under seal in care of Constable Fields, to Dr. Ellis, Toronto, public analyist. His report confirmed the suspicions of the Coroner and Dr. Sproule, who made the post-mortem of the body. The main question to solve is who administrated the poison. So far there is not a title of evidence to show that the deceased committed suicide, but every fact seems to point to one of the most heartless,

### COLD-BLOODED MURDERS,

having been committed in our neighborhood. that has ever stained the annals of crime in our country. We would not attempt to prejudice the public mind in so serious a matter, but as a public journalist, place all the facts we can gather before our readers.

The morning after the first sitting of the Jury, Constable Fields was dispatched to make search of any medicines or drugs which might be found in the house where the deceased came to her end, or in the possession of her husband.

#### BLIND COOK TEETS.

While going through his chest he found a bottle, half-filled, labelled—

"STRYCHNINE—POISON !"

This he secured. also a Life Policy on the life of Rosannah Leppard for four thousand five hundred dollars, payable to Cook Teets in the event of her death. While these circumstances supply positive evidence of Cook Teets having poison in his possession without objective use for it, and that it was the identical kind of poison which caused the death of his wife, they also supply the motive for the suspected crime. Yet there is one important link missing. Strychnine is a poison that generally acts very quickly, producing death in from ten minutes to four hours. The evidence so far goes to show that Cook Teets was not in the company of his wife for a period of twelve hours or more before her death.

##### VERDICT OF CORONER'S JURY :

The verdict of the Coroners Jury was as follows :

1st.—That Rosannah Leppard came to her death by poison.

2nd.—That the poison was strychnine.

3rd.—The Jury believe, from the evidence adduced, that Cook Teets feloniously administered that poison to her.

The Coroner, immediately upon the finding, issued his warrant for the arrest of Cook Teets. When he came into the hall in charge of constable Fields, the Coroner, at his request, read over the verdict, and on hearing the last clause, he was visibly affected—a spasm passed over his haggard features, which he attempted to hide, passing his hand nervously over his face and sighing heavily. This man may be innocent of the horrible crime but a crowd of circumstances like hideous spectres with outstretched fingers and mocking gibe, seem to say—"Thou art the man !"—*Flesherton Advance.*

Excerpt *Markdale Standard* (November 2, 1883)

# TO BE HANGED

### By the Neck till He is Dead!

# COOK TEETS!

### Found Guilty of Murder & Sentenced to be Hung.

Possibly the most intensely absorbing case tried at the Grey Fall Assizes this week, was the trial of Cook Teets for feloniously administering poison to Rosannah Leppard, his wife, last fall, the circumstances of which terrible crime was given at length in the columns of the ADVANCE at the time it transpired. It will be remembered by our readers that an inquest was held before Dr. Christoe, coroner for the County. From the evidence gleaned on that occasion, it was deemed expedient to send the stomach of deceased to Dr. Ellis, public analysist, Toronto. The inquest was accordingly adjourned pending the result. At the adjourned inquest the report of the analysist was handed in when it was ascertained that the stomach contained strychnine. In accordance with all the facts brought to light at this inquest, the jury brought in a verdict on the strength of which Cook Teets was placed under arrest and sent to Owen Sound gaol. The case was postponed at the Spring Assizes, and this week it again came up before his lordship judge Armour.

It is just a year since the terrible affair sent a thrill of horror through the community. The excitement was intense for the time, but as the weeks rolled on, the interest in the mysterious case flagged and finally almost died out altogether. Various were the surmises as to the possible result, the general opinion being that Teets would be acquitted.

On Tuesday night last, while stopping at the Coulson hotel, we were informed that the poisoning case would come up before the court next morning. Wednesday morning, found us wending our along the ice-clad streets in the direction of the Court house. On our arrival there, we found the prisoner Cook Teets, already in the dock, while sheriff Moore was calling out the jurymen, several of whom were refused by the Counsel for the defence, Mr. Masson, at the request of his client. In reply to the question—"Are you guilty or not guilty," the prisoner arose slowly to his feet and answered in a firm voice, "not guilty." The trial was then proceeded with

The prisoner, since his incarceration, has allowed his beard to grow, and it was some time before we could recognize in the venerable looking old gentleman in the dock—with his long flowing gray beard and heavy moustache—the man whom we had seen at the coroner's inquest a year previous, with his clean shaven face, tightly compressed lips, and almost rigid expression of countenance. For a time all the eyes in the crowded court room were fastened on him. One of his sightless eyes was inflamed and swollen, and it was evident he suffered much pain. At first he kept his eyes tightly bandaged with a large white handkerchief. but as the case proceeded, he manifested signs of uneasiness—now removing the bandage ; then replacing it ; now leaning his head on his hands and giving vent to deep sighs. Once he arose to his feet and seemed to be groping for somebody or something ; then he sat down and leaning forward with his head on the railing of the dock, seemed to be entirely absorbed in his own thoughts.

The counsel for the Crown, Mr. Alfred Frost, addressed the jury in a short, concise speech, in which he put the case for the prosecution very clearly.

The first witness called was Rosannah Leppard, mother of the deceased. The evidence of this witness was substantially the same as that given by her before Coroner Christoe and jury, with the exception of one or two important additions, viz., that she (witness) had heard the prisoner, while standing by the bedside of his dead wife, mutter to himself—"Poor Rosy, it was me caused this;" also "Poor Rosannah, I come down on you all at once." (sensation.)

While this witness was testifying, Teets expressed a desire to get near the witness box as he could not hear the evidence. He was then removed from the dock and placed in a chair near to his counsel.

Mrs. Leppard was subjected to a severe cross-examination by Mr. Masson, during which some rather unwholesome facts were elicited in reference to the chastity of two of her daughters ; but, as far as the case itself was concerned, nothing of a contradictory nature came out of it, and after having been in the witness box over two hours, she was allowed to take her seat. During this time the prisoner exhibited symptoms of great excitement, frequently wiping the sweat off his brow, changing his position and breathing heavily.

Bridget Leppard, daughter of the last witness, was then called. Several sharp glances passed between mother and daughter, while the latter was giving her evidence, and once the former raised her voice in what seemed an admonitory tone when she was checked by a bystander. The cross-examination elicited nothing of importance. The witness did not hear the prisoner say anything while he was standing by the bedside of the deceased. Cook stopped at the bedside of his dead wife perhaps half an hour.

Mary Ann Leppard, sister-in-law of deceased, was next called. She corroborated the testimony of her mother-in-law.

Dr. Sproule's testimony went to show that the brain of deceased was in a healthy condition. There was no natural cause to which her death could be attributed. The symptoms were strongly indicative of the use of strychnine poison. This poison, he said, caused death in from half an hour to three hours. His lordship asked the doctor several pertinent questions which were answered promptly and satisfactorily.

Several other witnesses were called, but the most important testimony against the prisoner was that given by Aaron Teeter. As our readers are all familiar with the statements made by him at the Coroner's inquest, however, as well as those made by other witnesses, whose names, &c. want of space compels us to omit, we need not more than barely refer to these facts here.

The prisoner's mother testified, as did also his sister, the former affirming that he knew her son had strychnine in his trunk or box, which he had obtained in the United States. Aaron Teeter did not see the poison while she was present at all events.

The meeting between the aged and infirm mother and her unfortunate son was an affecting one. The latter was especially deeply moved.

After hearing the evidence on both sides, the counsel for the defence, Mr. Masson, made a masterly address to the jury of over an hour's duration. He was followed by Mr. Frost, who, in his usual concise and able manner, clearly presented the facts for the prosecution in a speech lasting scarcely half an hour. This was followed by a resume of all the facts in connection with the case by his lordship, Judge Armour. He charged very wrongly against the prisoner, but presented the facts clearly and fully. The jury then retired.

Excerpt *Flesherton Advance* (November 6, 1884)

# THE LAST SCENE !

## Cook Teets Launched Into Eternity.

# HIS UNCONCERN !

*Protests His Innocence to the Last.*

### HIS LAST STATEMENT.

On Friday morning last, the 5th inst., at two minutes past 8 o'clock, Cook Teets was hanged in the court-yard of Owen Sound gaol. This was the first execution that has taken place in this County.

Notwithstanding the strenuous efforts of his lawyer, Mr. Masson, and some friends, to have the sentence of death commuted, a telegram was received on Thursday to the effect that the sentence of the Court would not be interfered with. How the condemned man spent his last night on earth, we know not; certain it is that he has all along manifested the utmost indifference as to his fate—*outwardly* at all events. When he became aware that the scaffold was in coarse of construction, is is said that he remarked to one of the gaol officials, that if permitted, he would save the County the expense of hanging him, if they would just stick a good strong pole out of his window !

By seven o'clock on Friday morning the limited number allowed to witness the execution, began to drop into the Court House. Shortly after that hour, the condemned man's spiritual advisers, Rev. Mr. Scott of the Presbyterian Church, and the Rev. Mr. Howell of the Methodist Church, were conducted by gaoler Miller to the prisoner's cell, where they administered the last sacrament. A few minutes afterwards two men past slowly through the corridors carrying a coffin, causing a shudder to pass through the small assembly. It was now clear daylight, and the gloom of the dismal court-yard was cheered up by the pleasant twittering of a number of sparrows perched on the eaves.

at twenty minutes to 8 o'clock the heavy doors leading to the gaol-yard slowly swung open with a dismal creak, and the spectators were ushered into the place of execution. In a secluded corner of the yard stood the gallows with all the dread paraphernalia of death—the rope, the trap slides, the lever, and, underneath all, the coffin. The snow had not yet melted away, except in places, and here it was damp and cold. The voices of the spiritual advisers were heard in earnest prayer, and shortly after our entrance, the deep boom of a church bell proclaimed the terrible fact that an immortal soul would shortly be ushered into the presence of the Great Judge who knows all hearts. The muffled sound of many voices, with an occasional suppressed burst of coarse laughter, filled in the void. With measured tread, the Chief of Police walked backwards and forwards before the scaffold—occasionally ordering some, whom curiosity prompted to examine the "trap" machinery closely, to "keep back." At ten minutes to eight the executioner, closely masked, mounted the scaffold, rope in hand, and proceeded to put everything in readiness. Five minutes later the unfortunate criminal, supported on either side by Revs. Scott and Howell, and attended by the Sheriff and policemen, entered the enclosure. With firm step and upright carriage he mounted the steps and stood on the fatal drop. He was neatly dressed in black, and wore a fur cap. While the rope was being adjusted by the executioner around his neck, Teets sprung the trap a little with his heels as though feeling whether it was firm, and exclaimed :—Gentlemen, this is the fatal board !'' He gave some directions to the executioner in a cool tone of voice, when Rev. Mr. Scott began to pray. Teets lips moved as if in response, and while Rev. Mr. Howell was delivering the Lord's Prayer, asked to be allowed to kneel. Ere the prayer had

been concluded, the black cap was placed over his head, and the executioner took his position at the lever. Scarcely had "amen" come from the preacher's lips, when the trap was sprung, and Cook Teets launched into eternity. Two or three convulsive shudders passed through his frame, and then the limbs assumed the rigidness of death.

Excerpt *Flesherton Advance*
(December 11, 1884)